Reverend Feelgood

Also by Lutishia Lovely

Sex in the Sanctuary
Love Like Hallelujah
A Preacher's Passion
Heaven Right Here

Reverend Feelgood

LUTISHIA LOVELY

Dafina
Books

KENSINGTON PUBLISHING CORP.
www.kensingtonbooks.com

DAFINA BOOKS are published by

Kensington Publishing Corp.
119 West 40th Street
New York, NY 10018

All Kensington titles, imprints, and distributed lines are available at special quantity discounts for bulk purchases for sales promotion, premiums, fundraising, educational, or institutional use.

Special book excerpts or customized printings can also be created to fit specific needs. For details, write or phone the office of the Kensington Special Sales Manager: Kensington Publishing Corp., 119 West 40th Street, New York, NY 10018. Attn. Special Sales Department. Phone: 1-800-221-2647.

Kensington and the K logo Reg. U.S. Pat. & TM Off.

ISBN-13: 978-0-7582-3865-8
ISBN-10: 0-7582-3865-7

First Kensington Trade Paperback Printing: February 2010
10 9 8 7 6 5 4 3 2 1

Printed in the United States of America

To my grandfather, Willie Hinton, Sr.,
who always encouraged me to write him a letter,
and to my father, Reverend Willie Hinton, Jr.,
who told a nappy-headed, ashy-knee'd little colored girl
that she could go anywhere, and do anything. . . .

ACKNOWLEDGMENTS

You would think that the more books I write, the fewer people I'd have to acknowledge. I mean, didn't I cover just about everybody in the first four books? In actuality, what happens is with every new novel there are more people to thank and more reasons to feel grateful. And while I've thanked some people in the past, there are some you just can't thank enough.

Like editor Selena James, for instance. So what that I just thanked her in *Heaven Right Here,* and in *A Preacher's Passion* before that, and in *Love Like Hallelujah* before that. This thank-you is for *Reverend Feelgood,* y'all, because her input and support were no less valuable in bringing this latest work to fruition. Behind every good writer is a great editor, believe that! Standing next to that editor is an awesome agent, Natasha Kern, and a fabulous, get-her-hustle-on-all-day-long personal publicist, Ella Curry, of EDC Creations. This is just part of "Team Lutishia" that is helping me take this brand to a whole nutha level!

Another big part of this team is my extended Kensington family: publicist Adeola Saul, Selena's assistant Mercedes Fernandez, copy editor Ellen Winkler, production editor Paula Reedy, cover designer Kristine Mills-Noble, along with cover photographer George Kerrigan, wardrobe stylist Denise Martin, and hair and makeup artist Lysette Drumgold, who gave those designers such great shots to work with. What draws readers to what's on the inside of a book begins with what's on the outside. Thanks for the great work. To the sales and marketing team who work so hard getting my books in as many stores and on as many websites as possible—I appreciate your efforts in making mine a household name!

I was very fortunate to be able to call my longtime friend

Carol Nichols regarding information on "all things Louisiana," where some of the Feelgood story line takes place. I still can't believe it's been so long since I've bitten into a beignet or sipped a hurricane. See you soon, Carol. I'm way overdue for a trip to N'awlins. . . .

Okay, let me put a disclaimer here and say I'm getting ready to start something. Because I'm getting ready to talk about what I feel is a writer's salt of the earth—readers. And not just any reader, but those collective groups of readers otherwise known as book clubs. *Baby!* Y'all sistahs and brothahs hold it down on the real tip, and I love, love, LOVE a book club. Y'all don't hear me, though. No, really, you don't even understand how deep this love goes! These readers will swim across an ocean, climb Mount Everest, and then head to the moon if there is a good book there waiting. And then they'll tell everybody else about it. They are the best fans and supporters an author can ask for. Every single book club out there is amazing, and aforementioned disclaimer in mind, I know I'm about to get into trouble by naming some, because I know I'll miss somebody, but these are the groups I've either met or interacted with recently, and without the naming of which, these acknowledgments would not be complete: Nikkea Smithers and Readers With Attitude (Richmond, Buffalo, and LA chapters), Tamika Newhouse and AAMBC, Lacha Mitchell and Woman To Woman Literary Sisters, Claudia Mosley and Sisterhood Book Club, TaNisha Webb and KC Girlfriends, Patricia Crowe and Ladies Of Color Turning Pages, J'Me Adams and Passion 4 Reading, Adrianne and Black Women Who Read, Tifany Jones and Sistah Confessions, Tee C. Royal and Rawsistaz, SBS (Sisters and Brothers with Soul), Women of P.U.R.P.O.S.E., Reading Is What We Do, Sister2Sister, Cedar Hill Divine Women Of Faith, F.A.M.E Book Club, Peace In Pages, Cush City, Page Turners, AA Book Lovers, People Who Love Good Books, Genesis, Phenomenal Women Of Color, and Carlos (Mikkar) and the Delaware Men Of Distinction Book Club. I just have two words: thank you. No, I have four: thank you very much!

Writing is a solitary endeavor, but I am blessed to have some wonderful authors in my life who make this journey one of camaraderie, mutual support, friendship, and fun! In them, either through personal relationship or literary inspiration, I've become a better writer, one who is proud to spell her name w-r-i-t-e-r. This list isn't complete, by any means, but it highlights those I especially appreciated during the writing of this book: mentor and phenomenal woman Gwynne Forster, the legendary Donna Hill (happy twentieth, Donna!), Renee Daniel Flagler, Trice Hickman, ReShonda Tate Billingsley, Shelia Goss, Alice Heiss, Venise Berry, Vincent Alexandria, Mary B. Morrison, and E. Lynn Harris. It was E. Lynn's hustle and success story that inspired me to independently publish my first book. (Sadly, just days after sending these acknowledgments to Selena, I received the news that E. Lynn had made his transition.) While I wish I'd been able to thank him in person, I am grateful to be able to thank him from these pages . . . where I believe he'll see this shout-out. And while E. Lynn Harris has written his last novel, his life and what it meant is forever written in my heart. There are more names to add to this list . . . next book, y'all!

Finally, as always, my thanks to Spirit, who has taken me on a wonderful, meandering journey from the religious to the spiritual, and has taught me that this entity is beyond names, denominations, definition, and/or description. Spirit is simply "all that is." I am all that I am, because of You. . . .

Prologue

The biggest religious scandal in modern American history was about to make headlines. This was an unfortunate fact for the Total Truth Association, an umbrella organization for several dozen ministries around the globe, which had one of its newest members and brightest stars smack dab in the middle of the controversy. Reverend Nathaniel "Nate" Thicke, senior pastor of the Gospel Truth Church in Palestine, Texas, had been caught on tape. And he hadn't been preaching the gospel.

King Brook, the interim president of Total Truth, paced his well-appointed church office as he talked on the phone. "We've got people threatening lawsuits, and several churches have vowed to pull their membership if we don't take decisive action—*immediately*. There's even talk of a federal investigation."

"Federal investigation?" Derrick Montgomery asked. Derrick was a founding board member of Total Truth and King's best friend. "Why?"

"Because some are saying the woman on the tape is under-age and that Nate may have crossed state lines to . . . be with her."

"No," Derrick answered. "She's legal. Barely, but she is."

"How do you know?"

"Trust me, I know. I'll fill you in when we meet in Texas."

King continued pacing. "Man, how in the *hell* could he have been so stupid as to sleep with jailbait, and then allow himself to be videotaped in the act? Especially right before he was to headline at our convention? His irresponsible actions have put the entire organization in the spotlight, and our reputation, maybe even our nonprofit status, in serious jeopardy."

Derrick knew how "stupid" could happen, and he knew King did too. A man often did foolish things when he let the wrong head make decisions. Still, Derrick understood his friend's frustration. Especially since King had reluctantly accepted the interim president position only after Derrick had pleaded with him to do so, and was therefore the unfortunate spokesperson at this auspicious time.

Total Truth's membership consisted of a variety of churches that had split from their traditional Baptist, Methodist, and Pentecostal roots, and adopted a less restrictive, more inclusive nondenominational position. Members under the organization's auspices recognized and practiced miracle healing, speaking in tongues, the prosperity message, and also more progressive spiritual practices such as the law of attraction, mantras, affirmations, meditation, and a controversial stance on homosexual tolerance within their congregations.

The sitting president had resigned unexpectedly following a death in the family, and Derrick, knee deep in an interfaith rebuilding effort that had him spending considerable time in Darfur, South Africa, had asked King to pinch hit. King was busy too. His church was in the middle of a major community development project, and his television ministry was flourishing. He'd been president before, when the association was in its infancy, so he knew how much time the role required. But Derrick assured King the position would be perfunctory—a couple conference calls, maybe a meeting or two, nothing more. And only for three months, until elections were held at the July convention. King had been two days away from passing the presidential baton on to a successor. And then the tape played.

King was not a stranger to scandal. As the handsome, forty-something pastor of Mount Zion Progressive Baptist Church in metropolitan Kansas City, he'd had to ask God for forgiveness more than once. Like Nate, he drew women to him like steel to a magnet. The two men even looked somewhat alike: both tall, dark, a study in rugged masculinity. But where King kept his black hair closely cropped, Nate let his texturized locks grow almost to his shoulders, and maintained a tidy goatee.

It was within this framework of understanding that King empathized, even as he denounced what his ministerial brother had done, even as he understood that decisive action would have to be taken to disassociate Total Truth from Nate's irresponsible actions.

"There's no doubt that Nate and his congregation will have to be completely severed from the association," King said. "We'll have to clearly and unequivocally break all ties with and support of that ministry."

Derrick listened intently, shifting the receiver from one ear to the other as he looked out the window of his home office and beheld a beautiful California afternoon. He passed a weary, deeply tanned hand across his handsome, clean-shaven face. It seemed that for the past five years there had been one church drama after another for him to deal with. Would the scandals ever end?

"I'll try to keep an open mind when we get to Texas tomorrow. Let's hear his side of the story," Derrick finally said. "But a picture is worth a thousand words. I hate to completely sever our relationship with his ministry, but unless he repents, steps down as senior pastor, and agrees to extensive counseling, we will have to. He was caught live and in living color. And the way it happened, fully exposed, before God and everybody . . . Jesus!"

"Kids in the sanctuary, church mothers, celebrities, the media." King plopped down heavily in the well-worn black leather chair behind his desk. "Lord have mercy. Somebody sure set out to ruin that brothah. Looks like they got the job done."

After making sure their travel plans for the emergency board meeting were properly coordinated, the friends hung up. But each man remained in his office—contemplating the catastrophe, and the possible ramifications for all involved—for a long time.

Derrick was especially troubled. It was bad enough that a pornographic video featuring a clear shot of Nate Thicke's glistening backside had been spliced into what was supposed to be a promotion of the Gospel Truth Church's holiday cruise. It was unconscionable that almost five seconds of the explicit tape was then seen by some of the record-setting twenty thousand attendees who'd gathered for the convention, before being abruptly stopped by a stunned yet quick-thinking technical director. And it was both shocking and devastating that Derrick had immediately recognized the woman moaning and thrashing beneath Nate's rhythmic thrusts, licking her lips as she turned her face toward the camera.

She was a former member of the ministry he headed, Kingdom Citizens Christian Center, and at sixteen—fast, feisty, and too much for her fifty-something parents to handle—had been sent to a Christian boarding school near Baton Rouge, Louisiana. That was about three years ago, Derrick figured. And he figured something else. Melody Anderson had moved again, to Palestine.

1

Generations

Three Years Earlier

Nate Thicke yawned, casually stretched his six-foot-three-inch frame, and gave the woman beside him a kiss on the forehead before getting out of bed. He strolled from the king-sized showpiece to the master bath in all his naked glory. At twenty-eight, he was in the best shape of his life, thanks to a mindful diet and the recent addition of a personal trainer to his church's official staff.

The woman in his bed, his administrative assistant Ms. Katherine Noble, admired his plump, hard backside and long, strong legs as he left the room. She especially loved how his dark brown blemish-free skin glistened with the fine sheen of sweat that had resulted from their lovemaking. They'd been lovers for a long time, and while she knew their relationship would never be more than that—had known from the beginning—she had fallen in love with him anyway. Even though she knew the day would come when he would take a wife and start a family. Even as she hoped he could continue to be her spiritual covering, her sexual satisfaction, as both his father and grandfather before him had been. Katherine had been a Thicke woman for generations.

Katherine rose and walked to a floor-length mirror that occupied a corner of the elegantly decorated bedroom, the black, tan, and deep purple color scheme her design. She eyed herself objectively, critically, turning this way and that. At fifty-three, her body easily looked ten years younger. It still held most of its firmness, her butterscotch skin was still smooth and supple. The stretch marks from her single pregnancy thirty-two years ago were long gone, rubbed away with cocoa butter and the luck of excellent genes. She tossed her shoulder-length hair away from her face, brought her image closer to the mirror. The fine crow lines around her eyes and on her forehead were deepening slightly, she noticed, and she detected a puffiness that hadn't been there five years ago. There was a slight sag to her chin, and even though she'd been the same weight for twenty-five years, it looked as if her cheeks were sunken, hollow, and not in a good way. These imperfections were not noticeable to the average observer. Most people who saw Katherine either admired or envied her for the attractive woman she was.

She turned to the side and continued her perusal, a frown accompanying her critique. Her butt had never been big, but it had always been firm. Until now. Now it hung loose and soft, like a deflated balloon, obeying the gravity that she tried to defy. A discernible dimpling of unwanted cellulite challenged her vow not to age. She cupped her cheeks, pushed them up, and thought about butt implants.

"Get out of the mirror. You're still fine." Nate walked from the bathroom into his massive closet and began to dress.

"I'm sure you say that to all your women," Katherine responded, without rancor. "But even if you're lying, it makes me feel so good."

Thirty minutes later, a showered and dressed Katherine sat across the desk from Nate in his roomy, masculine home office. She looked the epitome of decorum in her black skirt that hung below the knee, and a pink and black polka-dotted blouse with a frilly lace collar that tickled her chin. Her hair was pulled back in a bun, and black, rectangular reading glasses sat perched on her nose. Anyone entering would see a scene of utmost respectability.

A "matronly" older woman who had known Nate since he was born, Katherine had been considered the perfect choice as his assistant when he became senior pastor four years ago, the perfect barrier between him and all the young, single female members who clamored for his "counsel." Her position was the perfect cover for their ongoing liaison. No one ever questioned why she was in his home; no one guessed that she spent as much time in his bedroom as she did in his office. Of course, Nate's residence in a gated and guarded community was beneficial as well—very few eyes could pry.

"You had something you wanted to discuss with me?" Katherine asked after Nate had finished a call with a church deacon.

"Yes," he answered.

Katherine waited. In bed, at first, she had been the teacher, he the student. She had been the older woman, he the enthralled teenager. She'd been in control. But those roles had reversed a long time ago. Now he was her boss, and the more experienced lover. He was now clearly in control. So now, even though she could tell that his mind was in turmoil, she didn't push, but waited until he was ready to speak.

Nate cleared his throat and began toying with a paperweight on his desk. It wasn't so much that he was getting ready to talk with Katherine about what God had told him; she'd often been a sounding board. It's just that this time, he wasn't sure how she'd react to what he had to say.

"The Lord has spoken to me," he began in a tone of authority. "He has given me confirmation on who's to be my wife."

Katherine let out the breath she'd been holding. *Is that all?* she thought. At once, she quelled the surge of jealousy that rose to the surface, determined to not deny this woman what she knew she could never have, Nate's hand in marriage. It was why she'd denied her own feelings when Nate came to her some years ago and said he'd been led to become Simone's biblical covering. How could she protest his decision to have sex with her daughter? Katherine, along with the older Thicke men, had been Nate's mentors, his example, encouraging him to indulge his conjugal rights as a spiritual leader in their church. That's how he had wound up in Katherine's bed. And now, this is how she would always have a key to his home . . . as his mother-in-law.

Katherine was certain of God's message to Nate that Simone was to be his wife. After all, she was perfect. The two were good friends, had practically grown up together. At thirty-two, Simone had never been married and only had one child. Like her mother, Simone was a stunner, the family's Creole blood prominent in her features. Three inches taller than Katherine's five foot six, Simone had Katherine's beautiful hazel green eyes, a full pouty mouth, large breasts, and long black hair. She was educated and cultured, perfect "first lady" material for a prominent, up and coming minister. And to top all this off, Simone had the voice of an angel. Beyoncé, Rihanna, Mariah: these successful women had nothing on her daughter, either in looks or voice. This is what Katherine had envisioned on that first night when she knew Nate and Simone were sleeping together, when she had to make room for her daughter in her pastor's crowded bed. And now her dream was coming true!

Katherine reached over and placed her hand over Nate's. "Don't worry, Nathaniel. I knew this day would come. Everything is going to be fine, trust me. Simone is going to make a beautiful bride and a fabulous wife."

Nate's dark brown eyes met Katherine's hazel green ones. He forced himself not to squirm or break the stare. He had heard from God, and knew in his heart that his decision was right. For the first time since walking into the office, he blessed his longtime lover with a dazzling smile of straight, white teeth set against skin so dark and creamy smooth one wanted to lick it.

"Katherine, you're right, as usual. The woman God has chosen for me will make an excellent wife, and she will be the perfect first lady. But it isn't Simone."

Katherine snatched back her hand, stunned into silence. Within seconds, however, she found her voice. "Who could it be if not my daughter? There's nobody in our congregation who compares to her!"

Katherine thought back to Nate's busy schedule, and the increasing amount of time he spent ministering in other churches.

"Oh, my God, that's it. You've found someone outside of Palestine. Is it someone from Mount Zion Progressive, or one of those silicone-injected, weave-wearing minister chasers in LA?"

Katherine stood and walked to the window behind Nate's desk. Then she stopped, one hand on her hip, and swirled his chair around until he faced her. "You know I respect your anointing. I've never questioned your ability to hear God's voice. But, Nathaniel, I have to question it now. I'm positive that Simone is the woman you should marry."

"And I'm positive that it's her daughter, Destiny. Katherine, your granddaughter is the one who will be my wife."

2

Tangled, Tarnished Traditions

"A man of God has needs," Katherine said calmly. She emphasized the word *man* by drawing out the last letter in the word.

"I won't allow it," Simone replied with equal composure, looking at her manicured nails as if she were discussing the weather. "I won't let him sleep with Destiny. She's sixteen, still a child."

"She'll be seventeen in three months," Katherine countered. "Older than you were when you got pregnant."

Simone jumped to her feet. "But it's supposed to be me, Mother! That's what you told me, remember? And for the past four years, that's what I've believed. That once Nate got older, ready to settle down, it would be with me!"

"I also thought it would be you, baby, was sure of it. But God has spoken, and now we must heed the voice of His servant. You are no less chosen now than you were yesterday. You are the mother of our man of God's future wife. You'll always have an important role in the ministry."

At this point, Simone wasn't interested in Nate's ministry. To tell the gospel truth, she was worried about her role in his bed, a role she didn't want to relinquish.

"She's sixteen. I can't believe you, as her grandmother, don't find Nate's intention to marry her at this young age appalling."

Simone waited for Katherine to speak. When her mother remained quiet, Simone continued. "You might not have a problem with it, but I do. Destiny's too young," she repeated defiantly. "End of discussion."

Katherine sighed as she watched her proud, hurt daughter leave the living room. Simone had a right to be angry, Katherine knew, and she took her share of blame for stroking her daughter's expectation of becoming Mrs. Nathaniel Thicke, and first lady of the Gospel Truth Church. But she couldn't agree with her daughter that Destiny was too young.

Should I tell her? Katherine pondered. *Should I tell Simone the whole story about Nathaniel, and me, the Thickes and the Nobles, and our church's tangled, tarnished traditions?*

3

Something Noble

Katherine was twelve years old when she found out about the "man of God" and his special "needs." The lesson had been taught forcefully and thoroughly: initially painful, later pleasurable. Katherine was a quick learner. As she left her daughter's house, she barely noticed what rarely happened in Texas—a January snowfall. She got into her custom-colored, deep purple Cadillac and drove toward the Gospel Truth Church offices . . . and she remembered.

"Mama, Reverend Thicke touched me."

Naomi Noble closed her eyes briefly and took a deep breath. *And so it continues,* she thought. The pain she felt for her daughter was brief, replaced by a sense of duty and resignation. She turned to face her youngest child and only girl. "A man of God has needs, Katherine. I told you that, been telling you for years. Reverend Thomas Thicke is a man of God, a covering for the daughters of his flock. And only those who are special, chosen, are touched by him."

"But, Mama, it didn't feel good. It hurt."

Naomi stopped in midstroke, the doily she was crocheting momentarily forgotten. "Why? Did he put his peter in you?"

For a moment, Katherine was confused, wondering what a

disciple of Jesus had to do with what had happened in the pastor's office. "Peter?" she repeated.

"Peter, snake, ding-a-ling . . . Did he put his thing in you?"

"Oh, no, ma'am," Katherine answered, a blush creeping up from her neck to her scalp.

"Then how did he hurt you?"

Katherine bowed her head. She was too embarrassed to say what had happened, and when Naomi continued to stare at her, Katherine burst out crying and ran to her room.

Moments later, Naomi followed. Armed with the family Bible, she entered her daughter's darkened room and noted the curled up bundle underneath the quilt. Naomi pulled a chair up to Katherine's bed and spoke in a soft voice. "Katherine, baby, I need for you to look at me. What I have to say is important. I need to teach you what it means to be chosen."

When Katherine hesitated, Naomi continued in a soft yet stern voice. "Ain't a thing for you to be embarrassed about, Katherine. The man of God has needs, that's all, and certain daughters of the flock are chosen to help meet these needs. Reverend Thomas is being your spiritual covering, baby."

By now, any other mother would have been at this molester's house with a shotgun. But Naomi taught what she'd learned and experienced, actually condoning the unthinkable practice that had been passed down from her mother.

Katherine wiped her eyes and sat up against the backboard. "But Nettie told me it was nasty to let boys touch you . . . down there."

Naomi's voice rose. "What are you doing talking to Nettie or anybody else about God's business? Girl, you better learn to cover the man of God like he covers you . . . lest the Lord strike you dead, and me along beside you!"

The thought of losing her mother in such a horrid fashion terrified Katherine. "I didn't tell her about Reverend!" she wailed.

"Well, how does she know then?"

"'Cause last week . . . we were talking about boys."

"What boys?" Naomi hissed. "Who have you been whoring around with?"

"Nobody, Mama!" Katherine's eyes grew wide and tears threatened. How was it that she'd be a whore if a boy touched her but what had happened today was okay? "Reverend is the only one who touched me, Mama. I promise! But how come Reverend Thomas can do it, but it's bad if somebody else does?"

Naomi spoke slowly, enunciating every word. "Because Reverend Thomas Thicke is a man of God. He is your covering, protects us, keeps us safe. Hasn't he been almost like a father to you since your daddy run off?"

Katherine nodded. "Yes, ma'am."

"He's the reason we can stay in this fine house and I can buy those pretty dresses you wear. Because we're special, because *you're* special, child. Nettie ain't special, she's common. A man of God can't share with her what he can with you. When the man of God has needs, only special women, ones who are chosen, can take care of them. Do you understand?"

Katherine was beginning to. She nodded again, slowly.

"And don't you tell nobody about what goes on between you and the man of God, do you hear me? Nobody! Less the Lord strike me down and you along with me. That old, ugly Nettie don't need to know nothing about this here business. And she ain't your friend."

"But, Mama—"

"She ain't! She's acting like it now because y'all are still kids. But give it time, when she feels her flower blooming and boys start buzzing around it. Then she's going to be jealous of you. They all will. That's why you have to do like the Bible says: don't let your left hand know what your right hand is doing. I mean it, Katherine. Don't tell a soul."

Naomi had opened the Bible then, and quoted scriptures from the Old Testament. Scriptures that spoke of covering, sometimes a man with his own daughter, and then Naomi explained how such coverings were God's will. Much as her mother had when Naomi was Katherine's age, Naomi taught her daughter that what was wrong for other people was okay for them, because they were doing the Lord's work. After she put down the Bible, Naomi continued Katherine's education in being special, and how to please God's man.

It was another two years before Reverend Thicke's penis replaced the finger that had penetrated Katherine's innocence. By then she had become well versed in her role as a daughter of his flock. True to her mother's predictions, others became jealous, especially Nettie. Later, Nettie would have reason to hate Katherine, and that she didn't, even to this day, was why Katherine respected her more than any other woman. Their unlikely friendship had lasted for more than four decades.

Also true to her mother's prediction, Katherine became the topic of gossip and the object of scorn for most females in their small town. More than once, she was accosted by a church mother after coming out of the pastor's parsonage, especially when Thomas's wife, Mrs. Nancy Thicke, wasn't there.

"You ain't got no business in there when the Missus ain't home," one would say.

"She asked me to come over," Katherine would reply.

"Well, just what in God's name would she ask you to do while she ain't there?" another would demand to know.

Katherine would respond as her mother had taught her: "Something noble."

Katherine pulled into her parking space in the church lot and walked through the side door that led to the executive offices. The issue with Destiny was pressing, but her personal affairs couldn't interfere with church business. The pastor's anniversary was coming up in six months, and as always, Katherine intended to make sure it was the grandest one in the district. This year was especially important because representatives from a new, forward-thinking organization called Total Truth would be in attendance. Katherine hoped to align their ministry with these megachurch entities, in hopes of pushing Nate's star higher, faster.

Katherine had to focus on the anniversary for another reason—Jennifer Stevens. This new member had been at the church a little over a year and was already trying to act as if she ran things. The fact that she was from a big megachurch, Mount Zion Progressive, didn't impress or intimidate Katherine one bit. Jennifer wasn't the first twit who'd "heard from God" and changed her zip code to Palestine, Texas, in hopes of changing her last name as well. She'd seen many Jennifers come and go.

Katherine wasn't intimidated, but she was astute. She was paying close attention to how Jennifer was trying to weasel herself into Nate's inner circle, with her knowledge of the national church landscape, connections to the Total Truth board members, and tight skirts highlighting her big, juicy booty. The trysts Nate had with other church members were harmless. After all, old members knew the rules and, more importantly, knew that the Nobles ruled. *But this Jennifer chick, I'm going to have to slow her roll.* Katherine's brow knitted as she pondered how to make sure nothing and no one came between Nate and her Destiny.

4

Praying for Mercy

Nettie Thicke Johnson had already been praying for hours when the phone rang. *I need to get that.* She rose from her kneeled position at a chair in the living room and headed for the cordless phone in the kitchen. The phone had rung several times during her conversation with God, but since this was the first time she'd thought to interrupt their dialogue, the others had obviously not warranted her immediate attention.

Most speculated that the prophetic anointing that was on Nate's life came from the prestigious line of ministers on his father's side. That was only one of several mistakes one made where Nate's attributes were concerned. Nettie, his mother, was the one in the family with "the eye," the ability to prophesy so accurately that she could not only tell you the color of underwear you wore at the moment, but the pair you'd choose a week from now. Her son's brilliance was also courtesy of his mother, as was the compassionate heart that often got his lower extremities into so much trouble. Nettie knew her son well and had finally concluded: *Two out of three ain't bad.*

"Hello?"

"Nettie? Maxine Brook."

"Lord have mercy, Mama Max!" Nettie's mood immediately brightened at the sound of her voice. Maxine Brook had four children of her own, but she mothered almost everyone she met. Everyone loved her for it, and everyone affectionately called her Mama Max. "As I live and breathe, sistah, the Lord put you on my heart just yesterday. Told me you'd be calling."

"Well, chile, your hearing is good because the Lord sho put you on my heart a couple days ago. The Reverend Doctor has been ailing a bit, but I knew I'd call first chance I got. He's resting now, praise be to the Almighty, so here I is. How you doing, Nettie Jean?"

"Oh, tolerable. I can't complain."

"Gordon?"

"He's fine, too." Gordon Johnson was Nettie's quiet, hard-working husband of the past nine years.

"And the ministry?"

Nettie's sigh was barely audible. "God is good."

"God may be good but that quality don't always extend to church folk. Talk to me."

"Oh, Mama Max . . . you've been on this road long enough to know what the scenery looks like. It ain't changed since you and Mama first became friends."

Nettie's mother, Amanda, met Mama Max when both were minister's wives surviving harsh winters and even harsher congregations in the Texas countryside. Ten years her senior, Amanda became Mama Max's confidante, and Mama Max had known Nettie since she was a child. When Amanda went to be with the Lord more than a decade ago, after battling cancer, Mama Max stepped in and did her best to fill the shoes that no one else's feet could ever truly fill. She'd done a pretty good job of mothering though, supporting Nettie through crises and controversies, always there with a dose of "Mama Maxisms" and a listening ear.

"Naw, chile, you're right about that," Mama Max replied. "The felines might change from a pedigreed Persian to an alley cat but at the end of the day . . . it still comes down to pussy."

"Mama Max, you get on away from here with that kind of language!"

"Chile, don't act like I shocked you. You've been knowing me too long to think I'd change. So am I right?"

"About what?"

"About the problem revolving around puss 'n boots. Some woman's pussy and some pastor's boots?" Mama Max whooped at her own Maxism. "Nettie Jean, you're fifty-four, got three kids, and been in church your whole life. The truth ain't always pretty but it's usually pertinent. And you *know* I'm telling the truth."

Nettie laughed. "Well, there is a little something going on."

Mama Max crossed her legs and waited, took a sip of black coffee and looked out her picture window at the snow-covered lawns of a Kansas winter.

"It's Nathaniel. He's getting married."

"To who? When? How long has he known the girl?"

"Whoa, Mama Max, one question at a time. Her name is Destiny. They're going to have a long engagement, and he's known her since, well, since she was born."

"Known her since . . . Nettie? Are you trying to give me a heart attack so I can join your mama in paradise? You better explain yourself and quick, lest I be on the first thing smokin' outta Kansas for Texas. Nate may be grown, but he ain't past a good butt whoopin'." Even as she spoke, Mama Max picked up a newspaper off the coffee table and swatted the furniture twice—for practice.

"It's Katherine's grandbaby, Destiny."

"Katherine Noble? Lord have mercy, Jesus, and Mary, mother of God, why can't the Thicke men stay away from those Noble women?"

"Well, I could use your words to provide an answer, Mama, but I don't want to be disrespectful."

"Go ahead, girl. Tell the truth and shame the devil. It's puss 'n boots, baby, the man of God's ultimate weakness. From David to Sampson, Adam and every Thicke who's ever approached the throne of grace. You forget I been a preacher's wife for nigh unto fifty years. Married one and raised another. Now, it's many a saint who's been splayed by the split. And those Noble hussies are Satan's soldiers. You don't have to tell me, chile. I've been there. I know."

For Mama Max, the Noble name had been a curse word for most of her adult life. The acrimonious origins harkened back to a challenging time in Mama Max's marriage to her husband of almost half a century: the Reverend Doctor Pastor Bishop Overseer Mister Stanley Obadiah Meshach Brook Jr. She could remember the incident as if it had happened yesterday. Where: Dallas, Texas. When: 1963. What: the National Baptist Convention. Who: Katherine's mother's sister, Dorothea Noble. Why? Mama Max had finished a long day of conferences and teachings, and had foregone a dinner invitation with her husband in favor of a good night's sleep. She'd gone back to the hotel right after service and was already snoring when the phone rang.

"Sistah Brook," an unfamiliar voice had whispered into the receiver. "I don't mean to be nosy or rude, but I just saw your husband come into the lobby and I don't think he's headed to your room."

"Who's this?" Mama Max had demanded, suddenly wide awake.

"You can just say I'm my sister's keeper." Then the line went dead.

Mama Max jumped out of that bed as if lightning hit and started praying in tongues. "Give me the spirit of discernment, Holy Ghost," she intoned as she paced back and forth and around the room. After about fifteen minutes a number came to her clear as day: 915. Without hesitation, Mama Max slipped on her caftan, pulled on her slippers, and checked her always perfectly coiffed hair in the mirror before leaving the room and heading for the elevator. When she reached room 915, she knocked on the door. After a moment, a quiet voice asked tentatively, "Who is it?"

"It's your worst nightmare!" Mama Max had explosively responded. "Wife of Bishop Stanley Obadiah Meshach Brook and mother to his four children: King, Queen, Daniel, and Esther," Mama Max yelled for the world to hear. "Open up this door, you two-bit hussy. I think you've got something that belongs to me!"

"Mama Max? You still there? Hello?"

"Oh, baby, I'm so sorry. Memories just took me down hell's highway. Now what were you saying?"

"I was asking you to pray for Nathaniel, and this decision he's made. I think Destiny's got a good heart, and strange as it seems, I think she's God's choice for him, but she's still a child."

"How old is she?"

"Almost seventeen."

"Almost? Lord have mercy, Jesus, son of Mary, brother of James, Savior of nations. That boy of yours is playing with fire. Nate best be sure his sins don't find him out."

"I'm praying for mercy," Nettie responded.

"Well, pray without ceasing," Maxine replied. "Because the devil is sho 'nuff busy, and if that slew-footed horned scoundrel has his way? Chile, I get the feeling your son's gon' wind up needing more than mercy . . . a lot more!"

5

Duty Calls

Simone Noble allowed herself the luxury of stretching her five-foot-nine, one-hundred-forty-pound frame toward the ceiling. She had been tense for two weeks, ever since her mother's visit . . . and the news. Except for the previous weekend when he'd been swamped with meetings and putting out church fires, Nate had been out of town since Katherine told her about his intentions—that he would not only cover her daughter, Destiny, but marry her as well.

Any other mother would have been thrilled at this news. Nathaniel Thicke was a prime catch, by either secular or religious definition. But Simone Chastity Noble was not any other mother. She was the woman who'd left a well-paying job in Dallas, Texas, to move back to Palestine, and along with it, the very real possibility of going from the advertisement firm owner's employee to his wife. But when Katherine had called and suggested Nate might be looking to settle down, Simone hadn't thought twice about giving up what she had for what she could have. After all, ad firm owner Leon Bates's millions were no match for Nate Thicke's hammer—and potential to make millions. Simone had been blessed with the pounding of that tool on a few occasions, during breaks home from college and once just before she relocated to Dallas. At that time, Simone had never considered a relationship with Nate. Back then, she hadn't been ready to deal with being part of the then-named Palestine Missionary Baptist Church harem. Thinking it would spur him to change his ways, Simone had told Nate she was leaving, and that when he got ready to settle down, to give her a call. But he hadn't called her, Katherine had. In the end it hadn't mattered who called, but that the phone had rung with the message that Nate might be ready to marry. Simone put in a two-week notice and was back in Palestine a month later. That was four years ago, and now that Nate had finally decided to take a wife—Simone wanted to be that woman.

Simone looked around the room. Satisfied that the stage was set for seduction, she glanced in the mirror one final time before walking from her bedroom to the living room. She knew her look was impeccable; at her mother's urging, she'd spent a lifetime insuring this visage stayed intact. Her outfit was a simple, D&G design: a chocolate-colored pantsuit tailored to Simone's surprising curves for such a lanky body, paired with a tan-colored knit shell and matching pumps. She'd washed her hair just that morning and knew it was shiny and smelled of lavender, one of Nate's favorite fragrances. She'd just gotten a manicure and pedicure, and her flesh still tingled from yesterday's bikini wax. There was not a scar or blemish on Simone's body, not even a pimple. On the outside, she was the epitome of elegance and control. Inside, she was an emotional wreck.

She'd tried to handle the news about Nate covering Destiny the way Katherine had handled the news about him covering her. But she couldn't. Katherine had known there was no chance for marrying Nate, while becoming Mrs. Nathaniel Thicke had always been Simone's dream. Up until two weeks ago, she'd felt a marriage between them was inevitable. Even the vivacious, booty-full Jennifer Stevens hadn't ruffled Simone's feathers, despite the fact that she knew Nathan had covered her. Simone never thought she'd have to compete with a sixteen-year-old for her pastor's affections, much less her own daughter. But desperate times called for desperate measures. Now appeared to be one of those times.

Simone was startled out of her reverie and self-examination by the chimes of the doorbell. *He's here,* she thought, rising to open the door for her beloved. *I've got to find a way to show him the mistake he's making. Simply telling him won't be enough.*

"Hey, Nate." Opening the door, Simone hoped her voice sounded casual as she worked the two-syllable greeting around a bundle of nerves. She signaled him to enter, and then sauntered back into the living room. She took up an offensive position in the hallway between the combination living/dining room and kitchen and asked, "Would you care for some tea?"

Nate had a lot on his mind at this moment. He knew Katherine was still reeling from the news he'd shared about his decision to marry Destiny and from the fear that their sexual liaison might be over. He also knew that Simone was pissed about his decision, and he hadn't yet had time to think about how to approach the woman-child who'd captured his heart. Adding to this pressure was the fact that his self-help book was due to the publisher in thirty days, his church was bursting at the seams with new members signaling the need for a new building, and his five-year anniversary, where the Total Truth Association would officially welcome him and his congregation into their ranks as a member in good standing, was all happening in less than six months. Anyone would agree that there was a lot to care about.

"I'd love some tea, beautiful," he said to Simone. Not so much because he was thirsty but because the simple act of her making tea would hopefully chill out the tension he'd felt as soon as he'd entered the room, no matter how much Simone had tried to hide it. He figured the best way to deal with the situation was up front. With this in mind, he followed Simone into the kitchen.

"You're upset with me."

Simone was glad for this opening to discuss Nate's decision. Now she didn't have to worry about how to broach the subject herself. "Upset? That's putting it quite mildly, Nate. The nonviolent person you're looking at could probably render you unconscious with her bare hands. But what purpose would that serve besides messing up my nails?"

Nate laughed. Simone had always had that affect on him, the ability to loosen him up. While he believed that her daughter possessed it as well, along with every other characteristic he desired, he admitted that each Noble woman owned a particular uniqueness he enjoyed. With Simone, it was definitely her dry yet vivid sense of humor. For Katherine, it was her ability to nurture him, make him feel powerful and special. Nate had his pick of almost any woman at the Gospel Truth Church, but the Nobles and he shared a special bond. He knew that his father, Daniel, had taken Simone's cherry, even though Katherine had sworn him to secrecy after finding out Simone hadn't shared this news. Katherine obviously knew her daughter quite well because Simone had denied it when he finally asked her about it just two years ago. And even though Simone was aware of the Thicke-Noble history, how each Noble woman had been deflowered by a Thicke man, Nathan didn't think she knew as much as he did. Specific information had been given to him as a rite of passage when he entered the ministry—almost as instruction on his duty to cover not only the Nobles, but other female parishioners of the flock. It is this history that made Nate feel verified, justified, and qualified to introduce Destiny to the ways of womanhood, and to not only cover her, but to get her commitment to become his wife.

"I probably should have told you first about my decision, you being Destiny's mother and all."

"Probably, but it wouldn't change how I feel about it. First of all, Destiny is too young to marry anybody. Secondly, I thought when you walked down the aisle, it would be with me." *There it is*, Simone thought. The truth was out.

"Marrying Destiny doesn't have to change the relationship

between us," Nate said softly. "But I've heard from God, Simone, and Destiny will be my wife."

"I heard from God too," Simone said, not backing down one inch. She turned off the teapot and shook away the sudden image of pouring the boiling water over Nate's foolhardy head. Instead, the water flowed into two mugs, which she placed on a tray, along with a bowl of honey, a saucer of lemon slices, and a dish of butter cookies. Simone didn't miss the irony of the homey moment as she picked up the tray and left the kitchen.

Walking into the living room, she continued. "You know I'm the one who is best suited to serve you, Nate. Destiny is beautiful, I'll grant her that. She's also intelligent, charming, and refined. The apple doesn't fall far from the tree, does it? But I gave up everything to come back here and serve in the ministry because I realized this is where I belong. You are my heart's desire, Nate, and I'm not too proud to be very clear that it's you I want. I intend for the words we've penned together to come alive in *my* life."

Nate sighed inwardly as he sat on the couch and watched Simone prepare his tea: two dollops of honey and two lemon slices, just as he'd instructed her years ago. He understood Simone's disappointment, but he'd actually expected more outrage from Katherine; after all, they'd been together longer. Simone had always been like a best friend as well as a lover. For some unknown reason he'd thought she'd just shrug her shoulders and understand. He'd thought wrong.

Simone scooted closer to Nate and put her hand on his chest. "Nate, my darling, you know I can help ensure your success: materially and spiritually. We're a great team, you *know* this."

She smiled, licked her lips subtly, and kissed his cheek. In spite of his resolve to not cover her this day, Nathaniel hardened.

"The book I've ghostwritten is going to make you a bestselling author, I can feel it!" With that, Simone left the room, her genuine, dazzling smile still permeating the area after she'd gone.

Nathaniel watched her go with mixed emotions. Simone was one of the most beautiful women he'd ever met, her daughter notwithstanding. And in many ways, she was right. They were well suited for each other, spiritually, temperamentally, and especially physically. Nathaniel would never deny to anyone that he loved Simone, but he was *in* love with the daughter whom he hadn't yet kissed.

Nathaniel reared back on the couch and remembered the moment when he knew Destiny was meant to be his bride. It was a few months ago—three to be exact. His reflection was cut short by Simone reentering the room. Her eyes glowed as she walked toward him carrying a small box of papers. "I finished it last night," she said proudly.

Nate immediately sat up. "This is my book?" he asked.

Simone simply looked at him and nodded.

Nate got up and took the box out of her hands. "I can't believe you finished it already! When I told you the publisher had moved up the deadline—"

"Then meeting that deadline became my singular goal. I took my vacation time to finish it, stayed home all last week and worked on it every minute. I barely ate or slept," Simone gushed, remembering both the agony and the ecstasy of seeing Nate's dream come to life at the tip of her fast-typing fingers. "I'd do anything for you, Nathaniel Eli Thicke . . . anything."

Nate walked into the dining room and pulled out a chair. Running his hand over the cover page, he read reverently: "*Give Up Everything and Have It All,* by Nathaniel E. Thicke, Senior Pastor, the Gospel Truth Church, Palestine, Texas. All Rights Reserved."

He looked up at Simone with a gaze full of appreciation and gratitude. "I couldn't have done this without you," he admitted with undisguised pleasure.

"It's only the beginning of the things we can do together,"

Simone answered. "It was as if your very spirit flowed through me as I typed these words. I think I captured both your message and your voice, not only from our discussions and the tapes of your sermons, but from what I know about you. The Spirit fell as I typed, and I saw what God has in store for you. You're going to be big, Nate. One of the biggest preachers the world has ever known."

Nate scanned several pages while Simone talked, his heart swelling with gratitude at this accomplishment, his first book. Thanks to Simone, he had no doubt that he would meet his publisher's deadline. He was sure he'd find little that she'd have to correct. Now, Nate believed he owed Simone for two babies: the one she'd birthed sixteen years ago named Destiny, and the literary one she'd help birth right now.

He looked over at Simone, his dark brown eyes boring into her hazel green ones. "What can I ever do to thank you?" he asked sincerely.

It was the moment Simone had waited for. "Cover me," she said simply. "I need to be loved by the man of God." *And I need to try and fuck some sense into your head!*

Without another word, Nate stood and headed toward Simone's bedroom, shaking off the promise he'd made to himself to not have sex with anyone tonight. He was a Thicke man and Simone was a Noble woman. Satisfying her was his obligation. Nathaniel removed his tailored suit jacket as he walked toward her bedroom. He watched the way her derriere moved in the form-fitting slacks and was suddenly no longer sorry for the fact that . . . duty called.

6

Keeping Friends Close

Outside the patio door, a gentle wind stirred the dead leaves in the coral-colored clay flowerpots as unseasonably warm temperatures heralded February's arrival. But Jennifer Stevens didn't notice. She was too busy looking at the picture that had burned into her conscience from the moment her eyes beheld it the previous Sunday: the sly smile and secretive wink she'd seen her pastor, Nathaniel Thicke, bestow on Simone Noble's daughter. *Simone's daughter, for God's sake! A frickin' child!*

Too keyed up to sit, Jennifer rose from the table by the patio and walked outside. She wrapped arms, clad in a wool sweater, around herself. Despite the bright sun, there was a chill in the air—just like the cold she felt in her heart. Jennifer had been in church her whole life. She knew the games and how they worked, knew the signs of a member slippin' and dippin' with the pastor or some other senior sanctuary official. That's why she knew without a doubt that Simone Noble and Nate Thicke were screwing. *That bitch thinks she's God's gift to the universe.* But what was up with the wink?

"Forgive me, God," Jennifer said out loud. For all the sins her current mood enlisted—jealousy, envy, coveting, etc.— Jennifer truly loved God and tried to live the life of an upstanding Christian woman. Before happily succumbing to Nate's charms, she hadn't been with a man for almost ten years. But from the time Nate had preached at her former church a year and a half ago, Jennifer's focus had been singular: to be by his side. She'd prayed and prayed for a sign from God, one that Nate was meant to be her husband or at the very least that moving to Texas was God's will. After not getting a message from on high, at least one that she wanted to hear, she'd given a thirty-day notice at her job, gone online to find another one, and it wasn't long before she was moving from Kansas City to Palestine.

Jennifer had arrived at Gospel Truth Church with a written recommendation from her pastor, King Brook, and—she discovered shortly after her arrival—something to help Nate get what he wanted. A casual conversation with one of the members had clued in Jennifer to Nate's desire to become a Total Truth member. Jennifer had wasted no time in setting up an appointment, and remembered how making one with his assistant, Katherine, had been almost as hard as she'd imagined it was to see President Obama. *She's guarding the man so tough you'd think they were screwing.* Remembering that spontaneous thought gave her pause. And then she'd decided there was no possible way a man like Nate would be with a woman like Katherine. Granted, at one time Katherine had probably been a beautiful woman, like her daughter. But Nate had too many choices among the goo-goo-eyed females in his congregation to lay down with a heifah old enough to be his mother.

Jennifer had been so deep in thought that she jumped when the phone rang. "Hey, Patricia." Patricia Cook was the woman who'd told Jennifer about Nate's Total Truth member aspirations, as well as confirmed that Simone and he were screwing. Then she'd shared some news that Jennifer hadn't expected: that Patricia was screwing him too.

"Jennifer, something is going on, girl!"

"What?"

"I don't know. That's why I'm calling you."

Did Patricia catch the same wink I did, from Nate to Destiny?
Jennifer decided to keep her cards close to her chest and see
what more she could find out. "Well, I'm not sure I can help
you, Pat. Going on with whom?"

"Who else, girl? Nate."

"What makes you think something is going on?"

"Well, for one thing, he didn't come over last night. And
don't start in on me about sleeping with the pastor. I know it's
wrong but I can't help it. You haven't ever been with him so I
don't expect you to understand. But if you had, well, suffice it
to say you'd know why I'll never deny that man."

*Oh, but I have . . . and I know. That's why I'm keeping my
friends close and heifahs like you closer!* The truth was, Jennifer didn't
have female friends, per se. If a woman was older than twelve
and younger than sixty, she was considered competition. As
such, she was kept at a distance. Still, Jennifer knew how to
play the game. Women couldn't be friends, but sometimes they
were unwitting accomplices. Now was one of those times.

"Anyway, that's not why I called," Patricia continued. "I'm
calling about what I saw this afternoon, when I stopped by the
church during my lunch hour to drop off the flyers I did for
the upcoming all-night prayer service."

"Well, do I have to pay admission to view this movie?"
Jennifer impatiently exclaimed after Pat hesitated. "What did
you see?"

Patricia lowered her voice, even though she was alone in
her car and sure no one else could hear her. "Well, first I saw
Katherine and Simone out in the parking lot. It looked like
they were arguing. But when they saw me pull up, they tried
to act like they were just talking."

Jennifer stifled a sigh. "Is that all, Pat? A mother and daughter bickering isn't the most unusual sight in the world."

"Maybe not," Patricia continued in a conspiratorial tone.
"But it's who I saw afterward that makes this little tidbit interesting."

"Why? Who was it?" Having to pull this story out sentence by sentence was starting to get on Jennifer's nerves.

"Simone's daughter, Destiny," Patricia answered. "She was walking down the hall to Reverend's office, and if you ask me, her skirt was a little short for church. I don't care if she is a teenager. As soon as she got into the office, the door closed."

Both women were silent a moment, because both knew what could happen behind their pastor's closed office door.

Finally Jennifer recovered enough to find her voice. "About what time was this?" she asked.

"I took a late lunch so it had to be around two. What do you think it means? Mama and daughter argue while grand-daughter goes in to see the Reverend?"

"Girl, who knows?" Jennifer said. She wasn't ready to share her suspicions yet, but knew when the time was right, Patricia could be an ally.

"Do you think there's a chance that . . ."

"A chance that what?" Jennifer asked, more forceful than she'd intended.

"Never mind," Patricia sighed. "I don't want to even have an inappropriate thought about the man of God, much less voice it. You know the Word says, 'Touch not God's anointed and do his prophets no harm.'"

Well, had you kept reading that Word, you slut, you'd also have read something about not screwing a man who wasn't your husband. Jennifer quickly excluded herself from this scripture by re-minding herself that hers and Nate's was a "spiritual union" al-ready, and as such was not sin.

"That's what it says," Jennifer agreed. "Which is why we have to keep the man of God in our prayers."

After making plans to have lunch on Saturday, the two Gospel Truth members hung up their phones. Jennifer picked hers right back up. Because while she intended to keep the man of God in her prayers, she hoped the phone call she was about to make would also keep him in her bed.

1

Her Heart's Desire

"Look at that high-yellow heifah. She thinks she's cute."

Destiny Noble held her head high and ignored her classmate.

"Yeah, we oughta kick her ass, snatch that weave off her head. Thinking she's better than everybody, that bitch bettah recognize!"

Destiny's loudmouthed nemesis, Carmen, signaled her friends and began walking behind Destiny.

"Hey, Destiny!" a young man shouted from across the street.

"Hey, Adam."

Adam shot a mean look at Carmen before sidling up next to Destiny on the sidewalk. "Don't pay those fools no mind, baby girl. They're just mad they're not you."

Destiny shrugged, but was thankful that her best friend had come along when he did. Carmen was always threatening her, but Destiny wasn't afraid: partly because she felt Carmen was just full of hot air—hating on her because Carmen Cook's mother, Patricia, couldn't stand Katherine or her relatives by default—and partly because of the industry-strength Mace she always carried at the ready. Girls had despised her ever since she could remember. "Because you're chosen," her grandmother had told her. Destiny wasn't going to risk getting her face scarred up fighting, but she'd Mace the hell out of anybody who attacked her.

Adam unlocked his car doors and he and Destiny climbed inside. "Baby girl," he said once he'd started the car and rolled out of the school parking lot. "You want to go with us to the movies tonight? We're gonna check out Tyler Perry's new movie."

"No. I have to study."

"On a Friday night? Girl, you're already a straight-A student. What are you going for, teacher's pet?"

Destiny smiled. "Something like that."

Destiny and Adam kept up small talk until Adam dropped Destiny off at her house. After promising to hang out with Adam and his friends one day soon, Destiny jumped out of the car and ran inside. She'd managed to sneak Reverend Thicke's manuscript out of her mother's bedroom, and had made herself a copy. She was almost done, and the timing was perfect. Because later tonight, she was going to spend an entire twenty-four hours with the reverend. She knew this time would be special, and wanted to be as prepared as possible to impress him.

Destiny stopped in the kitchen, fixed herself a salad, grabbed a sparkling water out of the refrigerator, and hurried to her room. She was anxious to read the last chapter of Nate's book: "Now . . . Know It's Yours." She knew even before turning the page that this would be her favorite chapter. The title said it all. Her body had fairly tingled as she'd read portions of other chapters, so closely had the words mirrored ones she'd told herself, in one form or another, since she was twelve years old. That's when she'd gotten up to use the restroom in the middle of the night and had accidentally glimpsed her reverend's naked backside just before it turned the corner headed back to her mom's room. She'd been shocked, of course, and in true preteen fashion had gone back to her room and dissolved into giggles, covering her head with a pillow to muffle the sounds. After the embarrassment wore off, however, another feeling had replaced it. A feeling near her private area, one she'd never felt before. The more she thought about seeing his hard, round buttocks, the more the feeling intensified. Destiny had tightened her legs to calm the flutters, but had gone to sleep with a schoolgirl crush that was now full-blown love. The next year she began fantasizing about Reverend Thicke coming to her bedroom instead of her mother's. And she began employing some of the techniques her pastor preached about, such as speaking about what you want as if you already have it, believing to receive, and asking God without doubting that what you wanted, God could deliver. While other teenagers opted for children's church or skipped the main service all together, Destiny never missed a sermon. After one of his more rousing ones, where her pastor had spoken specifically about the power of mantras, repetitive declaration, she'd gone home, rewritten a childhood prayer, and began praying it that night:

> *Now I lay me down to sleep,*
> *I pray the Lord my soul to keep.*
> *God, one thing I want in life,*
> *That I will be Nathaniel's wife.*

She'd prayed that prayer every day since then, for over two years. And then, a few months before her recently celebrated seventeenth birthday, her grandmother—who at Katherine's insistence Destiny called Kiki instead of Grandma—had come into her room with news she knew would change her life.

"Destiny, you're a Noble woman," Katherine had begun after sharing small talk. "Do you know what that means?"

"I know what the word means: distinguished, magnificent, renowned. . . ." Destiny had responded, her 4.0 intelligence and straight As in English shining through in her answer.

Katherine smiled. "Yes, dear, it means all of those things. And for those of us who carry that last name, it means something more. It means we are chosen women of God, here to help the man of God."

"Reverend Thicke, I mean Nate?" Destiny asked softly. Even though he'd instructed her to call him by his first name at their first meeting, she still viewed him as her pastor first and foremost.

Katherine nodded.

"How?" Destiny asked, as her heartbeat quickened with the memory of seeing his backside going back into her mother's room. She prayed that that was the kind of help her Kiki was referring to. Upon hearing Katherine's response, Destiny knew her prayers had been answered.

Destiny finished the last chapter, closed her eyes, held the manuscript to her chest, and began reciting her customized prayer to God. She repeated it seven times, the number of completion Nate taught, and then opened her eyes and looked at the vision board she'd made the year before, on her sixteenth birthday. It was small, the size of a piece of construction paper, but specific in its intent. The theme was clearly *marriage:* cutouts of a wedding dress, wedding cake, platinum diamond ring, doves, and rice pieces she'd randomly glued on the page. In the center was a picture of her taken before a school dance, and a picture of Nate that had accompanied an article on him in the *Dallas Post Tribune*. Destiny remembered feeling a rush of happiness after she'd finished the project inspired after watching a movie called *The Secret*. She made sure to watch it after its executive producer appeared on *Oprah*. Looking at the vision board now, she felt that rush again.

Glancing at the clock on the wall, Destiny's eyes widened. Where had the time gone? The reverend would be here any minute. And where was Kiki? Destiny hurriedly walked over to where the vision board stood perched against her dresser mirror. She placed both it and the manuscript back in their hiding place: in a locked backpack under her bed. She didn't want her mother to know about the board, and knew she'd be furious about the copied manuscript. It hadn't been lost on Destiny that Kiki, not her mother, had taught her the "chosen" lesson. Or that when asked, Simone had suggested Destiny concentrate on school, and let her handle the reverend's "spiritual needs."

Two hours after Destiny had read the last page of Nate's book, she and Katherine prepared to leave her home. "Are you sure you have everything?" Katherine asked. She had no doubts she was more nervous than her grandchild, who seemed unusually calm.

"Yes, Kiki," Destiny said, smiling. "You already asked me, remember?"

"I'm just making sure." Katherine turned and looked at Destiny. "This is a special night. I just . . . I want it to be perfect."

Destiny felt an unexpected rush of tears and threw her arms around her grandmother. She had tried not to think about the fact that her mother wasn't here, that what Katherine had done for Simone, prepared her for the inevitable Thicke moment, Simone had not been able to do for Destiny. "Thanks for everything, Kiki," she whispered after the emotional moment passed.

The two women got in Katherine's Cadillac and headed to the private location where a town car was waiting to take Destiny and Nate to an equally private airstrip and the chartered plane that would take the two to a clandestine section of Key West, Florida. Of course these secretive precautions were not taken because the Nobles thought what they did was wrong, but because they felt others wouldn't understand.

"Are you nervous?" Katherine asked after a few moments.

"A little," Destiny admitted.

"I know you wished it had been your mother, but I'm glad

I was the one who prepared you for the covering. My mother did the best she could but, my first time was very unpleasant. Did you bring the oil?"

"Yes." The nerves Destiny had held at bay all evening began making their presence known.

"Remember to communicate," Katherine continued. "If it hurts, say so. If you want to stop, say that too. The man of God is a gentle man. Nate will . . . you'll be okay."

Destiny looked at her grandmother. She'd often wondered if there was any chance Nate and her had ever been together, and in this moment, she had to wonder no more. Her brows creased as an unexpected question leapt into her young conscience. *Was it right for Nate to be with so many women?* she pondered. *First her grandmother, then her mother . . . and now her?* Then another thought occurred to her, one that caused her to sit up straight and take a quick intake of breath.

"What is it, Destiny?"

"Kiki," Destiny began softly. "Do you think that Nate, I mean, does Nate do this with other women, besides . . . besides us?"

Now it was Katherine who had the desire to gasp, but she maintained an outward calm. She knew that much didn't get past her granddaughter, but sometimes she marveled at the child's astuteness. *She said "us." That means she knows that Nate and I . . .*

"It is not for us to question the activities of the man of God," Katherine said quickly, to cover a sudden and rare feeling of embarrassment where the Noble-Thicke legacy was concerned. "It is only for us to do our part. All of us," she added, letting Destiny know that Katherine knew what Destiny now understood. "Yes," she continued, deciding to be as forthcoming as she could, to tell everything, in a way. "In the past, I was covered by the man of God."

"But y'all aren't still doing it, right?"

"What did I just say about questioning?" Katherine coun-

tered, more harshly than she'd intended. She'd almost rid herself of any jealous feelings where Destiny was concerned. Almost.
"There are some things I choose not to share right now,"
Katherine continued more softly, remembering, among other
things, Nate's desire to be the one who told Destiny about
their inevitable union. "Just know that you are doing what
you're supposed to do, and that what is happening between
you and the reverend is sacred. Which also means it's private,
not meant to be shared. Don't tell anyone outside of this family
about your involvement with Nathaniel, Destiny. I know you're
a mature young woman, but others still view you as a child."

Destiny nodded but Katherine didn't see. "Do you hear
me? It is no one's business what goes on with the man of God,
and you have a responsibility to cover the man of God . . . because he's covering you. And not just physically, but spiritually
too. Do you understand?"

"Yes, Kiki, I understand. I won't tell anybody, promise."

Destiny had a million questions she wanted to ask her
grandmother, specific questions about the sex act that hadn't
been covered during her and Katherine's single talk on the
matter, questions beyond her comfort and his release. Destiny
wanted to know how to make Reverend Thicke fall in love with
her. She wanted to know how to make him want to marry her.
But somehow she felt her grandmother wouldn't welcome these
questions, much as Simone had preferred that Destiny leave
Reverend Thicke to her. The whole situation was confusing to
Destiny, and seemed to contradict some of the other teachings
she'd heard in church, like those covered when Miss Nettie spoke
to the women's group, for instance. But amid all of the per-
plexity, one thought was clear: Destiny wanted to become
Mrs. Nathaniel Thicke. Beyond that, she decided not to think
or worry about it.

The closer Katherine drove to the meeting place with
Nate, the more nervous Destiny became, the more unsure she
felt. *Will I be able to please him? Am I too young for him to love me?*

Will I say the right things? God, please don't let me come off looking immature and stupid! She took a deep breath and tried to slow her rapid heartbeat. But it was no use. Moments later, when they pulled up next to the town car and six feet three inches of perfection unfolded himself out of the backseat and held out his hand to take hers . . . her heart would have jumped out her chest had it not been for rib cage, muscles, and skin. And the flutters that the mere thought of Nate had invoked since Destiny was twelve years old were in full effect.

8

You Left Something

Nate and Destiny relaxed and waited for dessert. They were enjoying the luxury of a private chef and a dining experience in the palatial estate of one of Nate's supporters. Destiny's flutters had been replaced with a warm, fuzzy feeling at the pit of her stomach. Nate had finally regrouped from the stunning image of beauty that had left him speechless when, after changing for dinner, Destiny had descended down the home's spiral staircase. He'd known he looked dapper at the bottom of the stairs, having gone all out and sporting a casual but tailored Ralph Lauren suit. But he felt his handsome countenance was completely overshadowed as soon as Destiny placed a graceful, Christian Louboutin–clad foot on the first stair. She wore a form-fitting, designer original that hugged her young curves and emphasized the large pair of breasts she'd inherited from her mother. Her bare legs were free of spot or blemish, as was a face almost totally devoid of makeup. She wore her long hair swept up on top of her head, while wispy tendrils that begged Nate's touch danced around her face. She'd looked at him shyly, then quickly away, when she took his hand and followed him into the dining room. For the first time Nate could remember, his hand became clammy, and he suddenly wondered if he could even properly converse with, let alone get a commitment from the woman on his arm.

But all of this discomfort was an hour ago, before the first course of creamy chowder, followed by the arugula and strawberry salad that preceded the perfectly prepared lump crab cake, which set the stage for their main course, thinly sliced Chateaubriand paired with a heavenly potato and carrot soufflé. It was before conversation of Nate's background, his time as a Palestine basketball standout, his stint at Morehouse College, and the time he experienced his first kiss, with a fast and frisky schoolmate when both were just seven years old. In turn, there wasn't much Destiny felt she could share that Nate didn't already know, or was so boring it didn't matter. Still, at his insistence, she talked about her favorite subjects in school, her passion for music, especially classical, and then the conversation shifted to things they both enjoyed: movies, certain hip-hop and R&B artists, sports-oriented Xbox games, and barbequed ribs. Finally, Destiny shared a secret: a desire to do something special with her life.

"I think I'm named Destiny for a reason," she finished softly, boring into Nate's dark-brown eyes with her fiery green ones. "And I intend to make a mark in this world. I don't know how, and I don't know doing what, but I know it's going to happen."

Nate simply nodded, and fiddled with his fork. It was hard to believe this girl was just seventeen. She had a poise that women twice her age should envy and a calm disposition that belied her years. They'd talked several times over the past two months, and even met a couple times—either at Katherine's house or sometimes in his office at church. But since marrying Simone was not going to happen, Nate had honored the one request by her that he could fulfill: he'd waited until Destiny turned seventeen to cover her. She now wore the necklace of yellow diamonds that had accompanied the three-dozen perfect orchids delivered to her house on her birthday three months ago.

The conversation stopped as the chef delivered their fiery bananas foster dessert. They oohed and aahed over its deliciousness and for a moment were content to quietly enjoy the chef's superb culinary skills. After several moments, Destiny giggled unexpectedly, her eyes twinkling as she looked at him.

"What?" Whatever it was didn't really matter. Destiny's joy was contagious and Nate found himself smiling broadly, "cheesing," his old-school friends would label it.

"When did you know?" Destiny lowered her head and batted her eyes coyly, unconscious of the effect the act had on Nate.

"Know what?"

"That you were in love with me?"

"Who says I am?"

Destiny laughed again, this time low and throaty. It was the sound of a woman steeped in the art of seduction, though with Destiny, it came naturally. "C'mon, Nate . . . when?" she asked again, more playful this time. "You know you're in love with me. C'mon!" She leaned forward and rested her chin in her hand, watching Nate as if he were her favorite movie. Her eyes sparkled with mirth and unabashed adoration.

Nate leaned back in his chair and stared at the woman he couldn't wait to make his. He rubbed his chin thoughtfully, even as he almost felt like a kid again, like he was back in high school "macking" on a schoolmate. "November twenty-third, around four o'clock, in the church's activity center."

Destiny's mind raced back to November. It had been a busy time for her: studying tests given before the holiday break, Christmas shopping, and helping Miss Nettie prepare hundreds of Thanksgiving baskets that Gospel Truth gave to the less fortunate. But she couldn't fathom what had happened on the day Nate mentioned to warrant his love. Her brows knit in concentrated effort to recall the day.

Nate smiled at her determination. He would need a determined woman, who was also strong, smart, and savvy. Her age had been a concern initially, but with every passing day, each passing moment he talked to her or spent with her, that concern steadily disappeared. Now more than ever he was sure of what he'd felt that November afternoon: Destiny Noble would become Destiny Thicke.

"You wouldn't remember," he said, still smiling. "It was probably just another incident to you, another brothah trying to get with you, get your goodies."

"My . . ." Now a delicious, light shade of red crept from Destiny's neck to her cheeks.

"Ah, you're blushing . . . that's nice," Nate said. "It was just before Thanksgiving and you were at the church, helping Mama prepare the baskets. You walked outside to set a couple of them in the van. Adam's friend, the tall dude—"

"Butch?"

"Yeah, he followed you down the hall and asked you out. After your initial refusal, he asked how much it would take to get a date with you. Remember what you said?"

Indeed Destiny remembered. "I quoted Proverbs," Destiny said quietly, once again shyly diverting her eyes.

"You told him your worth was far above rubies," Nate said. "You looked him dead in the eye and told him the truth: that you were not only valuable, but priceless. I knew then that no one else could have you—I mean, could cover you first—except me. That you needed somebody who could not only protect you, but give you everything you so obviously deserve."

Destiny was quiet, a myriad of emotions roiling within her: excitement, anxiety, both joy and fear of what was to come.

"When did you know?" Nate asked, after a prolonged silence.

"Know what?" Destiny asked honestly.

"That you'd fallen in love with me."

"Who says I have?" Destiny said, throwing Nate's words back at him, but with a smile. "I was twelve years old," she answered truthfully.

Nate's brows raised in surprise. "Twelve?"

Destiny nodded. "I, um, accidentally saw your . . . your butt one night when you were walking down the hall to Mom's room. It was late, and I'm sure you didn't think I'd be up. But I'd used the bathroom and then gone in the kitchen to get some water."

Nate felt embarrassed that he may have sullied Destiny's innocence at such a young age. "I'm sorry," he said sincerely.

"Something happened when I got back to my room," Destiny continued as if she hadn't heard him. "I got these . . . feelings." She fixed her green eyes firmly on him now. "Where I had never felt stuff before. From that night, I wanted to know what love was, and I wanted to find out with you. So don't apologize, Nate," Destiny nearly whispered. "I'm glad I saw your, uh, that I saw you that night." Destiny licked her lips subtly, and continued to stare at him.

Nate's sword hardened at the sight of Destiny's darting tongue. "Well," he asked in a voice deeply seductive, "are you ready to see it again?"

Nate was everything Destiny's Kiki said he would be: kind, gentle, patient, and much, much more. Due to his size and her innocence, their intimate encounter had been largely yet thoroughly oral, with Nate playing Destiny's body as if it were an instrument: giving her previously untouched body orgasm after orgasm. For all her naiveté, Destiny's natural instincts were incredibly astute. She lavished love on Nate's manhood as if it were a piece of candy or succulent fruit. He quietly instructed, she studiously obeyed. Late the following morning, after a long bubble bath in the over-sized Jacuzzi, Nate once again took Destiny to bed. He knew he had to make her initiation into this exclusive, some might say taboo, circle complete. After much foreplay and even more lubrication, he opened her wide and began a slow, gentle journey, inch by inch, until he was all the way inside her. After she'd expanded to accommodate him, he plunged deep, to the hilt. Destiny muffled her cries, even as long nail marks followed her fingers down Nate's back. The tradition continued, even as a new dance began.

When the two arrived back at the meeting point near Palestine on Saturday night, they were absolutely and completely in love with each other. Nate had made this declaration, even as he told her of his plans to give their liaison a more permanent status.

"I know you're young," he'd said casually, as they enjoyed a picnic dinner by the sea. "So I'll wait awhile to do the grand proposal, and for us to make the official announcement. But I want you to know my plans right now, so you feel that, well, so that you know you're spoken for. I'm the only one for you now."

"'Spoken for,' what's that mean?" Destiny had asked.

"It means you're mine," Nate answered.

Destiny's heart had skipped a beat. "But how?" she pressed. She wanted so badly to hear the words she'd imagined. "Is that like being engaged?"

Nate shrugged.

"Nate," Destiny persisted, in the delicate, slightly whiny voice that she also used in the throes of passion, a voice for which Nate was already so whipped that if she used it and asked him to cut off his arm, maybe even his, well . . . he'd definitely cut off his arm if Destiny asked him to in that voice.

"Nate, please? What does 'spoken for' mean?"

Nate smiled, enjoying the cat-and-mouse game. "I'm sure Miss Straight-A student knows what that phrase means."

Destiny smiled. "Nate . . . I want to hear you say it."

"Say what?"

"That being spoken for is like being engaged."

"It's . . . something like that."

"We're going to get married?" Destiny asked. After a pause, Nate nodded again. "We're going to get married!" Destiny exclaimed. Then she had reacted like the woman-child she was:

she whooped, jumped up from her seat, and threw her arms around Nate. She'd run to the water's edge and then along the shore, shouting with happiness: "I'm getting married. Nate and I are getting married!"

"Well, not next week!" Nate yelled, after he'd risen from his chair and ran after her. Once again, her joy was contagious. They ended up making love right on the beach.

Destiny smiled at the memories, and at the sight of her grandmother's purple Cadillac that waited near the private airstrip. Getting in Kiki's car marked the end of the best weekend she'd had in her life. But it didn't matter. The weekend confirmed what Destiny had always known: Nate was the only one for her. But while fastening her seat belt, she frowned with the next thought: *I won't be the only one for him. There's Mama and Kiki and God knows who else.* Then Katherine's words overshadowed her own: *It is not for us to question the activities of the man of God.* Destiny knew that in time she'd have to give strong consideration to exactly what Katherine's statement meant.

In the immediate future, however, Destiny and Nate would have something else to consider, something that would overshadow who Nate was covering or who was covering Nate, for that matter. Because when they parted, Nate unashamedly admitted that he'd left his heart with Destiny. But he'd left something else as well. A baby.

9

His Will Be Done

March had come in like a lion, but it was not the only thing that roared. Destiny's pregnancy dominated the thoughts and spirited conversations of all who knew about it. A home pregnancy test had confirmed what Destiny suspected from a missed period, and what Nettie had believed after having a dream.

"The man of God has a need," Katherine said somberly. "He has covered us, and now we must cover him."

Silence filled the elegantly appointed dining room in which Katherine, Simone, Destiny, and Nettie sat. Within those present discomfort was thick, anger was apparent, fear battled faith, and yet love conquered all. Nate was noticeably absent but had wanted to be there. He was out of town, and had asked his mother to wait until he got back to have this meeting. But both she and Katherine had agreed that the discussion couldn't wait. After all, everyone knew where he stood on the matter. And almost everyone agreed.

"I still can't believe we're having this discussion," Simone said, her anger boiling over. She turned to her daughter. "Destiny, I know I didn't have *the talk* with you, but if I've told you once, I've told you a thousand times about protecting yourself! And Nate knows better. As many women as he—"

"I don't think anger or blame is going to get us anywhere,"

Nettie interrupted. "Destiny has already told us what happened, that they used protection, except for one time."

"Well, now we know for sure that once was enough," Simone said, trying without success to lose the anger and keep the sarcasm out of her voice.

"I'm sorry, Mama," Destiny said sincerely. "I didn't mean for this to happen."

Nettie reached over and covered Destiny's hand with her own. "Don't worry, child. There are a lot of 'didn't mean to' babies born every day. There's no way you could have known this would happen, but God knew. Before the foundation of the world was laid, God knew."

Katherine remained silent, for the moment having nothing to add to the conversation. Destiny's pregnancy news had thrown her for a loop as much as Nate's marriage plans had thrown Simone. Sharing Nate's bed was one thing. But for Destiny to have his child, that was something else. This was new Noble-Thicke territory. A baby had never been a part of their tradition. Katherine wondered how this addition would alter the rules.

"What are our options?" Simone asked quietly, looking from Katherine to Nettie.

"Options?" both Katherine and Nettie asked.

"None," Destiny said before either woman could speak. "I'm having this baby."

Destiny lifted her chin and sat up straighter, trying to quell the fear that mixed with excitement inside her. She was having Nate's baby! His first! Yes, there had been many women before her, but she was the first one to carry his child. And she was determined to deliver it. "I'm having it," she firmly declared.

"This isn't just your decision, Destiny," Simone responded. "Because this isn't just your problem. This affects not only a man but a ministry, an entire congregation." She took a deep breath to calm the nerves that had been bundled ever since she'd received the shocking news a month ago. "We do have other alternatives, and I think we need to examine them fully. One is abortion."

"Thou shall not kill," Nettie quickly countered. "Nobody should take a life that can't give one."

"That same Bible also says 'an eye for an eye.' It's the same one that talks about Saul killing his thousands and David killing his tens of thousands. And David was a man after God's own heart. There are times God ordered whole towns destroyed, and everybody in them. So sometimes God killed."

"But you ain't God!"

"Look, Miss Nettie, I don't want to argue the sin of abortion," Simone continued. "I just want us to look at this problem from every angle. There is also the possibility of adoption. I'm sure there are many families, many childless couples, decent, successful Christian couples who would love to raise this baby as their own." Simone turned to Destiny. "You're young, just seventeen, and there's no way you can understand the enormity of this situation. There's plenty of time for you to have a child, once you and Nate are mar—" Simone still couldn't get herself to say the word. "You can have a baby later, when you're older. Don't you want to go to college?"

"I can still go to college!" Destiny had heard about all she could take on the subject of being separated from the baby that she already loved more than life itself, even as her stomach was still as flat as a pancake.

"I can't see giving the baby away," Katherine finally spoke. "The Nobles have always stuck together. I can't see something bearing my blood being raised in somebody else's household without me having anything to do with it."

"I'm with you on that, Katherine. Blood is thicker than water and this baby's blood is Thicke."

"So why make this difficult?" Simone argued softly. "An abortion—no matter what anybody thinks of it morally—solves this problem quickly and quietly. We can go to another city,

another state. In less than twenty-four hours it will be over and
done with.

"The timing is just not right for a baby," Simone continued. "Too much is at stake. This is a critical time in Nate's ministerial career. He's poised to join the Total Truth Association,
which will give him a powerful national platform. He's about
to publish his first book, and the publisher is already talking to
him about a second one. The church is growing bigger every
day. We'll be building our first new sanctuary in less than two
years. Down the road, a child might be a beneficial addition to
Nate's life, but right now? It would be the worst thing that
could happen."

"Would you be saying this if it were your baby?" Destiny
asked her mother.

"Excuse me?"

"You heard me. Would you be so willing to kill it if it were
you carrying his child?" Destiny pushed back her chair and
stood abruptly. "I don't care what any of y'all say, because
nothing will change my mind. I love Nate, this is his baby, and
I'm having it." She looked at her grandmother. "Kiki, you're
always saying that a man of God has needs. Well, this baby of
God has needs too. And I'm going to be the mother who takes
care of them!"

Simone stood and faced her daughter. "You will do what's
best. This isn't just about you!"

"No, it isn't!" Destiny shouted. "It's about my baby. And the
best thing for it is to be born!" With that, Destiny turned and
ran up the stairs.

"Destiny!" Simone started after her.

"Let her be, Simone," Katherine said, even as the sound of
a slamming door added to the tension. Then, for a moment, all
was silent.

"She has a right to be upset," Nettie finally said. "And I'm
not just saying this from a Christian point of view," she told Si-

mone. "I'm saying it as the mother of the man you're so determined to protect, and as the grandmother of the baby you're so
ready to get rid of. We need to get out of the way and seek
God on this matter. Let His will be done. Man looks at what's
on the outside, but God looks at the heart. He knows the heart
of both Nate and Destiny. If we listen to God and follow His
instructions, we'll be a lot better off. Because sitting around
this table, we've all got ideas on who should do what. But we're
human. We may get it wrong. But God? Hmph. God never
misses the mark. He never fails."

10

Sleep in the Bed You Made

Later that evening, Simone reclined on the chaise in her bedroom. To the observer her body may have looked relaxed, but inside she was as keyed up as she'd ever been. After Katherine and Nettie left, Simone had tried to talk to Destiny. But Destiny had feigned illness and said she didn't want to talk. Simone had thought later that maybe Destiny really wasn't feeling good, and had once again knocked, with a tray of tea, soup, and crackers. Destiny had finally opened the door, just long enough to take the tray and thank her mother. Also long enough for Simone to see the telltale sign of crying in her puffy, bloodshot eyes.

Simone's heart clinched as she battled a range of emotions. Her mind went back to a similar time in her life, when she found out *she* was pregnant. Those circumstances hadn't been as different as Simone would have liked to imagine them. She too had been seventeen, about to go college, mind filled with thoughts of conquering the world. Destiny's father had similar thoughts, which is why being saddled with a child while a standout basketball player at Texas A&M wasn't on his agenda. He'd refused to believe Simone was pregnant with his child, and after marrying a French woman and moving abroad, she'd never seen or heard from him again—didn't even know if he was still alive, and didn't care to know. Back when she'd gotten pregnant, few people had abortions; it was rarely even thought of, much less discussed. There were many single mothers in Palestine, even in the church. And for those women the church and the community came together, often treating the children as their own. In those days, it was understood. You got pregnant? You had the baby. At the time her grandmother had told her to "sleep in the bed you made."

After the initial outcry of incredulity and anger, Katherine hadn't said much at all. It was later, when Destiny was three or four years old, that Katherine shared the thoughts that would slowly take shape in Simone's heart: that she thought Simone a perfect complement to Nathaniel, a woman who could bring out the best in him. Simone had pooh-poohed the idea at first. After all, she'd known Nate since he was young, had seen him at his awkward stage—tall, gangly, with a fade and pimples. It seemed that overnight he went from scrawny to scrumptious. And from that moment, women were everywhere. That's why even after their first sexual encounter, when Nate's oral prowess left Simone mewling like a newborn kitten and feeling oh so good, Simone kept her distance. Even after Katherine had told her about the Noble-Thicke tradition, Simone determined she wasn't the type of woman who shared her man. She went away to college, got a marketing degree, and eventually moved to Dallas. She was determined to make a good life for her daughter, and eventually find a man for herself. She was well on her way to doing that. And then Katherine called.

When Simone returned to Palestine and saw Nate, she was amazed and impressed at the change. He was younger than her, twenty-four to her twenty-eight, but he was handling the stressful job of senior pastor like an old pro. His lovemaking skills had gotten even better, if that were possible, and along with thoughts of marriage, Simone began imagining something else . . . a sister or brother for Destiny. She'd even joked with him about it, said that he and she would make some pretty babies. He'd joined in the laughter, but had insisted he wasn't ready to have a child, that he didn't want to become a father until after he was married. For that reason, he told her, he insisted on using a condom every time they had intercourse. A couple times she'd tried to get him to do it without one, but he had allowed no exceptions. Obviously, there'd been at least one exception—her daughter. Simone wasn't proud of how she felt, but if she were honest with herself, she'd admit that that was the reason she wanted Destiny to have the abortion. Because she, Simone, wanted to be the mother of his child.

Tears came to Simone's eyes as she acknowledged this truth, along with the fact that she would not be Mrs. Thicke. It was her daughter, her *pregnant* daughter, standing in the way. *And who am I to try and block her path?* Simone reluctantly thought. During the discussion at the table, Simone had convinced herself that an abortion was easier not just for Nate, but especially for Destiny. Simone knew all too well the difficulties of being a single mother. She wanted to spare her daughter this hardship, have Destiny experience the joy of being footloose and fancy free at this time in her life, instead of burdened with responsibility. Not having the baby was definitely in the best interest of Destiny's future, Simone again concluded. But her daughter, who was Simone's even change in stubbornness, didn't agree. She wanted to have Nate's baby, just like her mother also did.

"Marrying Destiny doesn't have to change the relationship between us." Simone remembered Nate's words from the time he'd come over, the first time they met after he announced his plans to marry Destiny. His lovemaking had been exquisite that day, she also remembered. He'd lavished love on every inch of her, seeming to stroke her very core. Simone tried to imagine Nate's words being true, continuing to experience the heights of ecstasy she did with him while he was married to her daughter. *But can I be satisfied with just his dick, knowing Destiny has everything else? How did Katherine do it?* Simone wondered.

Maybe I'll ask her. Simone knew that if she were to keep any part of Nate at all, she'd have to find a way.

Simone sighed, rose from the chaise, and walked from her room to Destiny's. She started to knock on the door, but when she put her ear up against it, heard nothing but silence. Simone decided that tomorrow was soon enough to begin mending the rift she knew the night's conversation had put between her and Destiny. It would be mended—Simone was sure about that. Because from the time Destiny was born, she'd been the light of Simone's life. Yes, she loved Nate. But she also loved her child. And at the end of the day Simone knew that nothing, and no one, could take away that love.

Nettie prayed quietly, fervently, in the holy language. She battered the gates of heaven with her petition, asking God for clarity, direction, mercy, and grace. Alternately, she would become silent and still, listening for God's voice. She knew He would answer, knew He'd make a way. He had never failed her yet.

While the baby news had stunned Katherine and Simone, Nettie was not at all surprised. She'd known about the baby at least a week before Nate decided to share the news, news that confirmed what she'd seen in a dream. It was the second time she'd dreamt about Nate's child.

Nettie stood and began pacing the room, intoning the Spirit with the holy language. And then she heard it: a clear directive. God was speaking and she dared not move, lest she miss a word or even a syllable.

"What, Lord?" Nettie asked out loud, frowning at the thoughts coming into her mind. "This can't be God," she said to the four walls, even though Nettie knew God's voice better than she knew her own. She'd known His voice since she was five years old, and had heard "someone" tell her to get out of the yard and run on to the porch of their Texas farm. Seconds later, a rattlesnake had appeared out of the knee-high grass at the yard's perimeter and, bypassing a petrified Nettie, slithered down the dusty road. When Nettie relayed the story to her mother, she kept peeling potatoes while responding calmly and simply. "That was God talkin', chile. Be sure and keep listening, you hear?"

That incident had happened almost a half century ago. God was indeed still talking, and Nettie was still listening, as her mother had asked. But God was talking crazy, and while it wasn't the first time and probably wouldn't be the last, Nettie could barely wrap her mind around the solution that had popped into her head.

"Well, I know one somebody who will know whether this is God or those jalapeños I put in my beans last night," Nettie said to herself as she walked to the phone. She quickly dialed the number and took a long swig of cola as she waited for an answer.

"Mama Max? It's Nettie. I hope you've got a minute, because I need your opinion."

"Well, chile, you know I got plenty of those," Mama Max promptly responded. "Go right ahead, baby. My time is yours."

"It's about Nathaniel. Remember a while back when you said he might need more than mercy?"

"Uh-huh."

"Well, that time has come."

Mama Max jumped to her feet. "Have mercy, Jesus. You're a strong deliverer, Father!" She didn't need to know the problem to join her prayers and faith with Nettie's.

"I've asked God about it, but what I'm hearing just don't make sense!"

Mama Max sat back down. "You say it don't make sense?"

"No, ma'am, not at all."

"Well, Nettie, when it don't make sense is usually when I know it's God!"

11

Handle Your Business

The four gentlemen dining at The Palm restaurant in Dallas—fancier than any restaurant in Palestine, though two hours away—had caused a stir from the moment they'd entered. Not that they noticed; they were too busy enjoying each other's company. But the eyes of every female had followed their entrance, and even those with a ring on her third finger, left hand seemed to find her eyes drifting now and again to the table of magnificent manliness at the back of the room. Any of these men alone could heat up a space, but seeing Derrick Montgomery, King Brook, Stanley Lee, and Nate Thicke together was confirmation that God meant his words when after creating man he said, "It is good."

Nate listened intently as Derrick reiterated the rules of membership to the Total Truth Association and the organization's primary purpose: to educate, inspire, and support its members and to ensure that the divine interpretation of God's Word and tenets be practiced within their congregations.

"As I've told you before, Nate," Derrick concluded, "you are an intelligent man and a talented preacher. I think you're going to go far in advancing God's kingdom."

"I second that," King said. "He can't help but be good though. Just look at his lineage. You remember when Reverend Thomas Thicke used to preach those midnight revivals? That man would preach so hard, even his suit coat would be dripping with sweat. He'd leave people lying all over the place, slain in the spirit. Pretty radical when you think about it, that he was practicing the laying on of hands in a church full of Baptists."

"Yeah," Stanley added. "But no one said anything because no one could deny his anointing."

King turned to Stanley. "I didn't know you'd heard Nate's grandfather preach?"

"Not in person," Stanley responded. "But my mother swore by him, had all his albums. You know when you can feel the anointing through vinyl, the man is bad!"

"I heard your father a few times too," King continued in a softer tone. "Nobody would second-guess God's timing, but it sure seems like that man left this earth too soon."

Nate nodded and smiled sadly. It was rare that he talked about Daniel Thicke. That a car accident had snatched his father away from him when he was sixteen, was the one thing for which Nate still blamed God. "I keep forgetting that you knew my dad."

"I didn't know him, really. He was eight, nine years older than me and since our churches were in different districts, we never had the opportunity to fellowship directly," King said. "I remember when I heard him the first time, at a convention. He couldn't have been more than twenty-one, but he had that audience in the palm of his hand. And could he sing? Man, that dude could blow! Even I was enthralled. Passed up a chance to go chase tail so I could hear him preach. And for me, as a horny thirteen-year-old, that was saying something!"

"Nate Thicke!" Derrick slapped Nate on the back. "Sounds like you're a chip off the old block, son."

"I can't tell you what an honor it is to become a part of Total Truth," Nate said sincerely. "I've got big plans for Gospel Truth, and I know that being in an organization like this, and hanging out with men like you, will help them to happen."

"Well, I think I'm speaking for not only all three of us board members, but the entire group of leaders Total Truth represents when I say that we will do all we can to help you reach your goals," King said. "And while it doesn't hurt to have a plethora of brothers with whom you can call on, there's no support better than that of a first lady. Being a pastor isn't easy, and being a single pastor is a particular challenge. But then, I bet I don't have to tell you that."

"Man, I already know!"

King waited until the waitress had delivered their desserts and then continued. "And I guess I also don't have to tell you that nothing can stall a minister's career faster than a scandal involving women."

Stanley shifted a bit uncomfortably in his seat. As the senior pastor of LA's Logos Word Interdenominational church, a Total Truth board member, and good friend of Derrick Montgomery, he was no stranger to drama. He also knew better than anybody at the table what a woman-induced scandal could cause. That the scandal-causing female had been his wife, and not another woman, had been a bitter pill to swallow. But that was in the past, he reminded himself. Both he and his ex-wife, Carla, had moved on, and remarried. Stanley knew that his present wife, Passion, was the reason he'd been able to move on so quickly. One couldn't underestimate or overstate the importance of not only a good woman, but the right woman by your side.

"I agree with Derrick that marriage is important," Stanley said. "But don't get in a hurry just for appearance's sake. Seek God on the matter, make sure to heed His counsel. And in the meantime, practice abstinence. Let your mind be fixed on sacred h-y-m-n-s, not sexy h-e-m-s."

The unexpected humor from a usually serious Stanley broke up the table.

"That was pretty good, man," King said, wiping his eyes. "The brothah's right though. In a leadership position, your behavior has to be stellar, above board."

Now it was Nate's turn to squirm. He honestly doubted he

could go more than a few days without sex, hadn't since his
first sexual encounter at the ripe old age of thirteen. And he
definitely wouldn't stop doing Destiny. He could get hard just
thinking about that tender flesh. Simone either, not that she
would let him. Or Katherine, or Patricia, or Jennifer or . . . As
Nate mentally checked off the list of women he was screwing,
he finally concluded that none of them could do without his
spiritual covering. He also concluded his brethren wouldn't
understand—just as Katherine had said. And she'd told him
something else too, shortly after Destiny got pregnant.

"Don't tell the men about her yet."
"What men?"
"Total Truth. Don't tell them about Destiny and the baby."
"Why not?"
"We can't tell anybody, Nate, remember? If you mention
her name, they're going to wonder where she is, why she isn't
at the anniversary celebration. If they find out she's pregnant,
you won't get voted in. Once the two of you are married, everything will be all right. Only then can everyone know. But not
right now; there's too much at stake. Keep your eye on the prize."

"Nate?" Derrick asked.
"Oh, sorry about that."
"You were a million miles away, brothah. Was it King's question that sent you there?"
"Uh, excuse me, brothah. What did you ask?"
"I asked what you thought about what Stan said, about
being abstinent."
"Not much," Nate answered truthfully. King laughed, Derrick smiled, Stanley frowned. "I mean, come on now, y'all know
the deal. A man's gotta get release every now and then."
"I hear ya, man," King said. "Because honestly, I don't know
if I could go without sex. Never had to, being married almost
twenty-five years."

"What about you, Derrick?"

"It would be a challenge. But that's why I said what I did about finding the right woman and marrying her. That act would make this a moot conversation."

"And until then," Stan pressed, "you have to live a celibate lifestyle." He leaned forward and spoke directly to Nate. "After next week you will not only be representing Gospel Truth, but you will be representing Total Truth. Anything that happens to you will happen to every member under this umbrella. Not only that, but you're a man of God representing the kingdom. How can you tell the young men out there to respect the women of God if you're cavorting in your own sanctuary?"

Nate didn't have an answer for him.

"A man of God must be above reproach," Stan continued. "So that your congregation can follow you as you follow Christ."

Nate nodded, but couldn't have disagreed more. He was sorely tempted to ask Stanley about his divorce, and what re-proach he was above that had led to his big pretty ex-wife stepping out on him. What was lacking in their bedroom that made her seek pleasure elsewhere? But he didn't. Stanley was a Total Truth board member and as such, deserved respect. Plus, Nate was barely in. This was not the time to ruffle any feathers, or bedspreads.

"Look, Nate," Derrick said. "Your profile is increasing, your star is rising, which means more eyes, especially female ones, are going to be fixed on you. Be careful not to let a moment of plea-sure ruin a lifetime of plans. Be wise and prudent in what you're trying to do. You're an intelligent man. I trust that you know how to handle yourself . . . and how to handle your business."

"I appreciate that, Derrick. I'll try and do the association proud."

As the men made their way out of the restaurant and to the stretch limousine that had brought them to Dallas, Nate's mind was on one thing: which piece of "business" he was going to handle just as soon as he got back to Palestine.

12

Tell Me the Latest

"Mama Max!" Nettie yelled as soon as she saw one of her favorite people in the whole wide world coming through the hotel's lobby.

"Nettie Jean!" Mama Max responded, working to move her size-eighteen frame just a little faster. Nearing three score and ten, she still liked to think she was as fast and feisty as any forty or fifty year old, and thanks to the twice weekly workouts she did with her daughter-in-law, Tai, this was sometimes the case.

"Lord, you're a sight for sore eyes, Mama," Nettie said, her eyes unexpectedly welling up with tears.

"Well, your eyes sure been viewing some sore situations lately," Mama Max said as she enveloped Nettie in a long bear hug. "But you just rest your soul," she added as she patted her coiffed bun and followed Nettie to the car. "Mama's here!"

Mama Max, her husband, the retired Reverend Doctor Pastor Bishop Overseer Mister Stanley Obadiah Meshach Brook Jr., along with their son and daughter-in-law, King and Tai Brook, KCCC pastors Derrick and Vivian Montgomery, and a host of others, had descended on the tiny town of Palestine for Nate's momentous fifth anniversary as senior pastor of the Gospel Truth Church. Nettie had been busier than she could remember ever being. It seemed as if she'd blinked and it was June, and time for the week of faith-filled festivities. Truth was, there had been a lot on her plate. She was glad to finally have Mama Max here in the flesh, her ever-ready and ever-resourceful sounding board.

"So, girl, tell me the latest," Mama Max encouraged as she got into Nettie's black on black Infiniti SUV and pulled the belt over her sizable stomach. She pulled her "sunshades," as she called them, out of her purse and put them on. The large white glasses completed her summer-go-to-meeting ensemble of an oversized, floral top in greens, pinks, yellows, and lavenders over white capri pants and one-inch flat sandals. Mama Max might be getting older but as she often told the younger women: "I'll carry style to my grave, honey-chile. . . . That and my purse!"

"Whew, Lord, it's hot here in Texas," Mama Max rattled on when Nettie failed to answer her question. "Hotter than red pepper sauce on a fireman's backside, and that's *while* he's fighting the fire!" Mama Max hooted at her own joke, generated purposely to lessen the uptight atmosphere.

"Mama Max, I'm so glad you're here," Nettie said, taking her right hand off the wheel and squeezing Mama Max's left one. "I thought I'd seen and heard it all, but what's going on in Palestine right now? It's a soap opera for real."

"Girl, you ain't telling me nothing. I been in church a long time. People watching *As the World Turns* think they're getting some drama. Hmph. They need to tune in to *As the Church Turns,* baby, walk into the nearest sanctuary and stay there for a Sunday or two. They'd see performances worthy of Grammys, Emmys, and everything else, and more mess than one can gather from a chicken coop first thing in the morning!

"So let's start with Simone. Will she be at the program?"

Nettie sighed deeply and jumped into the muck and miry saga of Noble and Thicke. "She's coming, and she's on program to sing. We're going to make the announcement at the early morning service on Sunday, and hope that will stop a few tongues from waggin'."

"And what is the reason you're giving?"

"Mark will be there too." Nettie sighed again.

"Girl, this situation is either God or good God almighty!"

"Either way, the train has left the station and is headed down the road."

"Mark Simmons," Mama Max murmured. "I ain't seen that boy since he was . . . what—a teenager I think? Lord, where does the time go?"

"Wherever it went, he's a man now. And a good one. The more I've had a chance to sit with this thing, the more I believe it is God I heard that night. I think Mark believes it too."

Mark Simmons was Nettie's nephew, Nate's cousin, and close enough in looks that the two could pass for brothers. Seven years older and three inches shorter than his preacher cousin, Mark lived in Baton Rouge, Louisiana, where along with being an active member of his church, he was a bank president with political aspirations. His wife had died three years ago, just months after being diagnosed with ovarian cancer. The loss had devastated him, especially since they never had the child that both had so desperately wanted. Since then, he'd thrown himself into his work and, after a nasty election, won a seat on the Baton Rouge City Council. He'd immediately established himself as a leader in the group, had gotten several of his proposals passed, and was already eyeing the mayor's job. It was this immersion in civic service, work, and counseling from his pastor that had finally started the healing from the profound grief of losing his wife.

"Mark later told me what he'd thought about that first phone call," Nettie said. "Given my previous stance on him and women, I wasn't surprised."

When his Aunt Nettie had called and said there was "somebody she wanted him to meet," you could have knocked Mark over with a feather. The Aunt Nettie he knew while growing up was the one who was always trying to keep him and Nate away from girls. And now she was playing matchmaker? Mark had been immediately suspicious.

★   ★   ★

"C'mon, Aunt Nettie, what aren't you telling me?" he'd prodded. "There's got to be more to the story for you of all people to be trying to set me up with a date. Not that I don't appreciate it. I still miss my wife. Not as much as I used to, but I still miss her."

Nettie's heart had hurt for him when Rhonda died, and now it swelled with hope and happiness, as it often did with anything involving this gentle, soft-spoken nephew of hers.

"She's a beautiful, smart, church-going woman," Nettie assured him, before giving Mark a rundown of Simone's background.

"She does sound good, Auntie. But if she is all that you claim, why isn't she married already?"

"Maybe God was waiting to give her to you."

"Oh, so this was God's idea, not yours?"

"That's right."

"Uh-huh."

"Look, you can be skeptical and ungrateful if you want to. I just thought you might like to have a five-foot-nine, perfect size six, long hair—her own, almost down to her waist—with a perfect little behind and nice-sized breasts and everything, but I was obviously mistaken, so I'll just let you go—"

"Now hold on, Auntie, not so fast." The physical description had finally awakened Mark's genuine interest. "Tell me more."

And she had. She'd told him almost everything—almost. She left out what she knew about the Noble-Thicke legacy. But there was one very important thing she didn't leave out.

"Her daughter's in trouble," Nettie had said, after answering every question that Mark had asked. "And honestly, Mark, that's one of the reasons she may be agreeable to marrying you."

"Okay, now we're getting to it. This is to be a marriage of convenience. I knew this story was too good to be true."

"It doesn't have to be," Nettie countered. "Sometimes love can grow where friendship flourishes. I never would have considered it before—you and Simone—but now that I do, I believe you two can be friends . . . and more."

"What's going on with her daughter?"

"She's pregnant."

"Okay, Aunt Nettie, I think I've heard enough. You had me going along with it until you brought up the fact that I'd gain not only a wife and stepdaughter, but also the title of grandpa at the ripe old age of thirty-five."

"It's Nate's baby."

Mark groaned. "How old is this woman? And how old is the daughter?"

Nettie answered his questions, and relayed to Mark the chain of events that had led to her phone call, including the fact that while Destiny had agreed to let Simone claim the baby initially, she and Nate would eventually raise the child.

"This is getting crazier by the minute. I'm going to get attached to a baby just to have it taken away from me? I don't know, Auntie. I don't think I can go through losing anything again. Plus, I can't have any type of controversy around me. You know I'm thinking about running for mayor."

"Ain't nothing controversial about loving a child. And you don't have to look at it as losing, son. You can look at it as gaining, like gaining a niece or a nephew. Even after Nate and Destiny get married, you and Simone can still be a big part of the child's life. And I don't think Simone is thirty yet. Y'all could have a child of your own. Will you at least think about it, about the possibility of meeting her?"

Mark had answered, after a pause long enough to drive a train through. "I'll think about it."

Mama Max digested the incredible news Nettie had just told her. "That man has a crown in glory," she finally said.

13

Gonna Be All Right

"Selling Simone wasn't as easy," Nettie continued, as she exited the highway where one of Mama Max's favorite restaurants was located. "But after I'd done my job, it was time for Katherine to do hers."

"Marry who?" Simone looked stunned.

"Mark," Katherine had answered calmly. "Nate's cousin."

"You have got to be kidding. I'll take care of Destiny's child until she and Nate get married, but when I get married, it will be for love."

Katherine was silent. *Sometimes you're too much like me for your own good,* she'd thought. It was Katherine's pride and desire to get the things she wanted the way she wanted that had her still living as a single woman at the age of fifty-three—that and Nate Thicke.

"Just meet with him, that's all we ask," Katherine coaxed. "What harm is there in having dinner with the man?"

"I'll eat with him," Simone responded. "I just won't marry him."

And then she'd met him, and found a man who was thoughtful, intelligent, and easy on the eyes. There was something in his quiet strength that made Simone feel protected and special.

The ice around her heart, and the idea of an arranged marriage, melted just a little at this first meeting, and a little more in their subsequent telephone conversations.

"Aside from taking the fall for my daughter, why should I up and marry a man I hardly know?" she'd asked during one of their late-night discussions.

"I'll make you happy," was Mark's answer. And he believed he could, and would, had felt that way from the moment he'd laid eyes on her. He'd make Simone Noble happy—or die trying.

But as usual when it came to Simone, Nate was the one for whom she'd finally made the decision. When weeks had passed and Simone had still not agreed to this cockamamy idea, Nate had called and asked one simple question: "Will you do it for me?" That's when she'd said yes. Because for Nate, Simone would do anything.

"Plans moved pretty quickly after that," Nettie continued. "Simone and Destiny will move to Baton Rouge. Well, Destiny is there already, taking summer classes. She'll continue her education at a private school, and after having the baby, will stay in Louisiana until an appropriate time for Nate to announce their engagement. After their marriage, when Destiny is say, nineteen, twenty years old, the child can become a part of their household."

Mama Max looked at Nettie as if she'd lost her mind. "Some people ain't working with the sense God gave 'em. How in the hello Mississipppi are y'all going to explain how Simone's baby suddenly disappears on one hand, and newly married Destiny appears with a three-year-old on the other? Folks going to put two and two together and get four for sure!"

"We're not going to put the pregnancy and birth in the Sunday bulletin, Mama. But Gordon said we shouldn't hide it either. Once Nate and Destiny are married, we'll simply tell the truth."

"Hmph. Ain't nothing simple about that truth."

"So that's about it," Nettie finished. "That's what's been going on in Palestine."

"That's about enough," Mama Max quickly countered. "The truth sure is stranger than fiction," she continued after a pause, thinking how crazy life was sometimes. "Because if anybody read about this in one of them there romance novels, they'd swear it couldn't happen! It's a good thing y'all are announcing it in the early morning service—"

"Katherine's idea—"

"Figures . . . She's used to sneakin' and creepin', God forgive me for the truth I just told. Just like her mama and her auntie," Mama Max continued, mumbling. "Pardon me, Jesus, for my gossiping tongue." Mama Max opened her purse and popped a peppermint just to collect herself. "But back to your son and her daughter. This is probably the best time to drop this news. With everything else going on, it just might get swallowed up in the other events, like the Total Truth ceremony and Carla coming to town. The news is going to send tongues a'waggin' for sure. But by the time they get around to talking about everything else that's happened during the week, maybe this story will just be one more thing that went on."

"Let us pray."

Mama Max nodded, taking everything in. She reached in her purse for another mint. "Want one?" she asked Nettie.

Nettie shook her head no. "Destiny is carrying the baby well, so thank God she was able to finish out the year here, nice and normal like. She's taking summer classes to hopefully graduate midterm next year, and has already filled out applications to attend either Grambling or Southern. For all that's going on with that child, I must say she's staying focused. She's got a good head on her shoulders too, was always helpful at the church, attentive in Sunday School. I like her."

"Unh-unh-unh."

"What, Mama Max?"

"God sure has a sense of humor, don't He? I mean, did you ever think you'd have a Noble in your family?"

"Please, they've been in my family a *long* time," Nettie retorted.

"Girl, don't I know that. But I mean, legitimately, by marriage, and that you'd actually be okay with it."

"I can't say that I would have guessed it, no. But I knew that Destiny would get pregnant, and I knew Nate would marry her. God told me that before they did."

"Well, goodness knows the Lord works in mysterious ways. The girl's mama, Simone, wanted Nathaniel, but who's to say Mark ain't the better one for her? Looks enough like Nate to be his brother. Girl could do worse. She could be marrying somebody who looks like that boy who had that there dating show. What's his name? Tasty or Savor or something or other?"

Nettie frowned and glanced over at Mama Max. "You mean *Flavor,* Mama? Flavor Flav? How in the world do you know about his reality show?"

"Girl, I've got grandkids and teens for neighbors. I've got to come up."

"You mean *keep up* or *catch up,* because *come up* means to get paid."

"Hmph. All three, child! I need to come, catch, *and* keep!"

Nettie joined Maxine in laughter this time, her heart feeling lighter with each moment spent in this wise woman's company.

"I'm just glad Nate's found someone to settle down with," Mama Max said. "He attracts women like honey does bees, just like King when it comes to that. And being the wife of a man with all that adoration, from women willing to do anything for the 'man of God,' is a hard row to hoe. I hope that child is up for the type of life she's chosen."

"Destiny's young, but she's got a strong countenance. And her mother, well, I think Simone did the right thing."

"Sho she did! She would have hated herself if the church

crumbled when she had it in her power to keep the part together for the sake of the whole. Y'all only got the one other
Baptist church here now, right? Mount Pleasant? And everybody knows old man Jenkins got one foot in the grave and the
other on an ice cube. No, this ain't the time to have a scandal
and see everybody turn Methodist by default. Jesus would
surely have to come back then.

"How in the world did y'all get Carla Chapman to speak
at the ladies' luncheon on Saturday?" Mama Max continued,
changing the subject. "I mean, she always was down to earth
and all, but with her show and special appearances and work
with the Sanctity of Sisterhood and so on, I don't know how
she finds the time to fit it all in."

"Jennifer Stevens, that's how we got her. She and Carla are
friends. It wouldn't have happened without her. And that's not
all. She's going to try and get Nate on Carla's show, and a few
others. Become his manager, in a way."

Mama Max's eyes narrowed. "Jennifer Stevens is a good
worker, I'll give her that. She was a dedicated member at Mount
Zion."

"I feel a 'but' coming."

"But she's got a thang for preachers. I had to set that hussy
straight about King."

"Oh, Mama, don't tell me King—"

"Chile, not on my watch. But I saw her walk away from
him one day, swinging that butt like a basketball. Man would
have to be dead not to notice. I followed her tail right into the
bathroom, told her that I had my eye on her and that she was
looking at a true cock-blocker if there ever was one."

Nettie whooped. "You said no such thing!"

"Said such and would say such again. Nettie, don't go wor-
rying yourself about Nate, his baby, the women, or anything
else. God will take care of him just like he does King. Everything will be all right."

Nettie pulled into the Get Back Fish Shack's parking lot.

The ladies made quick work of getting out of the car and inside. Gossiping and giggling had worked up both their ap-
petites. Mama Max burst into a big grin as soon as the aromas
from the restaurant assailed her nostrils, her mind already set
on what she was going to order. "Yes, praise the Lord, hallelujah, thank you, Jesus. As soon as I wrap my mouth around some
catfish and hot sauce, and throw back a hush puppy or two
with some cole slaw, everything is sho 'nuff going to be all right."

14

Do What You Got to Do

Jennifer stood at the back of the auditorium and looked out on her success. She'd been right about a lot of things since making the phone call that finally paved the way to insider status and a closer relationship with Nate Thicke. She now had his home office as well as cell phone number, a home that she'd visited and spent the night in just one week ago. Things were moving along as she'd hoped they would, and as she'd planned.

The phone call that laid the golden egg had been to Carla Lee Chapman, the former pastor's wife turned successful talk-show host whom she'd met and befriended as a Sanctity of Sisterhood organizer in Kansas City. Jennifer had been active in her church's various women's groups, and when founder Vivian Montgomery brought the SOS conference to Kansas City, she had been one of the first people Tai called to help put it together. That's where she'd met Carla, a down-to-earth, gregarious soul who'd clicked with Jennifer immediately.

Part of the friendship may have been that like Carla, Jennifer was thick in stature, or "big pretty" as Carla's husband, Lavon, described plus-size women. Another part may have been the realness with which over a dinner designed to hash out last minute SOS plans, Carla and Jennifer had instead found themselves talking about failed diets and unsuccessful relationships.

Like Carla, Jennifer had spent her early years looking for love in all the wrong places. But unlike Carla, Jennifer had yet to find her knight in shining armor, the one who would rescue her from single status.

Carla would never know that for a brief moment, Jennifer had thought that Lavon might have been that man. Lavon had also been a member of Mount Zion Progressive, before meeting Carla and moving to LA. And while she didn't think her pastor, King, would leave his wife and her first lady, Tai, she hadn't been able to resist trying to get a taste of that brown sugar. She'd been more than ready to sin on Saturday and repent on Sunday with that man. But Mama Max had nipped that pipe dream in the bud.

But now was Jennifer's moment, now was her time. Nate was single, successful, and more than able to move around all five foot seven, and one hundred seventy pounds of what she was working with. He'd proven that time and again. And now she was proving something: that she would be a powerful asset in his quest for success. Not only had she secured Carla as a guest speaker for yesterday's luncheon, a rousing success that had pulled ladies from across Texas and neighboring states, but she'd been able to get a commitment from Lavon as well, for a four-part series of Nate on the MLM Network, the network where everybody who was anybody wanted to be. And finally, her suggestion to move the anniversary from the church, which seated five hundred, to the city's community center, which seated almost fifteen hundred, had been a good one. That's the view she now looked out on, almost every seat filled with worshippers decked out in their Sunday best.

"Hey there, Sister Stevens. You're looking powerful pretty today."

"Deacon Robinson." Jennifer spoke with the same enthusiasm one would use to address a corpse.

The head deacon of Gospel Truth was not in the least bit unnerved, as his next statement revealed. "You know, I've been asking you out for what, about six months now? There might come a time when I stop asking, and when you realize what you've been saying no to, what you're missing, it'll be too late."

"Well, since I don't care to know what I'm missing, I guess I'll never realize."

Deacon Robinson chuckled, even as he straightened himself to his full five-foot ten, his sienna skin encased nicely in a silver-colored suit with striped shirt and matching tie. At fifty-seven, this lifelong bachelor wasn't a bad-looking man, and as the owner of a major construction company, he wasn't a broke one either.

"You're a feisty one, I'll give you that." He lowered his voice, and while looking like the epitome of propriety, dropped a bomb in Jennifer's ear. "You think the reverend is the only one with a big hammer, don't 'cha? Well, I'ma tell you something. An even bigger hammer is one not shared." He walked away without looking back, leaving a stunned Jennifer watching as he made his way to the front of the center, to start the afternoon's devotion service.

For her, the rest of the afternoon's festivities went by in a whirlwind of activity. There were songs by the mass choir, and an impromptu, surprise visit by gospel and R&B star Darius Crenshaw. There was the formal welcome and induction of Nate Thicke and Gospel Truth Church into the Total Truth Association, the reading of well-wishes from around the state and across the country, including a proclamation from the mayor of Palestine, and the blessings bestowed by a Texas native who many considered a legend in his own time, King's father, the Reverend Doctor Pastor Bishop Overseer Mister Stanley Obadiah Meshach Brook Jr. And finally, there was the message from Jennifer's former pastor, King Brook, who for every female in the room brought to mind an ice cream fudge bar: you just wanted to take a bite. But along with his wife, King arrived with a message that resonated within all their hearts: God's plan, God's man. The service lasted almost three hours, yet everyone thought that it ended too soon.

"Lord have mercy, my feet want freedom," Mama Max declared as she sat down heavily in an oversized chair. She pulled off her heels and rubbed her toes.

"Your son did his thing today, Mama Max," Nettie declared proudly. "I don't think I've ever heard him preach like that! And even though he has his own style, he's sounding more like his daddy every day!"

"Chile, don't you let him hear you say that. You know the last thing some sons want to do is be like their father."

"Well, when I congratulate him, I'll be sure and keep that in mind."

The VIP reception room was buzzing, with people making the rounds who hadn't seen each other since the last big conference or anniversary. Along with the elder Brooks, King, Tai, Derrick Montgomery, pastor of LA's megachurch, Kingdom Citizens Christian Center, and his wife, Vivian, worked the room like pros. Darius Crenshaw, a member of KCCC, and a few other prominent members, including associate minister and millionaire businessman Cy Taylor and his wife, Hope, had flown down to Texas to lend their support and add their welcomes to the newest member of Total Truth.

Katherine was in attendance, as was Simone and her newly introduced fiancé, Mark. Patricia was in the VIP room as part of the hosting committee, along with several other Gospel Truth females and Nate Thicke admirers. Their job was to make sure all of the guests were taken care of, that the food supply never diminished, and that libations flowed. But Patricia hadn't minded donning an apron. When one couldn't come in the front door, then you had to go through the side or the back. Without a doubt, the most popular guest in the VIP room was Carla Lee Chapman. Even in this VIP circle, she found herself signing DVDs and taking pictures. After an hour and a half of pomp and pleasantries, Jennifer was able to get a moment with her, alone.

"Carla, girl, you will never know how much you've helped

me. Nate is so excited about appearing on your show. And Lavon taping a series based on his book? I owe you big time. Thank you so much."

"Just thank the good Lord I'm here to serve," Carla responded, mimicking one of her grandfather's favorite lines. "But something tells me this excitement isn't just about expanding the ministry, if you know what a sistah is sayin'."

Jennifer didn't have female friends, per se, but if she did, Carla would be one of the few. She respected her, felt she could be real with her, and was happy to finally have someone with whom to share her feelings. "Something tells you right," she said easily. "Me and Nate are . . . dating, but not openly."

"Is he hitting it?" Carla asked without compunction.

Jennifer's broad smile was her answer.

"Well, if he can screw you in the dark, then why can't he wine and dine you in the light?"

"It's not that easy," Jennifer continued. "Nate has to be careful with his image, and women are everywhere."

"So you're not the only one."

Jennifer's smile was not present as she answered this question. "It's complicated. I'm not even sure I understand everything that's going on. But one of my hurdles was effectively eliminated today." She told Carla about Simone, and why she was happy to hear the morning service announcement about her relocation. "It doesn't mean I'm home free yet, but she was my main competition, and now that I'm becoming such an integral part of the ministry, things should move faster now."

Carla remained silent as she eyed a woman she had grown to like. Jennifer reminded her a lot of herself. That's why she wasn't going to pussyfoot around when it came to her thoughts on the matter. "So . . . are you helping him to build God's kingdom, or your own?"

"Both," Jennifer answered quickly.

"Well, be careful with that," Carla said. "Those kinds of plans can backfire when the motive isn't pure."

Jennifer copped an attitude. "What do you mean, my motives aren't pure? My motives are *very* pure. Yes, I want Nate to succeed, and yes, I want to be a part of this success—to help him build God's kingdom. Don't try and tell me that what I'm doing isn't right."

While Carla noted Jennifer's anger, she didn't respond in kind. She knew that anger masked fear, and self-doubt. She'd seen it too many times . . . in the mirror. "Girl, you know I'm the last one to judge anybody. I'm not calling your actions right or wrong. I'm just flashing a yellow light, that's all. So that you weigh out all the pieces of the puzzle as you're putting them in place."

Carla's comment made Jennifer think about another piece of the puzzle that she hadn't thought about until now: Destiny Noble. Jennifer suddenly realized that she hadn't seen her all week. Not in any of the youth presentations or any of the services. Destiny had been a fixture at Gospel Truth since Jennifer arrived, and now, on one of the most important weeks in Nate's short yet illustrious career, the child star wasn't there. *Very interesting,* Jennifer thought. Where was she? Her brows furrowed in thought.

"Don't mind me," Carla said in response to seeing Jennifer's scowl. "You do what you feel is right."

"No, Carla, I appreciate what you said, really. And I'll take your advice. I don't have many female friends, and I feel privileged to count you among the few I give that label. Just pray for me, okay? I love Nate, and I want to be with him. And I didn't enter into this lightly. Before him, I'd been celibate ten years."

"Jesus!" Carla exclaimed so loudly that people near them turned and stared. "I'm sorry, girl," she continued more softly. "But ten years? And then it was Nate, that fine, tall, manly brothah that woke that coochie up from hibernation? I don't even have to ask what that was like because I've got a colored girl's story close enough to relate. Whew! Ten years." Carla shook her head in disbelief and changed her tone. "You go ahead and try and get your man. Who am I to tell you how? Because going that long without some loving, I think even Jesus would understand that a sistah has to do what a sistah has to do!"

Jennifer and Carla confirmed their plans for later: a private dinner with Carla, Lavon, Nate, and Jennifer in Nate's home to discuss the book and the publicity rollout series. Later Jennifer would be surprised to find out that Katherine Noble had wormed her way into being present, and that Deacon Robinson had weaseled out an invite as well. But in the end, Jennifer still considered the day a success. She was the woman to the right of Nate at the dinner table, and before all was said and done, planned to be the only one in his bed, and in his life.

15

Two New Friends

Destiny steered her CLK Mercedes into the mall's compact parking space and turned off the engine. The sporty, ice blue luxury car with soft, ivory-colored seats, satellite phone, radio, and custom license plates that simply said DESTINY, was one of the many gifts Nate had given his baby's mother since learning she was pregnant. Her life had been a whirlwind since that night on the beach in the Florida Keys. For all her outer calm, at times the diverse and ongoing life changes threatened to unravel Destiny's sanity. But whenever she felt herself losing control she thought of the baby inside her. In this regard her mother had been right. It was no longer all about her. It was all about Nate's child.

At six months pregnant, Destiny still got her share of stares from both men and women alike. It was no different on this sunny and hot Saturday in August, as she walked into the Cortana Mall. For all of the changes Baton Rouge had endured due to Hurricane Katrina, changes that some said had not been for the better, Destiny still enjoyed the city, and the relative anonymity it gave her. She'd been here for a little over two months, and coming from the small town of Palestine, she relished not knowing anybody, and loved it even more that nobody really knew her. But she was sure many wondered. It had taken some finagling for Angel House, a staunch, Christian school known for its moral as well as spiritual leadership, to take in a pregnant student. But once they understood that Destiny had resisted the easy path of aborting her child and that the father had every intention of marrying her, they not only allowed her into the school but, after receiving her stellar transcript, allowed her to be fast-tracked so she could graduate in December of the following year. The study load was grueling, but Destiny relished the work. It kept her from being too lonely, and from thinking about who Nate was covering.

She had just sat down to enjoy a chicken sandwich and a smoothie when a shadow fell over her table.

"Who are you wearing? It looks designer," the stranger asked.

"Who wants to know?" Destiny countered.

The young, attractive woman sporting a compact yet curvy body and bouncy black curls was taken aback. Since leaving California and arriving in Louisiana, she hadn't met anyone with more attitude than she possessed. She was immediately intrigued, and impressed, especially since she'd seen this sistah before.

"Obviously somebody who's into fashion," she replied with just a touch of attitude. "I don't see much of that in this hick town." Without waiting for an invite, she sat down at Destiny's table. "My name is Melody, Melody Anderson. I've seen you at Angel. . . . I go there too."

Destiny sipped her smoothie and looked at the woman sitting across from her. Private by nature, she had become even more untrusting since becoming pregnant. She understood what was at stake if news got out that Nate was the father of her child. While she had no intention of letting her mother raise her seed, she was willing to go along with the ruse until she and Nate were married and curiosity had died down. The truth would come out, but only when the time was right. Still, aside from her mother, Destiny had no one to talk to in this new city. She'd cut communication with her friends back in Palestine, even Adam. Maybe it wouldn't hurt to have someone her age to hang out with.

"It's Michael Stars," Destiny finally responded.

"Hmm, I never heard of him. It's cute."

"Thanks."

"So what's your name?"

"Destiny."

"Why are you at Angel?"

"Same reason you are—to get my diploma."

"Girl, please. That's not why I'm there. If I had my way, I'd be back in LA, where I was enjoying school just fine."

"So what, did your parents move here?"

"Hell, no. And not being around them is the only good thing about being at that place."

"Dag, girl, I guess you don't like your folks."

"They're all right sometimes, just too religious and old-fashioned. My mama found out I was screwing. That's why she sent me here." Melody fixed a look at Destiny's stomach. "Guess your mama knows you're screwing too."

"Obviously."

"So is that why you're here?"

"Something like that." The more questions Melody asked, the more guarded Destiny became.

"Where you from?"

"Around here. I don't mean to be rude but I don't really know you and don't really like people all up in my business."

"That's all up in your business? Asking where you're from? Well, don't tell me then. Ain't like I give a damn. I'm just being friendly. What kind of smoothie is that? I'm hungry. And that chicken sandwich looks good. Shoot, I hope I'm not pregnant!"

She's funny, Destiny thought. Even though she was a little pushy and a lot nosy, there was something about Melody that Destiny liked. "How do you think you're pregnant, going to an all-girls school?"

Melody rolled her eyes. "Girl, don't even sit over there and try and act naive. I know you know how I think I'm pregnant. I've been fucking!"

"Yes, but who?"

"Well, look a . . . I don't mean to be rude, but I don't even know you and here you are trying to get all up in my biz-ness." Melody laughed to show she was teasing. Destiny laughed too. "But I don't care. You the first person I've met at the school who is worthy of my company, so I don't mind spilling the beanies. It's Josh."

Destiny frowned.

"Mr. Sanchez, or should I say Brother Sanchez, depending on whether he's wearing the teacher or pastor hat."

"The math teacher?"

"And youth pastor. Yeah, girl. We've been doing it for a good two months now. I know I'm not pregnant though. I'm on the pill *plus* we always use a condom."

Destiny shook her head. "You're crazy."

"Yeah, I know. That's why I'm fun to be around."

"Is that why you're going to summer school? To be around Mr. Sanchez?"

"No, I'm taking his hard-ass class again so I don't get held back! That's why I'm fucking him, a guaranteed A. Ain't no way I'm not graduating on time so I can get up out this bitch. Plus, it gave me a good excuse not to have to go home. I'm staying with one of the older women from church, got her all wrapped around my finger thinking I'm 'living for the Lord.' I told her I might become a missionary, and she actually believes that shit. That's how stuck on stupid that clown is. Hell, I don't even like the missionary *position!* And I got a part-time job here at the mall, so I can meet my next honey."

"You're a trip, Melody. Tell me about LA."

"You've never been there?"

When Destiny shook her head, Melody proceeded to de-scribe life in her city, and the experiences she'd racked up in seventeen short years. She ended with the story of what got her sent away, the tryst with the popular gospel hip-hop singer, Shabach.

"You know Shabach?" Destiny asked, with more than a little disbelief.

"Yes, I know him. I know a lot of gospel artists, regular artists, celebrities, athletes. See, I belonged to a megachurch in LA, called Kingdom Citizens Christian Center."

"With Pastor Montgomery? I know about y'all. I've seen him on TV several times. And Darius Crenshaw is y'all's minister of music!"

"Uh-huh. I've been over to his house and stuff. It's mad hooked up. Got a pool, a Jacuzzi. . . . And I've been to parties with him and Shabach."

"That sounds like so much fun! But wait, Shabach got arrested for having sex with a minor. Was that . . . ?"

"The one and only, darlin'. . . . He was my first."

Destiny was speechless, but Melody had plenty to say, and in Destiny's eyes her stock was rising with every sentence.

"I wanted Darius," Melody continued. "But you know he's gay. That's when I got with Shabach."

"But if he was really with you, how did the charges against him get dismissed?"

"Lack of evidence or some shit. I was glad he got out, for real. Even though I was underage, I knew what I was doing. I wanted to be with his fine ass. It wouldn't have been right for him to do time for something that really wasn't his fault."

"I bet your church was fun, huh."

"Sometimes, it was off the chain! Especially the choir. They put it down for real!"

"Wow, I'd love to go to a church like that. My church is big, but not that big."

"What church is that?"

"Gospel . . ." Destiny realized that in naming her church, Melody would know where she was from. "Gospel Truth Church," she finished. What harm could there be in Melody knowing her hometown? There were plenty of men there who could be her child's father, or he might even live somewhere else. A plan formed in Destiny's mind even as she continued talking. "It's in a small town in Texas, but the church is doing well because of the pastor. He's young and can preach good also, like Pastor Montgomery."

"Is he cute?"

"Uh-huh."

"Your baby daddy go to your church?"

"No," Destiny said quickly. "He lives in Dallas." *There. Dallas has ten times as many men as Palestine. This made-up father could be anywhere.*

"So tell me more about this fine preacher. What's his name?"

"Reverend Thicke."

Melody giggled. "Ooh, I like him already."

"You've heard of him?"

"No, but if he's anything like his name . . ." Melody laughed again.

Destiny hid her anger behind a laugh. "That's so wrong, thinking about doing a minister!"

"Girl, I told you, I'm doing one now!"

"You should probably stay with him then. Everybody and their mama is after Nathaniel Thicke."

The two new friends stayed at the mall for over two hours, chatting about everything and nothing at all. Melody wanted Destiny to drive them to New Orleans, but Destiny wouldn't take the chance of not being at the evening worship, where attendance was mandatory. They made it back to campus and got to church on time. While sitting and listening to Pastor Sanchez, Destiny could only think about one thing: that he and Melody were doing it. Sitting next to her, Melody could only think of one thing too: the fine hunk of dark chocolate she'd seen when she'd Googled the name "Nathaniel Thicke" that afternoon—and how she was going to get Destiny to introduce them.

16

Wanting Dessert

Simone and Mark sat across from each other, enjoying a light supper on the patio. September had brought a slight relief to the heat and humidity, but Simone was still thankful that the patio of Mark's lovely, four-bedroom split-level home was enclosed. Simone wore a simple white halter mini-dress with matching sandals, and nothing else. She knew the dress looked great on her, and from the way he'd looked at her when she walked into the room, she knew Mark thought so too.

"This chicken is delicious, Mark. How did you make it?"

"There you go again, trying to get me to divulge my secrets. Don't you know that's how I keep you coming back to my table, woman?"

"Even if you tell me, I'll keep coming back here."

"Maybe," Mark said softly. "But I'm not going to take that chance."

The air shifted then, as it often did when Simone and Mark discussed seemingly innocent and casual topics. It had been this way for the past almost four months, since they'd taken an overnight trip to Vegas and before a nameless judge and anonymous witness, said stilted, uncomfortable "I do's." Simone had moved into his home, and during the grand tour he'd shown her where she'd be sleeping: the guest room.

At first, Simone had been relieved. She wanted to be in Nate's bed, not Mark's. Still reeling from the hurt of Destiny's pregnancy and Nate's asking her to not only move but marry his cousin, Simone had welcomed the space, and the solitude it provided. She needed to think, sort out her feelings, and figure out why she no longer seemed in control of her life.

Leaving her job had not been difficult. Working at the small ad agency near Palestine had merely been a paycheck, and a diversion. Mark had insisted that in looking for a job in Baton Rouge, she take her time, had stressed that he was happy to take care of her financial needs until her cash flow resumed. He also told her that if she wanted a job at the bank, it was hers. These were gestures of kindness without thought of reciprocity. And the first act that made her look at Mark with different eyes.

The second time had occurred about a month later, when Simone had gushed over a living room set shown on television. It had led to a discussion about decor and various tastes and preferences. Mark's late wife, Rhonda, had decorated their home in a traditional country style, with lots of wood, floral prints, chintzes, and ruffles. Simone loved modern elegance, and immensely missed the sophisticated vibe of her Palestine home, which newly acquired tenants were now renting. The next day, Mark had given her a checkbook, and told her she could redecorate however she wanted. "If there's not enough in the account," he'd added before leaving for the office, "let me know and I'll deposit more."

And then there was the cooking. Simone had never had a man pamper her the way Mark did, and none of her former beaus had ever cooked her a meal. Certainly not Nate, who felt it his due to be waited on hand and foot. And it was, but for Simone, that wasn't the point. She hadn't known such a simple gesture could mean so much to her. That Mark's food was delicious was a bonus, but she would have eaten whatever he fixed, simply because he'd done so for her.

"I might have found a job," Simone said, changing the subject.

"Something you like?"

"Maybe. It's a small graphic design company, and they're looking for a manager. I sent them my résumé and they called today. My interview is set for next week."

"So would you be doing the actual designing, or overseeing operations?"

"A little of both, I think. But the woman I talked to didn't know much about the job description. She'd just been asked to set up the appointment."

"If it's something you really want to do, then good luck."

Simone shrugged. "It will be something to keep me busy."

"If you joined First Baptist, you could stay busy. They need somebody like you, Simone. Your ideas, heck, your mere presence would be like a shot in the arm for our church."

"I don't like Ed Smith. I'm sorry, Mark. I know he's your pastor, but I just don't."

"Pastor Smith says some crazy things sometimes, but he means well."

"Not the way he puts down megachurches, and people like Nate. He's a player hater, and it doesn't become him. And what's more, he can't see that his very attitude is why his congregation is shrinking instead of growing."

"That's why the church needs you, baby. We need new blood, new thinking. Ed Smith is the pastor, but his word isn't gospel. He answers to a board like every other Baptist minister. I agree with what you're saying though, about some of his pontificating. A lot of people are growing dissatisfied with Pastor and his negativity."

"Then why don't they, and you, find another church?"

"First Baptist carries a lot of weight, sweetness. Many of the city's Black movers and shakers attend there. It's a great place to network, and honestly, is a great asset when it comes to my political career. For all of Ed's faults, he's got a knack for making stuff happen, for knowing the right people. His Get Out the Vote campaign during the presidential election yielded thousands of new registrants." Mark finished the last bite of chicken and rice, then sat back in his chair. "So will you come with me on Sunday, and think about joining?"

"I'll go to church, but I'm not ready to move my membership. It's just not the same as . . . where I was."

Mark paused. "Still miss him, don't you?"

"I miss Gospel Truth. I was very active there, felt I had a purpose and was contributing to something powerful, something great. And yes, I won't lie. I miss Nate."

"Then why don't you go to him? Arrange some place for the two of you to meet. I told you, Simone. I won't stand in the way if he's who you want to be with. He's my cousin and I love him. I know him too, probably better than you do. I know what was happening between y'all. And I'm under no delusions here. I know the only reason you're in my house and at my table is because he asked you to do it . . . for him."

"That's why I came initially, yes. But now I'm here because I want to be. You're a good man, Mark, and I . . . I think you could help me forget about Nate if you'd just . . . make love to me."

Mark sighed. Didn't this woman know how hard it was for him to have her in his house and not take advantage of what was being offered on a silver platter? But he was falling in love with Simone, and because of that, he didn't simply want her body. When she lay beneath him, he wanted it to be because he had her heart as well.

"There's nothing more I want in this whole world than to make love to you, sweetness. Hopefully one day that will happen, and when it does, I think it will be absolutely incredible. But when that day comes, it will not only be because we're married on paper, but because we're married in spirit as well."

"But that's what the sex will do, help us to become closer."

"Sex might make us feel better, but it won't make us closer, not for long. Not as long as Nate has your heart, Simone, and it's clear that that is still the case. I love you, I want you, but I won't be his stand-in.

"There's strawberry shortcake for dessert. Would you like some?"

Simone watched as Mark walked into the kitchen. He really was attractive, she decided as he lazily put one muscled leg in front of the other. He was bulkier, but had a butt just like Na— *There I go again,* Simone thought. *Mark's right. I am still in love with his cousin.* She was angry with him too. Since leaving Palestine, Nate had only covered her once, a month ago, when he'd come to visit Destiny while Mark had been out of town. The other times he'd refused her, using the lame excuse that she was married to his cousin. "Since when has the fact that folk were family stopped you from getting your groove on?" she'd asked incredulously. "Or should I call my *mother* or my *daughter* for an answer to that question!"

The air had fairly crackled for a moment before both had burst into laughter. The irony of the question had definitely not been lost on Nate, and he'd promised her that the next time he was in town, he'd take care of her. And boy had he ever. The day after, she'd been sore from the lavish attention he'd paid her, from the more than eight hours they'd spent rarely leaving the bed. But Simone was a very sexual woman, used to regular intercourse. And while this was true, she was also a selective woman; Simone didn't sleep with just anybody. So this present situation presented a unique quandary. One she wasn't quite sure how to handle.

Simone and Mark finished dinner and then Simone insisted on stacking the dishes in the dishwasher, even though the housekeeper did the heavier cleaning. When she finished, she joined Mark, who was sitting on the couch. She sat down right next to him and laid her head on his shoulder.

"Thanks for dinner," she whispered in a voice filled with

seduction. "You're too good to me." She turned then and kissed him on the cheek.

"You're welcome," Mark said, even as he gently eased away from Simone and got up from the couch.

"I'm a man of morals but not of stone, sweetness. It's been a long time since I've had a woman and I'm sorely tempted to get inside that halter dress that has you looking so delicious. One of these days, when the time is right, I'm going to give all of this to you," he said, running a hand over the huge bulge in his pants. "I'm going to give you all of this, and all of me. But it won't be tonight. Pleasant dreams, Simone."

"I thought you said you'd take care of me," she said to his retreating back. "I thought you said you would make me happy!"

Mark reached the stairs and answered her without turning around. "It may not feel like it at this moment, but that's exactly what I'm doing."

17

Real Good

Verniece Childress and Anne Beck had a lot in common. Maybe that's why they were so close. As small as Palestine was, both women were from even smaller towns: Verniece from a farming enclave in Alabama and Anne from a Nebraska railroad town. Both had been raised in church and came from staunch, traditional Christian families. Both loved the Lord and wanted to serve Him. And both had ended up in Palestine for the same reason: Nate Thicke. But neither knew this yet.

For all their commonalities, there were differences. For one, Verniece was boisterous, where Anne was quiet and shy. Verniece loved church projects that put her in the limelight, while Anne was the worker bee behind the scenes. Verniece was light and short, Anne was dark and tall. Anne was already screwing the pastor, Verniece was still in the desirous phase.

But on this overcast Saturday in October, it was their commonalities that had them diligently working in the Gospel Truth sanctuary, helping to prepare for the next day's service, which included the baptism ceremony performed every second Sunday. They chatted amicably as they folded programs, placing an announcement insert and offering envelope into each one.

"It's amazing how God works, ain't it?" Verniece asked in her endearing southern accent. "I mean, one day I saw the man on television, and the next day I saw this ad for a job in Palestine, one that paid more than I was making in Athens. I knew that couldn't have been nobody but God what had me see that ad. I wasn't even looking for a job!"

"God is good," Anne said quietly.

"How'd you get here all the way from Nebraska?"

"My grandmother lives near here, remember? I came down to visit her three years ago and she kept going on and on about this new preacher. I wasn't going to church at the time but she kept bugging me to drive her over here. And I did. . . . Moved down three months later and been here ever since."

"You moved down here just to go to church?" Verniece asked.

"I moved down here to take care of my grandmother!" Anne responded in a rare show of feistiness. "Just like you moved here to make more money, right?"

"Girl, you know it!" Both women were quiet a moment, trying to believe their lies. Verniece continued. "So when you got here, there was what, just a couple hundred members?"

"Uh-huh. Reverend Thicke had just taken over the church the year before and from what my grandmother tells me, wasn't but a handful of members when he got here. A year later there were two hundred members, then three hundred, four, five, and you saw that we had to move his anniversary this year just to handle all the people. *And* add extra services."

"Was it easier to talk to Reverend in those days? You know, to make an appointment for counseling or whatever? Because I've been trying to get an appointment forever, and they keep telling me he's busy and to talk to one of the associate ministers. But Reverend Thicke is the shepherd of this flock. I don't want to talk to an associate minister. I want to talk to him!"

Anne looked at Verniece with eyes of understanding. "Back then, Reverend used to be at the back of the church at the end of service, shaking everybody's hand. You just had to walk up to him and ask him."

"Was Ms. Noble his assistant then?"

"Uh–huh. Grandma says their family has been at this church forever. But she wasn't controlling his calendar so much, like she does now."

"Did you ever get counseling from Reverend?"

Anne cleared her throat. "Uh–huh." Both women stuffed programs quietly for a moment before Anne continued. "I was in a bad relationship and didn't know how to get out of it. I mean, I knew how to get out but just not how to stay out. I'd leave, he'd come find me, apologize, and I'd get back with him. The last time I went back, things were okay for about a month. Then one night he came home late, drunk. When I asked him where he'd been, he beat me. He'd hit me before but this time . . . it was bad."

"Did you call the police? Have him arrested?"

Anne shook her head no, answering in a voice even softer than the one she'd been speaking in. "He said he'd kill me if I did, and I believed him."

Their conversation was interrupted by Katherine's assistant, Charmaine. "Sorry, y'all, but these building fund envelopes just came in. Ms. Noble wants them added to the programs. I told her y'all were probably almost done but . . ." Charmaine didn't finish the sentence, though her rolled eyes and facial expression communicated what she dared not voice—that what Ms. Noble wanted, Ms. Noble got.

"That's fine, Charmaine," Verniece said, reaching up and taking the box. "It's not like I have a hot date tonight or anything."

"Thank you."

Verniece watched Charmaine until she left the sanctuary, then looked around to make sure they were still the only ones in the room. "So what did Reverend Thicke do?"

Anne smiled, remembering. "He made me feel good, Verniece. I waited a couple days before I called the office, and the sistah who answered must have heard the urgency in my voice. She put me straight through. As soon as I told him I was calling because my ex had beat me, he told me to come down to the office—immediately. After I told him the whole story, he called the police department and spoke to one of his friends who works there. They went over and got my stuff out of his house and Reverend gave me money for a hotel room for a whole month, so I could get myself together. No one had ever been that kind to me. . . . I owe him everything."

Anne became quiet, remembering the rest of the story, the part she didn't share with Verniece. How Reverend had given her his cell number as well, and how she'd called him almost every night, saying she did so because hearing his voice made her feel safe. And how one night when she was especially frightened, he stopped by the hotel room . . . and covered her. It had happened regularly since then, mostly on Tuesdays if he was in town. Anne knew there were other women on other nights, knew that before Simone Noble got married, she was one of his main girlfriends. But with Nathaniel Thicke, you didn't care that he had other women. You just wanted to be one of them.

"What do you need counseling about, if you don't mind me asking."

Verniece sighed. "Honestly, I just need some di—direction for my life." *I can't believe I almost slipped and said what I almost slipped and said!*

Anne looked keenly at Verniece for a moment, then went back to folding and stuffing the programs. "It might take you a while to get an appointment, but be patient. And keep trying." Anne fixed Verniece with a knowing look. "Reverend Thicke is good at giving direction, Verniece. Real good."

18

You Be Careful

Jennifer and her sister, Anita, strolled along the well-worn path of the area in New Orleans known as the French Quarter. They chatted amicably as they took in the sights and sounds of Bourbon Street. It was a sunny afternoon, and while the temperature had dropped, it was still warm enough to need just a jacket.

"It's not quite like it was before Katrina, huh?" Anita asked.

"No, but they did a good job rebuilding it. It still has that special feel to it; I think people who don't know it as well as we did will still enjoy it. I'm enjoying it, sister. Thanks for the invite. I'm going to come down and see you guys more often."

"I told you that you needed a break. Ever since you moved to Texas, it's been work, work, work. You have to stop and smell the roses sometime."

"You were right, Anita. But I love what I do, especially as Nate's manager."

"Oh, it's Nate now? Not Reverend Thicke?"

"It's Nate when he and I are alone, or when I'm talking to my sister." Jennifer winked.

"Uh-huh. And how often are y'all alone?"

"Not as often as I'd like, to tell you the truth. But that's all

about to change. I think after next month, our relationship is
going to go to another level."

Anita stopped walking and placed a hand on her sister's
arm. "Just what are you saying, Anita? Are you sleeping with
your pastor?"

Jennifer didn't know how much she should share with her
older sister. Just two years apart, they'd always been close. But
Anita had always been conservative, especially when it came to
church matters and *especially* when it came to sex. She'd married her high school sweetheart, they'd graduated college, and
then got the house, the kids, the white picket fence . . . just
like you were supposed to. Jennifer didn't know if Anita would
understand that sometimes life was not always tidy, not always
wrapped in pretty paper with a perfect bow on top.

"Nate and I have a lot in common," Jennifer said. "Our
goals are similar and because of the work I did in Kansas City,
at Mount Zion, I have a lot of the contacts he needs to reach
these goals. It's brought us closer, and I believe he's beginning
to appreciate me in ways that go beyond the professional."

"Uh, so would that be a yes . . . or a no?"

Jennifer laughed. "After next month, it might be a definite
yes. We're going to Los Angeles together on a publicity tour to
promote his new book. I was able to line up some stellar appearances, if I must say so myself. So I'm really looking forward
to this trip, not just because of what it will do for Nate's career,
but because it will give us some quality time alone."

"As fine as that man is and as fast as those California women
are, y'all probably won't be alone for long. You be careful."

"These are so good," Melody said, biting into her second
beignet. "They should start a chain of these, you know, like
Dunkin' Donuts or Krispy Kreme."

"But I think that's what makes them so special," Destiny
countered. "That you can't get them everywhere. They are
good though, huh."

"I'm so glad to be able to really chill for a minute; you never know who's looking at you in Baton Rouge. Especially with Josh trying to be all up in my grill about where I've been and who I'm with. I'm getting ready to dismiss his clingy ass."

"How old is he?"

"Twenty-four."

"So I take it you like older guys. It seems that's who you're with mostly."

"Hell, yeah. They know what they're doing more than boys our age. How old is your baby's daddy? What's his name anyway? And why ain't y'all together?"

"Dag, girl. Why are you trying to—"

"Get all up in your business? Because your ass is always all up in mine and you don't see me acting like I'm on *CSI* or some shit. You acting like you got a case and somebody's trying to solve it. I'm just asking because I want to know."

Destiny gave the spiel she'd been practicing since meeting Melody in the mall. "His name is Bryan. He's twenty, and we're not together because he accused me of sleeping around, said the child wasn't his."

"Were you?"

"No."

Melody shrugged as she took the last bite of beignet and followed it with a swig of cola. "Don't trip, girl. Wait a few months after the baby, until you have your figure back and shit, and then take his ass on *Maury* so we can all hear, 'You *are* the father'!"

Destiny laughed.

"But wait until you can get back into your clothes. You'll want to look good on national TV. I'm going to make sure my stuff is tight!"

"You?"

"Girl, you know I'm going with you. I'll make sure I get noticed, start a fight or something on purpose, anything to get me on tape. People love that sort of drama. Then the next thing you know, instead of *I Love New York,* it will be *I Hate Melody!* Paper, paper, cha-ching. Feel me?"

"Whatever, Melody. C'mon, let's walk around. My son is kicking me. I need to put him to sleep." Destiny got up, put a hand at the small of her back, and stretched.

"You know it's a boy?"

"Uh-huh."

"What are you going to name him?"

"Benjamin."

"Why not Bryan?"

"Bryan?"

"After the daddy?"

Shoot! "Oh, him. No, I ain't naming my baby after nothing that won't claim him."

Melody held the door for Destiny as they exited the café. Looking up, Melody saw two handsome young men casually strolling down the street. She tapped Destiny with her elbow. "Girl, it's time to cross the street. I see the man who's going to buy me a souvenir."

Jennifer's fork hit the plate with a clatter. "I'll be right back!" She rushed toward the front door of the restaurant, just as a large party, including a woman with a stroller, was making its way in. "Excuse me, please! I need to get through! Move!"

Ignoring the startled, angry looks from the incoming patrons, Jennifer ran out the door. She looked up and down the street, crossed, and then looked up and down again. She put her hands on her hips and waited two, three, five minutes. Finally, she walked back to the restaurant, just as her sister reached the door.

"I was coming to look for you. What's the matter?"

"Nothing. I thought I saw somebody," Jennifer replied.

"Who?" Anita asked as they sat back down at their table.

"This girl who used to go to Gospel Truth."

"Oh, one of your friends from Palestine. Well . . . was it her?"

"She was gone by the time I got out there."

"Do you have her cell number? Maybe you can call her."

Jennifer simply nodded. Even though her appetite was gone, she took a bite of her salad. Her mind was reeling with what she was sure she just saw, a very pregnant Destiny Noble walking down the streets of New Orleans—either her or her twin sister! *What does this have to do with Simone abruptly leaving Palestine and getting married?* Jennifer kept looking out the window, hoping to catch a glimpse of her again. But no one resembling her nemesis's daughter passed by. She didn't look that far along, maybe four, five months, Jennifer figured. But then again, Destiny was tall and skinny. Sometimes women like that were further along than they looked. Jennifer turned into a human calculator, rapidly putting numbers and dates together, trying to determine when Destiny would have gotten pregnant. And would she have still been in Palestine when it happened? Because if she had been, then who was the father? A face immediately popped into her head. *No. Not Nate.* There was no way Jennifer would believe that Destiny Noble was carrying Nate Thicke's child. She was barely older than a child herself. Surely he wouldn't . . . But deep in her heart Jennifer knew that he would.

"Girl, let's go. You haven't heard a word I've said for the past five minutes."

"Oh, I'm sorry, Anita. I was just thinking about something, that's all."

"Does it have to do with the girl you just saw, or Reverend Thicke?"

"Unh-unh," was Jennifer's noncommittal response. Because the answer to that question was one she feared: that it had to do with them both.

19

Give Up Everything and Have It All

With the exception of some cable shows, a couple locally produced programs, and a few guest appearances on TBN, Nate was new to television. But one watching wouldn't know it. He seemed born for the camera, and the lens loved him. In the prep run before the actual airing, he appeared relaxed and natural, as if he was talking directly to the viewer. Nate's national debut, strategically scheduled during the Thanksgiving holiday when many people were off work and therefore watching, was poised for success.

Carla Chapman made small talk with Nate as the makeup artists blotted the oil from both their faces, and the stylist rearranged Carla's new hairstyle. After more than a decade of braids, Carla had finally listened to her friends, Tai Brook and Vivian Montgomery, and came into the twenty-first century with a sleek, straight weave that brushed her shoulders. The symmetrical cut and wispy bangs framed her face with a slimming affect, not that Carla was ashamed of any one of the one hundred eighty pounds she carried. Monique wasn't the only one who thought that big could be beautiful. Carla not only thought it, but proved it with both her outer and inner beauty every single day.

"Nate, you are working that turtleneck like a job. Lord, that tan color looks good on you!"

"Jennifer thought the sweater would be more personable than a suit. What do you think?"

"I agree. You want to seem casual, accessible to people. I think people are more prone to buy nonfiction when they feel as if they know the author a little bit. And after this segment, there's going to be a whole lot of sistahs wanting to know you!"

Nate's response was cut short by the producer counting them down to action: "Four, three, two . . ."

"Good morning, afternoon, evening, everybody. Wherever you are and whenever you're watching, have I got a show for you!" Carla continued in the down-home manner that had made her show a ratings winner and garnered an Emmy nomination two years in a row. Her intro referred to the challenges facing not only America, but the world, and how in such times, people became more aware of what they had, and what they didn't have. Often, she noted, depression set in with people convinced they'd never realize their dream of getting married, having children, landing that promotion or plum job opportunity, buying that home.

"*How* is often the big question, isn't it? How can I get what I want? Well, my guest today has an answer that might surprise you. He says that you can have absolutely anything you want, but you have to give up something first. Why don't I let him explain it? Please join me in welcoming first-time guest, motivational speaker, pastor, and now, author, Nathaniel Thicke."

The applause from the mostly female audience was enthusiastic, and more than a few of the members wore glazed expressions as they ogled the Adonis in their midst. Nathaniel looked like he was kicking back with an old friend as he shared the couch with Carla, an arm casually draped across the back and his left ankle resting on his right knee.

When the audience finally stopped clapping, Carla put her

hand on her hip and addressed them. "Oh my! That was some kind of applause. Have y'all already read the book?"

Nate joined in with the audience's laughter. They all got Carla's joke. The book's big debut was tomorrow, so Nate knew the chances of anyone in the room having read the book, besides Carla and Jennifer backstage, were slim.

"Nate, let's start with the title. It's really interesting. What do you mean by"—Carla turned the book out toward the camera—"*Give Up Everything and Have It All?*"

"First of all, Carla, thanks for having me on your show. You're even more beautiful in person than you are on TV."

"Ooh, suky, suky, now! Somebody go get my husband so I make sure I behave!" The audience laughed again. She continued. "Seriously, thank you. Lavon and I met Nate a while back," she told the audience. "And he is as impressed with him as I am. Now back to the book: *Give Up Everything and Have It All.* Explain that title."

"There are many ways to frame what I mean by it, but simply put: to get something, you have to give something. And often to gain something, you have to lose something. Now this doesn't have to be a bad thing. Most often what a person gives up pales in comparison to what they gain. For instance, I remember watching President Obama right after the election. One reporter asked what he missed about his old life. He said he missed the anonymity of being regular, taking a walk, going to the store, those kinds of things. But what he gained, becoming president of the United States, made what he lost worth it. Anyone in here agree with me?"

Sustained applause was his answer.

"In life, it's easy to become comfortable with what we have, so much so that we don't want to part with it, even when we sometimes know that to do so would be in our best interest. Say you're looking for your mate." A murmur, mixed with laughter, ran through the audience. More than one woman watching obviously hoped they were looking *at* him. "And you have this ideal, perfect man in mind," Nate continued smoothly, a sly smile his only acknowledgment that he was aware of his effect on the opposite sex. "But you've got this knucklehead, this nucka, sitting in your living room night after night. Or you're going out with someone who doesn't have even fifty percent of what you say you want. What would happen if you gave him up—released that which was comfortable and familiar? What if what you wanted was worth giving up everything to get it? And what if you were guaranteed to get what you wanted if you were willing to sacrifice everything. Would you do it?"

A camera scanned the rapt faces of women in the audience. Some were nodding, others thinking, a couple sistahs high-fived each other at a comment only they'd heard. "My book details, in ten easy steps, how to get rid of whatever you don't want—to make room for what you desire. I share how to lose the fear of the unknown, how to step out on faith and trust the universe, God, to deliver your heart's desire. Because I can tell you from personal experience that if you give up everything . . . you can have it all." He ended his comment with a dazzling smile.

Carla looked at Nate's smile and began fanning her face with her hand. "Whew, talk about having it all," she joked, knowing every female in the room and watching knew what she meant. "God gave some people extra, more than enough. I can't even think right now, y'all. We'll be back right after the break. Sit tight."

The hour flew by, with viewers loving Nate more with every answer. He was at once intelligent, engaging, inspiring, and warm. Even as this live show aired, the studio's switchboards blew up as did both of Jennifer's cell phones. As had become customary with many authors, he gave everyone in the studio audience a signed copy of his book. As was not customary, he stayed for forty-five minutes afterward posing for photos with them.

Before the month was out, Nathaniel E. Thicke would be an *Essence* and *New York Times* best-selling author—and his life would never be the same.

Reverend Ed Smith steamed as he watched Nate on *Conversations with Carla*. He wanted to throw up as he saw the women swooning over him. They were repulsive to witness—none more, he thought, than that whore of a former first lady, Carla. Ed had relished the day she got her comeuppance, when her husband threw her out of the house like yesterday's trash. Not that he liked him any better. To Ed, Stanley Lee was a heretic, a false prophet, just like the rest of those money-hungry preachers.

Ed snorted as Carla introduced Nate Thicke as, among other things, a motivational speaker. "So here he's a preacher," Ed said to the walls, "but in la-la land he's a *motivational* speaker." Ed's laugh was dark and sinister as he reached for the bottle of brandy and poured another shot. "I'll tell you what he is. He's a whoremonger and a pimp!" Ed turned and spoke directly to the television. "You took something of mine, and I'm going to take something of yours . . . like your ministry, you fake-ass son of a bitch!"

Later that evening, Jennifer and Nate joined Carla and Lavon in the Chapman home. Carla had fixed one of her legendary southern spreads. Tonight's included oven-fried red snapper, greens, fried corn—cut fresh off the cob—mashed potatoes loaded with cream cheese, sliced tomatoes, fresh corn bread from scratch, and a berry cobbler—blueberry, blackberry, raspberry—for the wee bit of stomach room that anyone had left.

"Goodness, gracious, Carla Chapman!" Nate exclaimed as he took a bite of the still warm cobbler that he'd chosen to have à la mode. "I didn't think the dinner could get any better than that fish and those potatoes and greens, girl. But . . . unh,

unh, unh . . ." Whatever he was going to say was forgotten as he took another bite.

"This food is stupid good, girl," Jennifer agreed, taking a small forkful of the sliver of pie, sans ice cream, she'd accepted. Being in LA the past two days had made her acutely aware of her clothes labels that read "size 16," as had her observation that Nate's eyes seemed to linger especially long on slender women. She'd decided right then and there to cut back on food intake and start exercising when she returned home. Then, after another bite of Carla's pie, she decided to skip that "cut back" for tonight. "I think I'll have one more, tiny, tiny slice."

Carla and Lavon simply looked at each other and laughed as Carla dished up the big slice she knew her sistah friend really wanted.

"I suggest we get started right after the holidays," Lavon said when conversation returned to business. "Have the four-part segment on your book air around March or April. Your being on Carla's show is going to keep the buzz going at least until then, so the series will just ride that wave."

"Sounds good to me, but what's important is what my manager thinks." He tweaked Jennifer's cheek as he said this, then kept his hand resting on her shoulder.

Jennifer's heart soared. Everything was happening according to plan. She tried to remain casual, even as it felt like Nate's hand was burning a hole in her blouse. "Lavon's the expert in this arena," she answered. "I think we should follow his advice."

"You know life as you know it is over," Carla said to Nate. "You're public property now, my darlin'. I hope you're ready because it can be a crazy ride."

"I better be ready, especially with a manager like Jennifer, trying to book me on every radio and television show across the country."

"It's important for PR, Nate. We've got to stay in their faces. Especially during the first three months of book sales.

Those are crucial, and will help when you negotiate the second book deal."

"You've already got plans for a second one?" Carla asked.

Nate nodded. "Publisher called me shortly after reading the manuscript for this one and said they were interested."

"Well, after today," Lavon said, "you can count that deal as good as done."

"The company is lovely but it's been a long day," Nate said as he wiped his mouth and laid his napkin on the table. "If y'all don't mind, I'm going to call it an early night."

The foursome continued their easy banter as Lavon and Carla walked Nate and Jennifer to the door. Jennifer hung back to let the men go down the hall first.

"You seem so happy," she whispered to Carla. "I saw those looks you and Lavon kept giving each other."

"What can I say? I'm madly in love with my husband."

"I'm so happy for you, Carla. You deserve it after all of the hell you went through."

The story was old news and there weren't many who didn't know about it. Carla had been the wife of and copastor with Stanley Lee, as well as a popular speaker on the Christian women's circuit, when she'd met and had an affair with Lavon, a producer invited to their church by her husband to create a DVD series. Pictures of them together had been taken and then given or sold to *LA Gospel*, a popular tabloid-style magazine geared toward the Black Christian community. The scandal had rocked that community, not to mention Carla's marriage and ministry. But just like the phoenix, Carla had risen from the ashes and was now having the time of her life.

"I appreciate your saying that, Jennifer, really. Going through that heartache, especially in public, wasn't easy. But I'll tell you what a very smart man said to me recently . . . If you give up everything, you can have it all."

20

California Dreamin'

Jennifer became quiet as she and Nate neared the elevator of their plush hotel in Santa Monica. She'd learned that Nate liked to be the aggressor where their "spiritual relationship" was concerned, so she waited, and hoped, that he would want to be with her.

"More messages came in while we were at Carla's," she said, pressing the elevator button. "I know you're tired though. You'll probably want to wait till morning to hear about them."

"Yeah, you're a slave-driver, woman. That schedule was brutal."

"But you were amazing. I can't believe how well you're doing. I mean, I'm not surprised, but it's just that you handle this whole Hollywood TV thing like you've been doing it forever."

The elevator doors opened and the two stepped inside. Once again, conversation waned. Jennifer tried not to think about what she wanted, and how much she wanted it. It had been two weeks since she and Nate had been sexual, but it felt more like two years. Nate was like a drug; the more you had of him, the more you wanted. It didn't help knowing that he'd been spending the time he wasn't with her with other women. She tried not to think about that now, just like she tried not to think about Destiny. Nate's reaction had been interesting though, she remembered, when she'd casually mentioned her a week after returning from New Orleans.

"I was visiting my sister in New Orleans last week and guess who I saw?"

"Who?" Nate had asked, nonchalantly, as he watched the football network.

"Destiny Noble."

Silence had filled the room.

"Did you hear me, Nate?"

"Hmm?"

Jennifer had walked to the couch then. "I saw Simone's daughter, Destiny, in New Orleans. Did you know she was pregnant?"

"Destiny?" Nate asked, still watching TV.

"Yes."

"Are you sure?"

"She was either pregnant or sporting a beach ball under her top. I wonder who the father is."

Nate had remained quiet a long moment. Finally he said, "I thought Simone told me her daughter was in New York, checking out some modeling agencies. I doubt it was Destiny you saw. No, I'm sure it wasn't her. Bring me some ice tea, please?"

And just like that, Jennifer's theory had been dissed and dismissed. While Jennifer had been certain the woman was Destiny, Nate's reaction raised doubt. Some days Jennifer believed what her eyes saw, other days she believed what Nate told her. Tonight, she chose to believe the latter.

"Well, I guess it's good night, then," Jennifer said, when they reached her room. Nate's suite was at the end of the hall. "Call me if you need anything."

"All right, Jennifer. Good night."

Jennifer's heart plummeted, but she kept the smile plas-

tered on while Nate scanned the card for her and opened the
door to her room. Such gentlemanly acts, done without thinking, were why women swooned over him. "Congratulations,"
she whispered just before she allowed the door to close.

She walked over to the bed and plopped down on it. Not a
woman prone to crying, she was surprised to feel her eyes water.
She didn't want to feel sorry for herself. She was in LA, with
the man of her dreams, living life like it was golden. Jennifer
decided to take a nice, hot shower, and maybe go downstairs
and listen to the jazz group she'd heard playing when they entered the lobby.

Moments after stepping out of the shower, her phone rang.
"You said call if I needed anything, right?" a sultry voice asked.

"Yes," Jennifer whispered.

"Well, I need it. Get down here."

Jennifer put down the receiver, squealed, and, donning a
sundress, sandals, and nothing else, hurried down the hall.

Nate finished his last in a round of calls, this one with Deacon Robinson, and then stretched out on the king-sized bed
and waited for Jennifer. He had sensed how bad she wanted him,
could feel her desire as they rode up the elevator. And even
though he'd enjoyed a morning quickie with one of Derrick's
members whom he often phoned when he was in town, he
had more than enough stamina to handle his very capable
manager. She'd done an excellent job, after all . . . and deserved
a thank you.

Jennifer tapped once before using the card she had to
Nate's room. She walked straight to the bed and climbed in,
not even trying to perpetrate a fraud. "I'm so glad you called
me," she said, before plunging her tongue inside Nate's hot
mouth.

He immediately slid his hands up her dress, placed them on
her bare, ample rump, and began kneading it slowly as he
ground himself against her. *Oh, yeah, this sistah's hot. It's going to
be good tonight!*

Jennifer stopped long enough to pull the sundress over her head, then lay down next to Nate. She placed her hand inside his boxers and was rewarded with the feel of his massive weapon, ready to aim and fire. She massaged it and his balls as their tongues dueled. Nate found a nipple, the suckling of which rocked Jennifer's core. She opened her legs to give him access. He reached over for a condom that was on the nightstand. And then the phone rang.

"Don't get it, Nate," Jennifer whispered frantically. "I can't wait for it, baby. I've got to have you now!"

"Hold on a minute, baby, I need to get this one." It was Nate's private phone, of which only a handful of people had the number. He had a feeling who might be calling. He was right.

Katherine started talking before Nate finished saying hello. "You've got to get to New Orleans, quick! Destiny's in labor. She's about to have your baby."

21

Uncommon

Benjamin Nathaniel Eli Thicke was a perfect child, from the top of his full head of thick, silky hair to the tip of his long, thin toes. Weighing eight pounds, seven ounces at birth and measuring twenty-two inches long, the child seemed to have inherited the best features of both parents. There was still time for them to change, but right now his eyes were a dazzling hazel green, a nod to Destiny's Creole roots. But after taking one look at his balls and the skin around his fingers, Nettie declared that the child would more than likely be dark, like his dad.

"Wow, he's growing so fast," Nate whispered, after Destiny had changed the baby and placed him in his father's arms.

"That's because it's been almost a month since you've seen him, back in January," Destiny replied, with just a hint of the whine that drove Nate wild. She'd tried to be understanding and take her grandmother's advice and not nag, but she was a new, young, teenage mother. She didn't care that everyone in the world wanted a piece of Nate Thicke, the rising star author. She wanted her man by her side.

"Dang," Nate said as his cell phone rang for the umpteenth time. He didn't even have to look at it to know it was Jennifer. She'd been acting funny ever since he left her hot and horny in his LA hotel suite. And he was sure she wasn't the only one who'd noted his increased absence from the church during the month of December, when he'd spent as much time as he could with Destiny and their son. But once the holidays were over, it was back to work with a schedule that was insane. Not only was he receiving constant invites from the broadcasting industry, but the offers to preach across the country had tripled. Carla had been right when she said the life he once knew was over. And she was also right when she'd later said that sometimes he'd want the old life back.

"Here, take him, baby," Nate said after his phone had rung three more times, followed by text message beeps. "This must be important."

"I know you're busy, but you need to carve out some family time, Nate, when you cannot be disturbed."

"You're right," he said over his shoulder as he walked into the bedroom and closed the door. He didn't want to take a chance that the baby would cry while he was talking to the wrong person.

Destiny shifted her hungry son to her other arm, pulled aside her top, and began to nurse him. All the while she thought about Nate—what was happening and with whom back in Texas while she continued to live in Louisiana. She'd checked Nate's phone earlier, when he was in the shower. As she suspected, most calls were from women—most she knew, some she didn't. She paid particular attention to names that showed up often. Katherine, Jennifer, Patricia, Anne, her mother, were all names she recognized. But one of them, Verniece, was new. Destiny suspected Nate was covering all of them. And for the first time since she fell in love with him at the age of twelve, she had a problem with that.

"Sorry about that, baby," Nate said as he exited the bedroom. "I'm glad I took it, though. It was Jennifer. They're having some type of faith-based function at the White House where ministers from various denominations are getting together to discuss pressing problems facing the nation. I've been invited!"

"Really? That's great, baby."

"You don't sound too excited."

"I'm happy for you, but I just wish I could be with you. I miss you, Nate. I miss us. I want you with me all the time. I wish we could go somewhere together, just the three of us, and be alone. I hate that the baby and me are here in Louisiana while you continue to live in Texas." Destiny's eyes filled with tears as she continued. "I just love you so much that when you're not here . . ."

"Shh, baby, don't cry. Shh." Nate picked up Destiny, who was still holding Benjamin, and headed to the bedroom. "I miss you too, baby, more than I can say. But we have to do it like this right now, just for a little while."

He reached the bedroom and took a now sleeping Benjamin out of Destiny's arms. He kissed his son on the cheek before lowering him into the bassinet. Then he walked over to the bed and joined Destiny. "You know you're my heart, right?" he asked her, as he slowly stroked her body until it flamed. "You know that I'm counting down the days until I can announce you to the world, let everybody know you're mine. No one else's, just mine." Nate ran his hand over Destiny's stomach, already flat again, barely three months after giving birth. "This belongs to me alone. Remember that."

"But you're not," Destiny whispered.

"I'm not what?"

"You're not just for me. You're with a lot of different women."

"Baby, you already know what that's about. As the shepherd of the flock—"

"You're their spiritual covering. I know, I know, Nate, but it doesn't feel good. I can't be with anyone else, but you can."

A surge of jealousy and anger ripped through Nate, so powerful it shocked him. Just the thought of Destiny being

with anybody else rocked him to the core. He stopped touching her and sat up. "What, are you interested in somebody?"

"No, Nate, but—"

"But what? Where's this coming from all of a sudden? This
is how it's been since you've known me. I know Katherine
talked to you about it, and probably your mother too. If I find
out there's somebody else, Destiny, whoever it is will pay a
steep price."

"There is nobody else, Nate, and I don't want anybody else.
I only want you. I don't know where these feelings are coming
from. I just know I want you to myself. What about other preachers? Do they cover their flocks too?"

"Look, don't worry about other preachers. And don't worry
about who else I'm with." Nate's voice softened as Destiny's
declaration of singular love for him calmed his ire. "Just know
that you're number one, baby," he said, spreading her legs gently and easing a finger inside her. "And that nobody else can
compare to this right here. Okay?"

"Okay," Destiny whispered, spreading her legs farther and
wrapping her arms around Nate's broad shoulders. Within minutes, Nate was inside her, driving deep as if to brand her, deeper
than she thought possible, making her cry with the pain and
pleasure of it all. But before the night was over he was gone,
back to Palestine and the whirlwind of activity that was now
his life.

He promised them a vacation soon, just the three of them.
That's what Destiny held on to as, after feeding Benjamin and
putting him down for the final time that night, she walked over
to the television and pulled out the DVD series she'd been
watching for the past month. She'd gotten them from Melody
one day, after spotting them in her room.

"What's this?" she'd asked after seeing a DVD entitled *An
Uncommon Woman—You!*

"Girl, please, that ain't nothing. Just some religious mess my mom keeps sending me."

Destiny scanned the copy on the front, and then turned it over to read the back cover. "Who is it?"

"She's Pastor Montgomery's wife, Vivian. Most people really like her, but I can't stand her ass."

"Why not?"

Melody told Destiny about a dance troupe that she joined at Kingdom Citizens, and then quit when Vivian insisted the girls take "spiritual etiquette" classes first. "She thinks she's all that, but she ain't."

"Do you mind if I watch them?" Destiny had asked.

"What? For real?"

"Might help me get extra credit in my morals class," Destiny had teased. But what had captured her attention was the title. Something about being "uncommon" had sounded pretty cool.

Destiny watched intently as on the DVD, Vivian encouraged the women in the audience to set themselves apart, to respect each other, to treat their bodies as sacred, and to live their lives by their own truth instead of following the actions of others.

That's it, Destiny thought, as she continued watching. That's what had changed since she had the baby. She no longer wanted to do what all the other women in Nate's life were doing, what her mother and grandmother were doing, what his manager and his choir director were doing. Destiny wanted to be uncommon. After Vivian ended her talk and the applause had died down, she asked the women present to join her in the Sanctity of Sisterhood motto, the SOS creed. Destiny listened, pressed REPLAY and listened again. She pressed REPLAY one more time, until she had it, and the next time she pressed it, she joined the ladies from the privacy of her living room:

"I'm uncommon, I'm unusual, I am not the status quo.
Set apart, an earthly treasure 'cause my Father deemed it so.
Yes, I am my sister's keeper, and it should be understood,
That together we stand united, the sanctity of sisterhood."

Destiny felt something happen as she said those words, and she said them again and again. She wanted to talk to someone about what she was feeling, about whether it was possible to be Nate's uncommon woman. She thought about her mother and grandmother.

Kiki won't understand, she thought. *She'll just tell me about the man of God and his needs.*

"Maybe Mama," Destiny said. She quickly called the home number and, when it went to voice mail, decided not to call the cell. Obviously, she and Mark were out.

Destiny paced the floor, continuing to bask in the light of this new truth, about being uncommon and original. She went to her computer and looked up the word uncommon. *Rare, unusual, special, exceptional* were some of the definitions. The more she read, the more excited she became. Destiny wished she could talk to Vivian Montgomery directly. Nate could probably arrange it, but Destiny needed advice right now.

Suddenly, Destiny stopped dead in her tracks. "That's who I'll call!" She went to her computer, clicked open the address book, and minutes later was dialing the number.

"Hello?"

"Miss Nettie? This is Destiny. I need to talk to you."

22

Big Daddy

"You're looking powerful pretty there now," Deacon Robinson said, as he watched Jennifer walk up the sidewalk toward the church's side entrance. "I had to wait just so I could open the door for you."

"You're too kind," Jennifer said, without much kindness.

"You don't know the half," the deacon responded.

"And I never will," Jennifer shot back, but this time she smiled.

Deacon Robinson opened the door for Jennifer and the two stepped into the church. "Time is running out for that date I've been requesting."

Jennifer had a million things going on in her head: trying to keep Nate's PR schedule straight, battling with Katherine, who was handling his preaching calendar and always trying to throw her weight around, and Verniece, Nate's latest addition, who'd had the nerve to actually call her out the week before.

"Just so you know," Verniece had said as she sidled up to Jennifer in the church parking lot. "Your days in Nate's bed are numbered."

"So you can count?" was Jennifer's quick retort.

"Yeah, and add too," Verniece replied without missing a

beat. "And when all is said and done, one"—she pointed to herself—"plus one"—she pointed to the church—"is going to equal two"—she pointed to Jennifer—"without you!"

Then she'd turned around and farted, actually farted, before she looked back once more, winked at an appalled Jennifer, calmly walked to her car, and drove off.

"Look, Deacon Robinson."

"Please, call me James."

"Look, *James*. I am sure you're nice and everything. But I don't date older men."

"Word has it that you're sleeping with Nate, and he's older than you."

Jennifer hadn't intended to be rude but the deacon had gone there. So he deserved what he got. "Let me rephrase that then. I don't date shriveled-up, dried-up old men. Is that clearer for you?"

"It sure is," Deacon Robinson said, as he calmly took off his glasses and pulled out a handkerchief to wipe them. "And if I meet a man like the one you just described, I'll be sure and tell him you're off limits."

"Deacon! Just the man I want to see!" Nate came around the corner and immediately put his hand out to one of his mentors, who was also head of the deacon board.

"Oh, hi, Jennifer," he said as an afterthought. Jennifer was chagrined, but remained quiet as she followed behind the two men and listened.

"I can't thank you enough for all your help with getting the plans together for our new church," Nate continued.

"Spring is just around the corner," Deacon Robinson said. "Perfect time to break ground."

"Well, we couldn't have pushed up the timetable without you. Now that you've bought out Axel, yours should be about the largest construction company in Texas. Am I right?"

"Largest in the southeastern states," Deacon Robinson corrected. "Will be the largest this side of the Mississippi in five more years."

"You don't say?"

"Yes, I do," Deacon Robinson said, cutting a look behind him and meeting Jennifer's eye.

Jennifer began to follow Nate and the deacon into Nate's office.

"Uh, give us a moment, Jennifer. I'll be out to talk with you after I finish meeting with Mr. Moneybags here."

Jennifer tried to tell herself that it didn't matter that the man she'd just insulted might be richer than she thought. She knew he owned a construction company, but had assumed its reach was limited to Palestine and the other surrounding small towns. She had no idea that Deacon James Robinson was *that* James Robinson, the owner of the SLR Construction Company, which had been on the news, buying up smaller companies like jelly beans. No wonder Nate treated him deferentially, and no wonder Deacon Robinson had so much swagger. He could put his money where his mouth was. *So what. Trying to hit on me when he's old enough to be my daddy . . . I don't care if he has more money than God, he's not Nate.*

He wasn't Nate, but he was important to Nate, Jennifer decided. That's why she would apologize to Deacon Robinson the first chance she got, and if he played his cards right, she might go on one date. "But only one," she whispered to herself, just as the door to Nate's office opened.

"All right, you take care, man," Nate said as Deacon Robinson stepped out of his office.

"Oh, I'm gonna do that, man," Deacon Robinson responded. He passed by Jennifer, tipped his hat, and walked on.

Jennifer entered Nate's office with a newfound respect for the deacon who thought she was "powerful pretty." Maybe she could use his attraction to her to help Nate secure additional finances, or other resources from James's company. As the afternoon wore on, Jennifer warmed to the one date she'd go on with Deacon Robinson. True, she wanted Nate to be her husband. But until then, Deacon Robinson might play a nice role as Big Daddy.

23

Strange Bedfellows

Nettie blew on the hot cup of freshly brewed coffee and got comfortable. Since the anniversary, she and Mama Max had pledged to try and talk at least once a week. So far, they were batting a thousand.

"When's the last time you seen that grandbaby?" Mama Max asked.

"Oh, it's been a while. Not since shortly after he was born."

"Now, that don't sound like the Nettie I know. The way you love children, I would have thought you'd be halfway raising him by now!"

"If Destiny were here, that would be the case. But with them living in Baton Rouge . . ."

"Yeah, well, I guess you've got a point there. She back in school yet?"

"Taking a full load of classes. Nate got her a full-time nanny, but Destiny ain't one bit happy about leaving her son all day, I'll tell you that. I told her a temporary loss was worth a permanent gain. She'll be glad she stuck with it once she gets her degree."

"How's Katherine handling everything?"

"Trying to control what she can, I guess. She hovers over

Nate like a mother hen. I've had a couple women come to me and complain about how hard it is to work with her."

"What are you going to do about it?"

"Me? What can I do?"

"You're Nate's mama. If any female is going to run that church before he takes a wife, it should be you."

"No, it should be *Nate*. Me and Gordon tell him all the time not to let that woman run his life. He's got to learn how to handle *all* his business. Plus, I know he's got a soft spot for Katherine."

"Why?"

"Because of Destiny and Simone."

"Lord have mercy . . ."

"Mercy, Lord."

"What you hear about Simone these days?" Mama Max continued after a pause. "Not trying to gossip, you understand. Just need to know what to pray about."

Nettie whooped. "Maxine Brook, you are too much! But that's precisely why I love you and don't want you to ever change. According to Katherine, Simone's doing fine. She hasn't been back here though, not since the anniversary."

"So her and Mark's marriage must be working out."

"I guess so. Katherine told me they went to Hawaii for the holidays. That sounds like working out to me. You said that Mark might be the better one for her. Looks like you're right, and that she's happy."

"And if not happy, maybe content at the very least."

"I sure hope so. She waited for Nate a long time."

"Chile, I still can't get over the fact that you and Katherine are friendly."

"Sometimes marriage makes strange bedfellows."

"Yeah, but that piece of strange was in your marriage bed."

"This is old water you're treading in, Mama Max. You know the story. That woman did me a favor sleeping with Daniel all those years, God rest his soul. Lord knows that having someone else to poke is the only way he left me alone. The man was insatiable."

"Yeah, I remember Amanda saying you didn't like that aspect of marriage too much."

"Truth be told, Mama didn't like it much herself. I remember her and Daddy arguing about it. I imagine she'd roll over in her grave if she knew I'd heard."

"So you and Gordon have passed the point of physical affection?"

"Oh, it's been done past. You know he's got ten years on me. The only thing on Gordon that rises now is his blood pressure."

"Ha! Chile, you oughta quit."

Nettie took a sip of her now cold coffee. "That's what I'm trying to tell you . . . we have!"

"So back to Simone and Mark. They take the baby yet?"

"No. Destiny won't let them."

"Now, that's a child who's acting like a mama!"

"Tell me about it. She's a sharp one, that Destiny. I've been counseling her."

"Do tell!"

"At her request, of course. She'd been watching some of Vivian Montgomery's DVDs and had some questions. I've been answering them the best I could."

"Well, with you for a teacher, and God for a guide, that child's gonna be all right."

"I think she might."

"I know she will."

"I think you're right."

"And if I'm wrong, don't tell nobody!"

24

Almost There

Simone was neither happy nor content. She was pissed and frustrated beyond belief. *Why can't I get over him?* she thought, throwing a silk-covered pillow at her reflection in the mirror of her newly redecorated bedroom. And why wouldn't Mark believe her when she lied and said that Nate no longer mattered?

It was only two in the afternoon, but Simone walked into the kitchen and poured herself a glass of wine. She walked to the patio door that led to the well-tended garden landscape. The magnolias were in full bloom, and when she opened the door, their fragrance immediately assailed her senses. Her mind roiled as she walked among the blooms. She wanted to love Mark; she *did* love Mark. But he still wouldn't have sex with her, not completely. He said he wouldn't, so long as she was *in* love with Nathaniel.

She'd sworn she wouldn't be with Nate again, that she was over him, and ready to move on with the wonderful man under whose roof she lived. But then the holidays came, and with it, Nate had brought his fine self to Louisiana. They saw each other while both were visiting his newborn baby. The child was just a month old then, and Destiny was still healing. There'd been an innocent look, a not so innocent touch, and two hours later, they were in a hotel and each other's arms.

Simone didn't know how Mark found out. She swore the man had eyes in the back of his head, or spies, or both. Nate swore he didn't tell him. But somehow he knew. That two-hour tryst changed Mark's vacation plans. He had refused to sleep with her, after acknowledging that initially this was to have been the place of their official joining. After practically begging on her knees, he'd pleasured her with his fingers, brought her to a powerful climax, and then spent the night on the suite's living room couch. Eventually, he moved from there to the bed, where after kissing him into a frenzy, he finally let her blow him. But he still refused to enter her. *I won't be in your body while he is still in your head.* Mark had said he wasn't made of stone. But after their week in Hawaii, Simone figured it was either that or steel. She'd gotten a lei, but hadn't gotten laid.

Simone finished her wine, left the garden, and went back inside the house. She wandered aimlessly from room to room, and ended up in Mark's large master suite. She walked around it slowly, touching his things, breathing in his scent. She lay down in his bed and remembered all of the wonderful things he'd done to her and for her. She made a mental list of why she was in love with Nate, versus why she should be in love with Mark. With Nate, she ran out of ideas after just seven things. But with Mark, when she got to twenty and fell asleep . . . she was still counting.

And that's how Mark found her—curled up on her side, in his bed, looking like a goddess. Mark fondled himself un-ashamedly as he stood there watching his queen. He thought about Aunt Nettie, acknowledging that she'd been right. God had wanted to give Simone to him, and He had. And as hard as it was to wait, Mark was determined to hold out until Simone could give him all of her.

God knows it was hard. Mark felt he hadn't masturbated

this much since he was a teenager. He wanted Simone more than he'd wanted any woman in his life. He'd lost count of the times he'd come close and almost given in. But his auntie's words stayed with him: *a temporary loss is worth a permanent gain.* He knew that if he had sex with Simone while she was still in love with his cousin, it would be a rebound romance, a charity screw. Mark was a good man and he knew it. When he loved, he loved for real and he loved for keeps. He'd already lost one woman, and he didn't plan on losing another. When he became one with Simone Chastity Noble, he planned to be the only one in her bed, and in her heart.

She's close, son. She's almost there. Those are the words Mark heard as he watched Simone for a few more minutes. He nodded to acknowledge His voice, then went to take a shower—a cold one.

25

Sharing Reverend

Verniece stared at the Scrabble board, trying to find a move. "I think this game is locked up," she stated firmly.

"Are you passing? Because I've got a move," Anne replied.

"Dang, wait. Let me see." The score was almost even. Verniece led by twelve points. But since among other letters she was holding the ten-point *q*, that lead wasn't saying much. "Okay, here's one, *t-a-e*." She wrote down her three points with a flourish, pleased with herself for finding a place for this unusual word on the jacked up board.

"*J-a-i*," Anne said calmly, playing on the *a* Verniece just put down.

That was ten points. Verniece's lead was cut to five. "This game is locked!" Verniece declared again. She was hoping Anne would concede the game.

"It's almost over, I'll grant you that," Anne said with a twinkle in her eye.

"You heifah! You know I've got the *q*!"

"Uh-huh, and I've got another play. You passin'?"

"You won!" Verniece declared, upsetting the board. Pieces of wood flew everywhere. They both burst out laughing, then got up and retrieved the pieces. In the end it didn't matter who won. Both ladies were just pleased to have something to do, and someone to do it with.

"What now? You want to order pizza?" Anne asked.

"That sounds cool. What movies you got?"

"Nothing new. See if there's anything down there you want to watch."

Verniece plopped down in front of Anne's small entertainment center to check out the movies stacked below the TV. She pulled out a classic and popped it into the DVD player.

Anne went into the kitchen to get them both a wine cooler. Soon the music from the movie's soundtrack filled the room: *Fair Eastside . . . by thy side we'll stand and always praise thy name.* "Ha! Good choice," she said, coming around the corner with the coolers and the cordless phone. "I love me some Morgan Freeman playing Joe Clark."

"Yeah, girl, 'cause Mr. Clark don't play!" Verniece said, mimicking one of the lines in the film.

"You know it."

After ordering a large supreme with extra cheese, the ladies settled in to watch a movie that both had seen a zillion times. Before long, however, their favorite topic of discussion, their pastor, gave them something else to "lean on."

"How many times have you been with him now?" Anne asked.

Verniece shrugged. "Enough to know I want to be with him a lot more times."

The women giggled.

"I told you he could do the dang thang," Anne said.

"You sure did. I'm glad that I was patient, like you suggested, 'cause that brothah was surely worth the wait. And that little tidbit about slipping a note in the handshake is what finally got me around Katherine the Cootchie Watcher."

"The way that old heifah guards Nate's dick, you'd think that she was hitting it."

"Do you think?" Verniece began.

"No!" both women screamed, and then dissolved into hysterical laughter.

"I know we're not the only ones," Verniece said after Anne had paid the delivery man who knocked on the door. "And I'm cool with that. Truth be told, most women in America are sharing their men, whether they know it or not."

"Uh-huh. Makes it a lot easier when you know that up front."

"Yeah, like that story that made the news, of those women who looked like they walked straight out of another century."

Anne looked quizzical as she took a bite of pizza. Then she remembered seeing it. "Oh, that polygamy case."

"Uh-huh. I saw them on one of them talk shows, talking like they were one big happy family, calling each other sisters. One man had like forty-five kids."

Anne thought a bit and then responded. "I think I could do that," she said.

Verniece rolled her eyes.

"No, really. If I liked the other women, we all were cool, the kids were well-behaved and everything, I think I could live like that."

"Not me. I'm a one-man woman looking for a one-woman man—believe that."

"I don't know. The women I saw seemed happy. They cooked together, did the chores together, each had different nights with the husband. When I was with my ex—boyfriend, not husband—there were times I would have gladly let somebody else have him so I could have some peace. Then again, there were times that *because* somebody was having him, I couldn't get a piece. So I guess that mess is complicated."

"Damn skippy it is. Like, what if we were living in that situation with Reverend Thicke, and you heard me and him huffing and puffing in the bedroom next-door. What would you do?"

"Heck, I'd probably come join you," Anne quipped. The

women laughed and high-fived. Then Anne continued. "But at least with the polygamists, everything is up front. There's no lying, no sneaking around, no down low. So if the research is correct, and women are sharing men whether they know it or not, and whether they like it or not, I'd rather know."

Verniece nodded. "I'm okay with sharing Reverend, I guess. It's not as if I have his ring on my finger. The only one I don't like is that stuck-up Jennifer Stevens. Ms. Noble, I can at least understand why she thinks she's in charge. Hell, the woman is as old as the church! But Jennifer? That bitch just got here. Thinks she's special just because she came from that megachurch in Kansas City."

"It's more than that," Anne said, in her calm, quiet manner. "She helped Reverend Thicke blow up. You can't deny that. . . ."

"Reverend Thicke would have blown up without her fat ass." Verniece waddled off her own sizable hindquarters and grabbed another slice. "I think she's the reason I didn't get on this year's anniversary committee."

"Oh, it don't matter. This year ain't gonna be like last year, with all the pomp and circumstance. Mostly it's every five years where they make the biggest fuss."

"Are you kidding? Our pastor is a *New York Times* best seller, girl. Everything he does from here on out is gonna be big!"

"I know one thing that's big," Anne said coyly, taking a large bite of pizza.

"Umm, I bet you're talking about a sausage that's not served on pizza!"

Neither one of these ladies were drinkers, and after two wine coolers apiece, the comment made them dissolve into a fit of giggles again.

"So what do you think I should do?" Verniece asked. "You know the best way to stay in Reverend's rotation is to do something big for the ministry. Your spot is secure, now that you've replaced Simone as the church's songbird. I'm so tone-deaf that even if I lip-synch, it's off-key."

The unexpected joke caused Anne to spew the last swallow of her strawberry cooler all over the couch. "That was funny, Verniece," she said, getting up to grab some paper towels. "You really should think about doing comedy, because *that* was funny."

"It may have been funny, but this is no laughing matter. Jennifer's traveling with him, you're a lead singer, Patricia is either hosting or heading up some committee every time the church doors open. What can I do?"

"Ooh, my favorite scene is coming up," Anne said. "Let's watch Joe Clark get out of jail. Then we'll put our heads together and come up with something."

26

Do the Right Thing

Katherine frowned as she pulled her purple Cadillac up behind the white Infiniti in Nate's driveway. *Jennifer.* It seemed as if every time Katherine turned around, if Nate was anywhere around, that woman was there. Gone were the days when few church members entered Nate's gated community, when Katherine would get busy with him before getting busy for the Lord. Those rendezvous now happened at her place because his house was like Grand Central Station, with everybody and their mama trying to get on Nate's gravy train.

Before Katherine could get out of her car and into Nate's house, another car pulled up beside hers. Katherine's frown deepened. "What is she doing here?" she asked aloud. The two women got out of their cars at the same time.

"Patricia, what are you doing here?" No hello, no preamble—Katherine cut straight to the chase.

"And good morning to you too, Katherine."

"Excuse me? Calling me by my first name is not only presumptuous, but from someone of your age and status, it's also disrespectful. Either *Ms.* or *Sister Noble* will do just fine."

Is that what Nate calls you when y'all are fucking? "Back home, we call the elder ladies of the church *mother.* Perhaps I'll call you *Mother Noble?*"

"And perhaps I'll slap the taste out your mouth."

"You put a hand on me and I'll—"

"Ladies!" Kirk said, opening the door before either woman's hand touched the knob. Kirk Meadows was Gospel Truth's twenty-four-year-old associate minister and newest addition to Nate's entourage. Hiring him to assist Nate full-time had been Katherine's idea, mainly to serve as a buffer between Nate and Jennifer. He was also her eyes when Nate and Jennifer went on PR trips, reporting back what she most certainly didn't want to know—that Jennifer rarely slept in her own room. Katherine deduced that so far his presence hadn't been that much of a barrier.

"Good morning, Kirk," Katherine said as she entered.

"Hi, Kirk," Patricia said, holding out her hand. "I don't think we've been formally introduced. My name is Patricia Cook. We'll probably be seeing a lot of each other around here."

"How's that?" Kirk asked, after shaking Patricia's hand.

Katherine turned the corner and then stopped to listen. *Yes, how is that?*

"I've just joined the building committee and will be working very closely with Deacon Robinson. We have a slew of meetings coming up. I'll be sitting in on all of them."

What? When did this happen? Why hadn't Nate told her about it? *And how in the heck was Patricia doing all this when she worked at the post office?*

"You're going to be a busy woman then."

"Tell me about it. All of this and I work nights."

Oh, so the hussy got her shift changed so she could stay in Nate's business. Well, we'll just see about this. Katherine continued down the hall, walked through the living room and into Nate's office. He and Jennifer were sitting there, sharing a laugh.

"Nate, can I have a moment with you, alone?" She looked pointedly at Jennifer.

"Is something wrong, Katherine?" Nate asked. When she didn't answer, he turned to Jennifer. "Give us a moment."

"Do you want me to check out the report while you two are meeting?" Jennifer asked.

"No, just hang out for a moment. This won't take long."

Once Jennifer had left the room, Katherine closed and locked the door. She bypassed the chair Jennifer had vacated and instead walked around to Nate's side of the desk and sat in his lap. "I miss you," she whispered before lowering her head for a kiss.

Nate pulled his head back. "Is this what you interrupted me and Jennifer for, Katherine? We were in the middle of something important."

"Oh, really? Please. I heard your laughter halfway down the hallway. In all the years we've been together, I've never felt neglected."

"And you feel that way now?"

"A little bit." Again, Katherine moved to join Nate's lips to hers. This time he obliged her. "Um, I feel something," she said after the slow, lazy kiss. She placed her hand on Nate's crotch. "I want this."

"Later," Nate said, kissing her lips at the same time he gently pushed her off him. "I've got business to handle now. So if that's all, send Jennifer back in. Let me know if James is out there and make sure I don't miss my conference call with Total Truth."

"Is that all?" Katherine said brusquely, figuring now was not the time to mention Patricia's new position.

"It's all for now," Nate replied, dismantling her anger with a single smile. "But I do have another, uh, piece of business. It'll be all yours later on."

After Katherine had done what Nate had asked her, she went into one of the guest bedrooms, closed the door, and pulled out her cell phone.

"We've got to do something," she said as soon as Simone answered the phone.

"About what?"

"The Noble legacy, baby. Nate's got people circling him

like vultures after dead meat. I don't trust that Jennifer Stevens as far as I can throw her, and you and I both know I can't toss her hefty behind. And guess who's here now, in his house?"

Simone stifled a sigh. "Who, Mother?"

"Patricia Cook! Nate is really lowering his standards, Simone, and getting a bit careless too, if you ask me. The other day I walked into his church office not long after Verniece left. You could still smell the sex in the room!"

Simone got up from the couch and began walking through the house. The man her mother was talking about was the one she was trying to put out of her mind—and on most days succeeded. More and more of Simone's heart was being occupied by a man named Mark. Now, she figured, was as good a time as any to tell her mother she was ready to trade the legacy for love.

"I don't know what you want me to say, Mother. My life is here now, in Baton Rouge. I was going to tell you this afterward . . . but this coming Sunday, I'm going to move my membership to First Baptist, Mark's church."

"Simone Chastity Noble, I know you didn't just say you were going to join Ed Smith's church. That bastard can't stand Nate!"

"This isn't about Nate. It's about me, and Mark . . . and our future."

"Are you telling me you don't still love Nate? Because I'll quickly rid you of that illusion. One can never get Nate out of her system, baby. That's just the way it is. Now, I understand making a life for yourself and Destiny's baby, helping to cover Nate until those two can get married. But in time, you can come back here, help with the ministry. We've moved up the building schedule and expanded floor plans to make the sanctuary larger. So much is happening, Simone! Nate needs you here."

"Nate has more than enough people to do what he needs done."

"Okay, then. I need you here."

"And where does Mark fit in to this equation?"

"Wherever he wants. He's family, Simone. I'm sure Nate will give him a prominent position in the ministry. We've got to circle the wagons now, because we've worked too hard on Nate's career to see some predator pussies come in here and snatch the spoils out of our hands."

Simone heard the front door close. Mark was home for the lunch she'd prepared. "I've got to go, Mother."

"All right, Simone. But think about everything I've said. And not just for me, but for Destiny."

Later that evening, Nate and Katherine lay naked in her brass canopy bed. She idly played with his now limp member, still throbbing from its powerful assault.

"Remember the first time?" Katherine asked softly. "Remember the first time we were together?"

"You mean when you robbed the cradle?"

"You were the one with the gun, as I recall."

Nate chuckled. "You came over and asked if Mama was home, knowing she wasn't."

"And you licked your lips and let me in."

"Then I licked *your* lips." Nate turned on his side, facing Katherine. He stroked her hair, damp with perspiration. "You blew my young mind with that blow job. Had a brothah's nose wide open!"

"Well, that clearly is not the case anymore."

"I'll always love you, Katherine."

"I know. When was the last time you talked to Destiny?"

"This morning."

"You keep in touch with her—good."

"She's the mother of my child. Of course I keep in touch with her."

Katherine rose up on an elbow. "Is that all she is to you now, Nathaniel? Your child's mother?"

"She's more than that and you know it. Destiny is the woman I'm going to marry."

"I know it . . . but does Jennifer?"

"Oh, so that's what's up." Nate flung back the covers and got out of bed. "You're jealous of Jennifer."

"I'm jealous of the time you spend with her, I admit that. But I'm not jealous of *her*. I am worried though," Katherine continued. She got out of bed, pulled on a robe, and joined Nate, who had pulled on his boxers and was now sitting on a love seat checking text messages. "Jennifer is a very ambitious woman. I don't have to tell you that manager isn't the only *m* title she's aiming for. She's aiming for Mrs."

"Well, like I said, that title's taken."

"For now, it is. You think it is. But the best laid plans are often waylaid. Be careful with her, Nate. Some women will do anything to be with a man like you."

"I've already got one mother, Katherine, and her name is Nettie."

"And always wear a condom," Katherine continued as if Nate hadn't spoken. "She looks like a baby-making machine that could get pregnant just thinking about it."

"I'll keep that in mind."

"And why in God's name would you put Patricia on the building committee? What expertise could she, a lowly postal worker, bring to the table of a multimillion-dollar construction project?"

Nate slowly looked up from his iPhone and fixed Katherine with a penetrating stare. "She'll bring whatever I ask her to bring to the table," he said. "Whenever I ask her to bring it. Any more questions?"

Katherine knew when she was being warned. And she also knew she'd put some things on Nate's mind. Getting Jennifer out of her church and Nate's bed was turning into a trickier proposition than she'd thought. But Katherine was determined to rise to the challenge.

She walked over, kissed Nate's temple, and used the final dynamic that worked to ensure her constant presence in Nate's life—praise. "No more questions, lover. Only assistance, and my undying loyalty. You're the handsomest, smartest, most intelligent man I know. When it comes to Gospel Truth, and my granddaughter, you'll do the right thing. I have faith in you, Nathaniel . . . always."

27

A Little Bundle

Patricia and Jennifer studied the menus at the Mexican restaurant.

"I think I'm going to get the combo plate," Patricia said. She put down the menu and took a sip of iced tea.

"I was looking at that," Jennifer said. "But the taco bowl looks good too."

"I've had it before. It's delicious."

"Okay, that's what I'll get."

Jennifer never thought it would happen, but she'd finally said yes to a lunch invite from Patricia. She hadn't changed her position on female friends. But getting on the building committee, one of Nate's pet projects, had upped Patricia's profile. *One day soon,* Jennifer thought, *the postal worker's alliance may be an important one.* So here they sat.

"What do you think about James?" Patricia asked, after the waiter had taken their order.

"Deacon Robinson? I don't think about him."

"You know he's rich, don't you?"

"Money ain't everything."

"It's a lot."

"Don't tell me you're interested in James Robinson. I'm thirty-two, and you can't be much older than me."

"Thirty-five."

"Well, that man's damn near sixty."

"Fifty-seven."

"That's damn near."

Patricia shrugged. "There's not much to choose from around here. He seems like a good, decent man. And he's smart too. I like that."

"What James Robinson is, is a dirty old man. If he's showing interest, it's just so he can get in your panties."

Patricia shifted in her seat. "Sounds like you're speaking from personal experience."

"Girl, that man has been asking me out nonstop. 'You're powerful pretty,'" Jennifer said, mimicking the deacon. "That's what he says every time he sees me."

"Oh, really?" Patricia didn't try and hide her disappointment. It didn't surprise her though. Jennifer was shapely and cute, with an outgoing personality that people loved. Patricia was more like the nickname her school classmates had given her, Plain Pat. She'd joined the building committee partly for Nate, and partly so that maybe the deacon would notice her.

"Do you really like him? I'm sorry, Pat. I shouldn't have told you that then. But don't trip. We never went out or anything. He doesn't hold a candle to Nate."

Patricia's head shot up. "What does Nate have to do with who you're dating?"

"Everything." Jennifer felt this was as good a time as any to start marking her territory, and see how much trust she could put in this new friend.

"You're dating the reverend?"

"We're very close."

"Reverend is 'close' to a lot of women," Patricia said sarcastically.

"Our situation is different."

Patricia snorted. "That's what we all hope."

The two ladies were silent as the waiter placed their orders on the table. When Jennifer spoke again, it was on a safer topic. "Yum. This taco bowl *is* good, Pat. It's delicious."

"I thought you'd like it."

"How's that combo plate?"

"The bomb. These enchiladas are spicy! I love how they seasoned the shredded chicken."

The women ate in silence a moment, but thoughts raced through both their minds at a mile a minute.

After eating almost a third of the food on her plate, Jennifer put down her fork and picked up her tea. "I might have to kick Katherine Noble's ass," she said evenly.

"You too?"

"I'm serious. I don't know who told her she was God's gift to the universe, but she'd better back off me. I am not the one."

"Who you telling? Would you believe she had the nerve to tell me to call her either 'Ms.' or 'Sister Noble'? I have a few titles for her all right, but she doesn't want to hear them. What did she do to you?"

"What she's always doing. Trying to block where Nate is concerned. She thinks I don't know that she had Kirk hired to spy on me and Nate. What she doesn't know is money talks and bullshit walks. I'm paying him to spy on *her* ass now!"

"Has he found out anything?"

"What I already knew—that Nate is screwing her too."

"That's disgusting. She's old enough to be his mama." As she said this, Patricia thought about James, and realized she probably should use a different argument.

"Tell me about it. Some men will put their dicks anywhere."

"She does look good though, for a woman in her fifties. I'm sure glad Simone found somebody and moved the hell on. If she had stayed here, she probably would have become first lady."

"Do you know that dude she married?"

"Mark? Not really. Seen him at church a couple times. It don't make sense for one family to have so many fine men."

"I wonder how their marriage is going."

"Must be going pretty good. I heard she had a baby."

Jennifer sat straight up. "What?"

"It's just rumor, but supposedly somebody saw her going into Katherine's house with a little bundle."

"When?"

"Oh, this had to be two, three months ago that I heard this."

That's Destiny's baby! is what Jennifer thought. "Interesting," is what she said. "What do you know about her granddaughter?"

"Destiny?" Patricia said with disdain.

"Uh-huh."

"Not much. I think she's in college."

"Where?"

Patricia shrugged. "I couldn't care less. Why are you asking?"

"I'm just curious."

"I could probably find out. Enter her name in our system and see if an address comes up. Want me to try and find her?"

"No. Like I said, I was just curious. She used to be a regular at the church and then disappeared all of a sudden."

"Now that you mention it, I don't remember seeing her when they prayed for the seniors graduating high school. But like I said, I think she went to college."

I think she went to have Nate's baby. And now Simone supposedly has a child? Jennifer didn't want Patricia to know it, but she definitely intended on locating Destiny's whereabouts, as well as the "little bundle." Even if the baby was Destiny's, Jennifer was almost sure that Nate wouldn't even think about marrying someone so young. But Carla had told her that some of the Total Truth members were nudging Nate to find himself a wife, a first lady for the church. If and when he responded to that nudge, Jennifer wanted to be the one to whom he said "I do."

28

The Buzz Begins

It was Nathaniel Eli Thicke's sixth pastoral anniversary, and Verniece's words proved prophetic. It was big—twice as big as his fifth anniversary. The guest speaker for this year's service was Total Truth board member Stanley Lee, pastor of Logos Word Interdenominational Church in Los Angeles, accompanied by his wife, Passion. Whether or not this had anything to do with the fact that his ex-wife, Carla, and husband, Lavon, Chapman were "unable to attend," one could only speculate. And Mama Max was sorely missed, especially by Nettie, but the good reverend doctor had been feeling poorly off and on for months. They decided not to chance his health to make the journey. But no matter; it seemed as if everybody else who was anybody else was there, including a spattering of celebrities and professional athletes. Yadah, the gospel girl group who'd nabbed Stellar and NAACP awards for best new gospel group, was a highlight. There were write-ups in all the major Texas papers, and many magazines from other regions, including *LA Gospel*, covered the event. And later, Katherine would concede that she'd never seen so many women in this area of Texas in her thirty plus years of living here. It was official. Nate had arrived.

And so had someone else—Simone Noble Simmons. The buzz began as soon as Anne, with a front row center seat in the elevated choir stand, noticed her entrance and sent a text message to Verniece. It continued as Simone, accompanied by her debonair husband, Mark, followed the usher down the aisle and sat in the first row. When Patricia found Jennifer in the VIP room and told her of Simone's arrival, Jennifer almost broke her neck trying to get to the main auditorium. She wanted to see if Simone had brought "her little bundle," and if she had, she wanted to examine said little bundle to within an inch of its life, and see if she saw Nate anywhere. There were necks craning, eyes cutting, tongues wagging. And later, only a handful of Gospel Truth members would remember the title of Dr. Lee's message: Eyes Stayed on Jesus. Most of their eyes had been on Mark and Simone.

After the service, the VIP room was full. Simone held Mark's hand as they were escorted through the doors into the room that had been transformed from a regular meeting room into a plush gathering place with deep-piled burgundy carpet and burgundy, blue, and silver silk panels covering the walls. Heavy hors d'oeuvres were strategically placed throughout the room, as were hot and cold drinks. An ice sculpture in the shape of a cross dominated the back of the room, backlit with blue strobes. And dominating the entire room was Nate Thicke, in his element as the center of attention.

Nate knew the moment Simone had entered the room, but kept talking to the *LA Gospel* reporter who was singing his praises. He noticed how she clung to Mark, and how possessively Mark held her. Nate knew he had no right to be jealous, and he wasn't, not too much, and not of the fact that Mark had Simone. No, he was jealous because the woman who had his heart above all others was not with him, standing by his side. He'd wanted Destiny to attend but Katherine had been adamant.

"It's not time yet," she'd said.

"Give it another year, son. She's just eighteen," his mother had echoed.

He'd expected Destiny to be devastated by the fact that she

couldn't attend this anniversary, especially after missing the one following the birth of their son, but she'd surprised him, something that was beginning to happen with frequency. "I think it's best," she'd said simply. Then she mentioned having to study for finals, and hung up.

On the other hand, Katherine had encouraged Simone and Mark to come. She'd said it was time that people saw her daughter again, with her husband, and that people knew about the baby. Even though the child attended children's church, with the babysitter, Katherine had no doubt that news of Benjamin's existence would be on the tell-a-church-member hotline before the benediction. Nettie agreed with Katherine when she suggested this information be handled low-key, that there be no formal announcement. "Let people assume, that way we don't have to lie," she'd said. Katherine's plan seemed to be working. Even James Robinson had come up to Nate and said about Simone: "It's a shame for a woman to have a baby and still look that good!"

"What's up, cuz!" Nate said when Mark and Simone were finally able to get through to him. He and his cousin hugged. They were as different as night and day, and didn't have time to talk much these days. But growing up they'd been as thick as thieves, and though just under the surface, the affection was still there.

"Excellent service, man," Mark said. "You're up there looking like you're somebody."

"I am somebody," Nate said in a voice mimicking Jesse Jackson. "Glad you two could make it." He leaned toward Simone and gave her a peck on the cheek. Her stiffening was subtle, but Nate noticed it anyway. "You're looking good, Simone."

"Thank you. I'm being well taken care of." She looked up at Mark, adoration swimming in her eyes, and then put her arm around him.

"Glad to hear that. But I heard something else that surprised me. That you're cavorting with the enemy."

"If you're talking about my moving my membership, yes, I joined the church my husband attends. My place is with Mark, wherever he is."

"Yeah, Simone. But Ed Smith? I've been trying to get Mark out of that church for years."

"He's a bit chagrined to learn that I have my own mind," Mark said playfully to Simone.

"I admit Reverend Smith can be a bit . . . judgmental at times. But there are some good things going on at his church," she said.

"Especially since Simone arrived. We've had five people join the choir in the last month just so they could sing with her. Attendance has increased too. Word of her talent is getting around."

"Well, I'm happy for you," Nate said sincerely.

Jennifer walked up and butted right in. "Simone! You finally came out of hiding."

"Hello, Jennifer."

She nudged Nate playfully. "Nate, I don't think I've met your cousin."

"Oh, my bad. Mark, this is my PR manager, Jennifer Stevens. Jennifer, Mark Simmons."

"Nice to meet you," they both said.

"Now where's this baby I've been hearing about?" Jennifer asked. "I can't believe that didn't warrant an announcement in the bulletin, Katherine being a staunch member of the church and all, and this being, what, her second grandchild?"

Simone answered, unfazed. "If I were still a member of Gospel Truth, then it probably would have been in the bulletin. But since I'm not, I guess it isn't Gospel Truth business." The way Simone looked at Jennifer made the real meaning clear—that it wasn't Jennifer's business either. Anyone watching from a distance would have observed a cordial conversation going on.

"How's your daughter?" Jennifer asked, giving as good as she got.

"She's fine."

Jennifer looked at Nate. "That girl graduated and got the heck out of Dodge, didn't she? Has she even been back to Palestine? I don't think I've seen her."

"I wasn't aware that you were looking for her," Nate said, as his eyes narrowed.

"Oh, I'm not. But she was a faithful church member, as I remember. Always active in the youth department. A church can always use good young Christians like her."

The tension was so thick it was a wonder anyone could walk through it. But Katherine's assistant, Charmaine, managed to do so, and tapped Nate on the arm. "Pastor Montgomery asked if he could have a brief word with you. He and his wife have to leave soon to catch their plane. They're waiting in the back."

"All right, Mark, Simone," Nate said, giving Mark dap and Simone another kiss on the cheek. "Thanks for coming by. We'll be in touch." He cut a brief yet stern look at Jennifer before following Charmaine to the back of the room, and the place reserved for the VIPs of the VIPs.

Jennifer watched him go, an involuntary shudder ripping through her. The attitude she'd felt from him just now was colder than the ice sculpture melting in the back of the room. It was a habit with Jennifer, talking too much. But something in her had snapped when she saw Simone and Nate conversing. Even with Mark there, she'd felt immensely intimidated. She hadn't intended to show that many cards, had meant to keep most of them, especially her suspicions about Destiny, in the deck. But if Simone's answers and Nate's attitude were any indication, she'd exposed them—face up. She sighed as she went to look for the *LA Gospel* reporter to make sure Nate's picture graced the cover of the issue featuring him. After handling his business, she would worry about reshuffling her cards.

★ ★ ★

"I'm sorry if I came off sounding like I was getting in her business, Nate. But I was genuinely curious about the child. Everybody was talking about it."

It was ten P.M., and Nate was experiencing a rare moment of having his house to himself. Jennifer was the only other person there. And if his mood was any indication, she wouldn't be there long.

"I didn't hear everybody talking about it. I just heard you. Mark is my cousin, Simone is my friend, and they were here as my guests. How dare you walk over and start grilling them as if you had the right. You're my manager, Jennifer, not my wife. And after that stunt you pulled, I'm wondering if your being in my employ is a good idea."

Jennifer realized if she was going to reshuffle cards, now was the time. Nate was even angrier than she thought he'd be, and she'd thought he'd be livid. "I was wrong, Nate. I don't know what came over me. You know how professional I am; your best interest is at the front of everything I do. I am so sorry for how I acted with them, and will do whatever you ask to make it right."

"And what was with the questions about Destiny? You don't even know her."

"You're right," Jennifer answered quickly.

"There's something you need to understand, because obviously you don't. I am the only one who handles my business, nobody else. And I'm the only one who knows my business. Other people might think they know, but they don't! My life is complicated enough. I don't need people around me trying to make it more so by being messy. Do you understand?"

"Yes, Nate, Reverend, I'm sorry." Jennifer wasn't aware she was wringing her hands. "Would you like me to fix you something, coffee, tea, or maybe some fresh-squeezed orange juice? Or I could run you a bath and give you a good massage. It's been a long day. I know you're tired."

"Yes," Nate answered. "I *am* tired, Jennifer. I'm especially tired of bullshit. And I won't have it. Not in my ministry."

"What can I do for you?" Jennifer whispered. "I'll do anything."

"You can go home," Nate said after a long pause.

Jennifer hung her head and headed for the door.

"But before you go, I need my keys back."

"What, the key to the office?"

"All of them."

Jennifer swallowed hard. "Even your house key?"

"Especially my house key."

From now on, Jennifer would be locked out of Nate's house. She only hoped she wasn't locked out of his heart.

29

A Love Song

It was almost midnight when, after dropping Benjamin off at Destiny's house, Mark and Simone arrived back at their home just outside Baton Rouge. For Simone, it had been a grueling day, especially mentally. She'd been all too aware of the looks and whispers, all too familiar with what was probably being said. Most of the women at Gospel Truth had little love for the Nobles. And as far as Simone was concerned, the feeling was mutual. That's why she'd ditched the town weeks after high school graduation. It had always been too small for her, full of small-minded people without enough business to leave hers alone. But while the day had been taxing, in another way it had been hugely beneficial. When she'd come face to face with Nate for the first time in months, she finally knew, without a shadow of a doubt, that she was no longer in love with him.

"Would you like some tea?" she asked Mark when they entered the living room.

"No, thank you."

"I know it's late, but would you like to watch a movie or . . . something?" Simone wanted to be near her husband any way she could; she wasn't ready to spend another night alone.

"Thanks, sweetness, but I think I'll just head to bed. You

were wonderful today, and the most beautiful woman in the building. Good night."

Simone stood still and watched the man she loved mount the stairs to his bedroom, his not theirs, as she wanted it to be now more than ever. This evening it became clear she not only loved Mark, but that she was *in* love with him. At first the need for sex had been purely physical. After all, Simone had had sex regularly since she was sixteen years old. This year was the longest she'd ever gone without intercourse. Here she was, married for the first time in her life, able to screw both legally and morally, and dealing instead with a forced celibacy. If this was God's sense of humor, Simone thought, she didn't find it funny at all. But now the need was much more than physical, it was spiritual. Her very soul was crying out for Mark's presence. But apparently his soul didn't hear.

Simone watched until Mark had taken the last step and turned the corner. Then she walked into the kitchen, put on water for tea, and mentally recounted the day's events. It had been good to see some of the people there. She knew Nettie's hug was genuine, and that while Deacon Robinson was a feisty rascal, he was a harmless one who respected her. The women who'd known her since she was a child oohed and aahed over Benjamin. And when they said he looked just like she and Mark, Simone had simply smiled. It had been good to sit in her mother's dining room and enjoy a light breakfast. Few would understand the relationship between her and Katherine; even she didn't understand it sometimes. But Simone knew that Katherine was mothering in the best way she knew how, and that love for her family was paramount. Katherine really liked Mark, Simone could tell, and the sense of normalcy had been extremely soothing, as the three had chatted while Benjamin slept in Katherine's lap.

But here you are back at home, and nothing's normal. Simone sighed as she poured the hot water over her tea bag and added lemon and raw sugar. As she mounted the stairs, her heart was heavy.

And there was only one person who could lighten it.

She walked past her door and continued to the end of the hall, and Mark's master suite. She raised her hand, but just before she knocked on the door, she changed her mind. She'd already invited Mark to spend more time with her tonight, and he'd turned her down. Simone didn't think she could handle another rejection. So she decided to just drink her tea and go to bed.

Mark stripped off his clothes and stepped into the shower, fully prepared to masturbate. *Not tonight, son,* a voice whispered into his mind's ear. *Your wife needs you.* Mark showered, lotioned his body, put on a robe, and sat in the sitting area of the immense master suite, thinking. Could he have really heard what he thought he heard?

Simone drank the tea but she didn't taste it. Her mind was in turmoil, her body hummed with unreleased passion. Thinking a hot shower would help, she hurriedly shed her clothes and stepped under the nozzle, letting the pounding of the hot water knead her tense muscles. But there were tense muscles the water couldn't reach, and only one person she wanted to knead them. She finished washing, dried off, lotioned herself, and crawled between the cool sheets.

The tears came of their own volition. Simone had lived a fairly charmed life by most standards, and aside from Nate, had gotten just about everything she wanted. Now she wanted someone more than she'd wanted anyone in her life, including Nate, and she couldn't have him. He was her husband, and she couldn't have him! *Please God. You know I love Mark and you know I'm now in love with him. Please touch his heart, God, and let him know that my love is true. I know he's been hurt, God, that he's afraid to love and lose again. Please let him know that I'm for real, God. My love is for real!* Simone tried to stifle the cry of anguish that tore from her throat. She buried her head in the pillow to suppress the sound of her sobbing.

Mark placed his ear against Simone's door. His heart clenched, both that she was crying, and that she was crying for him! He turned the knob quickly and walked inside. "Simone."

Simone's eyes flew open. She sat straight up in bed, too shocked to remember that she was naked. "Mark. What is it? I was just . . ."

"I know."

"I just prayed that . . ."

"I know. And before you called Him, He answered. And while you were yet speaking, He heard." Mark knew Simone had no idea of the picture she painted, with the night lights from the garden streaming through the bedroom window. She looked like a goddess, her hair tumbling over her shoulders, breasts jutting out in greeting. "I love you, Simone."

"I am *in* love with you, Mark Simmons."

Mark let the robe fall as he walked toward the bed. Simone's eyes quickly moved from his face to his manhood. It was glorious in its erection, bobbing before him like a sword ready to duel. Simone watched and waited, barely daring to breathe, lest she inhale too deeply, wake up and realize the moment was only a dream.

"The dream" climbed into her bed and on top of her. Simone relished the weight of Mark's bulk pressed fully against her. She couldn't get enough of him, as her hands moved from his hair to his shoulders to his taut buttocks. She opened her mouth and Mark's tongue plunged in, even as his long, strong fingers found her paradise and did likewise.

Mark kissed Simone over and again. He felt he could kiss her forever. But there were other areas of her body screaming for his oral attention, and he did not want to disappoint. He reluctantly left her succulent mouth and bent his head down to her weighty breasts, taking as much of one as he could into his mouth. He suckled and squeezed and nipped and massaged. Again, he could stay there forever. But there was more.

Honey, Mark decided, was what Simone tasted like as he journeyed past her navel and down to her thighs. Simone's breathing quickened, her body squirmed, telling Mark what it wanted, and where it wanted it. Realizing she'd waited too long for him to tease, he spread her legs and sunk his tongue into her heat. Simone shuddered uncontrollably, and grabbed the pillow that had stifled her sobs to now stifle her loud moans.

After his wife's second orgasm, Mark felt he could focus on his own needs. He rolled over and silently directed Simone to please him. She called upon everything she'd ever heard, seen, or learned to satisfy Mark as he had satisfied her. She worshipped his manhood as if it were a shrine, lavishing love on it as if it were an onyx scepter. She took in as much of him as she could, and thrilled as he moaned and thrashed. Tears came to her eyes as she loved her man, her husband, her beloved. And still, it wasn't over.

Mark shifted until he was at the edge of the bed, and then stood. He held out his hand, signaling Simone to come with him. Wordlessly she climbed out of bed, and together they walked down the hall, into the master suite. Mark picked up Simone and placed her in the center of the bed. He climbed on behind her, spread her legs wide and with one hard, deep thrust, joined them together as one. Over and over, with each powerful stab, he pledged his love and undying devotion. She climaxed once, twice, yet Mark continued, intensifying the heat with his increased rhythm, steering them both toward a mutually enjoyable masterpiece. When it happened, when they climaxed together, Simone swore she saw stars, she knew the earth shook, and was convinced an angelic choir broke out in song. Belatedly she realized the sustained note she heard—a perfect high C—was her own voice. It was for Mark, her song of love, and the only audible sound made during the entire time of this—Mark and Simone Simmons's first marital dance of love.

30

Gettin' with That

"Here you go, girl. Congratulations." Destiny shifted Benjamin into her other arm and gave Melody the gift-wrapped box.

"You got me a graduation present? Thank you, Destiny!" Melody hurriedly ripped off the paper and removed the box top. Inside was the Prada handbag she'd gone on and on about at the Mall of Louisiana a few months before. Melody screamed, jumped up, and hugged Destiny. Her abrupt actions scared Benjamin, who started to cry. "Oh, I'm sorry, baby. I didn't mean to scare you."

"He's all right." Even so, Destiny turned Benjamin away from Melody and began cooing and walking him back and forth. Destiny had noticed that for some reason, Benjamin wasn't too fond of her best friend.

"I can't believe you brought me this, girl! I'm still trying to figure out how you're living so large."

"I'm not."

"Yes, you are. Look at you, with your own house, a Mercedes, a nanny for your baby. You're going to college full-time, and you don't work. Why are you holding out with the info? What's his name?"

Destiny knew she'd never tell Melody or anybody else about Nate, and how he showered her like a tsunami with money and gifts. Guilt money, Destiny had told him once. To make up for the fact that during the past year, he'd rarely come to visit.

"I told you, Melody. I received scholarships. Plus, Kiki helps me."

"Dang, your grandma must have hella paper."

"It's not that big a deal, Melody."

"Yes, it is."

"So tell me, girl," Destiny began as she put her seven-month-old brown-skinned beauty into his playpen. "What are your plans? No, don't tell me. Now that you're free at last from the prison otherwise known as Angel House, you've probably already got a one-way ticket back to LA."

"I don't know. I'm thinking about moving to Dallas."

"Dallas? What's in Dallas?"

"That's what I'm thinking about finding out. I don't have the paper to live like I want in LA and I sure as hell ain't moving back in with my parents. You remember Roxanne?"

"The girl with the braces who says 'praise the Lord' after every sentence?"

Melody laughed. "Uh-huh, that's her. Well, her sister was here a couple weeks ago and I met her. She lives in Dallas, has a two-bedroom condo, and is looking for a roommate."

"And you'd want to room with one of Roxanne's relatives?"

"Don't get it twisted. Susie is nothing like Roxanne. Girlfriend took me to get some Asti Spumante and next she was asking if I knew where she could cop some weed."

"No way!"

"If I'm lying, I'm dying!"

"But have you been to Dallas, Melody? I think it would be pretty boring for somebody like you."

"Maybe, but I could hang for a minute. Plus, it would give me the opportunity to go to Palestine and check out that fine Thicke preacher. And don't think I ain't still mad at you for not driving us to his anniversary. We could have met Yadah!"

"You could have gone. I had finals."

"Yeah, but I don't have a car. And if Bobby don't buy me one like I asked, I'm gonna pack up the pussy."

"Bobby? What happened to Josh?"

"You didn't know? Josh is getting married. Some girl back in New Mexico, where he's from."

"Wow, that was quick."

"Not really. I guess they've been off and on for years and I was just a diversion. He didn't have enough money for me anyway. I've got bigger fish to try and fry—Thicke fish."

Melody's fixation with Nate was the main thing about her that bugged Destiny. She'd tried to dissuade her, telling her about the long line of women trying to hook up with her pastor. But Melody wasn't fazed. She believed she had what it took to move to the front of the line.

"Whatever, Melody. I'm trying to save you from a little heartache, but if you want to become a Nate Thicke groupie, you just go right ahead."

"Please, you know you're one too."

"How do you figure?"

"Because of the way you try and act like you don't have an attitude when I talk about him. But you do."

Destiny hid her shock. She thought she covered up her love for Nate brilliantly, but obviously she had so much of it that some was seeping through the cracks in her mask.

"Yeah, I'm a groupie," she said nonchalantly. "That's why I'm here, in Louisiana, getting my degree and taking care of another man's baby. Because I'm *so* in love with Nate Thicke."

"Well, maybe not. But don't try and act like you wouldn't let him hit it if he wanted to."

"And risk giving Benjamin a sibling? I've got plans, Melody. Men are the last thing on my mind right now."

"Well, I tell you one thing, that chocolate chip is on my mind, and if I ever get the chance, I'm gonna get me some of that."

Destiny didn't respond, and soon after Melody changed the subject. But what she said stayed on Destiny's mind, even after she'd dropped Melody off at school and returned home. *So many women.* With Nate, she knew it had always been like that. But did it have to be? *I'm uncommon, I'm unusual, I am not the status quo.* No, she resolved, what Nate had done in the past did not have to dictate what they did in the future. Destiny decided she didn't want to be just another woman. She wanted to be the only one. If Nate wanted to marry her, there'd be no more covering. The other women, including her mother and grandmother, would have to get out of his bed—and stay out.

31

Good Graces

Jennifer was heartbroken. It had been three months since the anniversary, and Nate still hadn't made love to her. He'd taken his keys back in June. This was September. How long was he going to stay mad? She'd said she was sorry! When it came to her acting as his manager, things hadn't changed. His schedule was busier than ever, and she still traveled with him. But now, at any given time, so did almost a dozen other people. He was almost always surrounded by a large entourage. And not only was her hotel room no longer right down the hall, as it often had been in the past, now she was usually in a different hotel altogether. She'd been downgraded, gone from first class to the business section. It wasn't coach, but she still didn't like it.

A knock on the door interrupted her thoughts. For a second, Jennifer hoped it would be Nate. *Maybe he's finally over his anger, and is here to make me feel good.* But a quick glance through the peephole killed that fantasy. Jennifer sighed, opened the door, and took the hamburger and fries she'd ordered from room service. "Maybe I should have gone with Kirk," she said out loud. But at the time, hanging out with him and the assistant from the *New York Times* hadn't sounded like her idea of fun. It's not that she didn't love traipsing through the streets of the Big Apple. It's just that she'd rather have done so with Nate.

Jennifer set the tray on the table and grabbed the remote. She munched on her fries and idly flipped through the channels. On one station, a well-dressed Black man was being interviewed. Jennifer turned up the volume, put down the remote, and took a bite of her burger.

"They're pimps," the Black man said. "Masquerading behind the Word of God."

"But you're a preacher too," the interviewer said. "How can you say such things about your peers?"

"Those megamoochers are no peers of mine. My peers are the handful of men and women in this country who still preach the unadulterated word of God!"

Jennifer rolled her eyes and reached for the remote. But the man's next sentence stopped her from turning the channel.

"There's one out there now, calling himself a motivational speaker. Lying to people about what they can have, getting their hopes up by saying they can have anything they want. As if God were Santa Claus and you just have to make your list and check it twice. But there's a catch," the man continued. "You have to buy his book first, see. You have to follow *his* magic formula. Well, does his formula come with a guarantee? If falling for his scheme and giving him your money doesn't get you what you want, can you get your money back?"

"Who is this fool?" Jennifer asked out loud. She knew the man was talking about Nate. Anyone familiar with his ministry or book would likely come to the same conclusion. As if the television heard her, the guest's name appeared at the bottom of the screen: "Reverend Ed Smith, Pastor, First Baptist Church."

"These are pretty powerful words coming from someone of your stature, Reverend Smith. But as always, you've been an engaging guest, leaving us with plenty to think about. Until next time I'm . . ."

Jennifer turned the channel and finished her meal. Then she sent a text message to Nate about what she'd seen. *Maybe*

by cleaning up any messes made by this Smith guy spouting nonsense,
I can get back into Nate's good graces, Jennifer thought.

Nate was quiet as he perused the portfolio in front of him.
In it were broadcasting entities with which he was familiar, and
names he recognized. Dana Owens was top-notch, no doubt
about that. She was easy on the eyes too, which always helped.

"You've been busy in the years since graduating at the top
of your class. You built all of this business up from your base in
Dallas?"

"No, Reverend Thicke—"

"You can call me Nate."

"Thank you, Nate. I honed my chops and garnered a large
share of my clients while working in Atlanta. I was part of a
megaministry there, as you know, and that is where I got a
foothold into the religious community. You see, I want my
firm to cover every area of our society, secular and spiritual. Although as a Christian myself, I am always pleased when I can
use my talents to advance a member of God's kingdom."

"It's obvious your talents are sizable," Nate replied, once
again browsing through a folder that along with her résumé
and letters of recommendation from prominent clients, also included newspaper clippings and magazine articles she'd been
able to secure for those she represented.

"What I'm really excited about," Dana said, as she continued to watch Nate page through her collection of accomplishments, "are the inroads I'm making internationally. The Internet
has made this a small world indeed, and ours is now a global
marketplace. I've developed solid connections in London, Paris,
Germany, and specifically for my religious clientele, I'm working on several networks in Africa. Has your book been trans-
lated?"

"They're releasing versions in Spanish, French, and German
next year," Nate replied.

"My contacts would allow you easy access to those markets, speaking engagements where you could get in front of the international audience. They can be pivotal to book sales. Not that you need my help with that. You were on the *Times* top ten for what . . . six months?"

"Seven, not that anyone's counting. I'm definitely interesting in expanding internationally, but I have to tell you, *yo hablo español y francés muy poquito.*"

Dana laughed. "You don't have to be able to speak other languages. The audience that comes to hear you will be able to understand English just fine."

Nate and Dana continued conversing, about both public relations and each other. Nate liked Dana. She was no-nonsense, and at forty-five, a seasoned professional with a plethora of contacts and associates in almost every promotional arena imaginable. She'd come highly recommended, and after their two-hour meeting, Nate knew he'd found what he was looking for. He held out his hand.

"Dana Owens, congratulations. As of this moment, you are my new manager."

32

Plain Pat

Patricia was tired. After months of burning the candle at both ends—working for the church during the day and the post office at night, with five hours of sleep in between if she was lucky—Patricia was feeling the strain. She eyed the clock angrily as she turned off the alarm, as if the situation was its fault.

Dragging herself out of bed, Patricia trudged to the kitchen, put on a pot of coffee, and headed for the shower. While under the invigorating flow of tepid, almost cold water, she replayed in her mind the afternoon's meeting with Deacon James Robinson.

"Well, now, Sister Cook, I appreciate your enthusiasm, your desire to help advance the kingdom. But I really don't see any type of paid position being created in this department, not in the foreseeable future, if at all."

"But what about once the actual building starts? Won't there be a need for a liaison between the church and the construction company?"

"Uh, Sister Cook, that would be me."

"Oh."

"Like I said, I admire your zeal for the Lord, but you've got a pretty good thing going at the post office. You say you've been there fifteen years?"

Patricia nodded. "Going on sixteen."

"I heard the post office paid well. How are the benefits?"

"They're pretty good."

"And the retirement package? Can you retire after twenty years?"

"Their program takes several factors into consideration, including age. I'm a long way from being able to retire, what with raising a daughter alone, and having to put her through college, starting next year. But the thing is, Deacon Robinson, working for the post office is just a paycheck, a means to an end. Working for the church, and with you, makes me feel like I'm doing something worthwhile, contributing to the greater good of not only the Christian community, but the community at large. Building this church will benefit more than Gospel Truth. It will bring in jobs, and open up opportunities for our young people. It blesses me to be a part of something like this."

Deacon nodded and stroked his chin as he listened to Patricia. She was a hard worker, and he admired her zest for the things of God. It was a pity he couldn't do anything to help her. "I tell you what," he said after a pause. "Why don't you bring your résumé the next time we have a meeting. I'll talk with Nate, and while I know there's nothing available right now, we'll put your information in our employment database so that if something comes that's a fit, you can be considered."

"I appreciate that, Deacon Robinson. My administrative skills are good and I'm an excellent organizer. I know I can be of some benefit to the ministry if given the chance."

That part of the meeting went okay, Patricia thought, as she finished dressing and packed her lunch. It was what happened during the final five minutes of her and Deacon's discussion, which, if she had it to do over again, would not have happened.

★ ★ ★

"Is there anything else?" Deacon Robinson had asked.

"Well . . ." Patricia hesitated, not sure if what she was about to do was appropriate. Her heartbeat quickened and she chewed her lip nervously. Unlike Jennifer, dealing with people in general and men in particular was not her forte. "Could I ask you a personal question, Deacon?"

"Sure, you can ask it. There's no guarantee you'll get an answer, though."

"I was just wondering why you never married."

Deacon Robinson's eyes widened in surprise. Patricia knew she'd overstepped her bounds.

"I'm sorry for asking, just wondered—"

"Well, now, that's a good question, Sister Cook. I guess you might say it's because I haven't found the right woman yet."

"Do you ever . . . I mean, there are a lot of nice women here at Gospel Truth."

Deacon's eyes had narrowed then. "There's one or two."

"Would you like to, uh . . . What I'm trying to say is . . . when was the last time you had some good home cooking?"

Another long pause had preceded Deacon's answer. "I like my own cooking just fine, Sister Cook." And then he'd smiled. "Is that how you got your last name?"

"No, marrying a fool and taking his name is how I got it. Kept it because of my daughter. But I can cook."

"Well, now, one of these days I'm sure the Lord will bless you with somebody who will appreciate your meals."

With that, the deacon had stood, shook her hand, and walked out of the meeting room.

Patricia pulled into the post office parking lot. She was ten minutes early and, instead of going inside and chatting with coworkers, she kept the radio on, listening to Willie Nelson sing about faded love. Few people knew that Patricia loved country music, but her mother was a big fan. Willie's words soothed her, and she tried to stop feeling sorry for herself. She knew she wasn't the most beautiful woman in the world, but she thought she cleaned up pretty good. She loved God, had a decent head on her shoulders, was a hard worker, and when she had one, treated her man like a king. There had only been a couple stead-ies in her life since birthing Carmen seventeen years ago. And aside from Reverend Thicke's occasional pity covering, there was no one now. Patricia wanted to change that.

If it had been Jennifer, he would have been all over the invitation, would have jumped at the chance to go to her house. But as Patricia clocked in to begin her shift, she reminded herself that while the deacon thought that Jennifer was "powerful pretty," to him she was obviously just "plain Pat."

33

Punanny on Lock

"Hey, baby girl, why don't you go ahead and give me your phone number so I can hollah at your fine ass."

Destiny smiled but kept walking. "I told you, Duane. I'm not available." She knew that Duane Higgins, the football standout and biggest man on Southern University's small campus, was not used to being told no.

"And I told you that there ain't nothing that nucka got that I ain't got more of. You know I'm going places, baby. I want to take you with me."

"I heard the scouts have been swarming the campus."

"Man, they buggin' a brothah for real! Offering millions in bonuses and shit, if I join their team now."

"Then why don't you?"

"Promised my moms I'd finish college. She's all set on me getting a degree."

"Sounds like you have a smart mom."

"She would love you, Destiny. C'mon, girl, one date! Your boy ain't here. What he don't know won't hurt him."

"But *I'd* know, Duane." Destiny reached her car and hit the unlock button. "See you later."

Destiny laughed as she started her car and headed out of the school parking lot. She liked Duane, felt that for all his posturing, he was a genuinely good guy. A couple times she'd actually entertained the idea of going out with him, just for something to do. She had several casual acquaintances but she was a private person by nature, and cautious about letting anyone get too close. Since Melody had moved to Dallas, hers had been a rather lonely life.

Well, speak of the devil. Destiny pushed the TALK button on the car's speakerphone. "Melody! I was just thinking about you."

"For real? I called your home phone first."

"I just got out of classes. What are you doing?"

"On my lunch hour. I just started a new job."

"A new job? What happened to the one at that upscale restaurant? I thought you said you liked it."

"Girl, that place was just a way for me to try and meet my next sugar daddy. It wasn't happening fast enough. Another opportunity came along and I took it."

"Oh, so you'll meet a sugar daddy on this job?"

"We'll see."

Destiny looked at her caller ID and found that, speaking of sugar daddies, hers was calling. "Melody, I'll call you back. This is, uh, Kiki calling." She hit her CALL WAITING button. "Nate, where are you?"

"Miss me, baby?"

"You know I do, all the time. Are you coming to see me?"

"Next week, and I can't wait. I miss you too, baby. How's our son?"

"Growing like crazy and trying to talk up a storm. I think he's going to be a preacher, like his daddy."

"And he'll be a good one too, especially being raised by such a smart, beautiful woman."

Destiny blushed and warmed all over. Nate could say one word and she was putty in his hands. The way she loved that man made no kind of sense.

"How's school going, baby? You still on track to graduate in three years?"

"Absolutely. That goal is what keeps me pushing."

"I thought it was the goal of being with me?"

Destiny laughed. "That too."

Nate's voice lowered to a sultry tone. "I know it's not easy, baby, our being away from each other. But I love you and Benjamin with all my heart. Everything I'm doing, I'm doing for us."

Their conversation was interrupted by the sound of a horn honking, loud and continuous. "I'ma follow you, baby!" Duane shouted from the open window of his SUV.

Destiny laughed and waved.

"Who was that?"

"One of my crazy classmates."

"What's his name?"

"Nate, it doesn't matter. He's just—"

"What is his name?" Nate repeated.

"Duane Higgins," Destiny said. She knew the name wouldn't get past her sports fanatical fiancé.

"The Jaguar's running back?"

"Yes."

"Are you seeing him, Destiny?"

"No."

"Are you sure?"

"Look, I said I wasn't. I'm not seeing anybody. And if you're going to question me like a detective, then I'm going to hang up!"

Nate took a deep breath and tried to calm down. It wasn't that he didn't trust Destiny; he just didn't trust all the men he knew she was around. He also felt guilty that he hadn't spent more time with her and Benjamin. The truth was, he was scared. Destiny had matured since going away to school and having the baby. She'd always acted older than her age, but there was a self-assurance to her now that made Nate feel vulnerable, like she didn't need him. Having the baby had only enhanced her beauty. The last time he saw her and she approached the bed wearing stockings, a garter belt, and nothing else . . . she'd taken his breath away.

"It's time for you to come home, Destiny. Back to me, and Palestine." Nate couldn't believe how fast time had flown. It had been more than two years since Destiny had left Texas, Benjamin was almost a year old, Thanksgiving was just around the corner, and his seventh pastor anniversary was as many months away.

"Midterms are next week. I'll be free after that if you want us to meet somewhere."

"Why not just come and stay at my house?"

"Nate, you know that wouldn't be good for your image. Some people have no business of their own, and that's why they're always in yours."

"Are you sure that's the reason?"

"Reason for what?"

"That you don't want to come here. Look, I'll fix it so nobody knows. While you're here, I'll conduct all my business at the church. Come here for the holidays, baby. I want you. I need you by my side. Will you come?"

"Okay, Nate."

"You're my destiny. You know that, don't you?"

"Yes, Nate. I know."

A little over a month later, that's exactly where Destiny and Benjamin were, in the gated community just outside of Palestine, Texas. Nettie and Katherine visited regularly, but aside from that, it was as if Destiny was cut off from the outside world. It was absolutely wonderful spending quality time with Nate, but she felt if she spent one more day inside this gilded prison, she'd climb the walls.

"Just let me go to the mall, or take Benjamin for a walk."

"Baby, you know I can't do that."

"Why not? These people don't know me."

"But they know me, and believe me, neighbors are watch-

ing the house. I think somebody on the block knows somebody at Gospel."

"Why do you say that?"

Nate didn't want to tell her the reason: that in a recent conversation Jennifer Stevens seemed to have an uncanny knowledge of who had been at his home and when they'd visited.
He thought after getting fired as his manager, she'd simply leave
the church, and the city. Instead she was at church every time the
doors opened, front and center. The last thing he needed right
now was a scandal involving his future wife.

"Look, after I conduct the New Year's Eve service, what do
you say I take my two favorite people in all the world down to
the Bahamas for a few days. Would you like that?"

"Of course."

"Now, can I get something I like?"

Destiny felt mixed emotions as Nate took her in his arms.
She'd mentioned her heart's desire to Nate, to be his one and
only. He'd said he'd think about it, and obviously that's all he
did. This visit confirmed that women in general and Gospel
Truth women in particular were still being covered.

"Not tonight, Nate," Destiny whispered. "Let's wait till
we're married."

"Baby, in the eyes of God, we're married now," he'd whispered, all the while kissing her senseless, and gently prying her
legs apart.

"No, Nate," Destiny said with her mouth, while the actions of her body defied her. Before she knew what was happening, her legs were spread wide and Nate was inside her,
pounding her, owning her, as he always did.

All too soon, it was time for Destiny to return to Louisiana.
"Nate, are you still covering other women?" she asked shortly
before leaving for the airport.

"Don't worry about other women," he'd answered dismis-
sively. "You're my number one."

Two hours later, Destiny placed Benjamin back in his car seat and buckled him in, as the plane prepared to land at New Orleans's Louis Armstrong International Airport. She was glad to be home, where she could think straight. True, she had loved every moment, every second in Nate's arms. He was everything she wanted in a man, and he treated her like a queen, plying her with love and gifts at every turn. There was no doubt in her mind that he was the man for her, and she still recited her daily mantra about being his wife. The trip had reminded her why she loved him, and how much.

But it had reminded her of other things, like his other women. No, they hadn't come to the home, and no, she hadn't attended any Gospel Truth services. But Nate's phone rang nonstop, and she could tell from his side of the conversation when the call was from someone he covered. He'd told her about Jennifer Stevens no longer being in his employ, but what Destiny had read when she'd Googled the name Dana Owens let her know that his new manager was one to watch.

And therein lay the problem: Destiny wanted to be a wife, not a watch dog. And she didn't want to be number one, she wanted to be the *only* one. Miss Nettie had told her what she would do in the situation, advice that lined up with the words of women she now considered mentors, women like Vivian Montgomery and Carla Chapman. Destiny remembered a show where Carla had told a young teenager with two kids to put her punanny on lock. Destiny doubted she could refuse Nate's sexual advances. She loved him too much, and was afraid of losing him if she said no.

Then something Miss Nettie had said during their last conversation sounded in her head, her answer when Destiny had relayed this fear to her. "You can do all things through Christ, which strengthens you," she'd said. Destiny knew good and well that to deny Nate and herself, she'd need God's strength. Clearly, hers was not enough.

"But how?" she whispered as she made her way to baggage

claim to retrieve her luggage. This time it was Nate's words that provided the answer: *give up everything and have it all.*

Destiny decided then and there to try and honor the marriage vows she'd someday speak. She would give up something she loved dearly, the intimacy she experienced with him. She would give up trying to please him. And give up the fear of losing him if she didn't give him what he wanted. In his book, Nate said that success rarely came without sacrifice. Destiny decided Nate was right. She would pray to God for the strength to do what was necessary . . . to honor and obey her husband . . . starting right now.

34

Wonderful and Wise

"How you doing, Mama Max?" Nettie asked when she answered the phone.

"Oh, tolerable. I can't complain."

"Then why haven't I heard from you since when, around Valentine's Day? That was almost a month ago! How's the Reverend Doctor?"

"You ask me, ain't nothing wrong with that man that getting back in the pulpit won't cure. He ain't been the same since he retired; I think all these ailments are just a result of him being sick about that! It's my daughter-in-law what's kept me busy. Tai had a scare just after the holidays when those fibroid tumors she's battled for years really started acting up. Three weeks ago, she had to have surgery and then had a reaction to some medication her doctor prescribed. I've been helping King with her and the kids. Barely had time to think, let alone talk to anybody who wasn't in the room. You was absent from my head, chile, but not my heart."

"Don't pay me no never mind, Mama. I'll be sure to pray Reverend and Tai's strength in the Lord."

"We appreciate that, Nettie. Goodness knows that prayer changes thangs. What about you? How you getting along?"

"Like you, I can't complain. Me and Gordon thinking about

taking a trip around Memorial Day. We haven't been on a real vacation in years. Thinking about going to either Florida or California."

"That sounds nice. Life's too short, girl. You got to take time out to enjoy yourself."

"That's what I've been thinking. And since this might be the calm before the storm . . ."

"Uh-oh. What's going on now?"

"We're all going to find that out in about three months."

"Why, what's happening in three months? Let's see, that'll be what . . . June?"

"Uh-huh."

"Nate's anniversary."

"Uh-huh."

"Lord have mercy, and don't forget grace. What's your son gone and done now?"

"He's making a formal announcement of his engagement to Destiny."

"Already?"

"That was my reaction. I think he should wait one more year. What's the hurry? She's got one more year of college and is adamant about finishing. And it's been so far so good where Benjamin is concerned. After the initial gossip, which wasn't that much, about Simone coming here with a baby, it's been quiet in that area, far as I can tell. Nate's doing so well with the ministry. They just broke ground on the new building, and his appearance on *Oprah* sent his book back to number one on that *New York Times* list. And he's conducting his first conference overseas, in London. He's got a lot on his plate right now, which is why I told him that now might not be the best time to announce it. But ever since Destiny came to visit him over the holidays, he's been adamant about taking their relationship public. I understand it partly. That girl is almost too beautiful for her own good, even more so since she had his child." Nettie chuckled. "First time in my life I've seen Nate nervous when it comes to a woman, but that little girl has got his number, you can believe that. He told me he'd think about what I said, but I know my son. Ain't no changing it when his mind's made up. And it's made up."

Mama Max paused and digested this information. "Well, now, I can't necessarily see anything wrong with that. The child is nineteen now, right? By the time they plan the wedding and everything, give folks time to get used to the idea, she'll be twenty and he'll be what, thirty-one? Now, Nettie, that just might work out all right."

"Let us pray."

"What's got your heart troubled, chile?"

Nettie sighed. "I just don't know what's going to happen when all these other women hear Nate's getting married. Some of them are bound to be upset. You know how the Thicke men carry on with women in the congregation, and unfortunately Nate has continued that tradition. Now I don't think he's made any false promises to anybody, but you know how we women are. We can imagine love where there is none and believe what ain't true. I just hope nobody goes and acts crazy behind the news, that's all."

"Crazy like what? Are you fearful for his life, Nettie?"

"Naw, after his daddy, Daniel, got killed, I asked God to give Nate a long life, so his son wouldn't have to go through what Nate went through. I believe God heard my prayer, and is careful to perform His word."

"Well then, short of death, don't worry too much about what'll happen to the boy. Whatever don't kill him will make him stronger."

"Ha! Mama Max, that's certainly one way to look at things, and that way feels a whole lot better than how I was looking at it."

"That's where your believing in God comes in, baby. You know how they say some people look at a glass and see it half empty, and others see it half full? Well, I say fill the glass up with faith, fill it to overflowing with belief in God. That'll quench the thirst of worry and douse the dehydration of fear."

"Maxine Brook, did anybody ever tell you that you are a wonderful and wise woman?"

"Yes, chile. But it don't hurt an old woman to hear it again."

35

Counting the Cost

Mark and Simone Simmons made a striking pair as they entered Fleming's Prime Steakhouse in Baton Rouge's upscale Towne Center. That's what Reverend Ed Smith thought as he watched them walk toward him. *What I wouldn't do to get a taste of that sugar dumpling.* He rose from his chair abruptly to stop the flow of his sinful thoughts.

"Mark, Simone, good to see you!"

"And you, Reverend Smith. Thanks for inviting us." Mark stepped forward and shook his hand, followed by Simone.

"Jackie will be joining us shortly. She had a conference call that ran late." Jackie Connors was a political heavyweight in the state of Louisiana. Her father had been a congressman for many years, and their family had been a part of the political landscape for generations.

"How do you like First Baptist so far?" Ed asked, once the waiter had taken their drink orders.

"There are many things that impress me," Simone answered truthfully. "Your community outreach programs are innovative and effective, and what the church is doing regarding the city's youth is to be applauded. They need direction, and First Baptist is providing that."

"We base our ministry on the word of God, not money, like that pimping preacher where you came from."

That Simone disagreed with Ed Smith's view on mega-churches, prosperity preaching, or abundance in the lives of saints would be a gross understatement. But arguing that point would be counterproductive to the reason she and Mark were here. "Well, I'm here now," she said, while blessing the minister with an engaging smile. "And grateful for the support you and this ministry are giving to my husband."

"Mark's a fine man," Ed said. "Just goes to show you that blood isn't always thicker than water and that sometimes apples do fall far from the tree! He and that scoundrel Nate Thicke are as different as night and day. It's a wonder that false prophet don't choke on his lying tongue. Why I—"

"Jackie!" Mark interrupted Ed and stood as he saw Jackie Connors hurrying toward their table. "Thanks so much for taking time out of your busy schedule to join us."

"You're more than welcome," Jackie said. "Sorry I'm late."

The foursome exchanged small talk while the waiter took their orders and refreshed their drinks.

"You know I'm one to cut to the chase," Jackie said, after the waiter left their table. "So if you don't mind, Ed, I'm just going to ask the question straight out." She turned to Mark. "Have you made a decision? Have you decided to run for mayor of Baton Rouge?"

Mark looked at Simone, who placed an encouraging hand on his arm. "Jackie, I've decided not to run for mayor."

"Oh no!" Jackie's disappointment was starkly evident.

"Now, son, you might want to reconsider," Ed said. "You're a born leader with a gift for speaking to the hearts of people. Our city needs you."

"Well, I thank you for that," Mark says. "I believe that I could be of some benefit to the people of Baton Rouge. But Simone and I have been discussing it, and she believes I could be an even bigger asset to the people of Louisiana."

Jackie and Ed looked at each other, and then at Mark.

"Jackie, Ed, I would like your help in running for governor, governor of the state of Louisiana."

Later that evening, Simone lay nestled in Mark's arms, basking in the afterglow of their lovemaking. "I'm so proud of you," she said softly.

"You should be proud of yourself. I would have never considered running for governor if you hadn't encouraged me, and made me believe I could win."

"I believe you can win because you're the best man for the job," Simone countered.

"It's funny, but before I met you, I'd taken some ministerial courses online and had toyed with the idea of going into ministry."

"Christians can minister in different ways, Mark. Some of the most effective ministries take place outside the pulpit. You're a man with godly principles, worldly intelligence, an excellent education: that's a powerful combination. It's funny that you mention the ministry though," Simone continued after a pause. "Because for a long time, I thought I'd eventually be a first lady." That she could say this, knowing that they both would think of Nate, proved just how far their marriage had come, how much they'd grown as a couple.

"Like you just told me, ministry comes in different ways. If I win—"

"*When* you win . . ."

"When I win, you'll be the first lady of this state. And win or lose," Mark said, pulling Simone closer, "you'll always be my first lady."

Not everyone was thrilled with Mark's decision to run for governor—or at least with his timing. Katherine sat at her dining room table, steaming just like the bowl of soup sitting in

front of her. She was totally unaware of the the Texas wildflowers
that had bloomed with only God's help in the lot across the
street—morning glories and black-eyed Susans visible from
her plate-glass window.

"What do you mean you can't come?" Katherine asked Simone.

"Just that, Mother. I can't come to Nate's anniversary this
year. There's too much going on right now. We're in the middle of planning a massive campaign."

"But haven't you heard anything I've said? Destiny and Nate
will be announcing their engagement. It's unconscionable that
you would think of not showing your support."

"I don't have to be there to support them," Simone said
wearily.

"I wonder . . . how much of this has to do with Mark's
campaign, and how much of it has to do with Nate marrying
Destiny instead of you."

"A year ago, it would have had everything to do with it,"
was Simone's honest answer. "Mother, you might find this hard
to believe because you're still in love with him, but I've moved
on from Nate. Yes, I will always love him. I'm getting ready to
be his mother-in-law, for goodness sake. Ha!" Simone couldn't
help but laugh at the irony of life.

"I don't find anything funny," Katherine said dryly.

"No, I guess you wouldn't. The truth is, something happened to me when I married Mark. Yes, I did it for Nate, and I
did it for Destiny. I thought we would be together a few years,
get through any scandals that Benjamin's presence might cause,
and then I'd come back to Palestine, and Nate, and take a number for a chance to sleep with him whenever he called. But that's
not my life anymore, Mother. I'll still do whatever I can to help
them, especially to help Destiny. But my life is no longer in
Palestine, with Nate and Gospel Truth. My life is here, in Baton
Rouge, with Mark."

"You still have time to change your mind," Katherine said. "They'll be making the announcement at the three o'clock service."

Katherine replaced the receiver and sat quietly. Her uneaten soup grew cold. She gazed out the window and finally took in the beautiful June day, and the flowers. Recent rains had turned everything green, a stark contrast to the brilliant blue of a cloudless sky. Katherine watched her neighbor's granddaughter ride her bike down the street. She was about twelve years old, Katherine imagined, the age when Katherine had been introduced to the Noble-Thicke tradition. She stood, walked to the window, and continued watching the girl on the bike. Her braids flew behind her, and the child laughed as a dog came to run alongside her. Katherine thought of her mother, Naomi, and Naomi's mother, Sadie, and the whole story she had yet to fully hear about what happened between Sadie and Nate's great-grandfather, Elijah, which had started it all.

Katherine wondered what would happen with Simone's break from tradition. Would the Lord strike her down for not serving the man of God? Could Destiny's marriage to Nate somehow stay God's wrath, if He determined Simone was being disobedient? And then there was the matter of Katherine's feelings, of being unsure she could handle standing in the church, alone and smiling, as the man she loved openly declared his love for another. It was a lot to bear. But for the love of her family and all things Thicke, Katherine would bear it, nobly, and not count the cost.

36

The Gospel Truth Faithful

The crowd for Nate's seventh anniversary had almost doubled from the previous year, and once again, the service had to be moved to a bigger building to accommodate the masses. Workers had toiled into the night to transform the auditorium into a place of worship, re-creating the backdrop that hung in their sanctuary, a Bible with a sword cutting through it, angel's wings above it, and these words emblazoned underneath: SPREADING THE GOSPEL TRUTH TO ALL NATIONS. Flowers decorated the altar area directly in front of the pulpit, and a temporary choir stand had been erected to the left of where the pastors and dignitaries would sit. Ushers were busy placing offering envelopes on each of the five thousand chairs on the floor and balcony. Assistants scurried to carry out the wishes of their superiors: from making sure there was water and glasses in the pulpit to carrying platters of cookies to the area designated for children's church. It was an organized chaos, overseen by Kirk and the associate ministers, and a horde of deacons taking their instruction from James Robinson.

Behind the scenes, in the room that was serving as Nate's office, all was calm. The door was locked, and he sat with Destiny perched on his knee. He repositioned her for a kiss.

"Nate, you'll wrinkle my suit!"

"It doesn't matter. You'll still be the most gorgeous woman in the room." Destiny gave in and allowed him to kiss her. "Nervous?" he asked after he finished.

Destiny nodded. "A little."

A lot, would have been a more accurate statement. *Beyond belief,* an even better description. If what she'd seen this morning was any indication, when she accompanied her grandmother to regular morning service, God only knew how the news of Nate's engagement would be received.

From the moment she'd stepped her foot out of her grandmother's brand new, lavender-colored Cadillac, all eyes had been on Destiny. Some women viewed her covertly, others flat-out stared. She'd prayed that she would run into some of her old schoolmates, someone familiar with whom to interact, but the few she'd seen had turned their faces, acting as if they hadn't seen her. This didn't surprise her really; she was tolerated at best by those her age during her time at Gospel Truth. Most of her friends had been women like Nettie, and others on the mother board. After visiting briefly with Nate in his office, she and her grandmother had been ushered down to the front row of the church. At first, you could have heard a pin drop. And then little by little the murmur, which had started at the back of the room with their entrance into the sanctuary, became an all-out cacophony. Some members didn't even try to keep their voices down.

"That's Simone's daughter, Destiny."

"Wonder what she's doing here."

"Hmph. I'll give you three guesses and the first two don't count."

Katherine had stood then, tall and regal, put her hand on her hip and looked around the room, staring into the faces of the naysayers and player-haters who dared meet her eye. Slowly the chatter quieted, and shortly after that, the organist began playing a lively rendition of "This Is the Day," an ironic selection since few were rejoicing and even fewer seemed glad.

Destiny could not have told anyone what the sermon was about. She'd been too busy trying to look as if everything was fine, as if she couldn't feel the eyes on her, sense the hostility aimed in her direction. A tall dark woman with a beautiful voice—Anne, Katherine later told her—had eyed her in a way that if looks could kill, she would have been dead and gone. Another short, light-skinned woman kept looking at her and laughing, then covering her mouth and talking to the woman beside her. The visiting minister had barely finished the benediction before Jennifer Stevens made a beeline for the front of the church where Destiny stood. She didn't make it though. She was stopped by security, detained until Destiny had been whisked through a side door and taken to Nate. All of this, and the announcement hadn't even been made yet!

There was a knock on the door. "Reverend Thicke?"

Destiny got up so Nate could unlock the door. "Yes, Kirk."

"The VIP room is filling up, sir. Pastors Montgomery and Brook want to see you. They're being entertained by your grandfather right now. But there's also a bunch of celebrities and reporters, all asking for you."

"Thanks, Kirk. I guess it's that time." He turned to Destiny. "Ready for your debut, Mrs. Thicke?"

"I'm not Missus yet," Destiny said, even as her smile showed that his comment pleased her.

Nate offered his arm. Destiny took it, and the two followed Kirk and a member of the security team down the hall to the VIP room. All heads turned as soon as Nate and Destiny entered. They were a dazzling duo: Nate, six feet three inches of dark chocolate, his newly trimmed hair and clean-shaven face effectively showing off his sharp features, wearing a tailored suit that fit as if he'd been born in it. And Destiny, just slightly shorter than him in her three-inch heels, wore an ice blue Jason Wu suit that was tailored to perfection and showed off an enviable hourglass figure and graceful calves. She wore her long black hair straight and away from a face that needed no makeup, yet had been even further enhanced by the professional artist who'd highlighted her vivid green eyes and bee-stung lips. In short, Destiny looked like a fairy princess, and Nate, the prince ready to ascend the throne.

After the pregnant pause where everyone drank in the vision this couple created, Derrick and Vivian walked up to greet them and conversation in the room resumed.

"Reverend Thicke!" Derrick exclaimed as he embraced his brother in Christ. "And you must be Destiny," he continued, offering his hand. "What a pleasure it is to meet you. This man has been singing your praises."

"And it's all true," Destiny said playfully. "Destiny Noble," she said to Vivian, who enveloped her in a hug.

"You are even more beautiful than Nate described," Vivian responded. "Being a first lady isn't always easy, but I have a feeling you are up to the task."

For the next thirty minutes, Nate and Destiny took a turn around the room, meeting and greeting, before one of the associate ministers let everyone know it was time for the service to begin. Nate and Destiny returned to his office, along with some of the visiting pastors. The others followed ushers to the special seating for distinguished guests. Patricia, who'd been a hostess, went to the bathroom to throw up. Seeing Nate all goo-goo eyed over a woman who looked like she stepped off a runway had literally made her sick to her stomach.

Destiny took a deep breath and braced herself for the entrance into the arena. Nate went with the other ministers to take his place on the elevated podium while she, along with Katherine, Nettie, Mama Max, and the ladies-in-waiting assigned to them walked to their reserved seats in the front row. The talk may have been no less active, but for Destiny it was easier this time. Perhaps because of the size of the auditorium, she wasn't as aware of eyes on her as she'd been in the smaller space. Then again, maybe it was because almost every time she looked up, Nate's eyes were on her, his smile reassuring, his wink comforting. What she'd prayed for was coming true, and everybody was getting ready to know it.

After the singing, praying, and acknowledging of Nate's accomplishments and service to God; after the offering had been lifted and the sermon had been preached; after the doors to the church had been opened and closed, visitors acknowledged and dignitaries announced . . . finally . . . it was time. After much discussion, it had been decided that Nate's grandfather, Thomas Thicke, would do the honors.

He slowly walked to the podium and began speaking at once. "It gives me great pleasure to stand before you and make a special announcement." The buzzing of voices began. "To testify to the wisdom, the constancy, and the faithfulness of God." The murmuring dimmed, as people second-guessed what they thought they knew was about to happen. "The word of God says that it is not good for a man to be alone, and that he who finds a wife finds a good thing." The buzzing began again, louder this time. "And I am happy that God has allowed me to live to see the day that my grandson, a true man of God working for the kingdom, found his good thing."

Thomas turned to Nate. "Come here, son." He then turned to Destiny. "Come here, daughter."

Destiny hesitated only briefly, and then stood, taller and more regal than her grandmother had that morning, and walked up to where Thomas and Nate stood.

"Ladies and gentlemen, I am here to formally announce the engagement of Nathaniel Eli Thicke to Destiny Nicole Noble. May God bless and keep this couple, as they walk toward marriage and a lifetime together."

Loud applause broke out from the two-thirds of attendees who were from other churches or out of town. They rose to their feet, giving the beaming couple a standing ovation. The musicians broke into an impromptu jazz version of Brian McKnight's song "Back at One." Shouts of "praise the Lord" and "thank you, Jesus" were heard from the section where the older women sat—the mothers of the church. One by one the pastors came forth to shake Nate's hand and lightly hug Destiny.

But not everyone clapped or considered the announcement good news. Scores of women's hearts broke as their improbable fantasy was dashed. True, most of them had never even met Nate Thicke in person, but as long as he was single, they could dream. As long as there was no one physically by his side, they could put themselves there. But today, that spot had been officially taken.

And then there were the Gospel Truth faithful, women who had allowed themselves to believe that being intimate with Nate would grant them special favor. They hadn't cared that Nate didn't marry them, as long as he didn't marry anybody else. Verniece gasped when she heard the news, and then burst out crying. She could only hope those watching believed hers were tears of joy for her pastor. Patricia, whose stomach had quieted during the service, felt the roiling again, and left the sanctuary. Anne sat stunned, trying to look normal, a smile pasted to her face that was as fake as snow in Miami. Katherine stood with both sad and happy tears streaming down her face.

These women sat in different areas but shared a common thought: *Will Nate still cover me?*

For one woman, the stakes were higher than a romp in the sack. When Jennifer Stevens had been tossed out of Nate's office and out of his bed as well, she'd surprised everyone by not leaving the church. She believed that staying would prove to Nate that being at Gospel Truth was about more than her being his manager, being in the limelight. She wanted him to see that she could take her just punishment, and wait—as long as it took—for Nate to forgive her. She'd remained faithful, and was at the church every time the doors opened. She'd doubled her offering and given liberally to the building fund, doing her part to advance Nate's dream. But now, as she sat in the back of the auditorium, she saw her own dream slipping farther and farther away. How far she had fallen, from last year when she was a VIP of the VIPs, to this year when she'd barely gotten a seat. Amid the accolades and well wishes, and through the benediction, Jennifer sat there and remembered: when she first arrived at Gospel Truth, Nate's elation when she booked Carla for the luncheon, their exciting times in California, Chicago, and New York. The way she felt when she was in Nate's arms.

"No!" she said out loud as she finally stood on her feet to leave the half-empty area. *I'm not going to give up on Nate, or on us. There must be something I can do to prove I belong in his life.* As Jennifer exited the building and walked to her car, an idea began to form in her mind, a way that Nate would know beyond a shadow of a doubt that Jennifer's love was genuine, that nobody could have his back the way she did. She didn't even go home to change clothes. Instead she filled up her gas tank, ordered a fish sandwich from a drive-thru, and hit the highway. It was time for another visit to Louisiana.

37

The Pleasure Is Mine

"Baby, are you sure you have to go back today?" Nate followed Destiny from the bathroom to the bedroom.

"I told you, Nate. I've got school."

"I don't want you to leave. I need you."

Destiny stopped packing and looked at her fiancé. "Do you want me here now, meaning I'll have two more years of school, or do you want me to take summer classes so I can graduate by January?"

"Yes."

"Very funny, Mr. Thicke."

"Baby, things happen when you're around me. You're like a good luck charm." He walked up and grabbed her from behind. "And you're so soft, and smell so good." He wrestled her onto the bed and got on top of her. "Uh-huh. I've got you now. You're my prisoner, baby. My prisoner of love."

"Nate, stop playing. I'm going to miss my flight!"

"Which would make me a happy man."

"I'm serious. Stop, Nate. There's something I want to say to you. It's important."

Nate gave Destiny a quick kiss, rolled off her but remained seated on the bed. "So, talk."

Deciding the bed wasn't the best place for what she was

about to say, Destiny slid off it and began to pace the floor. "I want you to know that what I'm about to say . . . the decision I've made, I didn't come to lightly. I've really thought about it."

Nate's heart lodged in his throat. "You're leaving me?"

Destiny walked over and cupped his cheek. "I never want to leave you, baby. I want us to be together forever."

Nate's sigh of relief was audible. "Okay. What then?"

"I've asked you to do something for me, and if we're to be married, it has to happen. I don't want a whole bunch of women in our marriage bed. Now that we're engaged, I want to be the only woman you sleep with. And if I'm not the only one, then I won't sleep with you."

"Destiny, why do you keep bringing this up? You know my duties as shepherd of the flock. Katherine and Simone never—"

"I am not Kiki, and I am not my mom. I don't agree with what they've told me about your covering other women. I've read the Bible for myself, and it talks about the man of God having only one wife."

"You've been reading the Bible . . . ? What, you're the expert on religion now?"

"I'm the expert on how I feel, and what I want. It's all I'm asking, Nate. If you want me, you'll have to give up the other women. I know it's a lot to sacrifice, but it's what you've taught me through your book, that great sacrifice can bring great rewards. And Miss Nettie—"

"What's Mama got to do with this? Is that who you've been talking to, who has been filling your head with all kinds of nonsense?" Nate jumped off the bed and stormed over to the phone.

Destiny rushed behind him. "No, don't, Nate. Don't call your mother, and don't blame her. Yes, I've talked about this with your mother. I knew her opinion would be different than what the women in my family believe. But I came to this decision on my own, Nate. The same way you're so adamant about my not being with anyone else? That's how I feel about you." Destiny walked over to where Nate stood and hugged him. "Give me the chance to be the only one who satisfies you. Maybe I'll be enough."

The intercom in the hallway beeped. "Reverend, Ms. Owens is on the line."

"Thanks, Kirk." Nate looked at Destiny a long moment. "That's my afternoon appointment," he said with a sigh. "I'd better take it."

"Think about what I said, Nate. And let me know your answer."

"Joe is here with the limo. Stop by my office before you leave."

Three hours later, Nate sat in his church office, looking comfortably chic in a crisp, ivory-colored suit and silk pullover. The jacket lay draped over the chair behind him. He wore no tie. Glancing at the clock, he closed the building update Deacon Robinson had provided. After looking at the same page for five minutes, he finally admitted this was not a good day for intense thinking. His mind was still on Destiny, and her request.

The truth was, Nate loved Destiny more than life itself and would do almost anything for her. But he was clear on certain responsibilities he had regarding females in and around his congregation, had been since being groomed for ministry by his grandfather at age sixteen. He wondered how could he get Destiny to understand that? *Maybe Katherine . . .* His phone rang, and minutes later, a well-put-together Dana Owens walked into his office. One would never know it was almost ninety degrees outside. She looked cool as a cucumber in a mint green pantsuit, black pumps, and shades. Another woman came in just behind her.

"Good afternoon, Dana," Nate said, rising from his seat and coming from behind the desk to hug her. "I'm glad you were able to find another flight out."

"I am too. I was so bummed that I had to miss your anniversary yesterday. I didn't want to miss this meeting as well."

"How was your niece's wedding?"

"It was beautiful, really."

"Well, you were sorely missed from the festivities, but you were where you were supposed to be. And who is this attractive young lady?" Nate asked, with hand outstretched.

"This is my assistant, Melody Anderson. She was a big help in Nashville, where I just came from, so I brought her along to help me here as well."

"Melody, nice to meet you."

Melody held out her hand and said with a voice of professionalism, "Reverend Thicke, the pleasure is mine."

38

Good Lovin'

"I'm still in shock."

"Me too."

"I mean, where the hell did she come from?" Verniece plopped down on the couch in Anne's living room, flipped through a few pages of *Ebony*, and then threw the magazine on the coffee table in front of her. "Damn!"

"I told you she used to live here and has been away at college. Maybe his being married won't matter," Anne suggested. "Maybe he'll still be with us."

"I doubt it. With a wife in the picture, everything's getting ready to change. Has he called you since the anniversary?"

"No, you?"

"No, but it's only been a month."

"Yeah, but before he used to call almost every week, or every two weeks."

"Have you called him?"

"No."

"Why not?"

Anne shrugged. "Scared, I guess. Don't want to hear him tell me not to call any more."

Both women were silent, pondering their potential loss.

"For some reason, I just can't see Reverend Thicke being married," Anne said. "He's too much man for just one woman."

"Why she have to be so damn beautiful and shit? Skinny as hell—no offense, Anne—with that long-ass hair."

"You know that's a weave."

"No it ain't. I talked to one of the church mothers who's known her since she was a little girl. That's that bitch's real hair."

"Taking my good dick away . . . I want to snatch her bald-headed."

"That's real talk right there. She's messing with my feel good." Verniece picked up the *Ebony* again and began thumbing through it.

Anne picked up the remote and began flipping through channels on a muted television neither woman watched. "I wonder if there's anything we can do about it."

"About what?"

"About Reverend Thicke. Him sharing is one thing, marrying is another. I wish I knew more about this chick, how to contact her, for instance. Because I'd let her know in no uncertain terms that her wearing his ring wouldn't change a thing, as far as I'm concerned. I'll still come running every time Reverend calls. And every time we screw, I'll make sure she knows about it."

"Ooh, I wish I could call her," Verniece agreed. "She thinks she wants to be married to Nate, wants to be Gospel Truth's first lady? Hmph. Not after I get done talking to her, she won't. I'll describe Nate's dick down to the mole under his balls . . . ask her if she knows how he got that little scar on the inside of his left thigh. By the time I get done with her, she'll be running her little narrow ass right back to wherever it is she came from."

Verniece scooted off the couch and retrieved her purse from the dining room table. She pulled out her cell phone.

"Who are you calling?"

"Reverend Thicke." Verniece put the call on speakerphone. Both women barely breathed as they waited to see if he'd pick up.

"Hello?"

"Hello, Reverend, it's Verniece."

"Hello, Verniece. How are you?"

"I'm okay, and you?"

"Excellent. What can I do for you?"

Verniece's eyes grew wide as she looked at Anne.

Ask him! Anne mouthed.

"I was just wondering if you could . . . I mean, I know you're engaged and all but . . ."

"Do you need something, Verniece?"

"Yes." Verniece swallowed. "I've been feeling really depressed lately. I need your counsel. And I need . . . to be covered," she said softly. There was a long silence on the other end of the line. "Reverend, are you there?"

"I'm in Dallas right now. I'll be back on Thursday and will call you then."

"Thanks so much, Reverend. Good-bye."

Verniece got off the phone, shrieked, and started dancing around the room. "Did you hear that? Thursday night, baby! I'm gonna get some good lovin'!"

"Praise the Lord," Anne said, joining Verniece in a dance around the room. "Guess that means I'll call him next week, if I haven't heard from him by then."

"Ha! I bet that girl thinks Nate's all faithful and everything, that she's got him wrapped around her finger with her beauty and her poise. But obviously I've got him wrapped around something because he's coming back for the nana!"

"For the Gospel Truth nana," Anne repeated.

"Ha!" Both women laughed hysterically, until they could barely catch their breath.

39

Ready to Tell

"You're something else, you know that?" Nate spoke over his shoulder as he stood in front of the mirror, buttoning his shirt.

"Is that a good thing?"

"What do you think?"

Melody rolled off the bed and strolled naked over to where Nate stood. She put her arms around him from behind. "I hope it is, because you've got me hooked on you already. When can I have some more?"

Nate laughed. "My goodness, Melody. You make me sound like a sandwich or something!"

"Yeah, and I've never had anything that tastes so good! When can I have some more?"

Nate finished dressing and turned around to face her. "I'm a very busy man, Melody, and I'm engaged. I'm glad I was able to make you feel better, but I can't make you any promises on this happening again. Now hurry up and get dressed. I arranged a late check-out, but you need to be out by two P.M."

Instead of getting dressed, Melody sat down on the bed and changed the subject. "Your fiancée's name is Destiny, right?"

"That is correct."

"Lucky woman."

"No, I'm the lucky one. Now get dressed."

Fifteen minutes later, Nate left the room. Melody waited a few minutes to be sure he was gone, and then walked over to the closet to retrieve the video camera she'd turned on and hidden shortly before he arrived. She rewound the tape and played back a little, to make sure it had recorded. A big smile spread across her face when she saw that it had. Since filming herself having sex with Shabach years before, Melody often videotaped her intimate trysts. Watching them later was a turn-on for her—*And the things that man did to me!* There was no way this was going to be the only time she was with Nate Thicke. No wonder Destiny had kept that kind of loving a secret. Melody couldn't wait to get home, watch it, and remember how good it felt all over again!

An hour later, Melody was in her preowned Honda, barreling down Interstate 35. Her thoughts were racing faster than the seventy-plus on the speedometer. She'd been shocked but not surprised when she'd seen the pictures from Reverend Thicke's anniversary, and the subsequent engagement announcement that made headlines across the Christian community and in the secular arena as well. *I knew it,* she'd thought when she'd seen her former classmate standing poised and elegant beside her pastor. Melody found it interesting that there had been no mention of Destiny's son. Which brought to mind another question. Just who was Benjamin's daddy? Was it some guy named Bryan, as Destiny had told her, or was the daddy named Nate? After all, she'd lied about liking him, lied about fucking him. What else had she lied about?

Melody reached for her hands-free device and placed it over her ear. As soon as it was attached, she dialed the familiar Louisiana number. She'd waited this long to see if Destiny would phone her, and again, wasn't surprised to not get a call. *She knows I know now. The cat is out the bag.* Her friend may have felt the need to keep her life with Nate a secret, but Melody felt exactly the opposite. She had just been sexed to within an inch of her life, and she was getting ready to tell Destiny everything.

40

Love Yourself

Simone reclined on a chaise in the enclosed patio, listening with restrained patience to a rare rant from her normally unflappable mother.

"I need you to go over there and talk some sense into her," Katherine said in a raised voice. "That girl is a Noble. And you're her mother. You can get her to understand that what Nate is doing is what the Thicke men do, is a part of their calling. She's getting ready to mess up everything, behind some nonsense. And I know Nettie's got something to do with Destiny's new attitude. The next time I see her, she's going to hear a thing or two. All the years her husband covered me, she never said a word. Well, now is not the time for her to start talking!"

"I've already talked to Destiny, Mother, right after she found out about Nate sleeping with her friend. And I'm convinced the decisions she's made are her own and no one else's."

"Nate slept with that Melody hussy months ago! You need to go over there again and talk some more. She's taken his ring off and has threatened to call off the engagement. Nate is beside himself."

"Then why isn't Nate over there? It seems to me if anybody should be doing the talking, it's him."

"She still won't take his calls."

"Finally, a Noble woman who can actually refuse a Thicke man."

"That's not right, Simone, and you know it."

"All I know is that Destiny has to live her own life, just like I'm now living my own life. A life without Nate," Simone continued, her voice soft. "Have you ever thought about it, Mother? Meeting somebody, getting married again? You're still attractive, with so much to offer. Perhaps if you met somebody—"

"Then what? I'd stop sleeping with Nate? I will be with the reverend as long as he needs me. And it's a good thing too. Because the rest of you Nobles seem ready to abandon him when he needs us the most."

Katherine's words had the desired affect. Simone was no longer in love with Nate, but she still loved him, and wanted what was best for his life.

"Everything we've ever dreamt for Nate has come true," Katherine continued. "To go to the next level, Nate needs to be married. It's important for men of God of his stature to have a wife, the right kind of first lady. You and I both know that woman is Destiny."

"Mother, I know that Noble women have been with Thicke men for generations. But you've never told me why."

"I don't know the whole reason, but Destiny will. I visited old man Elijah the other day, and he said that soon, the whole story would be told. I'm as interested as you about the missing pieces—why when a Thicke calls, a Noble answers."

"But the man is almost ninety-five years old. When is 'soon,' and what if he dies before that time comes?"

"He said there are papers in his personal effects that tell everything, and he's bequeathed them to one of us . . . eventually we'll know. Now will you help me? Will you talk to Destiny?"

"Yes."

★　★　★

Later that evening, Simone sat at Destiny's dining room table. "Is he asleep?" she asked, when Destiny reentered the room.

"Finally," Destiny said.

"He's a beautiful boy. Looks so much like Nate."

Destiny let out a deep breath.

"And you," Simone added.

"Kiki send you over here?" Destiny eyed her mother as she asked the question.

Simone nodded. "Nate's . . . having a hard time without you."

Tears came to Destiny's eyes. "It's hard for me too."

The silence was loud as both women wrestled with their thoughts, and feelings, and the legacy.

"At one time I felt as you do," Simone said finally.

"How?"

"That if I were to be with Nate, I couldn't share him."

"What happened?"

Simone shrugged. "I fell in love with him, and I convinced myself that Nate's being with women in the congregation was something I'd have to learn to live with. After all, Mother did it. She knew when he covered me. Grandmother Naomi did it, when Mother began with Thomas Thicke. But clearly, you're different, Destiny. You're the first one of us who has actually refused to accommodate what has gone on for years. I asked Mother about that tonight, how this whole thing started with the Thicke men and Noble women."

"What did she say?"

"That Elder Elijah knows, and that when the time is right he'll tell us. But I think it has to do with some type of promise. Other than that . . . I don't know."

"Am I wrong, Mommy? Am I wrong for wanting Nate to myself?"

Now there were tears in Simone's eyes. "I don't think so, baby," she whispered. "Not long ago, my answer would have been different, as you well know. But knowing what I now know and having what I now have, with Mark . . . God knows I want the best for Nate. But you're my daughter, and I want you to be happy.

"I never thought I'd feel the way I do right now, thankful that I'm with someone other than Nate. I thought he hung the moon and the stars—"

"He didn't?"

"I think he may have placed a planet or two." Both women laughed.

"I guess I'm here to say two things," Simone continued. "One—talk to Nate. I'm not saying you have to do anything you don't want to do, but just talk to him. Hear what he has to say. But the second thing I want to tell you is . . . follow your heart, Destiny. Listen to God. It seems that's what you've been doing so far, and I believe it's working for you. I know we Noble women have an interesting history, an interesting relational dynamic not understood by those outside it. But above all else, I am your mother. I love you. And I know you love Nate. I just want you to always be able to look in the mirror . . . and love yourself."

41

I Said Yes

"Hey now, Nettie. What you know good?" Mama Max waltzed around the kitchen preparing homemade rolls, tickled to pieces she could both cook and talk on the phone with the hands-free device her grandson had both bought and showed her how to use.

"Know quite a bit. Don't know how good that is. I just got off the phone with Destiny, and the you-know-what is about to hit the fan."

"What is it, problems at school?"

"No, she whizzed through her finals and except for walking across the stage, this coming May, she's all through with college. Got her degree, with honors."

"Business administration, right?"

"Something like that," Nettie said. "Anyway, she has decided to come home, to move back to Palestine, praise the Lord. Nate is crazy over the thought of losing her."

"Isn't that good news? What's gonna hit the fan behind news like that?"

"She's moving back, but not in with Nate. She asked if she could stay with me. And I said yes."

"Whew, Lawd have mercy, and Joseph say grace. I can smell the stink all the way up here in Kansas! Ooh, and I'm about to smell some burning rolls." Mama Max was silent as she hurried over to a drawer, pulled out an oven mitt, and quickly removed the perfectly done rolls from the oven. "Nate is not going to like that news, not one bit! But tell me this. Why is she staying with you, Nettie? Why not Katherine?"

"I think you know the answer to that question, Mama Max. It's gonna take all the discipline that child's got to hold her ground with Nate. Now I love my son, but you know how forceful and persuasive he can be. Over at Katherine's, I think she'd feel vulnerable. But here, she knows I've got her back."

"She bringing the baby with her?"

"Not right away. Benjamin is going to stay with the nanny in Louisiana. Simone is busy helping her husband win that election but has promised to help watch him. Destiny will go back as often as she can, and once they get married, which will hopefully be sooner rather than later, they'll bring Benjamin into their household, ask the church's forgiveness for the sins of omission and commission, and hopefully move toward a happily ever after, if there is such a thing."

"Well, I for one don't think Nate should have a problem with what she's asking," Mama Max said. "Word get out that the preacher is shacking up, be all kinds of trouble. And she's right about wanting him to stop all this cavorting with other women. Shouldn't be too hard to do with a gorgeous girl like her lying right next to him, there for the taking. Men sure can make a mess of thangs sometimes."

"Well, that's the other thing. She wants to abstain from being with Nate again until they get married."

"What did you just say? Are you sure that girl's a Noble? I didn't know any of them could spell abstain, let alone practice it."

"Destiny's got a mind of her own, and a pretty good one, if you ask me. She loves her grandmother, but she doesn't want to be like her, doesn't want to share her husband. I'm encouraging her to stick to her guns."

"Your son's not going to be too happy with you. You know that, don't you?"

Nettie sighed. "Yes, I know. But right is right, Mama Max, and while I kept my mouth shut, I never agreed with what old man Elijah started, all the Thicke ministers spreading themselves across the congregation. And even though I looked the other way knowing Daniel was with Katherine, telling myself it was just as well since I didn't want it no way, it hurt to know he was fooling around. I saw the sly looks from the women he covered, felt their smug attitudes as they watched me walk to the front row as the wife of the pastor. I had the title and the prestige that goes with it, and I took my rightful place on Sunday mornings. But the rest of the week belonged to other women, especially Katherine. If Daniel hadn't died, I strongly suspect he would have divorced me and married her."

"Now, Nettie, you don't know that."

"I know he loved her something fierce. And I know she would have been more than happy to take my place in the front row. I shed many a tear behind the fact that I knew Daniel didn't love me like he did her. And if I can keep Destiny from feeling that kind of sorrow, and at the hands of Daniel's son no less, then I'm going to try and do it. It might be time to write a new chapter at Gospel Truth. Katherine's granddaughter just might be holding the pen."

Mama Max and Nettie were silent a moment, contemplating the winds of change that were always blowing from church to church. "Wonder what Katherine's going to have to say about this? Have you talked to her?"

"No, and don't plan to. Destiny's a grown woman, and can live where she wants. Katherine ain't had much to say to me for the past couple months anyway, ever since Destiny asked her to stop sleeping with her fiancé! Can you even imagine having to ask your *grandmother* a question like that? Katherine called and accused me of influencing the girl. I told her I'd done no such thing, and when she kept flapping her jaws I told her she needed to take six months to tend to her business, and use the other six months to leave mine alone."

"Ha! I can imagine Miss High and Mighty didn't like that."

"Didn't matter to me whether she liked it or not. I meant every word." Nettie looked at her caller ID. "Oh, Lord, this is Nate calling. Might as well get this conversation over with."

"Just remember you're the mama. And a child never gets too old or too tall to whup."

Nettie was laughing when she clicked over to the other line. "Hey, Nate."

"Hey, Mama! What's so funny?"

"Just got off the phone with Mama Max. How are you doing, son? You sound happy."

"Are you kidding? My baby's coming home. I'm ecstatic!"

"I bet she's pretty happy too. Have you talked to her today?"

"No, I just landed and saw that you'd called. I'll call her next. Have you talked to her?"

"Yes, she called me this morning."

"You know, I want the two of you to spend some time together when she gets here, Mama. I need you to show her how to make those apple cobblers."

Nettie laughed. "I'll be more than happy to, son. As a matter of fact, your wife asked me this morning if the two of us could spend time together, so it looks like you two are already on the same page."

"I think that's great! She'll be traveling with me, of course, but when I'm in town, you're welcome to stop by the house anytime."

"That's why I left that message for you to call me, Nate. Because there's been a change of plans for when Destiny returns to Palestine."

"What do you mean a change in plans? She's still coming in December, right?"

"Oh, yeah, she'll be here December nineteenth, in time for

the church's first holiday ball. But when she arrives, she'll be moving in with me."

"What?" Nate was sure he'd heard incorrectly.

"Destiny asked me if she could stay here until the two of you get married, and I agreed."

"Mama, I don't like this. Sounds like you're trying to get in my business. You don't belong in between me and Destiny."

"I'm not between anybody, son. I was here in my house minding my own business. Destiny called me. She voiced her concern at how it would look to Gospel Truth members for her to be living with you before you married. I'm surprised this wasn't your concern, you being the senior pastor and all. But she asked if she could stay here, and I said yes. I'm going to fix up your old room, and you can visit here . . . as often as you'd like."

Nate raised the privacy petition in the limo. "How much have you been talking to Destiny? Are you the reason why she's so fixated with . . . my duties as pastor?"

"Anything Destiny is fixated on is your doing, son, not mine."

"Because you know my responsibilities, Mama. I am the shepherd of this flock and being the spiritual covering for my members—"

"I brought you into this world, boy. Don't preach to me. And don't try and tell me about the Thicke tradition. I could tell you a thing or two."

"What you need to do is tell Destiny that her place is beside me. I can't believe you're interfering like this, Mama. You never interfered with Daddy's affairs."

"You don't know what I did and didn't do where your father was concerned. And this isn't just your business, Nathaniel. My name is on the membership roll at Gospel Truth, and I live in this town. What you do affects me and a whole lot of other folk."

Nate took a deep breath and tried another approach. "You know what, Mama? Destiny spending time with you might be a good thing. You've been a first lady, and from what I remember, always handled yourself with style and grace, even though I know you knew that Daddy was . . . what Daddy's responsibilities were to the flock. You can teach Destiny how to be like that."

"Destiny doesn't need me to teach her anything. But it looks as if she could teach you a thing or two, starting with the decorum of not shacking up with your wife-to-be while leading a congregation!"

"That's it, Mama. This conversation is over. I'm going to call Destiny and try and get her to see reason. She's moving in with me, period. And then I'll call you back. In the meantime, Mama, you need to think about everything I've said."

"And you need to think about what *I've* said. I've been a silent observer to the Thicke goings on for over forty years, and all the time held my tongue. But no more. Destiny is welcome to stay with me. That is, if she's still interested in being your wife after the foolishness you're getting ready to talk to her."

Nate looked at the phone and then did something he'd never before done in his life. He hung up on his mother.

42

It Needs to Be Holy

"Hey, D, you there?" King had placed Nate on hold shortly after finding out the nature of his call, to get his best friend and fellow counselor on the line.

"I'm here and at your service, brothah."

"Good, good. I've got Nate on the line. He called for my advice on a situation he's dealing with, and I thought he'd benefit from your counsel as well."

"I'll do what I can. How are you, Nate?" Derrick took a seat in his home office and said a silent prayer as he waited for the conversation to continue.

"Honestly, Derrick, I've been better. And I really appreciate both of you taking the time to talk with me. I know how busy your schedules are."

"That's part of our mission in Total Truth," King said. "To be here for each other, mentor each other, especially when there's a need. Why don't you fill Derrick in on what you just told me."

Nate gave a very brief recounting of his conversation with Nettie: basically that he wanted Destiny in his home and his mother out of their business. "We're already married in the eyes of God," Nate concluded. "Besides, I'm moving to an exclusive community with live guards twenty-four hours a day. No one who doesn't live in the community will be able to get in to see me without my permission. So the members most likely won't even know she's there."

"God will know she's there," Derrick countered. "And now so will King, myself, your mother, her family. Nate, there is absolutely no way I can condone your living with Destiny before the two of you are married—not as a pastor, a member of Total Truth, or a man. That woman is deserving of your respect, which includes having her best interest in mind, not yours."

"Wait a minute, Derrick—"

"No, you hold on. You called for my advice and I have to give it to you straight. Your mother is right, Nate. Now I know this isn't what you want to hear, maybe not what you expected. But you are the high profile minister of an up-and-coming megachurch. You're a best-selling author soon to have a television broadcast. All eyes will be on you, and what they see needs to be holy.

"When you finally told King about Destiny having your child, and he subsequently told the board members, there were some who felt you'd betrayed them, because you hadn't been totally forthcoming during your confirmation. But because of your plans to marry the mother, they allowed your membership to stand. Folks are watching, some of whom would like nothing better than to see you fall. Don't give them that chance, Nate. Move up the wedding if you have to, but make sure when Destiny moves her things into your new home, that she enters the right way: as Mrs. Nathaniel Thicke."

Nate was silent so long both King and Derrick thought maybe he'd hung up. But he hadn't. He respected these two men on the phone to the utmost, and would heed their counsel. Perhaps begrudgingly, and only temporarily, but he would listen to their instruction. "What do you think, King?" he finally asked.

"I agree with Derrick, man. Moving Destiny in before the two of you marry isn't wise, especially right now, at such a crucial time for the ministry. And believe me, I understand your wanting her by your side, in your home, *and* in your bed."

"Speak to it!" Derrick said.

Nate laughed. "Well, my brothahs, I'm not going to lie about that."

"You might as well not," King said. "I've been there. I know. Destiny is a beautiful woman and if it were me, I wouldn't be able to get the ring on fast enough to hit that fine—"

"Uh, yeah, King," Derrick interrupted. "I think Nate gets the picture. But there is one other thing, Reverend Thicke. And if you thought your mother was in your business, then that shoe is going to fit me in about two seconds. We've been dealing with a particular topic in our men-only meetings that I need to bring up here. It's about abstinence outside marriage."

"Derrick, I'm telling you now . . . that's not going to happen. I've been active since I was thirteen, man. Ain't no way I'm going six months without it, especially with my woman ten minutes away."

"And there's the matter of any other woman who might be, uh, enjoying your favors. She needs to go, too. Destiny deserves to have all of you, man."

"Y'all are putting a hurting on a brothah! But there's something you two might not understand. At Gospel Truth, I have some spiritual relationships that are a part of tending my flock."

"Man, don't even try it," King countered. "The only spiritual relationship is the one between you and your wife, Nate. All of the other ones are just pussy."

King and Derrick shared what they knew of other ministers who maintained "spiritual relationships." They offered scriptural viewpoints to the contrary regarding these beliefs, even as King empathized with Nate, and shared times when he'd been unfaithful.

"If you want your marriage with Destiny to not only last

but be an exciting, productive, loving union," King concluded, "you are going to have to commit to her and only her one hundred and fifty percent, every day, for the rest of your life."

The three men talked for over two hours, holding nothing back of what they felt about Nate and Destiny, and what they expected of him as a fellow minister and member of the association. Nate argued his points, but Derrick and King were unrelenting in their position. By the end of the conversation, Nate had agreed to abide by the rules of Total Truth, and to six months of marital counseling from Derrick, King, and their wives.

"It's for your own good," Derrick said finally.

"It's because we love you," King added. "So what do you think, man? Do you think you'll be able to make it until the wedding in June?"

"What I'm thinking," Nate answered seriously, "is that we need to move the wedding up to Valentine's Day."

43

House Cleaning

The week following his conversation with Derrick and King, Nate scheduled a meeting with a very exclusive group of Gospel Truth members. Along with marital counseling, the two seasoned pastors had delivered some sage ministerial advice. Nate planned to implement their suggestions immediately, one of which was to trim and tighten the inner circle around him. There were only seven people around the table, Deacon Robinson, Nettie, and Katherine among them.

"I'm making some changes, effective immediately," Nate said, after Deacon Robinson had opened the meeting with prayer. "We're getting ready to shore up the leadership in this ministry, strengthen its backbone and foundation, so we can withstand the growth that is sure to continue, as well as the challenges that come along with such growth. Some of these changes are also a result of my impending marriage, and the addition of an amazing first lady to our congregation. I want to make sure that my wife is welcomed into this church and given the same respect, love, and deference as I am now afforded. Her comfort beside me is of the utmost importance. I will not tolerate otherwise. Now, these alterations are few, yet crucial. And unless I am given impeccable arguments by one of you to the contrary, these decisions will stand."

Nate took a moment to look around the room, meeting every eye looking back at him before continuing. "As of today, every appointment, meeting, phone call, and request of any kind, from any member, concerning me or the executive office, must go through Katherine and/or her office. No exceptions. Any and all calls for counseling, prayer, or any other ministerial guidance from a female member is to go through my mother. In due time, my wife will undoubtedly become a significant leader in the women's ministry. Until then, Nettie Thicke is the woman in charge. Any questions so far?"

There were none. "I have a list of members whose presence I feel no longer works in this ministry's best interest. There are no new names, but a couple I want to reiterate. Jennifer Stevens is no longer a member of the executive committee, the public relations or marketing department or any active department in this church. I'm surprised she is still attending, but since that is the case, I want everyone to understand she is a member, nothing more. No access by her to any of the offices is to be allowed. Deacon Robinson, make sure you get with security so that they understand these are my orders where she is concerned. It has also been brought to my attention that Kirk Meadows has developed quite an alliance with Jennifer. At this very moment, he is being given his walking papers, after which he will enjoy the same status as Jennifer—a member to be considered hostile and potentially dangerous to the ministry. I want the ushers and security to keep an eye out."

Nate read off the names of several others and also discussed the forthcoming announcement about Benjamin. After those around the table voiced their opinions, and a few other pressing church issues were discussed, the meeting was adjourned.

Nate was on a roll. He went directly from that meeting to his office, where he went through his electronic Rolodex and pulled several numbers. His calls were methodical, the conversations succinct. When he had concluded them, several women around the country and the Gospel Truth faithful, including Patricia, Anne, and Verniece, knew without a shadow of a doubt that they had been covered by Nathaniel Eli Thicke for the last time.

44

Talk to Me

"I don't know what to tell you, Jennifer. If the office said the tickets are sold out, I guess they're sold out. But that's just for the sit-down dinner with Reverend. There's a general dinner happening at the same time, in the larger ballroom where the Christmas program will take place. You won't have any problem getting in there."

"But that's just it, Pat. I have to be at that dinner with Reverend. I've already told you why. I need to talk to him, don't have his new number, and the office is guarding him tighter than the pope."

Since he'd announced his engagement six months ago, not being able to talk to Nate was only one of several things that had changed. Almost immediately afterward, so had all of his phone numbers. A lock had been put on the door leading to the executive offices, and additional security staff and assistants had been hired to manage the growing number of people wanting Nate's attention or affection—or both.

But Jennifer would not be denied, not now that she had concrete proof of what she'd believed all the time, that Nate was the father of Destiny's baby. It had taken months of snooping, miles of travel between Palestine and New Orleans, and twenty-five hundred dollars in bribe money paid to a hospital clerk, but Jennifer had in her possession a copy of Benjamin's birth certificate. She had it in her power to ruin Nate Thicke because Destiny had given birth when she was just seventeen. That meant Nate was having sex with her before she was legal. She didn't know about Louisiana but in Texas, sixteen was statutory rape. Jennifer was determined to let him know what she knew, and to assure him that she could be trusted. After all, many people would take this type of information and sell it to the highest bidder. Jennifer would show him that she was different, that she was looking out for him. And then she would show him that she could look out for him better than Destiny.

"Please," she pleaded with Pat, one of the few people of the inner circle with whom she still communicated. "I know there's an extra ticket lying around somewhere."

"If there is, I don't know about it. Sorry, Jennifer, I'm busy and really need to go."

"Oh, so it's like that, huh? You're too busy for a friend? You know what? You've changed since you've started working full-time at the church. When you were a lowly hostess, and I was Nate's manager, you always had time for a phone call, lunch, anything to keep in the loop about what was going on with the man we both were screwing. But now, since it looks like I'm out and Destiny's in, you no longer have time for me. Guess you'll be trying to get her number now. Well, let me tell you something, sistah. Looks can be deceiving. You would be wise not to count me out."

"I'm not counting you out, Jennifer, and I'm not trying to blow you off either. It's just that Deacon Robinson is waiting on this report I'm typing. If I hear of anybody with an extra ticket, I'll call you."

"Never mind. I bet I know who'll have a ticket that I won't have to beg for. You handle your business while I give your boss a call."

"You do that, Jennifer."

Jennifer ended the call and immediately called the church

offices. Unlike Nate, Deacon Robinson's private line number hadn't changed.

"What can I do for you, Sister Stevens?" Deacon Robinson asked after her greeting.

"What?" Jennifer purred. "No 'powerful pretty' greeting for me today?"

"Well now," the deacon chuckled. "Seeing as to how I can't see you, that type of greeting over the phone would be an assumption. An accurate one, I'm sure."

Jennifer smiled. *This is going to be easy. Can't believe I didn't think to call him first, instead of player-hatin' Patricia with her mousy looking self.* "They say beauty is in the eye of the beholder," she continued. "And if I may be so bold, it would be my pleasure for you to behold my beauty next month at the church's holiday ball."

"I'll look forward to it," Deacon Robinson said after a slight hesitation.

"Wonderful! I knew I could count on you."

"You can probably count on many people to behold your beauty, Sister Stevens."

"That too," Jennifer laughed. "But I knew I could count on you for a ticket to the dinner. I'm sure you're all too aware of how difficult they were to get, that they were sold out within a week."

"Excuse me, Sister Stevens, but I think we have a misunderstanding here. You don't already have your ticket? You're not already going to the ball?" Deacon Robinson knew that she wasn't; Nate wouldn't have allowed it.

"No, but I am now. And I must say I'm looking forward to your finally getting the date you've been asking for forever."

Deacon Robinson cleared his throat. "But that's just it, Sister Stevens. In this conversation, I didn't ask you. You asked me. And while I'm flattered, I'm rather old school. When it comes to women and dating, I like to do the asking. Now, if you're at the festivities, I'll make it a point to greet you. But I don't have an extra ticket."

"Deacon Robinson, I'm sure a man of your importance could get another ticket if you asked for it."

"On the contrary, Sister Stevens. All of the tickets for Reverend's dinner are not only sold out, but there's a waiting list for cancellations. They became a hot item after a few celebrity names were leaked who would be attending. If you'd like, I'll transfer you over to the secretary who can put you on the waiting list."

For an entire month, Jennifer tried and failed to secure a ticket to the coveted preball dinner with Nate and his fiancée. Now she stood steaming, watching with the hordes of others who stood across the drive from the ballroom entrance, hoping to glimpse someone famous, or their beloved pastor and soon-to-be first lady as they exited their limos. She watched with loathing as well-dressed couples in tuxedos and gowns beamed for photographers the church's PR team had hired, before showing their ticket and making their way inside.

Her breath caught in her throat when Nate arrived. He looked dashing in his tailored, navy tux, and Destiny was positively radiant in a Vera Wang original. The onlookers cheered, most of them having fallen in love with Destiny's beauty and charm. *But will that love continue when they find out she was a teenaged whore?* Jennifer glowered as she watched them pose for the cameras and wave at the well-wishers. When her attempts at getting a ticket failed, she had tried everything to reach Nate directly, including sending a certified letter to his home. It had been returned, unopened.

She remembered the last phone call. She'd told his secretary that she was Jennifer Stevens, his former manager, who wanted to talk to him about a small but significant matter that had happened in New Orleans approximately two years ago.

She'd had the secretary repeat the message back to her, and asked that it be delivered verbatim. She'd sat and waited to hear his voice on the line, sure that with the baby hint he would take her call.

After a few moments, the secretary returned to the line. "The Reverend says he is unavailable to speak to or see you, now or in the future. He suggested you make an appointment with one of the associate ministers regarding any matters you'd like to discuss."

Now that she'd seen the first couple's grand entrance, a frustrated Jennifer decided to leave the throng of onlookers and go home. After witnessing the exclusive set entering for their private dinner, she had no desire to be one of the regular people at the program later on. She made her way around the crowd, crossed the drive, and was just about to enter the elevator for underground parking when a couple exiting their limo caught her eye. It was a stately and elegant looking Deacon Robinson, with a date. Jennifer's eyes narrowed as she beheld the woman on his arm, complementing him nicely in a simple black dress with beaded shawl. Perhaps it was intuition or coincidence, but the woman suddenly looked up and caught Jennifer staring. Patricia's brows arched slightly before she turned to walk with Deacon Robinson into the hall.

Jennifer sat in her car, her fingers tapping out an erratic beat on the steering wheel. She refused to cry, because that would be acknowledgment that she had been defeated. Why couldn't she get Nate to talk to her, to let her back into his life? If he married Destiny, she would take the leftovers—being covered whenever he could. Because the truth of it was she was in love with Nate Thicke, more than she'd ever loved anyone else. "I'll try one more time to get him to talk to me," she said out loud as she started her car. "And if he won't listen . . . I'll just have to find someone who will."

45

What God Has Joined

Destiny couldn't believe it—her wedding day had arrived. From late November, when Nate had phoned with the news that he couldn't wait until June to marry her, until now, life had been a whirlwind: moving from Louisiana to Nettie's house, a barrage of meetings with Katherine, Simone, and a resort wedding planner, romantic yet innocent moments with Nate, caring for his son, and teleconferenced counseling with the Montgomerys and Brooks.

The counseling was definitely strengthening Nate and Destiny's bond. Each had been encouraged to let go of past attachments and expectations concerning the other, and to squelch individual desires that didn't benefit both. "Constant communication is a must," Vivian had stated during their first conversation. "Talk about everything, all the time. Don't give a negative thought or assumption a chance to grow."

"Destiny? Are you okay?" Simone knew they had time, but Destiny had been in the bathroom for forty-five minutes.

"Fine, Mom. I'm about to get out of the tub now."

"Remember to rub yourself liberally with that oil I brought you," Katherine added from her perch in the resort suite's massive living room. "You want your body to feel like silk tonight."

"The way Nate's been sniffing around my house since she's

been here?" Nettie replied as she gazed out the floor-to-ceiling windows. "That girl could feel like steel wool and he'd still be happy!"

"Mother, Nettie, would you like a cup of tea? I brought a special lavender blend to help calm our nerves."

"That's probably a good idea," Katherine said as she joined her daughter in the kitchen. "After all that fussing I did about not having a big church wedding, I'm actually glad we're here. Everything is so convenient, and with the resort handling all of the wedding details, this feels like I'm on vacation!"

It was true. Katherine had not been pleased with her granddaughter's decision to marry in Turks and Caicos. She had wanted Nate and Destiny's wedding to rival the biggest Texas had seen. Katherine's wedding ceremony had taken place in Naomi's living room, and no family witnessed Simone and Mark's hasty Las Vegas exchange. So Katherine's dream of being a part of an elaborate wedding ceremony had rested in Destiny. But her granddaughter had had other plans.

"Five hundred! I want a big marriage, Kiki, not a big wedding," she'd said, echoing her new mentor Tai Brook's words. This after Katherine had suggested the number as a proper amount of guests for someone of Nate's stature. Kiki had thought the Rosewood Mansion on Turtle Creek would have been an adequate backdrop, followed by a sit-down dinner and dancing with a live orchestra. Their counselors had encouraged a more subdued joining, especially in light of the fact they already had a child. The plan was for them to marry quietly, honeymoon, and then announce both their marriage and Benjamin the Sunday following their return. King would come from Kansas City to make the announcement along with Nate, and to show his and Total Truth's support for what would at the very least be seen as an instant family and at the most could be viewed as a scandal.

"Destiny, the masseuse is here," Nettie said after answering the knock on their door. "The hair stylist and makeup artist will come in an hour. It's time to get this show on the road, darlin'."

The relaxed atmosphere in the women's suite was in total contrast to the party central mode taking place with the men. Mark and Nate played a trash-talking game of dominoes, while Thomas entertained Derrick and King with zany stories from the many weddings over which he'd presided.

"So the man asked his friend how to spice up his marriage, and the man told him to have an affair. The man said, 'But what if my wife finds out?' His friend told him that we were living in the twenty-first century, so he should just go home and be up-front with the woman. So he did. 'I want to have an affair to spice up our marriage,' he told her. Nate's grandfather Thomas paused with great relish to deliver the punch line. "His wife looked at him and said, 'I already tried that . . . it don't work!'"

At exactly seven P.M., Destiny entered a flower-filled garden, and outshone the most exotic bloom. Her gown was simple yet stunning, a pink Maggie Sottero original, with yards of taffeta and exquisite beading. Her hair was pulled up in a loose chignon, with tendrils falling artfully around her face and down her back. The jewelry she wore were gifts from Nate: the necklace from her seventeenth birthday and the three-carat princess diamond engagement ring he'd given her Christmas Day. Tears came to her eyes when she saw Nate. She could have fainted with joy.

In the absence of her father, and in light of the history with Nate that both her mother and grandmother shared, Destiny had chosen to walk to her man seemingly unescorted. But privately, Destiny had asked God to be by her side, and she felt His presence keenly. An unusual calm enveloped her as she closed the distance between herself and her future. The slightest smile danced around her lips, and her eyes twinkled.

Nate's heart stopped as he watched Destiny come to him. *She's beautiful, and she's mine.* While he'd felt he couldn't bare it, he was grateful for the three months he'd gone without sex. Derrick had been right—it made him want Destiny all the more, and allowed him to look forward to a very special wedding night, in a way he couldn't have, had their intimacy continued uninterrupted. He had to change his thoughts to cool his growing ardor, so he turned to Nettie, winked, and then turned back to his bride.

As Thomas Thicke officiated, a dozen witnesses looked on. In addition to Nettie, Katherine, Simone, and Mark, Nate's two sisters, Destiny's best friend Adam—with whom she'd reconnected—the Brooks, the Montgomerys, and the young wedding planner who'd become Destiny's friend all beamed as Nate and Destiny exchanged their vows. Elder Elijah had expressed his desire to attend, but a nasty bout of pneumonia prevented him from making the trip. For the marrying couple's family members who were present, however, the significance of this occasion was not lost on them. For the first time in their long, sometimes laborious, often lascivious, intertwined history, a Noble woman was marrying a Thicke man.

After repeating the traditional wedding vows, Nate and Destiny completed their ceremony with their own declarations.

"I remember the moment you captured my heart," Nate said, his eyes shining with unshed tears. "And from that cool November day until now, my heart has beat only for you. You are the better half, who has made me a better man. You are the amazing woman who has ensured my lineage through our beautiful son, Benjamin. And you are the woman whom I will love into the afterlife. Without a shadow of a doubt, baby, you are my destiny."

Destiny wiped away tears as she collected herself to say her vows. For a moment, she wondered if she could get through them, when all she wanted to do was weep with joy. But with a deep breath, she once again felt the presence of Spirit. When she spoke, her voice was soft, but strong.

"It seems I've loved you forever, Nathaniel Eli Thicke. You

were not only my first love, but you've been my only love. My singular prayer to God was to become your wife. God answers prayer." Destiny stopped a moment as the tears threatened again. "Now I have a new prayer: that from this day forward, to be the only woman you'll ever want or need. Because there's one thing for sure: you are the one and only man for me. There's never been another, and there will never be another. You are my now and always."

By now, a couple of the men and all of the women were wiping away tears. Even Reverend Thomas had to clear his throat before closing the ceremony. "And now, by the power invested in me," he boomed in his eloquent preacher voice, "I now pronounce you man and wife. What God has joined together, let no man put asunder."

46

Bliss

Nate stared at Destiny's freshly showered, naked body. He was drowning in love for her, even more since coming together for the first time in three months. They'd barely made it inside their suite before he was all over her, taking off her dress as he hungrily kissed her, hastily removing the lacy white panties she wore. He'd stripped off his tuxedo, leaving it in a heap next to Destiny's ten-thousand-dollar designer gown. That he was treating such expensive clothing so carelessly hardly mattered. All Nate had wanted was Destiny, and within minutes of entering their suite, he was inside her.

That was two hours ago. Now, he lay next to his wife, feeding her grapes, strawberries, and kiwi from the fruit tray that had accompanied their elaborate room service dinner. Destiny glowed with adoration as she ate from her husband's hand . . . and fed him.

"I apologize for the urgency with which I . . . consummated our marriage," he murmured, placing whispery kisses along Destiny's neck and shoulders. "But I needed you so badly. . . ."

Destiny turned and placed one of her legs over his. "You never have to apologize for making love to me, Nate. Fast, slow, however we do it, it is always wonderful."

The two lovers were quiet a while, listening to the CD of love songs that King and Tai had compiled for them as part of their wedding gift. One particular song Destiny had played over and over. It was by a group she'd never heard of and that Nate barely knew.

"What's their name again?" she asked.

"Switch," Nate replied.

"I love this song," she whispered.

Nate kissed her, and softly sang the newly learned lyrics in her ear. ". . . so good, I know you won't forget it. There'll never be a better love . . ."

Once the song ended, Nate rolled on top of Destiny. "We've had fast," he said huskily, flicking her nipple with his tongue. "Now I'm going to love you slowly, my destiny. I'm going to love you until we can no longer move."

Destiny's giggle was swallowed up as Nate's warm mouth descended on hers. He ravished her mouth with his stiff, skilled tongue. She moaned as he found her pleasure button and teased it with his finger. "Come on," he said. "Let's heighten our pleasure."

With that, he lifted Destiny from the bed and walked through the bedroom's already open patio doors.

"Nate! What if someone sees us?"

"No one will see us. This area of the beach is available only to the guests in this home." A millionaire friend of Derrick's had told Nate about the villa, a privately owned, ten-million-dollar masterpiece with every luxury imaginable. As Nate spread the blanket out on the sand, he made a mental note to call and thank Cy Taylor.

"Come lay down," he said to Destiny. After she complied, he knelt before her and, starting with her toes, began licking her skin as if it were candy. The wetness from his tongue combined with the subtle warm island breeze and sent Destiny's desire into orbit. She climaxed almost immediately, as soon as

Nate's tongue found and parted her feminine folds, and he melded his mouth to her sweetness. But Nate wasn't finished. He had only just begun.

"I love you," he whispered, as he directed her onto her knees, where he continued his oral assault. He was determined that no part of his bride's body would miss his touch this night, that he would love her as thoroughly and completely as humanly possible. He slid between her legs and continued to suckle her. From this position, however, Destiny could add her note to the love symphony, and she immediately placed her mouth over his massive instrument . . . and began to play.

After almost an hour of foreplay, the two lovers once again became one. Destiny's eyes never left Nate's as she slid down onto his long, hard shaft. Nate knew he beheld a goddess as he watched her breasts sway with her movements, as she rose and fell, over and again, matching Nate's upward thrusts. He held her hips and led the dance, sometimes slow and leisurely, sometimes fast and intense. They made love in old positions and invented new ones. They moved from the blanket by the ocean, onto the patio, and after making love there, went back into the house . . . for more.

"Nate," Destiny panted, once he'd laid her on the bed. "It's too much love; baby. I can't . . ."

"Just a little more, my destiny," Nate pleaded in a whisper. "I can't get enough of you." Nate placed several pillows under her hips, and then spread her legs and entered her a final time, setting a slow leisurely rhythm as he kissed her breasts, her face, ran his fingers through her hair. His thrusts were deep, to her core, with him pulling out to the tip and plummeting slowly, so that she could feel every inch of him, and every ounce of his love. Destiny's weariness fled as passion once again ignited. Their eyes never left each other as after several moments Destiny once again felt the tremors of an oncoming climax.

"Nate, I love you!" she whined before going over the edge

of an orgasmic cliff. She grazed his skin with her fingernails as he pushed even deeper, ascending to a frenzied pace before he too went free-falling. Afterward, he stayed inside her, lay on top of her. And the two went into a blissful sleep—totally spent, totally satisfied, totally still.

47

Trading Videos

"Damn, girl, I can't believe you did this!" Kirk said, as the image of two naked bodies came onto the screen. He stood next to Melody in her Dallas apartment, in front of the television.

"I told you I did it," she replied smugly, before turning the video off after less than a minute had passed. "Just wanted to show you enough so you'd know it was true."

"I can't believe Reverend let you roll tape. Him being all high profile and what not."

"He doesn't know, and nobody else will either," Melody said, as she put the DVD back in its case and tossed it on top of a pile of other movies. "Watching myself on tape is a private fetish. And just so you know . . . it'll be you and me on camera tonight. You down with that?"

Kirk nodded yes, even as his mind whirred with possibilities.

Melody had met Kirk two weeks ago, when she'd driven to Palestine to see Destiny. The two hadn't spoken since her explicitly informative phone call back in August and since then, Destiny had moved and changed her cell number. Melody had gone to Palestine to try and reach out to her old friend. She hadn't expected Destiny to jump up and down at the news of her sleeping with Nate, but she hadn't expected Destiny to to-tally sever their friendship either. From what Melody had heard, Nate was screwing several women in his congregation. She didn't think it was that big a deal. Destiny did.

"You knew we were engaged, Melody. Why did you sleep with him?"

"I didn't know it was to you," Melody had lied when she realized how upset her news made Destiny. "I only found that out afterward. That's what you get for keeping your little se-cret, for not letting me up in your biz-ness," Melody had added playfully, hoping to bring their camaraderie back.

"You're all up in it now though, aren't you?" Destiny spat back. "And you couldn't wait to call and tell me. Is this how LA bitches treat their friends? Sleep with their men and then brag about it?"

"Girl, please. You act like I'm the only one fucking your man. Plus, to hear you tell it, there wasn't anything going on with you and your pastor. You should have told me up front that you were in love and shit. Then maybe I wouldn't have done it." In reality Melody knew that not only would she still have done it, she would do it again.

"Look, girl," Melody continued when Destiny didn't re-spond. "I'm sorry for sleeping with your man. It won't happen again, okay?"

"No, Melody," Destiny said in a voice filled with sadness. "It is not okay."

That had been the end of the conversation. The next time Melody called Destiny, her number had changed. Melody began to feel the full impact of what she'd done. Had gaining another notch on her man belt been worth losing a friendship?

Melody went to Palestine that Sunday hoping a sincere, face-to-face apology would make a difference. But when she'd arrived, she'd found out Destiny and Nate were on their honeymoon. She'd learned this after stopping at a gas station and flirting with a cute guy whose name she later learned was Kirk. He told her of his former connection with Nate, and that he used to be a member of Gospel Truth. She'd asked him where she could find something good to eat. He'd showed her, first at a restaurant and later at his apartment.

Melody walked to her closet, pulled out an outfit, and laid it on the bed. "I'm going to take a shower," she said to Kirk. "Want to join me?"

"Naw, let me lay here and chill a minute. I'll take one when you get out."

"Well, make it quick cause you're taking me shopping."

Kirk watched Melody's massive assets as they jiggled behind her. *She's young, but she's been around,* he thought, remembering their wild sex. A woman like Melody wasn't someone Kirk would ever get serious about, but her kind had their advantages.

Obviously the reverend thinks so too, Kirk thought derisively. *Preaching on Sunday, pumping on Monday.* "And he had the nerve to fire me for inappropriate conduct to the ministry?" The more Kirk thought about his unceremonious firing, the angrier he became. "Muthafucka couldn't even face me himself," he mumbled. "Had one of his staff members do that shit." Kirk was angry, and hurt. He'd looked up to Nate Thicke, had thought to follow in his footsteps, go to seminary and eventually become Gospel Truth's number-two man. Nate had led him to believe that was possible, had said he was looking for strong men to help him lead the masses. As associate minister at Gospel Truth, Kirk had felt important, respected. That's why he'd had Nate's back, even after he began traveling with the ministry and learned of Nate and Jennifer's intimate affair. He'd assumed there were others, but he never would have guessed his suave pastor would be with somebody like Melody. Kirk shook his head. That fast girl was barely legal, and had been passed around more than grape juice during the Lord's Supper.

The longer Kirk thought, the madder he became. *He's the reason I'm in the shape I'm in.* Because of the conditions surrounding Kirk's release, the church had given him no severance pay, and he was not entitled to unemployment benefits from the state. Kirk had always lived above his means, and once he'd started working for the ministry, visiting Nate's home and seeing how his mentor lived, his spending had gone into overdrive. He'd maxed out all of his credit cards trying to stay in designer wear, and had leased a high-end car he couldn't afford. Now his apartment complex was threatening eviction for nonpayment and he was hiding his BMW so the dealer couldn't repossess it.

"That man owes me," Kirk said, eyeing the pile of DVDs on the floor. "And I'm about to get mine."

Kirk and Melody left the apartment, went shopping, ate, and then returned to her home. Not long afterward, Melody set up the camera in the bedroom and Kirk tried to put on the performance of his life. When he left the house several hours later, Melody had a new video to add to her collection. And Kirk had one of her videos to add to his.

48

First Family

Gospel Truth's temporary edifice was packed to the gills. Even in the overflow, there was not an empty seat to be had. It was Nate's first Sunday of preaching since getting married, and the official unveiling of the church's new first lady. It seemed every member on the books had shown up to see for themselves the woman who had finally captured their pastor's heart.

There was an organized chaos happening behind the scenes, in the executive offices. Destiny chatted with Tai Brook and Tai's college-age daughter, whom Tai thought would be good for Destiny to know. Nettie, Katherine, and the nanny fussed over little Benjamin. Nate and King Brook had their heads together on the other side of the office. Associate ministers came and went with messages for their pastor. Reverend Thomas Thicke studied his Bible in a corner, various security personnel monitored the halls, and the hostesses were busy restocking the table of light breakfast fare that had been spread.

"For Destiny's sake, I hope this goes well," Nate said. He'd shown a rare case of nerves ever since entering the church.

"Think positive, my man. And remember that church folk can be fairly forgiving, especially when a Christian in question does the right thing. Sure, some will be upset that you kept your child a secret. But I believe most will support you, now that the two of you have married."

Thirty minutes later, the party from the executive offices joined the parishioners in the main sanctuary. The only ones still behind the executive office doors were King, Tai, Nate, Destiny, and a member of security.

"You look absolutely amazing," Nate said, hugging Destiny lightly.

"It's because I'm standing next to you," she replied.

"Whatever happens out there, remember I love you."

Destiny kissed Nate lightly on the mouth. "And I you, Reverend Thicke."

The applause began as soon as members spotted Destiny walking beside her husband. The church came to its feet, as the couple and King Brook made their way to the pulpit. Tai joined her daughter and Katherine, in the first row. Nate and Destiny beamed as they accepted the show of appreciation. Nate finally held up his hand in an attempt to quiet the crowd. The clapping went on for several minutes, however, becoming louder after Destiny leaned over and gave Nate a peck on the cheek, with a couple whoops thrown in for good measure.

King walked to the podium and reached for the microphone. "Praise the Lord," he said, motioning for the audience to quiet down. "Ladies and gentlemen, saints and soldiers for the Lord. It gives me great pleasure to present to you the Gospel Truth first family—Reverend and Mrs. Nathaniel Eli Thicke!"

The clapping started again, accompanied this time by the newly formed Good Gospel band, the church's in-house music team. They played a lively number that the younger members knew was a song from gospel's newest darlings, Yadah.

After the clapping subsided for a second time, Nate joined King at the podium while Destiny went and sat between her grandmother and her mother-in-law.

"Isn't she lovely?" Nate said, gesturing to his wife. "Isn't she wonderful?" he continued, as some began to clap again. "Isn't she precious?" he added, before breaking out in a dazzling smile. "Okay, y'all, I'm going to leave Stevie Wonder alone this morning." He paused a moment, becoming serious. "First and foremost, I want to thank God for the gift he's given me, my destiny." Nate winked at his wife, then looked out over the crowd. "Today is indeed a moment of celebration. And for me, it is also a time of confession." A very soft rustling began in the crowd. "My heart is a bit heavy because of a secret I've been keeping from you, my church family. It was wrong of me to do it, and today I want to right this wrong, and ask for your forgiveness."

At this statement, some members whispered loudly among themselves while others stared openly at Destiny.

Nate took a deep breath. His voice remained strong. "A couple anniversaries ago, some of you met and admired a beautiful little boy, a child brought here by Simone Simmons, Destiny's mother, and her husband, Mark. Many of you, most of you I'm sure, assumed the boy was hers. At my request, she did nothing to dispel this assumption. But I stand before you today with the truth: that child, Benjamin, is my son—mine and Destiny's."

For a split second, the audience was stunned into silence. "Oh, my God," Verniece cried from the back of the sanctuary. That utterance opened up a flurry of other reactions as people all over the church began talking at once. Some people even stood up to get a better look at Destiny, only now their looks were of condemnation instead of admiration. One woman got up and walked out of the church, creating a chain reaction in which several other women, and a few men, followed. The voices grew louder as members took sides. Those who in mere seconds had decided to forgive their pastor began shouting at the ones who clearly hadn't. Nate stood motionless, unsure of what to do.

King looked out at the beginnings of World War III and decided to take control. He walked to the podium, gently took the microphone from his shell-shocked brother, and turned to face the crowd.

"This is the house of the Lord," he said with authority. "And you will respect God's house!'

The firmness with which he spoke brought an immediate hush over the audience. "This news is understandably upsetting to many of you," he continued, in a softer tone. "I'm sure you have questions, comments, concerns. Some of you may feel hurt, others betrayed by your pastor's actions. And you have a right to your feelings. Reverend Thicke's actions were wrong. But the true test of a Christian, and of this church, is not how you react in times of triumph, but rather how you respond in times of trial, like right now. Your brother has asked God for forgiveness, and has been forgiven. He has come to the Total Truth Association and asked for forgiveness, and has been forgiven. And now, he stands before you. Will you forgive?"

This question was argued for hours, even days after the service—from member to member and coast to coast. It seemed everyone and their mama weighed in with an opinion. Fortunately for Nate and Destiny, the people who mattered in their lives forgave them. But what would really put a hitch in their giddy-up were the ones who didn't.

49

Come Sunday

Conversations with Carla was on but Jennifer wasn't watching. She couldn't have cared less about the guest who had children she couldn't control. "Join the crowd," she muttered before switching off the television. Jennifer felt she hadn't been in control since Reverend Thicke had left her life. To make matters worse, the savings she'd built up while earning the big bucks managing Nate had dwindled. Another month, two tops, and she'd have to get a job. Getting a job meant that she'd have to leave Palestine. The more Jennifer thought about it, the more she realized she should have left town months ago.

Relocating had been her intention in December, right after seeing Pat and Deacon Robinson together at the dinner party. On top of seeing Nate and Destiny, this surprise coupling had been almost too much. Belatedly, Jennifer had realized she liked the attention Deacon Robinson had paid her. She never took him seriously, not beyond the number of zeroes she guessed were behind the first number in his bank account. But she'd felt a twinge of envy seeing Patricia on his arm, and that had surprised her. She'd thought about him later that night, how kind he was, and patient. James Robinson had diligently asked her out for months, even as "powerful pretty" continually refused his advances. He'd said one day the invites would cease. And they had.

Actually, James had had little opportunity to ask Jennifer out, since she hadn't been to church since before Nate's wedding. She'd gone a few times after Destiny arrived, but couldn't stand to see everyone fawning over the soon-to-be first lady. She went to the other Baptist church in town a couple times, but their service was so boring and the pastor so old that one time he closed his eyes while sitting in the pulpit and Jennifer thought he might have died. After then, she'd relied on television for her weekly Word, watching famous ministers from all over the country—and Nate.

The weeks of inactivity were beginning to take their toll. Jennifer began overeating, letting herself go. It had been weeks since she'd had a mani-pedi and her hair could definitely use a perm. She realized she was entering into a depression, but wasn't sure how to stop the downward spiral. *I've got to get myself together,* she thought to herself yet again.

But not today, she decided as she reached for the copy of *LA Gospel* that she'd scanned a thousand times. A beaming Mr. and Mrs. Nathaniel Thicke adorned the cover while a pictorial spread of their island nuptials took up four pages and the centerfold inside. She tried to view the pictures dispassionately, and it was starting to hurt less each time she viewed them. But she kept imagining herself in the photo, in place of Destiny, by his side. *I was so close . . .* Jennifer angrily turned the magazine page, determined to turn a page in her life as well. She knew she had to move on, but how? Where should she go? Returning to Mount Zion Progressive Baptist Church didn't appeal to her, although her pastor, King Brook, had said she was welcome.

Jennifer kept thumbing through the magazine, making herself read the articles she'd previously ignored. There was an informative one on Shabach, who'd rededicated his life to

Christ after being cleared of rape charges. There was a large ad, and accompanying advertorial about SOS—Sanctity of Sister-hood—a popular women's conference that was holding its annual retreat in August. For the first time, the retreat would be held out of the country, in Mexico. The resort sounded beautiful and the topics relevant. Carla Chapman was listed as one of the speakers. *Maybe I'll go,* she thought.

Jennifer yawned, stretched, and thought about what she could fix for dinner. She was just about to put down the magazine when a small article near the bottom of the next to last page caught her eye. It was about the gubernatorial race in Louisiana, one in which a decidedly right-wing, conservative Republican incumbent was being challenged by a moderate Democrat openly running on Christian principles. "Now that's a switch," she said out loud as she continued reading. Her mouth flew open when she read the name of the candidate: Mark Simmons. *Simone's husband!* She continued reading and grew more intrigued when she read a quote from Mark's pastor. "I told Mark that God belonged in politics as much as the devil did. And we all know the devil is constantly walking the halls of political buildings everywhere. I fully endorse Mark Simmons. He is a man with the right principles and values to lead Louisiana toward a new day."

The pastor's name sounded familiar but at first she couldn't place it. And then she remembered: the hotel in New York City and the television interview she stumbled upon. That's where she first heard Ed Smith speak, and now she knew where he pastored, in Baton Rouge. The wheels started turning before Jennifer could get off the couch and go to the computer. She needed to schedule a hair appointment and go buy a new suit. Because come Sunday, Jennifer would once again be in church.

50

Pulpit Pimps

"Be not deceived, God is not mocked. Whatsoever a man sows . . . that shall he also reap!" Reverend Smith preached with fervor, mopping sweat from his brow with a large, white handkerchief. "If you sow greed, you're going to reap greed."

"Amen!" various members of the congregation shouted.

"Preach, preacher!" one of the deacons encouraged as he stood up.

"If you sow lies, you're going to reap lies. If you sow fornication, you're going to reap fornication. If you sow false doctrines, you're going to reap false doctrines. But if you sow Jesus!" Reverend Smith held the first syllable until dozens more members had jumped to their feet. "If you sow Jesus, then you'll reap Jesus. You'll reap peace, a peace that passes all understanding."

"Say it!" yelled someone from the choir stand.

"You'll reap joy!"

"Hallelujah," an elderly church mother agreed.

"You'll reap everlasting life. With Jesus! Jesus! Jesus!"

Reverend Smith's sermon ended amid furious clapping and cries of joy. The choir, small but boisterous, began singing a Baptist hymnal, *Jesus Is All the World to Me.* Reverend Smith walked to his chair, sat, and rested his forehead against steepled fingers.

He's got a wide reach for someone so small, Jennifer thought as she observed the minister she'd researched online. She'd learned this compact man, five-seven, eight tops, Jennifer guessed, was a mover and shaker in the Baptist denomination and the state of Louisiana. His church managed several programs that bene-fited the city, including education for the homeless, food banks for the hungry, and a low-cost thrift shop for others in need. The big, round glasses he wore, along with his near-bald head and flowing white robe, gave him the countenance of a fly, es-pecially as he sat bowed and hunched over. Jennifer stifled the urge to laugh. Fortunately, her attention was diverted as an as-sociate minister stood and opened the doors to the church, inviting anyone wanting to give their life to Christ or become a member of First Baptist to come and sit in one of several chairs that had been hastily placed down front, near the pulpit.

Jennifer watched a middle-aged woman and a teenaged girl make their way to the area where the young associate min-ister beckoned. She also recognized Simone Simmons, stand-ing in the front row next to her husband, Mark. *They look alike,* Jennifer concluded, thinking of Nate and the man at whom she now stared. *Except he's bulkier, and a bit shorter, I think.* He also had the slightest traces of gray appearing at his temples, which gave him an air of gentility and importance somehow.

After the benediction, Jennifer shook hands with the woman seated next to her and pondered what to do next. The answer made itself known as she watched Reverend Smith, along with two associate ministers, make their way to the farthest aisle against the wall and begin walking toward the entrance. At the same time, she noticed that Mark and Simone followed a small group of people to a side door and walked through it. Imme-diately she remembered when she'd been ushered through side and back doors, into various church's executive and VIP areas, where she'd waited as Nate held court, conducted interviews, or visited with the pastor. The seed of bitterness that had lay dormant in her soul since her ouster, and had grown roots while looking at Nate's wedding pictures, grew further in this moment. She remembered why she'd come to this church, what she and Reverend Smith had in common: they both despised Nate Thicke.

Jennifer tried to ignore her aching feet as the line to shake the pastor's hand inched forward. Instead, she focused on the reverend, and how he seemed to connect intimately no matter who greeted him, from children to old people, male and female alike. As she drew closer and could hear his comments, she was impressed at how he seemed to know little tidbits about each person who shook his hand, something personal, or something he remembered.

"I haven't forgotten about that grade card you're going to show me, Bobby," he said to a pimply faced teenager.

"Tamika, I'll be by on Tuesday to pray for your baby," he promised a young mother.

"Miss Fields, I do believe that's a new hat," he complimented an elderly member. "You're looking mighty fancy!"

Jennifer began to see how this caustic minister could maintain a loyal following. Ed Smith made people feel special. "This is my first time at your church and I really enjoyed it," she said when she finally reached him.

"Well, then, hopefully it won't be your last," Reverend Smith replied.

"I especially appreciated what you said about reaping what you sow, and about certain ministers sowing questionable crops. I used to work for a popular church, and I know what you're saying is true."

"Is that so?" Reverend Smith said, suddenly intrigued.

Jennifer lowered her voice so that the member waiting behind her couldn't hear. "I'd rather not say his name here, but you are well acquainted with his ministry. I saw you on a talk show in New York several months ago. You mentioned some things that . . . pertained to the church I attended."

Reverend Smith's eyes narrowed as he peered at Jennifer. "What's your name, sister?"

"Stevens, Jennifer Stevens."

The minister motioned to one of his associates, who pulled out a card and handed it to Jennifer. "Give my office a call in the morning," Reverend Smith said. He then turned and greeted the next parishioner, effectively ending their brief but pivotal chat.

At five minutes till the hour, Jennifer pulled in to the First Baptist parking lot. She wanted to be exactly on time for her three o'clock appointment with Reverend Smith. Jennifer stepped into the administrative area of the church, which was in a building behind but connected to the larger sanctuary. She was greeted by a lone secretary and directed to the pastor's office, a few feet beyond where the elderly woman sat. It was refreshing not to have to deal with the hoopla that now surrounded Nate's ministry, or that she knew outsiders experienced at Mount Zion. Here she'd simply announced her name and been directed to the senior pastor's domain.

"Sister Stevens," Reverend Smith said as he walked around the desk. He offered his hand, which Jennifer shook.

"Good afternoon, Reverend Smith. Thanks for agreeing to meet with me."

"I found your comment yesterday very intriguing," the minister answered honestly. "Can I get you something to drink? Coffee? Tea?"

"Whatever you're having is fine."

Reverend Smith hit his intercom button and asked the secretary to bring two coffees. Then he rocked back in his chair and looked at Jennifer.

"I take it you are no longer with this ministry you mentioned yesterday?" he asked.

"No, Reverend Smith. Once again, I'm looking for a church home."

"You say 'again.' Have you been moving around, Sister

Stevens? Because in order to grow spiritually, you need to be planted, in good ministerial soil you understand. You need to find a place and stay there so your instruction can be steady and strong."

"That had been my intention when I joined Gospel Truth."

At the mention of Nate's church, Reverend Smith stopped rocking in his chair. "You belonged to Nate Thicke's ministry?" he asked quietly.

"Yes, sir. I also worked as his manager, helping him promote his first book. Without wishing to beat my own drum, it was my work that helped make *Have It All* a best seller."

Reverend Stevens rubbed his chin, continuing to observe Jennifer as the secretary brought in a tray of coffee with sugar and cream. The silence continued as each doctored their brew, a liberal dose of sugar and cream for the reverend, a small amount of cream, no sugar, for Jennifer. They each took a sip, and then looked back at each other.

"I believe your coming here is an answer to my prayer," Reverend Smith said after a moment, and another sip of coffee. "I've been toying around with an idea for the last year or so, but didn't know exactly how to get the project started, or what steps to take after that. I think you just might be the perfect person to help me. This is a personal project of mine, still dealing in ministry but separate from the church."

Jennifer remained quiet, trying to guess what kind of project the minister could possibly be talking about. She didn't have to wonder long.

"I could use someone with your experience, Sister Stevens. It just so happens that I want to write a book myself. One that deals with what I've been espousing in my sermons, as I did yesterday. It's a message I've been delivering for the past several years now, about the false doctrines that have sprung up and become the more popular ministries, the ministers leading thousands of congregants to hell every Sunday morning. They're an abomination in the eyes of God, and somebody has to call them out without fear and without holding back. Sister Stevens, I'm the man to do it."

Jennifer hesitated. With all of Nate's faults, and the way he'd treated her the past few months, a part of her still cared about him. She wished that weren't true, but it was. Did she want to be a part of something that could cause him problems? Did she want her name attached to a work that criticized megaministries? Most of the Total Truth ministers ran mega-churches. What would Reverend Smith say about these pastors she admired?

"I'm not sure, Reverend Smith. I don't believe all mega-churches are bad, nor do I believe all megachurch pastors preach a message that is unbiblical. I guess I'd have to hear more about what the book would entail, before I could decide whether or not it is something I could be a part of."

Reverend Smith leaned forward and put his elbows on his desk. "Sister Stevens, we're living in the last days. This is no time for foolishness, no time to be fearful about standing up for God. I should add that you will be well compensated for your time and expertise, and we could probably find you a paid position in the ministry as well. What I'm trying to say is, you'd be treated like the queen in God's kingdom I know you are, if you decide to help me do His will."

"So I'm right. This book is about megachurches and mega-pastors?"

"Sister Stevens, the title will say it all. This book is going to be about pulpit pimps."

51

A Higher Standard

Verniece made a sound of disgust as the movie credits began to roll on the theater's large screen. "That was just okay," she said to Anne. "If it wasn't for the fact that Derek Luke was in it, I'd demand my money back."

"He does look pretty good," Anne agreed.

"Pretty good? Girl, please. If that fine box of chocolate wasn't too young and already married, I'd move to California just to try and connect."

"Ha! Well, good luck. You'd be joining the millions of others who've moved there with that same intention, trying to date a celebrity."

The women continued talking about the movie, what they liked and especially what they didn't, all the way to Anne's car. Once they'd reached it and got inside, she changed the subject. "You want to go get something to eat?"

"I will but I shouldn't."

"Why not?"

"Haven't you noticed me gaining weight? Ever since I stopped feasting on that Thicke meat, seems like I keep on eating but can't get full."

"You need to come back to church, Verniece," Anne said.

"Why? So I can sit there and think about how much I

can't stand that ho he married? Just seeing her makes me sick, looking all beautiful and acting all perfect, after her butt's been screwing the man on the regular, got pregnant, and then took care of Nate's baby on the down low . . . behind all our backs? And I'm supposed to stay at that church and watch Reverend Thicke in the pulpit like what he did was all right? That shit is scandalous, Anne, and you know it. If he was so serious about wanting forgiveness, why didn't he ask for it back then, when the girl was pregnant? Why did he hide them, wait until their relationship was too legit to quit, and then lay his sins down on the altar? I, for one, didn't believe the 'forgive me, I was wrong' hype. And I'm not alone."

"But like King Brook said, Verniece, if God can forgive him, maybe we should too."

"I'm not forgiving him. And I'm not going back to Gospel Truth."

"I know what you're really mad about. You're mad because Reverend won't cover us anymore. You need to just find somebody else and get your release. 'Cause that's what's got you all frustrated."

"Well, that Nate is no longer hittin' the honey pot definitely does not help matters. I can't lie about that."

"But he's a minister, Anne. He's supposed to be held to a higher standard than us regular Christians. And you know good and well if some regular church folk pulled the same crap that Reverend and his hoity-toity wife just pulled, they'd be given the left foot of fellowship right out the church. It's just like that one minister was saying the other day. It's time to get the pimps out the pulpit."

"Who was saying that?" Anne asked.

"Reverend Ed Smith, out of Baton Rouge."

"Reverend Smith is the last preacher you should be listening to," Anne countered.

"Why? What do you know about Reverend Smith?"

"More than I care to share, trust me."

"Dang, sounds like all of these preachers are jacked up."

"A good number are," Anne said after a pause. "But I believe there are true men and women of God out there too, ones who are living the word they preach about on Sunday."

"Oh, really? Then where are they at?"

Anne thought about an answer for a moment. "You tell me and then we'll both know."

52

Direct and Protect

Lifting the phone from her cheek, Nettie wiped away tears as she relayed the events of a few Sundays ago, when Nate's secret was revealed, and her grandson was introduced to the congregation. "I didn't realize what a burden carrying that secret had been," she admitted. "I guess since the child was in Baton Rouge and not here, it was easier to ignore the situation. There's fallout for sure, and we've lost members. But overall, it looks like Gospel Truth will weather this storm.

"But I am so proud of Nathaniel, Mama Max. It's almost a miracle how he's transformed his life. You know the history of the Thicke men, and for the first time since I've known the history of it . . . one of them is remaining faithful to his wife, has become a one-woman man. I've always known the power of prayer, but God has really showed out this time, praise His holy name!"

"Oh, He's worthy!" Mama Max said in agreement, wiping tears from her eyes as well. "It ain't easy being a man of God. The weight of the world is on their shoulders sometimes. People always talking bad about preachers, but they don't know the half of what they deal with, of what it's like to be called. I married one and birthed another—"

"Same here—"

"And I can tell you from experience that these men, whatever their faults, are carrying out the will of God the best that they know how."

"Well, just look at the Word, Mama Max. Some of those men did terrible things, at least how we look at it, and their names are sho 'nuff written in the lamb's book of life. David and all the men he killed and the women he slept with, Saul killing his thousands, Samson and all the folks he slew, kings ordering the killing of children, fathers sleeping with daughters, Peter denying Christ and then cutting off a man's ear in anger. . . . I could go on and on. And these are our examples! These are men whose stories made it into the Good Book. Folks these days too quick to cut a preacher down and toss him out. But those folks couldn't begin to bear the burden of the saints.

"The minute a preacher shows he's human, we want to crucify him. But what about all the other times, when they are living the Word, doing what they're supposed to? What about the millions of preachers who are living by their Christian conviction and standing on their principles? Where are the articles about them? Who's shining the spotlight on those living *right* for God?"

Nettie was silent, and in a rare moment of affectionate reflection, missed her first husband, Daniel. *For all his faults, he was a good man.* Nettie had seen of him what few others saw: the tears he shed, the pacing he did in the middle of the night, trying to figure out how to minister to the flock in a way that would best benefit them. They hadn't seen how he was with his children, especially his son. And they hadn't seen how he had loved Nettie, stayed with her, even when she didn't share his passion for physical intimacy, even as he fell deeply in love with another woman who did.

"Nettie, you all right?"

"Fine, Mama, just letting my mind roll back."

"Just as long as you don't do that too often. Like that old

baseball player Satchel Paige used to say: 'Don't look back. Something might be gaining on ya!'" Mama Max whooped. "So what's next for y'all? I guess it's the anniversary and then Nate's big night at the Total Truth Conference."

"Yes, and we're celebrating this one in the new sanctuary, praise the name of Jesus."

"Lord, y'all been busy down there in Texas. I don't see how Nate does all the things he does."

"James is the one responsible for the building coming in on time and on budget. That man is a blessing to the ministry, for sure."

"Deacon Robinson?"

"Uh-huh."

"Wonder why that man ain't never been married."

"Hear him tell it, ain't never been tempted!"

"Mercy, Lord." The two women chuckled. "But he's a powerful man of God," Nettie continued. "If he ever does marry, she'll be blessed."

The women continued their conversation, about Nettie's husband, Gordon, and his recent talks of retiring, Mama Max's husband, the Reverend Doctor Pastor Bishop Overseer Mister Stanley Obadiah Meshach Brook Jr., and his talks of coming out of retirement and preaching again, their minister sons and managing daughters. Mama Max vowed that she and the reverend doctor would be at Nate's anniversary next month, and Nettie vowed she'd be there two, and twenty pounds lighter if the good Lord helped her. As often was the case, the two ladies ended the call in prayer.

"Father God," Mama Max said, "once again we thank you for this time of fellowship. We thank you for our health and strength, and for your goodness and mercy, Lord. And we ask you, Lord Jesus, to look after our sons, and all men and women of God who are on the battlefield. Direct them, Lord. Protect them, Jesus. Amen."

53

Naming Names

Jennifer and Ed Smith sat in the den of Ed's stately home. For all his talk about money-hungry preachers, Jennifer had noted the reverend wasn't living too badly himself. His was a southern style home, with large columns out front, black shutters against stark white exterior paint, chandeliers in most of the rooms, and perfectly finished maple floors. Here in the den, they sat in rich leather chairs, burgundy, and drank coffee from fine bone china. A cleaning woman kept Ed's house immaculate. It had been clear to Jennifer from her first visit to his home that Ed Smith didn't think all money was bad, especially the money that could provide this lifestyle.

"I like how the book is coming along, but I think we ought to name names," Ed said. He was pacing the floor with excitement. "Especially since you have proof that the man was committing a crime. Now, we'll have to double check, but I think Nate broke the law when he slept with the girl who's now his wife. You say she had the baby at seventeen?"

Jennifer nodded. "I'm pretty sure. . . ."

"Then he had to have been with her when she was sixteen. And they may have gotten together when she was even younger." Ed Smith clapped his hands with relish. "Exposing this won't just make my book a best seller, it will finally knock that bastard off his high horse."

"And it could also lead to a lawsuit, Ed. We have to be careful."

In the two months since starting to work for Ed Smith, Jennifer's priorities had shifted. Leaving Nate's ministry had been extremely painful, but she'd learned a lot—such as what she did and did not want. She wanted a man, but she didn't want to share him. She wanted to be a part of a high-profile ministry, but she didn't want to just be an employee. She'd also learned that making snap judgments could be costly, such as the one she'd made about James Robinson. She could have been living in the lap of luxury right now, the way she imagined Patricia was doing, but she'd dismissed him as a "dirty old man." Jennifer was determined not to make the same mistake twice, so when Reverend Smith, who was a widower, asked her out to dinner after their second meeting, she'd said yes without hesitation. And that dinner is where her transformation had begun in earnest.

She hadn't meant to tell Ed about her and Nate's sexual liaison. But he had a way of coaxing out information, showing genuine concern for her and her feelings. He could tell there was more to the story involving her dismissal from Gospel Truth. And before the night was over, she'd told all.

"Men like him prey on women like you," Ed had said softly. He took her hand in his and continued. "They take and take and never give. Look at him. You made him who he is with that best-selling book. And as soon as he didn't need you anymore, what did he do? Kicked you to the curb, as the young folk say. And believe me, Jennifer. You're not the only one. Look what he did to that poor girl—stole her innocence, saddled her with a child, and then, when it was convenient for *him*, went and married her so he'd look good. Soon as the time is right, he'll drop her too and get another one. I know those Thicke men. Knew his daddy, Daniel. He carried on right under his wife's nose. Most folks tried to act like they didn't know, but I knew what was happening over there in Palestine. Had a cousin who went to the church for years. Men like him need to be *uncovered*, Jennifer."

Jennifer had almost flinched at his use of this word. "That's what Nate said he was doing with me and the other women," she said softly. "Covering us."

"He's covering up, that's what he's doing. But you and I, working together, can pull off those sheets."

54

No Replacement

Patricia yawned loudly as she unlocked the door to her home. She was weary, not only because of the ten-hour day she'd just worked, but because of the continued uncertainty about her life. After a year and a half of working herself to the bone and even with her new job in the ministry, she was no closer to having a fulfilling personal life than when she'd worked at the post office. Deacon Robinson was rarely in the church office when she was there, and seemed in no hurry to establish a relationship. They'd attended the ball together and had coffee a couple times afterward, but that was it. And even though she knew he'd been swamped with the sanctuary's completion, she couldn't help but wonder if not only lack of time but lack of interest had kept them apart.

On top of this dilemma, Patricia had been busy dealing with her daughter. Carmen had chosen the worst possible time to hang out with "those no good thugs" her mother always warned her about and had gotten herself arrested on drug and weapons charges. The attorney had assured Patricia that Carmen's charges would more than likely get reduced, if not totally dismissed. She'd simply been at the wrong place at the wrong time, with a boy she'd gone to school with. But a zealous prosecutor was trying to tie her in as a knowing accomplice to drug dealing.

Patricia walked to her daughter's bedroom door and quietly opened it. Carmen was in bed, asleep. Patricia sighed, closed the door, and walked down the short hallway to her own bedroom.

Where did I go wrong? she asked herself as she undressed. Granted, Carmen's dad was rarely around and Patricia worked, perhaps too much, to be able to afford their home and those things her daughter wanted. Even with little time together, Patricia felt she and Carmen were reasonably close. It wasn't until their conversation after the arrest that she truly became aware of how much distance there was between them.

"I'm very disappointed in you, Carmen. Hanging around those hardheads, getting arrested. I raised you better than this. I've worked too hard—"

"I said I was sorry, Mama. I don't really want to hear this right now."

"I just spent three thousand dollars that I didn't have bailing your ungrateful butt out of jail. You will sit there and listen to whatever I've got to say, do you hear me? This is what happens when you have no direction in life. You end up in places you shouldn't be, doing things you shouldn't do. I brought you those brochures on junior colleges. Have you looked at them?"

"Mama, I don't want to go to college."

"Why not, Carmen? You're a bright girl!"

Carmen had simply shrugged and kept text messaging.

"Then what about that job fair I told you about? Did you go?"

Carmen's answer had been an exaggerated sigh, one that pushed Patricia precariously close to beating some sense into her daughter and risking possible arrest herself!

"I'm not going to have you lay up here and not do any-

thing to contribute to this household. You've got such potential, Carmen. Why are you not motivated to do anything concerning your future? Just look at your former classmate,
Destiny. She got her degree in three years and—"

"Don't nobody want to hear about what Destiny's got!"
Carmen had interrupted. "You used to couldn't stand Destiny
or her grandmother, and now you're throwing her degree in
my face? Maybe because like those other women, you got
some counseling from her husband, your *pastor.*"

Patricia had slapped her then, hard, across the face. She had
always been the epitome of discretion when it came to the few
relationships she'd had since Carmen was born, had never introduced her dates or brought a man home. She knew Carmen's comment was based on gossip the child had heard, but it
still stung. As did the fact that while she'd given it every effort,
she still longed for Nate. She missed him loving her, missed his
tender caresses. Even though sometimes he'd only covered her
once a month, he'd do it so well that its memory alone took a
sistah through the other twenty-nine, thirty days. But Nate had
declared himself a changed man—no longer servicing the female flock.

*I'm thirty-seven years old, God. I don't want to live the rest of my
life alone.* Patricia lay down, hoping that things would heat up
between her and James Robinson. Except for him, it didn't
look as if there was a replacement for Nathaniel Eli Thicke's
affections anywhere in sight. Not that anyone could truly replace Reverend Thicke. No other man in the world could
make a woman feel that good.

55

Two Former Friends

Melody watched as the Sunday worshippers filed out of Gospel Truth's beautiful, newly completed, three-thousand seat sanctuary. Even though she'd specifically come to try and talk to Destiny, she had really enjoyed the service. The ones conducted at Angel House were unexciting, the pastor's drone perfect for putting people to sleep, which with Melody's secretive Saturday cavorting, he'd done often. She hadn't realized how much she'd missed charismatic expression: the joyous hand clapping, rocking live band, colorful congregants, and excellent oratory delivered by a fine preacher.

And Melody realized something else: she really missed Destiny. She had been a lifesaver at a time Melody had thought she'd die of boredom. From their mall meeting on, she and Destiny had been best buds of sorts, both in a town that wasn't big enough to hold them. That's why she'd finally talked Kirk into delivering a note to one of the head ushers he knew, who in turn was to deliver it to Destiny. She only hoped the message reached its target.

Melody followed a security guard as he went around to the side of the massive new Gospel Truth sanctuary. Kirk had told her that Nate never exited from the front of the building; he'd get bum-rushed. So following her instincts, she made her way past the newly installed fountain, with water spewing forth from the mouth of a winged angel, and stood watching the door from which she hoped her friend would emerge.

Her instincts paid off. "Destiny!" she shouted, smiling and waving her hand. "I've got a present for Benjamin!"

Destiny kept walking and Melody's heart fell. Then Destiny whispered something to Nate, who looked over at her. Melody could only imagine what either he or Destiny were thinking at that moment, but she couldn't worry about that. *He's had so many women, he probably doesn't remember me anyway.* Still, she held her breath, waiting to see what would happen.

Nate motioned to a security guard who walked over to their car. Now there were three sets of eyes staring at her. The burly man nodded curtly and began walking toward Melody. Suddenly fear replaced uncertainty. *Are they going to arrest me for trespassing or something?* Melody had experienced a brief encounter with the law, when her mother had reported her as a runaway. Those few hours in a detention cell were enough for her to know she didn't want to ever again be behind bars. She began backing up, and was just turning to run when the guard's voice stopped her.

"Lady Destiny would like to speak with you."

This comment stopped Melody in her tracks. She whipped around with a smile on her face, and followed the guard down the path to where Destiny stood waiting. She stopped about a yard from where Destiny stood. For a moment, the two former friends simply looked at each other.

Melody held out a gift bag covered with multicolored teddy bears. "I know it was a while ago . . . but I remembered his birthday, November twenty-third."

Destiny looked at her friend, and then at the gift. She stepped forward and took it. "Thank you."

A pause and then, "I miss you, Destiny."

"I miss you too."

Those simple words bridged the acrimonious gap between

them. The two former friends rocked back and forth as they hugged each other, tears in their eyes.

"I'm so sorry for what I did," Melody said when they finished embracing.

"I know. I read your note."

"I'm really happy for you, Destiny. Look at you, a first lady! But I always knew you'd be somebody really important." Melody noticed how her friend had changed. She seemed older, more mature.

"So what's up? How is everything?"

"All right, I guess. I'm still working for Dana, but like I said in the note, not on Nate's stuff. She landed Yadah as a client, so I'm primarily working on stuff for them."

There was an awkward silence as both women pondered words unsaid.

"Lady Destiny," the guard said as he approached. "The reverend is waiting."

"I've got to go, Melody. But leave your number with the guard here. I'll try and call you." When Melody looked dubious, Destiny continued. "I've had to forgive a lot of women for . . . things in the past. And I've had to be forgiven. So . . . I forgive you. I'll call. Promise."

The two women shared another quick hug before Destiny hurried to the limo and Nate, who waited inside. Melody quickly wrote her number on a piece of paper and handed it to the guard. The windows were tinted, but still she waved frantically as the limousine passed her. And while she couldn't see the person behind the pane, she was sure Destiny waved back.

Several hours later, Melody was on her knees near the entertainment center in her living room, going through stacks and stacks of DVDs scattered around. Destiny's new lifestyle had given Melody more than a few things to think about. Her life, for instance, and just what she planned to do with it. There was one thing Melody knew for sure: she wanted to be big, wanted to join people like Kimora Lee Simmons in the fab lane. But now, she knew something else—she didn't want to get there just any kind of way.

That's why she was looking for the tape of her and Nate screwing. She knew better than anybody how it felt to be caught on tape. It had been years, but she'd still not quite gotten over the fact that her mother had watched part of the nasty tape she'd made of losing her virginity with one of gospel's hip-hop darlings, and still prayed every day that her dad would never find out about it, let alone see it. She continued her search with renewed vigor, planning to destroy all of her sex tapes, but especially the one with Destiny's husband. As it was, she regretted having shown it to Kirk. Thankfully, she thought, he was the only other person who'd seen it.

Melody's hand stopped midreach. *Kirk!* She became frantic then, throwing DVDs everywhere, going through her CDs, running into her bedroom to look on those shelves and back to the living room, which now looked as though a tornado had passed through. After several more moments of frenzied searching, she raced to the phone.

When Kirk answered, Melody was breathing heavily, almost beside herself with dread.

"Hey, Melody, can I play on your instrument?" Kirk answered cheerfully, playing off her name as he often did.

"I tell you what you can do, Kirk," Melody shouted. "You can tell me what in the hell you did with my video!"

56

Not Even Death

Nate swatted Destiny playfully on the behind as she took their son from his lap so he could get back to work. He watched her graceful movements as she left his home office, still somewhat unbelieving of the gift God had given him. Nate was successful, but he'd never known he could feel this complete. *This is what it feels like to have it all.* He smiled and turned back to the computer where he was reading the final draft of his second book: *Go with God and Have It All*. Dana had been right, the ghostwriter she'd found was brilliant, taking his words and turning them into prolific passages that made a complicated message simple and mere perfunctory words profound. He bolded a passage he wanted changed and then chicken-pecked the new phrasing he preferred next to it, in red, as the writer had instructed.

"Yes, that's it," he said out loud after reading the new text. He kept reading and was almost to the end of the chapter when the phone rang.

"Reverend Thicke!" King boomed after Nate answered. "Are you ready to turn the place out next month in Miami?"

"I'm just a simple vessel for God to use," Nate replied in mock humility. Everybody, including Nate, knew he was one of the best orators the church world had seen this century.

"Everybody is so excited for you, man. The board can't believe how attendance to the conference has increased since placing your appearance in the ads. We're expecting upwards of twenty thousand attendees this year—our highest number yet. I believe your being one of the main speakers is part of the reason for the increase. Everybody wants to find out how to give up everything and have it all."

The two men laughed at the reference to Nate's first book. "How's the new one coming?" King asked.

"That's what I was working on when you called," Nate answered. "It's set to be released about the same time the first one was, during the holidays."

"Perfect for that gift-giving time, huh?"

"I think that's what my publisher is hoping."

"It doesn't matter when it comes out, Nate. Anything with your name on it is a best seller now. I couldn't believe how many dignitaries attended your anniversary this year. And being featured in *Ebony*? Man, Jakes better look out!"

"Please, T. D. doesn't have to worry about a thing. I'm a long way from the success of Potter's House. But I'm grateful for where I am, what I have. What about you, man? I know your schedule has been rough, filling in as president for Total Truth."

"It hasn't been too bad. Derrick told me I'd just have to preside over a few meetings and calls, and so far he's been right. Another month and we'll be electing a new president, which is the reason I'm calling. I think you could give the association the shot in the arm it needs, attract new, younger members, up our profile. What do you think?"

"Wow, King, I don't know what to think. At only three years in, I'm still the new kid on the block. I appreciate your confidence, but with everything going on with my ministry right now, I don't know that I could give such a position the attention it deserves."

"I know your life is crowded, Nate. But do me a favor and

think about it. I'm going to run the suggestion past the board during our teleconference next week."

"All right, man. But remember, I've made no promises. I'm still a newlywed. On top of everything else that's going on, I have to carve out a generous amount of quality time with my wife."

"For sure, brothah. But I have a feeling there's nothing that can come between you and Destiny."

"Not even death shall separate us, King. I love that girl."

51

My Decision Is Final

"Don't do it, Jennifer."

"Why not? The Word says the truth shall set us free."

"Yes, but whose truth?"

Carla had been on the phone with Jennifer for thirty minutes, ever since she'd finished the last page of the manuscript that Jennifer had sent overnight express. Jennifer was hoping to book a spot for Ed Smith on *Conversations with Carla,* and at Carla's request, had sent what would be the subject matter.

"Anybody remotely familiar with the church world will know this book is talking about Nate Thicke. And there are barely veiled references to Derrick as well as your former pastor. How could you even think about instigating this kind of drama? When you know this book is sensationalized and filled with half-truths?"

"Is it a half-truth that Nate got Destiny pregnant at seventeen? Because if it is, that little half-truth is going on three years old now, and Destiny's twenty. You do the math."

Carla took a deep breath and sat down on the chaise on her balcony. It was a beautiful June day in sunny California and only something like this conversation could turn it cloudy. "Why, Jennifer?" she finally asked. "No, let me tell you why. It's because you're still hurting behind that man and what you perceive he did to you. But you went into that situation with your eyes wide open, Jennifer. You knew Nate's reputation, and you still went for him with everything you had."

"If I remember correctly, it was with your encouragement."

"Excuse me?"

"Do what you gotta do . . . Remember that advice?"

"Yes, and that was spoken in the same conversation where I said to be careful, and that sometimes plans backfired. Do you remember that?"

Jennifer became silent. She did remember. She remembered a lot of things that she'd tried to forget since meeting Ed Smith. There were so many things she liked about him, and especially his ministry. He was an important man in Louisiana, and when she was with him, she felt important too. He treated her kindly, with respect, and while once or twice he'd hinted at being attracted to her, he'd kept their relationship professional. His actions were always above reproach. He'd promised her a prominent place in his ministry once the book came out. And lately Jennifer had been contemplating a prominent place in his life.

"Look at it this way, Carla. Ed Smith will be a ratings bonanza. Challenge him on the parts of the book you disagree with. Heck, even have Nate on to refute the charges. Girl, your ratings would go through the stratosphere! You'd probably beat Oprah, Ellen, and Dr. Phil combined."

Carla was silent for a long moment. "Have you forgotten, Jennifer? I've been on the other side of that ratings bonanza, when it was my life, my scandal from which publications and networks benefited. And from that perspective, I can assure you, the ratings aren't worth it. I'm trying to help you avoid going where I've been. Because just like with Nate, these plans you're hatching with Ed might not turn out the way you want."

"I'll get exactly what I want," Jennifer countered. "After marketing this book, I'll be able to write my own ticket. And I might even get a husband in the process. He's a little old but his money and status are timeless. Not to mention that because of the way the royalty contract is written, I'll have a nice little nest egg of my own."

"But, Jennifer . . . What good is it if a man gains the whole world but loses his soul?"

Jennifer didn't have an answer for that. "Good-bye, Carla."

It had taken Jennifer two weeks to come to a decision, and now that she had, she was ready to act on it without further delay. She used the key Ed had insisted on giving her and entered the stately foyer.

"Ed!" she said, announcing her presence. She'd never found him in any state except polished and professional, but she never wanted to chance stumbling upon him naked or in some other embarrassing condition.

Ed hurriedly hid the brandy bottle and shot glass that had been on his desk and reached for the powerful mouthwash he used. He was closer than ever to exacting revenge on his nemesis and getting a godly woman to be by his side, unlike the other one, who was too weak to stand by him, who didn't have what it took. "In here," he intoned, spraying on cologne to add to the cover-up. "Is that the woman of God?"

Jennifer's smile was tentative as she turned the corner. "Hello, Reverend Smith," she said.

"What's with this 'reverend' stuff," Ed replied in mock indignation. "I thought we were way past being on a first name basis."

Jennifer laughed nervously. "You're right, we are."

"So to what do I owe this pleasure? I rearranged my schedule right away when you called me. You're a priority, you see. I knew something serious had happened when you asked for time off. Now I'm here to help in any way I can."

"I appreciate it." After sitting down, Jennifer took a deep breath. "Ed, I've made a decision about the book, *Pulpit Pimps.*

I can't do it, Ed. I can't endorse it and I can't promote it. As of today, I can no longer be a part of the project."

Ed rubbed his chin as he digested this information. A slow boil began in his stomach, and his hand shook slightly. He hid his anger behind a smile and a soft voice. "Dear," he began, "I understand your hesitation. It takes great courage to go up against Goliath. But we have the Lord on our side."

"Are you sure about that, Ed? Are you sure this is about God? Because I'm not at all sure anymore. I agree with some of the things you say, but I know these men, and I'm convinced they love God as much as you and I do." Jennifer paused, sat up straighter in her chair. "I've prayed about it, and my decision is final. I will not be a part of this book."

Ed slowly rose from his chair and began pacing back and forth. "Well, now, Sister Stevens, this is quite the surprise, I must say. But then again, maybe not. See, anyone who lies down with the devil is liable to become one of his minions, unable to totally escape from his grasp." He stopped directly in front of Jennifer. "But if you continue with me, help to expose that liar for who he is, *that* will be the act that breaks the bondage, Jennifer. And then you'll be free."

Jennifer stood, and in her flat shoes was almost eye to eye with the diminutive preacher. "I've said what I came to say, Ed. I'll pick up my personal effects from the church offices tomorrow."

Jennifer backed up and turned to leave. She never saw the first fist coming.

58

Ego and Pride

Kirk met his friend, the usher from Gospel Truth, in the parking lot of a convenience store. Anxious to hear the news, he jumped out of his car as soon as he saw him pull into the parking lot.

"So did he do it?" Kirk said by way of greeting. "Did your boy do what I asked him?"

"He said he did."

"What do you mean, he said he did? You didn't see it?"

"I saw the reverend fucking your girl. But I don't know if he spliced it into the promo, dog. Even with the money, that's some messed-up shit to do right there."

"So did he give me back the half I gave him then? 'Cause if that muthafucka mess with me and my money . . . it's about to go down!"

Kirk had become increasingly bitter since Melody broke up with him, almost obsessed with extorting money from Nate, even though he was now making plenty of his own. Creating near perfect IDs and other documents for illegal aliens was big business! But with Nate, it was a matter of his ego, his pride. Nobody dissed him and got away with it. And that's what had happened the one and only time he had called the church offices and Nate had taken the call.

"Look, *Reverend* Thicke, trust me when I tell you, I've got something to bring you down, dog. You're going to have to pay the piper for it to disappear, feel me?" He'd proceeded to tell Nate about the tape with Melody, and that it would cost half a million to get it to go away.

Nate had laughed in his face. "Kirk, do you really think I'm going to take your threats seriously? You need to get your life together, man. And find another church home where you can continue your spiritual growth. In the meantime, you're also going to have to find another swindle, brothah, because that dog ain't huntin' here."

Kirk had then taken the demand down to $250,000, and given him two weeks to contact him with how to pick up his money.

"You don't have to give me two weeks, Kirk. You don't even have to give me two minutes. Tape or no tape, I will not be blackmailed. And one more thing. I've been a preacher for a long time, but I haven't always been saved. Don't threaten me again."

The click of Nate hanging up had been his good-bye.

"So talk to me, son," Kirk said with agitation. "Either show me my copy or give me back my money."

The usher looked into the distance for a long time. "You got my cut?" he finally asked.

Kirk smiled, and opened the black bag he carried. "That's what I'm talking about." He pulled out a wad of bills and a small video camera. "Let's see the media ministry's finest at work."

59

The Promo

The conference crowd was still buzzing about Nate Thicke, their newest star. He'd turned the place out the previous night with a rousing sermon that the audience ate up: Having It All. Everything with his name on it was selling out: books, audio CDs, DVDs. The convention-goers had fallen in love with both him and Destiny. In the church world, they were royalty, and Nate had definitely delivered a message from the King. The accolades began before he'd finished his sermon and hadn't stopped.

"Congratulations again," King said, coming up to shake Nate's hand. "You give any more thought to the presidency?"

"I talked it over with Destiny and we'll have to pass this go round. Too much going on, man."

"I figured as much."

"Reverend Thicke!" Derrick said, as he joined King, Nate, and several other ministers preparing to enter the American Airlines arena. The two men exchanged a soul brother's handshake as small talk continued among them. "That cruise your church is sponsoring sounds good," Derrick said. "We might have to think about doing one."

"It's selling out, thanks to Dana and her ad placement. Plus, my media team created a two-minute infomercial. It's going to play tonight."

Shortly thereafter, the team of ministers, more than thirty of them, entered the buzz that was the arena. Some of them took their place on the podium, others went to the front rows, which had been designated for the clergy. The mood was festive as gospel artists of every genre set the stage for a glorious night of praise. As the offering was being lifted, various promotional pieces began to play.

First came a video about the convention marketplace, where tapes and DVDs of every service could be purchased. Next were videos promoting various ministries, including one of SOS.

"Oh, here's the promo," Nate said to Derrick, when he saw a picture of a cruise ship with the words "Gospel Truth's Gospel Cruise" transposed over it. Both men turned to watch.

"The Gospel Truth Church invites you to sail the sea with the saints!" The announcer's bass voice was crisp and convincing. "Join Reverend Nate Thicke and his wife Destiny as they—"

The sound stopped, and the picture of Nate and Destiny smiling at the camera was replaced with another—a clear shot of Nate and another woman, obviously in the throes of passion, and a panning of the camera down to his backside—and then the screen went blank.

"What the hell?" Derrick said, totally forgetting that for this week this arena was the house of the Lord.

"What? What?" King had momentarily turned away from the screen to talk to the minister behind him, and had missed the five seconds of ass flashing.

Unfortunately, thousands of convention-goers hadn't. The arena went into an instant uproar, even as King raced to the microphone to try and restore order. He held the microphone and looked at the masses, his mind temporarily blank. *They just saw Nate Thicke's bare behind, humping a woman who is not his wife. What can I say to that?*

Derrick joined him at the podium and took the microphone. "Saints, saints, please, I implore you to take your seats
and calm down. Remember, we are still in a place of worship
and God deserves to be respected."

That may have been true, but nobody heard it. Some people
were trying to wrap their minds around what they'd seen, others
believed there was no way they could have seen what they'd seen,
and the ones who hadn't seen were trying to imagine what the
image they missed looked like. It took a full ten minutes before
Derrick was able to get a majority's attention and speak to the
crowd. In that time span, Nate, Destiny, and their entourage
had been whisked through a side door and taken backstage.

"On behalf of the Total Truth Association, I sincerely apologize for what just happened. We are as shocked as you are, and
I guarantee you we will get to the bottom of it. We must be doing
something right, because this is definitely the work of the devil,
and he only bothers people who are on the move for God!"

This comment brought some of the saints back around,
while others were lost for the night. Mama Max's husband and
the night's featured speaker, the Reverend Doctor Pastor Bishop
Overseer Mister Stanley Obadiah Meshach Brook Jr. took the
bull by the horns, promptly changing his message to fit the
moment. When he told the still-confused congregation that
the title of his message was "Get *Behind* Me, Satan," the attendees were all ears. He preached his heart out, mixing humor with
stern rebuke, cautioned the saints against gossip, and warned
them to keep their minds stayed on Jesus.

Well, they may have kept their minds stayed on Christ but
their mouths were stayed on Nate's glistening backside caught
on tape, and the mystery woman who was not Mrs. Thicke. It
took less than two hours for the news to be all over the Internet, and by the next day, rumblings of an X-rated video by best-
selling author Reverend Nathaniel Thicke were on the six
o'clock news.

60

We Fall Down

The somber faces on those gathered around Nate's conference room table were in stark contrast to the elated expressions these same men had worn the week before. The same men who'd clamored for a photograph with him could now barely meet his eye. Nate totally understood—he was still in shock himself.

The first half of the meeting had been filled with rants and raves about how disappointed the board was with him, how irresponsible he'd been, why his singular moment of thoughtlessness now jeopardized all they stood for, and exactly what they expected him to do about it.

"The good news, if there can be any," Derrick offered, after the last minister had voiced his justified chagrin, "is that the fast-thinking of the technical director prevented this from being much, much worse. The tape was stopped so quickly that most people didn't know what they were looking at until after the screen went blank. Then they wondered if they really saw what they thought they saw. Many folk talking right now didn't actually see anything at all. The convention director immediately pulled that copy of the promotion, and Nate has not only fired his entire media staff, but had professionals check all other tapes in his possession. And I'm not exactly sure how he can be so certain, but he assures me that there remain no copies of this . . . incident . . . that can be recopied and sold for gain."

A few of the men shifted in their seats, but no one responded to Derrick's attempt at a silver lining.

King spoke into the silence, looking Nate in the eye. "We're all in agreement that decisive action has to be taken, to send a message to you, the Total Truth membership, and the Christian community at large. As of this moment, your membership and that of Gospel Truth Church is suspended. Should you not follow our mandates fully and to the letter, it will be permanently revoked.

"You must resign immediately as senior pastor of Gospel Truth. There must be a formal, public apology, both to your members and to the nation. You and your wife must undergo at least one year of extensive counseling, after which you must perform one thousand hours of community service, for this association, preaching the importance of abstinence, the wages of sin, specifically fornication, and the sanctity of marriage.

"Furthermore, you must provide restitution for any and all expenses that may arise out of lawsuits, court proceedings, counterpromotions, restorative public relations, and/or any legal, executive, or practical action taken as a result of this unfortunate event. All decisions concerning this matter will be handled by the board, and our recommendations are not up for discussion or debate. They are final."

King breathed a deep sigh. He loved Nate like a brother, and it hurt him to his heart to punish him, but it had to be done. "Nate, are there any questions?"

Nate stared straight ahead for a moment, and then stood. "I have no questions, but I do have something to say. I am not proud of my past actions, including the ones that led to this meeting. I didn't always believe it, but my behavior was wrong, and after being counseled by two stellar soldiers for God, specifically Derrick Montgomery and King Brook, I changed my ways. It doesn't change the outcome, but for the record, that tape was made, without my knowledge, before I married my wife, and during the one and only time I spent with . . . that other woman. But as God is my witness, Destiny Nicole Thicke is now and will forever be the only woman in my life."

When the men around the table remained silent, Nate turned to Derrick, who was sitting to his left, and held out his hand. "I'm deeply sorry, my brother. I've sinned against God, and the church. Will you forgive me?" Derrick looked at King, then back at Nate, before foregoing the handshake and instead rising to embrace his fallen brother. "I forgive you," he said.

Nate went around the room and repeated this admission to each of the board members present. His words were heartfelt and sincere, and his genuine humility and regret were felt by everyone in the room. When he'd finally embraced the last minister, he turned, still standing, and faced the table. For the first time since the meeting began, all eyes were on him.

"I accept the full recommendation of this wise and just board. I hereby tender my resignation from all Total Truth committees, and on . . ." Nate's voice broke and he stopped to regain his composure. "On Sunday I will tender my resignation as senior pastor of Gospel Truth. Regarding the other points outlined in your mandate, gentlemen . . . I will do all that you have asked."

61

Remember Rahab

Melody sat in her car, staring at the house in front of her. Nate's mother's house, and her last possible chance at redemption. She'd been almost inconsolable since hearing what had happened, and since Destiny had refused her phone calls and once again had her number changed. Not that Melody blamed her. She didn't have to imagine the embarrassment and shame Nate and Destiny felt for what had happened—she felt it too. Even without knowing exactly what had been seen at the convention, and hearing that the tape had run only a few seconds before being stopped, she still felt incredibly guilty. None of this would have happened, if not for her.

Melody looked around and slouched even lower in her car. She was wearing a hastily assembled disguise—a wig and sunglasses—because she didn't want to chance being seen, especially in Palestine. She was practically in hiding after being accused of ruining Nate's ministry and receiving anonymous death threats. She wasn't sure who the calls were from, but because of the underground tape from her previous high profile tryst, more than a few people knew who she was. Over twenty-thousand people had been in the arena. The calls could be from anyone, anywhere.

A tear rolled down Melody's face as she remembered the

hurt on her mother's face when she admitted to seeing her own daughter on tape. Now, Melody sat near the door of another mother who, because of her, had witnessed her son in a similar position. There was no way, Melody thought, she could imagine how his mother was feeling. But she couldn't leave Texas, couldn't go back to California without letting Mrs. Thicke know how sorry she was. With resolve, Melody placed her hand on the door handle and opened it. She walked up to the house as fast as she could, not giving herself a chance to turn back.

"Mrs. Thicke?" she asked, when a slightly plump woman with a troubled face opened the front door.

"Who's asking?" she said directly, but not unkindly.

"My name is Melody and I really need to talk to you. I—I am the woman in . . . in that tape," Melody finished in a whisper. "I'm sorry," she continued, tears streaming down her face. "I didn't mean for nobody to ever see what I did. Mrs. Thicke . . ." Melody couldn't continue for sobbing, and almost crumbled at Nettie's knees.

Nettie reached down and grabbed her hand, almost having to drag a petrified and limp Melody across her door jamb. There were many emotions warring for dominance in Nettie's heart, and she was battling back to allow those of compassion and forgiveness instead of anger and resentment to lead the way. Thankfully, she wasn't totally unprepared. The Lord had spoke to her during her prayer time and had said simply, "Remember Rahab." Nettie hadn't understood this cryptic message . . . until now.

Nettie led a still-sobbing Melody to her new, floral couch— ironically part of the new living room suite gift from Nate and Destiny—and gently guided her to sit down. She walked over to the coffee table and a box of tissue, pulled one out and put it in Melody's hand, and placed the box on the couch beside her. Still not speaking, Nettie went into the kitchen and put on a pot of coffee. Unconsciously, she began humming "Just a Closer Walk with Thee," and by the time the coffee had finished percolating and she'd fixed a tray with an urn, cream, sugar, and two cups, she was ready to talk to the woman who'd helped ruin her son's life.

"You say your name is Melody?" she asked, after she'd placed the coffee tray on the sofa table behind them and taken a seat on the opposite end of the couch.

Melody kept her head down, but nodded.

"Well, you can call me Miss Nettie or Mrs. Johnson. I'm remarried from Nate's father."

When Melody didn't respond, Nettie walked back around to the sofa table. "You take cream and sugar?"

"No, ma'am. I can't accept anything from you. . . ."

"You must not be from around here. Child, I'm southern. It would be sacrilegious to come into my home and I not offer you something. You look like a cream and sugar girl, am I right?"

Melody nodded, and a few more moments were taken up with Nettie fixing their cups. Once she'd handed Melody hers and sat back down, she took a sip, and then asked simply, "Why did you do it, Melody? Why did you make that tape of you and my son?"

Through a barrage of tears, Melody started at the beginning, with the first tape, admitting how watching herself have sex on tape had become somewhat of an addiction. "I was only with Nate one time," she concluded. "And I never, ever meant for the video to get out."

Nettie digested Melody's story for a moment. "Then how do you suppose it got out, if you didn't intend it?" she softly asked.

"Kirk," was Melody's equally soft response.

"Our Kirk? The minister from Gospel Truth?"

Melody nodded and took a tentative sip of the coffee Nettie had prepared. She then told her about the one time she'd showed a part of the tape to Kirk, because he didn't believe that she'd slept with his pastor. She didn't tell Nettie what Dana had recently heard through the grapevine, that Kirk's house had been ransacked, all of his videos seized and all of his electronic equipment destroyed. "He deserves whatever he gets," had been Melody's response when Dana told her. And then Dana had told her something else. She was fired.

"Kirk was mad at Nate, Reverend Thicke, for letting him go without severance pay. But this isn't Kirk's fault, Miss Nettie. It's mine. If I had never shown him the tape, none of this would have happened." She started crying all over again, hurting more than she ever thought she would, feeling sorrier than she ever thought she could.

Miss Nettie sat down her cup and moved next to Melody. "It's going to be all right," she said, taking the young woman in her arms and rocking her like a baby. "Everything works for good to those who love the Lord and are called unto His purpose."

Melody cried harder, wrapping her arms tightly around Miss Nettie. Melody had no doubt her own mother loved her, but Bernadette Anderson wasn't a particularly demonstrative or affectionate woman. Miss Nettie's was the type of absolute acceptance that had been missing from her life. Melody couldn't remember the last time she'd been hugged this way—the way a person who looked past your faults and saw your needs hugged, the way amazing grace hugged, the way unconditional love hugged.

The two women stayed this way a long time. As Nettie comforted Melody she thought back to God's whisper, and Rahab's story. How the prostitute hid the two spies whom Joshua had sent to survey the land, and that through her act of kindness, she saved her whole family. What God was telling her, Nettie believed, is that God could use anybody . . . even a prostitute.

Finally, Melody pulled back, wiped her tears and blew her nose. "What can I do, Miss Nettie? Destiny won't talk to me and I'm sure Nate won't either. But I want to let them know

I'm sorry. And I want to make up for the pain I've caused. Do you think that's possible? Do you think there is any way I can right this terrible wrong?"

"You can live your life for Jesus," Nettie said simply.

"But, Miss Nettie, I don't know how to do that."

"That's all right, child. God will help you," Nettie responded. "And so will I."

62

God Don't Like Ugly

"Girl . . . can you *believe* everything that's happened?" Anne had barely made it through Verniece's door when she began to speak.

"Well, you know what they say," Verniece said, walking back to the couch and flopping down on it. "God don't like ugly."

"Ooh, Verniece, you know that's wrong. I don't care if you've left the church. He's still a man of God."

"Whatever. He stopped covering his flock, which by his own words was a part of his responsibility. I begged him not to stop servicing a sistah. He refused. And look what happened. He stopped fucking me and he got fucked."

Anne stopped on her way to the couch. "Verniece, if you don't stop talking like that I'm going to leave your house. I will not be here when your disrespectful butt gets struck by lightning."

"All right, girl, you're right," Verneice said as Anne sat down beside her. "I do feel sorry for Reverend, to be truthful. He is anointed. One can't lie about that. And now he's been stripped of his church, his title, everything. It's a shame."

The two women tended their own thoughts a moment. And then Anne spoke again. "And what about Patricia? I told you she left, right?"

"Unh–unh."

"Yeah, girl. She and Katherine got into a little fisticuff—"

"Not fisticuff—"

"Fist-i-cuff, sistah—"

Verniece whooped and sat straight up. "When? Where?"

"Last Sunday, after church. A whole bunch of people saw it. They say Ms. Refined and Reserved Katherine Noble kicked Patricia Cook's ass!"

"Stop—it. Girl, you *know* you lying!"

"Hmph. I'm telling the gospel truth and yes the pun is intended. One hostess's mother said Patricia gave her notice at the church the next day, said she was moving to Dallas to join the Potter's House."

"Dang, she has to be put back together again, like Humpty Dumpty? Katherine must have pulled out a big can of whoop ass."

Anne laughed in spite of herself. "Verniece, you a fool."

"Ooh, girl, I almost forgot the main reason I asked you to come over. Look at this." Verniece walked to her dining room table and picked up a copy of a small newspaper article. "Here, check this out."

"What's this about, Reverend?" she asked.

"It's about a reverend, but not Nate. Read it."

Anne took the piece of paper. "A prominent Baton Rouge minister was questioned and released yesterday following an alleged assault at his home. Sixty-one-year-old Ed Smith—" Anne gasped and stopped reading.

"Keep reading!" Verniece prodded.

Anne read the rest of the brief article silently, about how Jennifer Stevens had filed charges against Reverend Ed Smith following an altercation she said had occurred in his home. The minister was denying all charges and prominent city leaders and church members were standing by his side.

"They're liars, all of them," Anne hissed. "I've got no love lost for Jennifer, but no woman deserves to get beaten. And that asshole beat her. I know he did."

"How are you so sure?" Verniece asked, concerned for her friend's sudden change in demeanor.

Anne turned and looked at Verniece. "Because Ed Smith is the man I ran away from. The man Reverend Thicke counseled me about and protected me from. That's why Ed hates him, and is always talking against him. And that's why no matter what he does and wherever he is, Reverend Thicke will always be my pastor. That man saved my life."

"Dang," Verniece said after taking in all that Anne had said. "There are so many no-good men out there. But I know some good ones are out there too. I just wish I knew where they were." Anne's melancholy mood had rubbed off on Verniece, and now tears filled her eyes. "I'm sorry for what I said about Reverend Thicke," she added, through her tears. "God forgive me."

Anne took Verniece in her arms. "We'll get through all of this together, sistah. No matter what, we've got each other, right?"

Verniece nodded against Anne's shoulder, as Anne comforted her friend, rubbing Verniece's back. Soon, Verniece's tears subsided, but she didn't break the embrace. Instead, she scooted closer to Anne and kissed her neck. Anne's hand stopped—for a moment. And then she began again, kneading Verniece's shoulders this time. Verniece kissed Anne again, this time on the cheek. "We'll always have each other," she whispered, before placing her mouth over Anne's and sealing this pledge with a searing French kiss.

An hour later, the women lay naked in Verniece's bed, and in each other's arms.

"Are you sorry we did that?" Verniece asked quietly.

"I'm not sure," Anne replied. "Something happened when

you kissed me and I—I've never felt this way before." Anne finally turned to face Verniece. "No, Verniece, I'm not sorry. Does this mean we're lesbians?" she asked while caressing Verniece's face.

"I think it means we're lovers," Verniece responded, with a shrug.

Anne looked deeply into the eyes of her new partner. "Then let's do it again."

63

Thanks for Asking

Jennifer felt no joy as she read the latest issue of *LA Gospel*. It was all there in black and white—the rise and fall of Nathaniel Eli Thicke. She wouldn't have been surprised if someone had paid Melody Anderson to make the tape. Jennifer knew about Melody from the time Shabach was arrested, the hip-hop artist she'd met in Kansas City when he appeared at a concert sponsored by Mount Zion. Later, an LA connection had filled her in on the details. But she'd never seen the tape her connection claimed was out there.

Ed might be behind this, she thought as she finished reading the article and closed the paper. *And even if he's not, he's over there gloating, happy beyond belief that the man he hates has finally been brought down.* "I'm glad I didn't do it," Jennifer said aloud, thinking about the book she'd helped write, praying it would never see the light of day. She reached up and gingerly touched a still swollen jaw, which along with a black eye, busted lip, bruised ribs, and dislocated shoulder, had all come courtesy of Baton Rouge's prominent, popular minister, a man that few would believe capable of what had occurred. Had it not happened to her, she wouldn't have believed it either. Aside from his reputation, which was stellar, Ed Smith wasn't a big man. Jennifer had been surprised at how strong he was. She'd tried to fight back, but that had only made him angrier. That's when she'd gotten the dislocated shoulder . . . and the bruised ribs, from his kicking her after he'd knocked her down. . . .

Jennifer shook her head and reached for the remote, determined to stop thinking about what he'd done to her. She'd filed charges; now it was up to the courts. And from the slew of dishonest witnesses who had vouched for his being somewhere else at the time she'd said the beating occurred, it was quite possible that he would walk away scot-free. *I bet I'm not the first,* Jennifer thought, having forgotten already to not think about it. *And I won't be the last. But one of these days, he'll get his. . . .*

A knock on the door startled Jennifer. She'd rarely ventured out of her house since the incident—only for food and to visit the doctor. Just a couple people knew she was back in Palestine, and she would only be here long enough to heal, pack her things, and return to Kansas City.

Her eyes widened as she looked through the peephole. She turned and leaned against the door, wanting the company, but at the same time not wanting anyone to see her like this. *But after what I did to him, he's still here to comfort me. Just like a man of God.* She turned and slowly opened the door.

Her visitor's eyes narrowed, and he looked at her a long moment. The briefest of frowns flitted across his face, before he forced a smile to replace it. "You're looking powerful pretty, Sister Stevens," James said softly, his eyes shining with compassion. He stepped into the room and Jennifer fell into his arms. She hadn't truly felt safe from Ed Smith and his threats of retaliation if she didn't drop the charges. But now she did. In James's arms, she felt she could stand up to anybody, or anything.

"Thanks so much for coming, Deacon Robinson."

"Please, call me James."

"Thank you, James. Your visit means the world to me."

They moved quietly to the couch and sat down. Jennifer turned off the television.

"I heard about what happened, and had to come by. I'm awfully sorry for your pain. I know Ed Smith, have for a long time, and I believe you when you say he did it."

"I never would have dreamed he was capable of being so violent."

"That's because he hides it well behind that polished persona. Just like he hides the fact that he's an alcoholic."

Jennifer stared at James. "I suspected it, but didn't know for sure. I never saw him take a drink, never smelled it on his breath. But one time his eyes were bloodshot and he was talking rather strangely. The thought crossed my mind then, but only for a moment."

"Yes, that's why Nate stopped dealing with him. When he first took over the ministry, Ed came here and offered to be Nate's mentor. Nate was familiar with First Baptist and its community outreach and was excited to learn how to incorporate similar programs into Gospel Truth. But the more time Nate spent with him, the more convinced he became that theirs was not a good liaison. He backed away, and turned down an offer to join a networking union Ed had founded. Then something happened with one of our members, something involving Ed, and when Nate took steps to protect this member . . . well, suffice it to say Ed didn't like it."

"I bet I know what he did, and I wish I could talk to that member," Jennifer said softly.

"It's not my place to talk someone else's business," James replied, "but you be encouraged. This isn't over. The Word says vengeance belongs to God, and that whatever's right, He'll pay." Deacon Robinson looked at his watch and stood. "Sorry, but I have a meeting. I just had to stop by after hearing the news, to ask if there is anything I can do, or anything you need."

"You can pray for me, Deacon . . . James. Other than that, I'm okay. But thank you so much for stopping by."

"There's one more reason I stopped by, Sister Stevens."

"Please, call me Jennifer."

"As you wish . . . Jennifer. I know you're feeling a bit under the weather, presently. But when you're in better health, say in a month or so, would you do me the fine pleasure of joining me for dinner?"

"Why, James, are you asking me out on a date?" Jennifer answered coyly, smiling despite the pain in her jaw.

"That is exactly what I'm doing," the deacon responded.

"Thank you for asking," Jennifer answered, reaching up to hug this patient, persistent man. "I accept."

64

First Lady

"Be sure and stay in touch with me, baby," Simone said. She acknowledged Mark, who walked up behind her and massaged her shoulders, offering his quiet support as she talked on the phone. "You are such a strong woman. I am very, very proud of you. I love you, Destiny. Let me know when you get there, honey, so I know you've arrived safely. Good-bye."

Simone placed the cordless phone back on the base and then joined Mark on the couch. "I put on water for tea," he said, taking the woman he loved into his arms.

"You're too good to me," Simone answered as she snuggled against him.

"How's she doing?"

Simone sighed. "She's trying to sound strong for me, and so is Nate. But I know they're both hurting. This was a devastating blow, to say the least. It has to have shaken Nate to the core. Before the tape played, he was unstoppable."

"There's no denying this was a huge hit," Mark admitted. "But sometimes people have short memories. And the church world can be forgiving, especially when people do what Nate did, own up to his mistake and take the punishment—like a man. After all, Christians aren't perfect, just forgiven. Nate's young. His best may still be yet to come."

"I hope you're right," Simone said. "For Nate's sake . . . and my daughter's."

The tea kettle whistle sounded and Mark rose to fix the tea tray. He loved doing these simple things for Simone, loved taking care of her, especially now. He'd always been a sensitive, nurturing man, something he often got teased for growing up. He'd protected unpopular kids from the bullies and cried when his pets died. He still cried at sad movies or sad moments, as he had when he found out about Nate.

"One cup of tea for my one and only," he said, setting the tray on the ottoman and preparing Simone's cup.

"Look at me, being served by the governor of Louisiana. I am special indeed."

Life had changed dramatically for the Simmonses since Mark won one of the tightest elections and biggest upsets in Louisiana's colorful political history. The opponents had demanded a recount, but when the dust settled, his victory stood. That this Democrat had won in a staunchly Republican state, even running as he did on a conservative, godly platform, had felt like a divine act. Mark's schedule had filled up overnight, and Simone was thrust into the political limelight. Fortunately the people and the cameras loved her, especially since she played up her familial connection to the state, as well as her Creole roots. Her parties were coveted, and her social secretary was constantly turning down invites to teas, dinners, and the like. Aside from mandatory social functions, Simone had decided to focus on her husband and his needs the first year. His needs—and those of their unborn child.

Mark settled back on the couch and pulled his wife back against him. He wrapped his arms around her expanding belly and nuzzled her neck. "How's my son doing?" he asked.

"Mark Junior is rather active today. I think he's excited because his daddy's home."

Mark's heart expanded with love and joy. He'd wanted a child for so long and he'd especially wanted a son. "Are you sure you want to name him after me? Granted, I'd love a junior, but your opinion counts too."

Simone turned into his arms. "There can be no greater honor than for this child to bear your name," she said. "Ooh!"

"What is it, baby? What's wrong?" Mark became alarmed, his heart jumping into his chest.

"Nothing, darling. Calm down. I didn't mean to frighten you. Your son is simply fluttering his agreement."

"Is that how it feels?" Mark asked, putting his hand under her blouse, directly on her stomach.

"Yes. You probably can't feel anything yet. He's too little. Give it another month or two. Then he'll visibly make his presence known, with a foot or a hand in my side."

Mark kissed Simone on the forehead. "I think I should call it a night. My flight leaves at seven-thirty in the morning."

"Can't you call in sick or something? I hate it when you're out of town."

"Oh, baby, don't make me sad. You know I'll do anything for you."

Simone stood up and held out her hand to Mark. "But you can't call in sick—you're the governor."

"And you're the first lady."

"I am, huh?"

"Yes, you are."

Simone smiled as she followed her husband up the stairs. She never could have imagined a life like this. For many years, she'd thought she knew what she wanted. But God had another plan, a better plan. She chuckled, remembering how hard she'd worked on Nate's book, thinking the labor had been for her, when instead it had been for her daughter.

"Why are you laughing?" Mark asked as they reached their bedroom and he began undressing her.

"I'm just so happy," Simone responded. "Because I have you, Mark Simmons, and you are more than I ever dreamed."

65

Something Noble:
Part Two

Katherine stood naked in front of her bathroom mirror. She eyed herself critically, turning this way and that. She leaned in closer to the glass and observed her face. There were a few more wrinkles, and a mole where there hadn't been one before. She stepped back and cupped her breasts. She turned to the side. To her chagrin, even with the squat exercises an infomercial had suggested, her butt was still sagging. Nate had told her she didn't need implants. But she knew all those Hollywood women with perfectly round tushes weren't born that way. She'd even read once where Diana Ross used to wear a prosthetic-type device to make her hind end look bigger. *Maybe I'll try that. . . .*

Katherine walked into her closet, pulled on a satin, kimono-style robe, slipped into heeled house slippers covered in rhinestones, and walked out of her bedroom. She ended up in the living room, by the large picture window, looking out at a humid Saturday in August. She looked out her window at the world around her, and for the first time in a long time, wondered where she fit in.

It had been a month since "the incident," when in an uncharacteristic display of lost control, she'd combined wrestlemania with amateur boxing and ended up rolling in the newly mown Gospel Truth grass. She still couldn't believe it had happened. All her life she'd been ridiculed by other women, the object of either their jealousy or disdain or both. In times past she'd ignored the haters. But on a warm, sunny Sunday one month ago, that hadn't been the case. Katherine was still waiting for the embarrassment to come, for the regret she thought she should feel as a result of her actions. But when she looked back on that Sunday afternoon, all she felt was . . . vindicated. After all, Patricia Cook had started it.

"Hello, *Katherine*," Patricia had spat sarcastically as she exited her car just as Katherine was walking past. She relished the fact that *Sister*, *Mrs.*, or *Noble* was nowhere in the greeting.

Katherine turned and glared, said nothing, and kept walking.

"You must be feeling fairly adrift, since you've lost your job as watchdog. Now that Nate's gone, I'm surprised you're still bold enough to show your face around here."

Katherine quickened her pace, annoyed that because workers had blocked off part of the lot to landscape it, she'd had to park almost a half block away from the office doors.

Patricia laughed, glad to finally be able to tell this woman what she thought of her. She'd held her tongue because of James and because of Nate. Well, James was no longer a consideration and Nate was no longer here.

"Yeah, your granddaughter always thought she was above my child. Miss High and Mighty, acting as if she owned the world. And where is she now? With the biggest fornicator in all of Texas, probably working on another illegitimate child."

Katherine whirled around. "Better a fornicator than a felon!" she hissed. "Destiny on her worst day is better than Carmen at her best. And you can say what you want about me, but you would do well to keep your mouth off my granddaughter *and* my son-in-law."

"Son-in-law?" Patricia was shouting now, playing to a gathering crowd. "Don't you mean your lo—"

The last three letters were muffled as Katherine's Louis

Vuitton bag connected with Patricia's mouth. A stunned Patricia stumbled back, but recovered quickly. She charged Katherine like a wounded animal, screaming like a banshee. Katherine got off another good whack before Patricia grabbed her hair. The two women tousled, even as security worked to separate them. The women worked themselves away from both men and tumbled to the ground. Patricia had a death grip on Katherine's mane until Katherine sunk her teeth into Patricia's forearm. "Ow!" That caused Patricia to release Katherine's hair, which gave Katherine time to wind up for another Vuitton strike. When the security guard snatched the bag instead, Katherine took off her shoe without missing a beat, unaware that her blouse was ripped, her mouth was bleeding, and she'd lost three nails.

"Don't—you—ever—talk—about—what's—mine!" she screamed, punctuating each word with a heel connecting with some part of Patricia's anatomy, and a couple blows landing on the security guard trying to subdue her. "As long as you're Black and paying taxes, don't do it," Katherine panted, finally restrained by a guard who looked as if he too had just done battle.

Just as the fight ended, Deacon Robinson had rushed out of the administrative offices and up to Katherine.

"What on earth is going on here?" he'd exclaimed, looking from her to Pat and back.

Katherine had flung back her disheveled hair, straightened her shirt, put on her shoe, and wiped blood from her mouth. Then she calmly turned and answered him. "Something noble."

Deacon had merely raised his eyebrows and opened the office door. Enough said.

66

Elijah Speaks

Nate and Destiny held hands as they walked through the garden entrance of the assisted care facility where the family patriarch, Elijah Thicke, resided. Nate felt a twinge of guilt. It had been almost a year since he'd visited his ninety-five-year-old great-grandfather, and months since they'd talked on the phone.

They got off the elevator and Nate knocked on the door. After a long moment, a slightly stooped over but spry old man opened it. Whatever greeting he'd intended died on his tongue as he beheld Destiny. He blinked his eyes rapidly and walked closer. His once six-foot frame was now around five-ten, so he had to look up at her. And then he knelt down and ran his hand over Benjamin's face, who was sleeping in his stroller. He stared at the child so long that both she and Nate became slightly uncomfortable.

"Well, old man, are you going to stand there and ogle my wife and child all day, or are you going to show some southern hospitality and invite us in?"

Nate's joking comment snapped Elijah from his revelry. "You'll forgive an old man his imaginings, won't you?" he said as he led the couple back inside his humble yet cheerfully decorated abode. The sun, filtered by sheer white curtains, shone brightly from the east window. Potted plants lined the shelf just below it. The simple, leather furniture was covered with brightly knitted throws, and the smell of a pipe—Elijah's one admitted vice—clung to everything.

"Still growing weed, I see," Nate joked, walking over and inspecting the plants. His great-grandfather had grown his own herbs for years, something he'd learned from his grandfather. Some were medicinal, others for cooking. All looked healthy and vibrant, a tribute to Elijah's green thumb.

"Long as I don't smoke none of 'em, I should do just fine." Elijah continued to look at Destiny. "You must be the reason this boy is still smiling," he stated simply. "A man can handle anything with the right woman by his side."

"I've heard so much about you," Destiny said, bending down to hug him. "I love the way you've decorated," she added, looking around. "Those throws are nice. Do you mind if I lay Benjamin on one of them?"

"Lay him right here," Elijah said, pointing to the couch. "As for the covers, those are presents from the women around here chasing me. You know a good-looking man is hard to find, especially when the one looking is eighty years old." Laughing at his own joke produced a coughing spell. Nate helped Elijah over to the couch and sat him down next to where Benjamin lay. Destiny poured water from a pitcher on the counter and handed it to Elijah.

They sat and waited while Elijah drained the glass. He stared into it for a moment, his countenance becoming at once serious and reflective. When he looked up, it was at Destiny, and there was a twinkle in his eye.

"You look just like her," he began, in a once strong voice that was now raspy. When Destiny looked questioningly at Nate, Elijah continued. "Your great-great-grandmother, Sadie. You're almost her spitting image."

"Sadie. My mother's mentioned that name. I don't know much about her though."

"Trust me, child. There's a lot to tell. A lot of wonderful

things that I'll share one day. But she's why I called you, Nate, and asked you over. Because now, after all these years, I can do what I promised, and honor her request."

Now it was Nate's turn to look puzzled. "I don't understand, Gramps," Nate said, using the second most popular name he called Elijah. Simply "Elder" was the first, and how most everyone addressed him.

Elijah cleared his throat and continued. Anyone watching could see his body was there, but his mind was far away, in another place, another time. Destiny and Nate again looked at each other, then back at Elijah. And waited.

"She was fourteen when I first saw her," he began again. "And I lost my heart right then, just like that." He snapped a bony but still-strong finger. "Her family had just arrived here in Texas, from Louisiana, part of the Negro elite. Her father was a doctor, you see, and their family way above my station." Elijah smiled wistfully. "But that didn't matter to her.

"I took a job with her father, being a handyman of sorts . . . delivery boy. I didn't care what he asked me to do, as long as I could sneak a peek at his daughter. I was nineteen with a bullet, randy as all get out, and I admit, that lady had me tied up in knots! First time I got her alone, I asked her to marry me. It was also the first time I'd talked to her, but that didn't matter! I knew I loved her, wanted her to be my wife. She wanted it too. That was the happiest day of my life.

"The next day was the saddest, or almost. She told her mother about my proposal, and when I stepped on their property the next day, it was to the sight of a shotgun pointed at me. Her old man told me to get off their property and not come back. I tried to explain that my intentions were pure, that I desired to be a preacher, and had no plans of doing anything unseemly until she and I were married. But I was randy, you understand, and I wanted to marry her right then. We married young back in them days, so what I was asking wasn't out of bounds. At least to me.

"But it was to him. I was off limits for many reason: poor, uneducated, and too dark. See, back then the light-skinned people would marry their own kind, to keep their color pure. I can't say I blamed them exactly. They often got treated better than folks who looked like me." Elijah stopped and looked at Nate, and then over at Destiny, and smiled. "Anyway," he continued, "I snuck back over there first chance I got and one of the new workers told me they'd shipped her off, back to Louisiana to stay with an aunt.

"I was beside myself, and as soon as I'd saved up train fare, I went after her. It took me two weeks but I finally found out where she lived. I got a note to her through one of her classmates. See, just 'cause I didn't have a fancy, formal education didn't mean I was illiterate, and didn't mean I wasn't smart." Elijah winked. "I could get anything I wanted when I set my mind to it." Elijah's joy faded. "Except her."

"She met me at the place I wrote in the note and, boy, were we happy to see each other. We talked for hours, pledged our love to each other"—Elijah looked over sheepishly—"and kissed like fools. That's all we did though. Like I told her daddy, I intended to marry her before . . . anything else happened.

"Well, you can 'bout imagine what happened. The aunt found out. Within a week, Sadie was gone again, this time to upstate New York, where they married her off to a prominent Black doctor up there, somebody's family that her daddy knew. Her friend, the same one who'd passed the note, told me all this. See, Sadie had told her about me, and our plans to get married. She knew Sadie loved me, and tried to help as best she could.

"New Orleans is the last time I saw her. But I heard from her one more time, in a letter she wrote to me and gave to her friend. She'd been married two years by then, had a baby. But she professed her undying love for me, and said she wanted to put an end to the nonsensical thinking that had kept us apart. She told me that one day, she'd return to Palestine, with her daughter. And that I needed to marry and have a son, so at least if not us, our children could be together. She asked me to continue this tradition until our love had come full circle, and there had been a baby born out of that love—with both Noble and Thicke blood running in its veins."

At that exact moment, Benjamin stirred and opened his eyes. He stared intently at the watery brown ones staring back at him, and then reached up to touch the stubbly gray whiskers of a foreign yet intuitively familiar wrinkled chin. And then he went back to sleep.

"It's done, now," Elijah said, his voice cracking, his hand stroking Benjamin's arms and face. "I did it, Sadie. I kept the promise. I'll come and join you now."

Epilogue

One year later . . .

"Baby, it's for you!" Destiny kissed her husband as she handed him the phone.

Nate smiled, and his heart swelled as he watched her go. He was so thankful to God for her, and for His love. After his butt had made its unceremonious appearance at the Total Truth Conference, Nate hadn't known whether he would ever smile again, and he certainly doubted he could be happy. But as his gramps used to say, it was a long road that didn't have a turn in it. Once again, his road had turned, and he was experiencing happiness like he'd never known.

"Hello?"

"Nate Thicke!" King's voice boomed over the phone. "How's life in paradise?"

"Why don't you come over here and find out!" Nate and Destiny had extended open invitations to the Brooks, Montgomerys, and others to visit them at their new home whenever they wanted. Turks and Caicos was indeed a paradise, and they loved hosting their friends and showing them around. "Mark and Simone just left two days ago," Nate continued. "With little

Mark Junior. That boy's not out of diapers and they're already talking about having another."

"You sound good, man," King said. "Island life is obviously agreeing with you."

King was right. Turks and Caicos had been the perfect place to heal from all that had happened. At first, Nate had felt out of sorts—too much time on his hands after going nonstop for years. Nettie had encouraged him to stop focusing on the bad and find the good. And once he began looking, there was plenty to see. One of his biggest blessings was that money was no problem. His best-selling novel and sell-out DVD series had made him financially secure. So after long conversations with his Mama, Derrick, King, Grandfather Thomas, and God, Nate had embraced his new life and opened himself up to another way of serving the Lord. He was almost finished with his third book, and had plans for yet another. His publisher had wisely delayed releasing the second one, until now. So far, bookstore orders were strong, and Carla had already booked him to be on her show. "Make your comeback with Carla," she'd teased him.

Carla had been a sage and understanding ear following his downfall, and since Nate and Destiny moved, a regular visitor and good friend. She and Lavon flew down once a month, and Lavon's production company taped Nate's ongoing public service announcements for Total Truth, regarding abstinence, the dangers of promiscuous sex, and the sanctity of marriage.

"The association needs you," King was saying when Nate began listening again. "We've put out a few feelers, mentioned your name here and there to gauge the reaction. People are impressed with how you've handled this thing, brothah. How you left everything, quit ministering publicly, got the counseling, expressed your remorse and your recommitment to fault-less leadership. The brothahs are ready to welcome you back into the fold. And we'll support any move you make toward reclaiming Gospel Truth as your ministry."

Gospel Truth. That had been his hardest task, resigning his position as senior pastor. For the first time in over seventy-five years, someone other than a Thicke was leading the congregation. He felt he'd let down not only God, but his family also.

Fortunately Gramps had set him straight. "It's done, move on," he'd said simply. Two weeks later, Elijah Rutherford Thicke had gone on to be with the Lord . . . and with the only woman he'd ever loved.

"It looks like Gospel Truth is doing all right," Nate said finally. "I think God might have other plans for me."

"Well, it seems as if you're preoccupied, Nate, so I'll let you go. Just know that Total Truth and your brothahs in the ministry are here when you need help with whatever you decide to do; and that you have a place at our association table."

"Thanks, man. That means a lot."

Nate hung up the phone and went in search of his wife. He found her lounging by the pool, which was less than fifty yards from their pristine private beach. Even after all this time, her beauty still dazzled him, and after hearing Elijah's story, it humbled him as well.

"Do you have room on that chaise for a Thicke man?" he asked, lying down and placing her on top of him.

"Always," Destiny said, kissing him thoroughly and feeling his ardor grow. "Oh, by the way, Kiki called. She said she had to cancel her plans to come down next week. She's met someone."

"Is that so?" Nate asked, a wide smile on his face. "In New Orleans?"

"Yes, at one of Simone's soirees."

"I'm glad she accepted Simone and Mark's offer and moved to Louisiana. It always puzzled me that she stayed in Palestine."

Both Nate and Destiny knew the reason why Katherine had stayed; neither felt the need to voice it.

"I've been wondering about something," Destiny said instead. "Having to do with Elder Elijah's story."

"Uh-huh." Nate nuzzled Destiny's ear.

"His and Sadie's love story explains why the Nobles and Thickes got together, but what about the covering of all those other women?"

Nate frowned, and took his hands from around Destiny's waist.

"Now, don't be like that, baby. You know I'm past all that. But I'm curious. How did that tradition start?"

Nate pondered how to share with Destiny what Elijah had told him in a visit when the two men were alone. "It's a long story," he began. "But the short version is that while the Thickes managed to always be the first lovers for Noble women, we never could marry y'all, until now. Apparently there was a Noble tradition of marrying within a certain class and color. That's why my grandfather, Thomas, didn't marry Naomi, because she ended up marrying a light-skinned lawyer. And that's why Katherine married that Hopkins dude. The Noble-Thicke love is why none of those marriages lasted, and why Katherine never took Hopkins's last name. If my father hadn't died"— Nate hesitated—"I think he and Katherine would have married."

"He would have divorced Miss Nettie?" Destiny was incredulous.

"My father was in love with your grandmother," Nate said simply. "And Mama knew it. But I don't think Daddy could help that he fell in love with Katherine. Just like how I can't help loving you." Nate wrapped his arms tightly around Destiny and continued. "Later, that same friend who'd tried to help Sadie and Gramps encouraged him to get married, told him she knew that's what Sadie wanted. He went through his entire congregation trying to douse the flame that Sadie had lit. He gave many women physical comfort, but he never got relief, though those women never let him forget how much his loving was appreciated. Wasn't ever an abundance of men in Palestine, and we Thickes, well, it's been said that we're pretty good at making love."

Destiny raised up and playfully slapped Nate's chest, even as she ground herself into his manhood.

"Gramps finally did marry my great-grandmother. He loved, but was never again *in* love. I guess nobody can douse a Thicke flame but a Noble. Anyway . . . that's how covering the flock started."

Destiny kissed Nate again, and before long, his hands were underneath her skimpy bikini bottom, kneading her lush backside. Their kiss deepened. Destiny sat up and took off her top. Her full breasts were aligned with Nate's mouth. He immediately took advantage.

"Come here, you," he drawled huskily. "Let's take this, uh, conversation inside where I can really *talk* to you, understand?"

"Are we getting ready to try and make a little Sadie?" Destiny teased. After visiting with Elijah, Destiny told Nate that that's what she wanted to name their next baby, if it was a girl. So that a Sadie could finally bear the Thicke name.

"We're going to try and make a bunch of little Sadies," Nate murmured, picking Destiny up and placing her on the dining room table. "And I'm getting ready to have my favorite dish." He took off Destiny's bikini bottoms, spread her legs, and sat down in the chair between them. Soon, Destiny was hearing harps and seeing stars and being reminded that one could have heaven right here.

Later that night, after another round of lovemaking, Destiny cuddled up next to Nate. "Guess what I remembered today," she whispered in that slightly whiny voice that drove Nate wild.

He pulled her tighter to him. "Hmm."

"The first time we were together, in the Florida Keys. I asked when you fell in love with me. Do you remember what you said?"

"Of course. I said November twenty-third. . . ."

"Yes!" Destiny said excitedly, knowing Nate understood. "Benjamin's birthday!" Which they'd discovered from the per-

sonal effects Elijah had bequeathed them—including the tat-
tered, yellowed promise letter—had been Sadie's birthday too.

"They say the spirit is eternal," Nate remarked. "Maybe
your great-great-grandma had a little sumpin', sumpin' to do
with us being us. You think?"

"I don't know." Destiny sighed. "But if she did, I owe her a
big thank you." Destiny was silent a long moment.

"You feel all right?" Nate finally asked.

"I feel amazing," Destiny said sleepily, feeling the effects of
their lengthy session of physical intercourse. "How do you
feel?"

Nate turned on his side and pulled Destiny into him,
spoon style. "Baby, there are no words for how I feel, how you
make me feel."

"C'mon," Destiny teased. "There are millions of words and
you're the world's greatest orator. Think of one to describe
how you're feeling."

"That word hasn't been invented yet, baby, the word that
expresses what your love does to me. Now stop talking and go
to sleep, or else I'll tap that spot again."

Soon, her even breathing told Nate that his wife had followed orders. But Nate stayed awake a long time, thinking
about Elijah and Sadie, and the love affair that had come full
circle. Then he thought about Destiny's question, and realized
the answer was simple. He leaned over and whispered into his
sleeping wife's ear, "I love you, baby. You make me feel good."

Author's Note

Palestine is a real town in East Texas; however, I've taken creative license in placing buildings and other locations in the story line that in actuality do not exist. While I once attended a "Palestine Missionary Baptist Church," this church was in Kansas City, Missouri, not Palestine, Texas, and in no way resembles the church now renamed The Gospel Truth in this writing. Thank the good Lord for that! :)

REVEREND FEELGOOD

LUTISHIA LOVELY

ABOUT THIS GUIDE

The following questions
are intended to enhance
your group's reading
of this book.

DISCUSSION QUESTIONS

1. Katherine was sexually molested when she was twelve years old, an act that her mother, Naomi, later justified. How do you think this impacted the way Katherine raised her daughter? How did this impact Simone? And Destiny?

2. Nate was taught that it was his pastoral right to sleep with female church members, and many were more than happy to oblige him. How much blame do you place on those who slept with him? Is it less than his, more, or equal?

3. The legal age for consent in Texas, regarding sexual activity, is seventeen. Is this an appropriate age for sexual relations? Why or why not?

4. Nate had Katherine's permission to sleep with Simone. Was it wrong that he did so? Why or why not?

5. Destiny believed it was her fate to be Nate's wife. What do you think?

6. What are your thoughts on modern spiritual practices outside of traditional Christianity practiced by Total Truth congregations, and by Destiny, such as the newly packaged "law of attraction" message, meditation, visualization, affirmations, mantras, etc.?

7. Simone wanted Destiny to have an abortion. How much of this was from her selfishness and how much was from a genuine concern for her child? What would you have done in this situation?

8. Stan Lee encouraged Nate to live a celibate lifestyle. What are your thoughts on single ministers? Should they date and, if so, how? Is it okay to date a woman in the congregation? To have sexual relations outside of marriage?

9. Simone married Mark out of a sense of obligation to her daughter and Nate. She ended up with a good marriage and a godly man. Did she deserve it?

10. Jennifer plotted both to be with and then to destroy Nate, but ended up with Deacon Robinson. Do you think she deserves him? What are your thoughts on their considerable age difference? Do you think this union will last?

11. Patricia sincerely loved Deacon Robinson. How do you feel about the fact that, at least for now, she's alone and feels forced to start over in a new city?

12. Verniece and Anne's friendship turned into something else. Do you think these women are lesbians? Is it possible to have a same-sex relationship and still be straight? Still be saved?

13. Verniece believes that like various cultures and religions (such as the polygamist Mormon groups), many women are sharing their men. What is your view on her perspective? Would you rather know or not know that your mate is not exclusive?

14. After Melody's video surfaced, Nate lost his ministry. Do you think he should have been forced to leave his church and Total Truth?

15. Even though Melody is only seventeen, she's got quite the sexual history. She purposely went after Nate, even

knowing of his relationship with Destiny. How much do you blame Nate for having sex with her?

16. Melody went to Nate's mother, Nettie, for forgiveness, and Nettie forgave her. Do you think she should have offered her forgiveness? Do you think Melody was sincere in wanting to change her life?

17. Nate's mother, Nettie, advised Destiny, and Destiny ended up becoming her daughter-in-law. What advice do you think made the difference in this outcome?

18. Reverend Ed Smith was very judgmental toward megachurches and megapreachers, yet he had his own faults. What are your thoughts on Jesus's first commandment: judge not, lest you be judged?

19. One of the historical barriers to a Noble-Thicke union was the issue of color within the Black community, specifically the argument of light versus dark skin. Do you think this is still an issue today? Why or why not?

20. It was an amazing story that Elijah finally shared with Nate and Destiny. What do you think of the promise he made to Sadie all those years ago? What do you think of soul mates?

Lutishia Lovely once again takes a smoldering journey into the scandalous and occasionally sanctified lives of people who go to church but aren't always 100 percent Christian in . . .

Heaven Forbid

Coming in August 2010 from Dafina Books

Here's an excerpt from *Heaven Forbid*. . . .

1

If God Can't Fix It . . .

Anyone watching the two men conversing quietly in the corner booth of the dimly lit restaurant would have thought their discussion serious. They would have been right. The seasoned seventy-something, gray-haired minister, looking important and dignified in his black, double-breasted suit, listened intently as the younger man, displaying a rugged handsomeness in his navy blue, tailored Kenneth Cole design, used his manicured fingers to underscore a point.

"Number one," Stan Lee said, his long, thick forefinger in midair, "*all* sexual misconduct is sin, whether or not your members want to hear it. Before you came and laid down the law, the Gospel Truth congregation was way out of hand, from the pulpit to the vestibule. You know I'm right about it. Two, it takes a tight rein to straighten out this kind of mess. And number three, Doctor O, I think you are the only preacher alive who can hold the rein tight enough to put this backsliding church back in line with the Word." Secretly, Stan wished the doctor could put somebody else in line—his wife. But that was another story.

Obadiah, officially known as The Reverend Doctor Pastor Bishop Overseer Mister Stanley Obadiah Meshach Brook, Jr., and affectionately called "Reverend Doctor O," nodded his head in understanding. He liked this young man's fire and fervor when it came to strong morals, and he couldn't help but agree with him. Doctor Stanley Morris Lee, pastor of the Los Angeles Logos Word Church, was a prolific preacher in his own right. Obadiah affectionately called Stan his namesake, even though he'd gone by his second name, Obadiah, since childhood. He respected the Logos Word ministry and viewed Stan as a spiritual son.

And Obadiah knew that Stan spoke truth: the Gospel Truth Church was in a gospel mess following the nationally televised scandal of its former pastor, Nate Thicke, and it took a preacher well worth his salt to pick up the shattered pulpit pieces. Something of this magnitude was the only thing that could have pulled him out of retirement, though truth be told, he'd missed the pulpit and was glad to be back.

Obadiah ran a hand over his weary eyes as he remembered the fiasco. How one of Nate Thicke's many women had managed to secretly videotape them during a sexual tryst, and how a portion of said tape was spliced into a holiday cruise promotion that was then shown during a national church convention. For about five seconds, Nate's glistening, bare backside had been seen by many of the 20,000 attendees before a quick-thinking technical director stopped the tape. It didn't matter; the damage had been done. Nate was forced to resign, and his mother, Nettie Thicke Johnson, had immediately placed a call to her good friend Maxine, Obadiah's wife. Nettie, like Stanley, had been convinced that someone of Obadiah's stature, experience, and wisdom was the only one who could lead the congregation back down the straight-and-narrow path. Goodness knew that during Nate Thicke's pastoral reign, the members—and the minister—had gone buck wild.

Obadiah cleared his throat and leaned toward Stanley, his powerful orator's voice near a whisper. "I know in my heart that every rule I've put in place and every change I've implemented at that there church is absolutely necessary. Narrow is the road that leads to salvation," Obadiah continued, his voice rising slightly as he quoted scripture. He looked around the sparsely populated dining room, took in the rich chestnut walls accented with deep red—covered chairs and tablecloths, and sipped his coffee. "But as right as I am, the church is failing. The Sunday offering is shrinking faster than a jackrabbit's peter. And I'm losing the regular parishioners, especially the young folk. That's why I brought you here, to lead a revival and staunch the flow of fleeing fornicators. If they end up over at that funeral home Jenkins is masquerading as a house of God, Thomas will turn over in his grave."

Stanley's chuckle was low and deep. "Aw, c'mon now, Doctor O. Why are you so hard on Reverend Jenkins? He's doing the best he can. Besides, he's older than you are, and most of his members have probably been with him the entire forty years he's pastored that church."

Obadiah let out an uncharacteristic snort but remained silent. He didn't care to share the beef he had with Reginald Jenkins, a beef that went back those forty years of which Stanley spoke, a situation where Reginald took something that at the time Obadiah thought belonged to him.

"Young women don't listen to old men like me," Obadiah said after a pause. "Especially since I'm telling them to close their legs and take the 'for sale' and 'for rent' signs off their hot-to-trots and whatnot. This medicine will go down better coming from a young, handsome man such as yourself." He looked over at Stanley, took in the sleek, bald head, the smooth, honey brown face, the square-jawed strength settled under dark brown eyes, and nodded his approval. "Yes, they'll listen to you."

Both men paused while the waiter came and took away their dinner dishes. They declined dessert but said yes to more coffee.

"I'm going to come with the unadulterated word of God," Stanley continued. He leaned back casually in his seat while his countenance remained serious. "I'm not going to leave them with any questions in their mind. When I get done this week, they'll understand that being saved and sanctified means no fornication, no adultery, no pornography, and definitely no masturbation." His lips curled into a snarl as he all but spat out the last word, several unfortunate memories rising up unbidden in his mind. "If these women *and men* want to call themselves children of God, then they've got to live holy!"

The wives of Stanley Morris Lee and Stanley Obadiah Meshach Brook were visiting at home, and having their own conversation on sexual matters from quite a different point of view.

"He hates it!" Passion said passionately. "How can a grown man, with three kids and oversized, working plumbing, if you know what I mean, abhor the natural act of sex so much? I just don't get it, Mama Max."

Passion had been sitting on the plush, chenille sofa, but now she paced back and forth across the carpet in Maxine Brook's living room.

"Humph, that would be a blessing for some women. There's plenty more that could go wrong in a marriage, child. Now lookie here. Is the man hitting you, abusing you?"

Passion stopped in her tracks. "No, whatever would make you ask that question?"

"Because I want to know, that's why."

The truth was, she and Stan had begun to argue more, and once, just once, he had advanced toward her as if to strike. But he hadn't. "No, Mama Max, Stan isn't abusive."

"Is he a responsible man, keeping food on the table and money in the bank?"

"Yes, ma'am, but . . ."

"But nothing. Is he a good father to his children?"

"The ministry keeps him busy, but yes, when he's around them, he's a good dad."

"Then count your blessings and get you a good book to read at night. Drink some of that camouflage tea so you can sleep easy."

Passion didn't try to hide her smile. "You mean chamomile, Mama Max?"

"Yeah, that too. Drink it and cool your feisty behind down!"

Passion returned to the sofa and sat close to Mama Max. "But Mama, I *like* making love. I want to share physical intimacy with my husband, not continue with this forced celibacy that Stanley has mandated. I was celibate for five years before I got married. I don't intend to be horny and wanting with two-hundred pounds of prime beef lying next to me! I'm sorry to be so blatant, Mama Max, but I haven't been able to talk about this with anyone."

"No apology needed, Passion, you can speak your mind in my house. Now, I can tell you're frustrated, and I wish there was something I could say to make you feel better. I haven't felt the flame of desire for nigh unto twenty years, and was never too crazy about the act of procreation when Reverend and I were busy creating King, Queen, Daniel, and Esther. But as a wife, you do have certain rights. Have you tried talking to Stan about it?"

"Until I'm blue in the face," Passion said, standing to pace again. "But he won't even have the discussion anymore; says that as a first lady, I shouldn't have such animalistic desires.

"It's not like Stan can't perform. Our sex life was fairly good right after we got married. Nothing too risqué, you understand, and only once, maybe twice, a week. But we did it."

"And then what happened?"

Passion hesitated in her answer. She respected Mama Max and her counsel, but could she share everything with her? Like what she'd discovered in Stan's luggage after he'd returned from a ministers' conference three months ago? And how, upon further investigation, she'd found similar items hidden in a rarely used gym bag on a top shelf in their garage? And how any doubt as to the use of these items was cleared up when Passion came home one day, early and unexpected, and was shocked senseless by what she had seen? Passion decided she wasn't ready to tell anybody what she'd learned about Stanley Morris Lee . . . she was barely able to admit this truth to herself.

"Passion, baby . . . you all right? I asked you a question, about what happened to change how you and your husband . . . know each other."

Passion shared what she could. "Stan has been traveling a lot, so I didn't really notice it at first. When I finally asked him about it, he made excuses. Then, about three months ago, he started spouting Bible verses and using scripture and religion as the foundation for denying me what is rightfully mine. He hasn't touched me since, and has made me feel guilty for wanting something perfectly normal!

"Things can't go on this way," Passion continued, almost to herself, as she looked out Mama Max's large picture window and beheld a beautiful Texas fall afternoon. But the burst of color from the autumn purple ash tree in the Brooks' front yard, the profusion of purple, red, yellow, and orange, were lost on Passion. Her eyes weren't looking at the scenery out front, but rather at a scene from her past, the pictures she'd taken with her cell-phone camera that had changed so many lives. She felt a strange camaraderie with Stan's ex-wife, Carla Lee, now Carla Chapman, along with the guilt that never totally went away, guilt from what she felt was her part in Stan and Carla's divorce.

"Passion, you need to take this burden to the Lord and leave it there," Mama Max said into a room that had suddenly become overwhelmingly quiet. "God can fix whatever is broken."

When Passion turned to face Mama Max, there were tears in her eyes. "I sure hope so, Mama," she said in a whisper. "Because if God can't fix it, a divorce court can."

Shortly after divulging her dilemma to Mama Max, Passion asked to be driven to the guest pastor condo. Her marital admissions had made her tired, and she wanted to spend some quiet time alone with just her thoughts before Stan arrived. Once inside the comfortably decorated abode, Passion undressed quickly and took a shower. She had no reason to believe that tonight would be any different from all the others, but she wanted to be clean . . . just in case.

As Passion walked into the closet to don a nightgown, Stan's unlocked luggage caught her eye. Without pausing to think, she stepped over to it and lifted the lid. Inside, everything was compartmentalized and organized, much like Stan's life. His underwear, including briefs, were neatly folded, his socks paired and lined against the side. Not wanting Stan to know that she'd snooped in his belongings, Passion gingerly lifted the undershirts, T-shirts, and casual polos. She ran a hand inside the zippered compartment and came up against belts, handkerchiefs, and ties. She was just about to pull out her hand when her fingers felt something else.

Passion closed her eyes and took a breath. She slowly pulled out what her hands clutched. Swallowing, she opened her eyes and sighed. The pink silky fabric was trimmed in frilly black lace. Passion didn't have to hold them up to know, but she did, anyway. It was just as she'd expected. The ladies panties were extra large . . . just Stan's size.